OVERDRAFT

THE ORION OFFENSIVE

OVERDRAFT

THE ORION OFFENSIVE

JOHN JACKSON MILLER

47N⬦RTH

Originally published as a Kindle Serial, April 2013.
Cover Illustration by Paul Youll
Book Design by The Book Designers

Published by 47North
PO Box 400818
Las Vegas, NV 89140

ISBN-13: 9781477807521
ISBN-10: 1477807527
Library of Congress Control Number: 2013933888

To my father,
who showed me how the world worked

EPISODE 1:
GREENMAIL

1

There was life in outer space, but you didn't want to get it on you.

"*Spore, three o'clock!*" Hearing the call, Bridget spun and pointed her rifle. Her armor's systems took it from there, targeting the laser beam within angstroms of the Spore's most vital place. Crimson energy flashed. An instant later, the greenish boil went gray and shattered, surrendering its peculiar life to the asteroid's night.

"Confirm kill," Bridget said into her helmet mic. "Eyes wide, people. Where there's Spore, there's more."

"Right, Chief," her flanker responded.

Bridget Yang knew the Spore wasn't really a spore, but "Exotic Formation Seven-Alpha" didn't scream omnivorous alien terror. She didn't come up with the names. She just did the shooting—or, at least, she carried the gun close enough to do its job. No drone could do this work. Not even out here, on an airless clump of rock orbiting Altair, a star that had been just a twinkle in humanity's sky forty years earlier.

Humanity had reached the stars and found them open for business. But just as the pioneering sea traders of Earth's past had disturbed strange natural enemies, things weren't any different in 2138. Chief Yang and her armored teammates were needed.

No one knew where the space-borne Spore had come from, or how to curb its appetite; Earth had simply joined the Signatory Systems Pact in part to combat it. "Surge teams"—surgical strike units like hers—had proved the best defense by far.

Laserfire flashed from beyond a shattered wall in the devastated compound. *O'Herlihy*, Bridget thought. A glimpse at the data feed projected against her helmet's faceplate confirmed it: her other fire team had found another small outgrowth. Specimens of Seven-Alpha ranged from pea-sized to gargantuan; the largest Bridget had ever seen had been chowing down on a moon…or what was left of a moon when she and the traders had found it.

But large or small, each lump of Spore had something like a nucleus inside its transparent membrane. Where a precision shot caused the mindless beings to disintegrate, even a slight miss released living particles that took root promptly on anything nearby. That was where the technology helped—and it did now, as she spotted another splotch of green. As she touched the trigger, the systems in her HardSHEL armor unit kicked the suit's internal servos into gear. Bridget became a puppet, her arm and rifle smoothly guided into the exact position for a perfect shot.

It was almost too easy. All her teammates had to do was bring their weapons reasonably close to their targets—and then decide to fire. That final decision was one no professional would ever give up to a computer.

"Not much fun this way," her flanking gunman said, watching Bridget's body return to her control.

"This isn't supposed to be fun," Bridget snapped. "You want laughs, Dinner, look at yourself in the mirror after you get out of the shower." It was known throughout the barracks that Arbutus Dinner had more hair on his body than a sheepdog. "I don't care that it's easy," Bridget said. "I care about people not screwing up. If this gear can help…"

Her eyes suddenly flashed onto the feed from the surveillance drone hovering meters above them. She turned her head. "Watch it, Stubek!"

Someone *was* screwing up: the rookie in the rear. A bulging growth of Spore to her right, Lynn Stubek went into a firing stance, ready to fire a point-blank shot. But she triggered her weapon before her boot could adhere properly to the asteroid's low-gravity surface. The motion of her servo-assisted arms shifted her mass enough that her shot went a centimeter wide. The beam lanced the Spore, which ballooned outward—alive and more dangerous than ever.

"No!" Stubek saw the goo on her gun first and threw it aside. No good. It was on her armor, too.

"Dammit, Stubek!" Bridget slung her weapon and stood fast. Her armor's systems identified and highlighted other Spore fragments tumbling in the low-gee. It would be seconds before she could navigate through them to Stubek. The rookie fell to the rocky surface and writhed, clawing frantically at the splotches on her breastplate.

"That won't work," Bridget said. "Burn! Burn!"

Stubek's eyes fixed on her discarded rifle, glowing as the metal-loving organism feasted. Her armor's composite coating was distasteful to the Spore, but nothing known was truly proof against its appetite.

"*Burn!*"

"I can't remember," Stubek howled, rattled. "I can't remember the command!"

Bridget threw her rifle aside. Seeing a meter-wide path between the drifting particles of Spore, she dove forward, letting the servos guide her. Her arms wrenched painfully as the suit stretched and moved her limbs into a bizarre contortionist's swim through the darkness. Landing beside Stubek, Bridget ripped the foil towel from her utility pack. Wiping clean the external override port on Stubek's armor, Bridget keyed in her code—one half of the confirmation. The chief's voice was the other half. "Surge Altair, Yang, commanding unit Stubek, Lynn. *Burn! Burn!*"

Bridget tumbled clear as a blaze of energy enveloped Stubek's form. Half the megawatts in Stubek's armor redirected to its skin, cauterizing the Spore in a silent sizzle. The chief's visor went dark, adjusting against the flash.

Rising, Bridget saw Dinner and the other two members of her fire team directing tiny laser bursts at the remaining globs. Stubek lay on the ground, her armor a fused ceramic cocoon. That was why it was a last-ditch method; it made million-dollar units into mummies.

Bridget looked down at the rookie. "You're all right. Your unit says so."

"Don't worry about me," Stubek said, catching her breath. She forced a chuckle. "I'll just lie here."

At least she's got a sense of humor, Bridget thought as she stepped over the immobilized trooper. For this sweep, she'd brought Stubek over from Hiro Welligan's crew, hoping to try to undo any bad habits her most slapdash squad leader had probably instilled. She'd make Hiro retrieve the woman and pry her out of the suit. It'd serve him right.

Incompetence had nearly killed them all this week. Four days earlier, the parent Spore had first attacked the asteroid facility. It should've been an easy defense for Bridget to mount with their technology.

Only she didn't have it. Having returned from another action, Surge Team Altair was outfitted with its high-grav armor. The correct gear for asteroid combat was supposedly on its way to them. But some idiot at the provisioning center had sent armor for the wrong species. Only Bridget's quick thinking—and her team's willingness to stuff themselves into combat suits meant for their starfish-like Uutherum allies—had saved the whole asteroid from being digested.

They had nearly been killed by a clerical error.

Bridget was still livid. More so now, triple-checking what was left of the place she'd called home for two years.

"Heard you lost one, Chief." Michael O'Herlihy led his wedge of warriors around the corner of a half-eaten wall. He looked around, his toothy smile visible through his faceplate. "So where *is* the rookie?"

"Staring at the stars and thinking it over," Bridget said.

"I want y'all to learn from that," he told his team. "Wanna feel worthless fast? Just lose a firefight with a germ."

Bridget smirked. O'Herlihy and his drawl always cheered her up.

One of their jokes was that she was more Irish than he was. Bridget was the black-haired and green-eyed daughter of a Chinese Greenlander father and a mother from Kilcorney; O'Herlihy had grown up in Little Arkansas, just outside Beijing. And never stopped growing, it seemed; the man towered over her even without a battlesuit.

His team looked no worse for their recon. "What have you got?" Bridget asked.

"There's a spot where everything caved in," he said, drawing on his hand with a gloved finger. A mark appeared on the map display inside Bridget's helmet. "Back near the unit's storehouse. It's a god-awful mess, Chief."

Bridget wasn't surprised. That was where the Spore had first awakened. A small amount had come in on a bangbox, the basic cargo unit for space travel, somehow slipping past the inspections at the interstellar transit station. *More incompetence.*

"Found a 'box that looks intact," O'Herlihy said. "Fell in when the ground collapsed."

Bridget's eyes narrowed. "Show me."
O'Herlihy started to write on his hand.
"In person," she said.

* * *

Bridget stood over the maw filled with undigested rubble and
bits of steel that had once been her team's home. There it was,
all right: a bangbox, half buried in the pile, its frame reflecting
the floodlights from their suits. The 'boxes were twice the width
of an old-time railroad car; sixteen light-years away, similar
containers were running on maglev tracks between every major
Earth city.

"No signal," she said. The container should have been broadcasting what it was and what it held. "Must be damaged."

"The hard way, then," O'Herlihy said, grinning. He handed
his rifle to Dinner and scrambled down into the mess. The top of
the 'box's door frame could just be seen. Bracing himself against
the container, O'Herlihy began digging, heaving the rocks away
as if they had as little mass as they had weight.

A red light flashed in Bridget's helmet. Falcone, her expedition's administrator, was paging. She ignored this call, like the
others. Corporate impatience had no place while security forces
were in the field. Yet, the clean-up phase of the operation seemed
finally done—

"*Gaahhh!*"

Bridget looked into the crater. Green bubbles blasted from
a gash in the 'box, spreading into the vacuum and spattering
O'Herlihy, who stumbled backward.

"Spore!" At the cavity's edge, Dinner and the others called
down. "*Burn! Burn!*"

O'Herlihy struck the ground, verdant paste smeared on his faceplate. Bridget heard him start to recite the code that would trigger his own armor to react as the rookie's had earlier.

Then she took another look at the green globules, boiling from the container.

"Wait a minute," she called, leaping downward. "Mike, wait!"

"Chief!" Dinner yelled. Bridget clambered into the pit, heedless of the spray hitting her.

"Wait!" She scrambled to O'Herlihy's side. Two flicks of her right ring finger called up the spectral analysis tool, and a beam of light from atop her faceplate washed over her companion's midsection.

That's not right, she thought, examining the readout. She knelt over O'Herlihy. The man struggled as she neared. "Bridgie, are you crazy?"

"Hush," she said. She opened her utility pack and withdrew a plastic tube. Quickly, she scraped up a clump of the green substance from the armor's surface. Then she inserted the vial into the feeder port just below her helmet's mouthpiece and cycled the vacuum lock. The port was a means of getting oral antidotes into the environment suit; now, Bridget used it to bring the would-be death organism to her mouth. She stuck out her tongue.

O'Herlihy's stunned eyes locked on hers. "Chief, are you nuts?"

Licking her lips, Bridget ignored him. Her human taste buds confirmed what her electronic sensors had told her. It made no sense.

And then it did, all at once. Bridget Yang realized there was much more to what had happened to her base than anyone had imagined.

She started climbing back out of the hole, more furious than before.

On his knees, O'Herlihy gawked. "You're crazy, Bridgie. You're gonna die!"

"Nope," Bridget said, looking back on the seeping 'box. Anger flared in her eyes. "But I *am* going to kill someone!"

2

Executing two million. Pow!

With the whispered command and a wiggle of his little finger, Jamison Sturm set forces in motion millions of kilometers away. Once again, his split-second decision had changed the lives of countless people he'd never met. If some suffered—well, that wasn't his problem. Details were for those on the ground.

Another hundred thousand executed. So long, London. Bang! Bang!

"Yes! Think I beat the close," he announced, blue eyes beaming under straw-colored brows.

"You're the champ, Jamie."

"The champ presses my shirts," he said, thrusting his arms toward the trading floor's rounded ceiling. "I am *King God America!*"

And he felt like it.

But now he had to wait. Even a king was subject to the laws of physics. Jamie slid back into his chair and downed the dregs of his coffee. *It was easier to trade stocks in the old days,* he thought as he watched the countdown on the isopanel before him. Back near the dawn of electronic trading—a century and a half earlier—even someone selling a single share could expect confirmation within seconds. Meanwhile, Jamie had a

trillion-dollar portfolio to manage—and another three minutes to wait before he learned whether the six billion dollars
he'd just moved got where it was going. What kind of service
was that?

Of course, he *was* on Venus. Or rather, in orbit above its far
side, or dark side, or whatever they called it. It always looked the
same to him: a shining white rainbow over a sea of nothing. It
rose outside his window every eight minutes as the part of the
station that held the trading floor rotated; it made for a disori-
enting sight, but it was the only way to simulate gravity. But why
look? Jamie knew there wasn't anything to see down on Venus.
The true action was elsewhere.

Out there.

In the stars, obviously—but also at home, on Earth. Home
was a minute and thirty-six light-seconds away and getting closer every moment, as Venus approached perigee. The
return window couldn't come quickly enough for Jamie, whose
sixteen-month duty shift was at an end. In four days he'd be
landing in Socorro; in five, he'd be departing Barcelona for the
ferry to Ibiza. There, his skinny white butt would bake for at
least a month. Retiring at thirty-one was a little later than he'd
always planned, but the extra year—or two, in Venus account-
ing—was worth it.

Forty billion dollars worth it. Yeah, that'd be worth leaving
the game in his prime for. He still loved it, of course. There was
no one better, not that he'd ever met. But there was no sense
being greedy.

An alert from his deskstation jolted Jamie upright: confirmation from the London exchange. There was no waiting on *that*
end, at least. The algorithm he'd sent had successfully executed
his complex series of trades in less time than it took for the sound
of the chime to reach his ears. It was done.

Jamie pulled a comb from his gray vest and ran it through his slick blond hair. Sensing his act, the liquid crystal displays surrounding his workstation became a three-way mirror.

He called across the aisle. "Dinner, Selena?"

The young Thai woman in the other cubicle simply growled.

"Not an answer," he said, straightening his tie.

"It's the same answer," Selena said. "Even when you're at the table, you never leave the desk. Some of us have other interests, Your Highness."

Before Jamie could respond, a flash came from outside the station, bathing the trading floor in green light. The camera images of Jamie disappeared, replaced by a stream of data. He turned, aware. Had his all-important shipment come in?

Selena spoke calmly and efficiently. "I see it. Eighteen 'boxes at Charlie."

That's not it, he thought. "Manifest?"

"Thulium. Independent traders—we're just the carrier. Arcturus contracts at ten?"

"I'm on it." By habit, Jamie flicked his right hand to bring up a digital report. He dismissed it without a glance. The Quaestor Corporation's technical advisory program had analyzed the incoming payload and made its recommendations; Jamie already knew what they were. And now Quaestor's Earthside financial arm would know, too—as soon as the speed of light allowed. He punched a key.

Another billion dollars. Bam. Bam.

Jamie knew what he was doing, and he knew it wasn't at all fair. Known by the giggle-inducing nickname "whirlibangs," the five interdimensional transit stations orbiting Venus received thousands of containers—known even more provocatively as "bangboxes"—from Signatory worlds every day. By a fluke of twenty-second-century physics, there was no way to know what the containers held until they arrived in normal space. Like artificial gravity, instantaneous communication was still the stuff of science fiction.

And so Venus had remained the combined customs office, immigration stop, and quarantine for the Solar System. Its orbit was near the "sweet spot" where the circular tracks that hurled 'boxes through the dimensional ether functioned best. That wasn't so sweet for humanity, which resided inconveniently on the next planet over—but it was delectable opportunity for Jamie. By keeping a watch on the whirlibangs from Ops Station, Quaestor and the other outfits on the curved floor of the bourse had a three-to-seven-minute jump on Earth's markets. Even if their individual expeditions hadn't brought back the goods from afar, they could certainly trade based on what the markets would do with the new information.

It was an ancient game. By the time the nineteenth-century West Coast newspapers reported what European ships in Boston Harbor held, the markets of the East had already acted. That advantage vanished in later years, with shipping manifests cabled or radioed in advance and computerized trading programs angling for a millisecond's edge on pricing.

But interstellar trading had been going on since the 2110s, and even now, nobody had a clue what was coming through the portals next. It had always flabbergasted visitors to Ops Station. Conveniently named for both the goddess of abundance and its function, Ops was the Solar System's eye on galactic commerce. And yet no one there had any idea what would arrive next. One 'box might carry home a Girl Scout troop, the next ten metric tons of Arcturan lymer guano.

It was no way to run a space railroad.

The saving grace was that the Ops traders got to see the produce of the Orion Arm firsthand—and that gave them here a chance to alter their firms' holdings before Earth's market reacted. It was enough to lure young MBA Jamie to enter Quaestor's training program—and, later, to overcome his stark raving terror at space flight long enough for the mercifully brief transit. He'd feigned the flu during the flight in, sedating himself for the whole trip. The meds for the return were already in his briefcase.

He'd be loopy but happy. And rich beyond measure.

The confirmation chime from Earth sounded. "You beat the Praetor guys," Selena said.

"So what else is new?" He grabbed the cowbell under his chair and gave it a triumphant jangle. Down the line, a broker for their largest competitor swore. Jamie responded with a loud raspberry.

He'd grown to hate these people over the last few months—which was only fair, given the number who'd hated *him* immediately. It didn't matter. It had never mattered. He hadn't come for the companionship, and certainly not for the coffee. All the targets Quaestor had set for him, all the bonus thresholds? Just a game, designed to waste his youth and talent. It took other traders years to realize that. Jamie had figured it out—and acted.

It was all going to be worth it. Let someone else have Trader of the Year. Sometime tonight, the deal of the millennium would close. *His* deal. He'd be able to buy his own coffee farm.

Or maybe even Colombia.

Jamie stood and checked the glistening digital figures imprinted on his palm. The time display generated by the nanoids implanted in his skin was keyed, as always, to New York. He looked nervously outside to Charlie, the closest of the transit hubs, motionless in its wider Venusian orbit. The whirlibang's giant wheel of girders sat silent, exterior lights on the rocket roller coaster blinking as it sank past the transparent pane. There was nothing more futile than watching for a shipment to arrive. Yet he was powerless to do anything else.

Jamie slumped back into his chair.

Why wasn't it here?

✳✳✳

Jamie woke with a start when the chime sounded. He didn't know how long he'd been sleeping at his station; he'd collapsed there so many times in the past that the caterer had started bringing his breakfast directly to the trading desk. But he knew what this particular chime meant: he'd programmed it to sound whenever a single 'box arrived from Altair.

This was it. He stood, heart pounding, and reached for his binoculars.

It was the most beautiful thing he'd ever seen. From across the void, it looked like any other container: cold, gray, and metallic. Seventeen meters long, five meters across, and five meters high. One of countless bangboxes whipping around the Orion Arm.

But this one had forty billion dollars inside.

Jamie sat down and breathed deeply. He'd planned this all along. In seconds, the container, now in normal space, would broadcast its contents across a secure channel to Ops Station. Logistical operators would order a robotic space tug to latch on to the 'box. On receiving orders from the container's owner aboard Ops, they'd direct the tug to a waiting rocket transport already connected to a cluster of other containers bound for Earth. The "last kilometer" would take far longer than the trip across deep space.

After sneaking a look at the rest of the trading floor, Jamie returned his attention to the screens. Activating an interface he'd never used before, he spoke his identifying code and the serial number of the 'box. "Owner, Cowbell Capital Investments. Sturm, Jamison P., proprietor. Destination for this container: receiving yards, spaceport of Johannesburg. Container contents…"

He stopped.

He lifted the binoculars again. *No, that's not right.*

He tapped the microphone attached to his collar. "Logistics?"

"Yeah," a male voice responded.

"This is Ja—I mean, this is the owner of the 'box just in from Charlie. Your tug should be taking it to the *Nördlingen*, right?" He tried not to let his voice waver.

"Not unless you want your passengers dead, sir. That transport has no life-support hookups."

Jamie goggled. "Passengers?"

"Yep. We're clipping on a taxi shell to bring them to Ops."

That was exactly what was happening, Jamie saw. He was almost afraid to ask the next question. "Why here?"

"Because they want to see *you*."

3

Jamie had a theory about his professors back at NYU. Whether they lectured in person or on isopanel, every one of them got dressed directly out of the laundry basket. And in the dark. But the man who now exited the elevator into the receiving area looked as though *he'd* gone through the tumble dry along with his clothes.

Zero gravity was rough on the fashionable: Jamie knew that well. Arrivals to Ops entered through the despun docking port at the center of the torus. Then they went from zero gee to the point-eight of the rotating habitation rings in a leisurely lounge car ride. Unless, that is, the passenger was in a hurry, in which case the elevator ride was the equivalent of an Apollo splashdown. A professional bearing seldom survived. This guy looked as if he'd never had one in the first place. The gray-haired man in his fifties blew his nose into a crumpled handkerchief. Red eyes looked up. "Jamison Sturm?"

"Present."

"Leonid Falcone," he said, wiping his brow with the rag.

"Leo," Jamie said, not sure whether to offer his hand.

"That's *Mr.* Falcone," came the gruff reply. Falcone looked back inside the lift. "These guys are with me."

Jamie looked up at the man's companions, both enormous. He wondered for a moment whether the Cowboys had scheduled an exhibition game in the commissary before recognizing the dress khakis of Quaestor's security detail. "You brought an escort?"

"This is Corporal O'Herlihy and Private Dinner, from my expedition's security detail."

"Private Dinner?" Jamie couldn't help but laugh. "What, no one else showed up?"

The looming Hawaiian glared down at him and growled. "That's right. Make fun of my name."

"Sorry." Flustered, Jamie looked back at Falcone. "I'm sorry. What's this about? You came from Altair?"

"Were you expecting something from Altair, Mr. Sturm?" Bleary eyes glared at him.

Jamie stammered. "Well, I…" Falcone began walking. "I'm the administrator of the Altair Sunward Product and Equipment Center."

"ASPEC," Jamie said. "I've heard of it." Prodded by the men-mountains, he followed. They passed through the main receiving lounge, and Jamie felt the stares of people he'd lived with but whose names he'd never learned. Falcone was indifferent to them. "We need to talk."

"Yes, but I don't have an office—"

"Forget it," Falcone said, waving his hand past a wall-mounted electronic reader. A door snapped open, and Falcone led Jamie into an area he'd never been in before. The trading companies had offices for debriefing arrivals from deep space here, but Falcone walked past the Quaestor rooms toward one normally reserved for independent traders.

Jamie pointed behind him. "Don't you want to use—"

Falcone stood with the door open. "I don't think either of us want the company to hear about this." He stepped inside and took a seat behind a desk.

O'Herlihy and Dinner grabbed Jamie by both arms and slammed him into the chair across from Falcone. Smarting, Jamie looked up, aggravated. "Look, I don't know what this is about, but I don't have to take this!"

Falcone ignored him. He took a portable isopanel from his pocket. "Sturm, your job isn't to move product, is it?"

"I—what?"

"You're a hedger for the company," Falcone said. "When you see that a supply of something is about to hit the Earth market, you make sure it doesn't bite Quaestor in the ass."

"It's more complicated than…" Jamie began to object. Feeling the eyes of the beefy guards on him, he calmed down. "Yeah, basically. Quaestor's got expeditions across the Orion Arm, but we're not the only ones. What we don't bring in ourselves, we need price protection against. So the firm buys, sells, and holds everything known to man—and a bunch of stuff known only to your bug-eyed-monster friends." He looked up at the guards. "No offense."

"None taken, smartass," O'Herlihy said. Dinner just smirked.

"So you deal with Quaestor's Earthly holdings." Falcone looked up from the isopanel, suspicious. "But you're not tipping anybody to the goods we're about to ship through the whirl-ibangs ourselves."

"Tipping?" Jamie straightened. "Of course not. That'd be illegal. Not to mention physically impossible!"

"Hmm."

Jamie didn't like where this was going. Falcone knew something. Or rather, he knew Jamie knew something. Yes, there wasn't any dimensional shortcut for information—no ethereal way of sending information instantaneously across trillions of kilometers. Only matter could make the trip, and only a specific amount of that. But while Quaestor didn't have contact with its traders in deep space, those reps all had their orders. Sure, a licensed Quaestor merchant dispatched to send back iridium from Regulus might send back kegs of Lehosian soup instead; dealers had to be able to make decisions on the spot. But more than likely, she'd send back iridium. And like all the Quaestor hedgers, Jamie had a good idea of what the company was searching for at any moment.

Well, better than a good idea.

"Let's cut the crap," Falcone said. "I think you're in the trading business for yourself."

Jamie rose. "I don't have to take—"

Falcone slapped the isopanel on the table. "Son, I think you'd better have a look at that."

Sweating, Jamie read. Destinations. Cargos. Account numbers. Instructions. After just a few lines, Jamie's heart was in his shoes.

"You've been playing a shell game, my young friend," Falcone said. "You're moving product out there, beyond the whirlibangs. Our company's product—back and forth, from star to star. You've been doing it for months."

Jamie shook his head. "No, no. I told you, I'm just a market specialist—"

"Some specialist." Falcone snatched back the electronic manifest. "Somehow, you got into the Altair expedition's requisitioning system—*my* expedition—and ordered a bunch of material for the security team's warehouse." He nodded to Dinner and O'Herlihy. "These guys' place."

They glared at Jamie.

Falcone continued. "You had containers of excess supplies shipped into Surge Altair's warehouse. But then you ordered them shipped back out again. Regulus. Porrima. All over. As soon as you heard here where the demand was out there, you sent the goods—and the sell orders—to our merchants on the scene. They conducted those trades like any other business. And you…" Falcone paused. Jamie's elbows were on his knees. "You all right, son?"

Jamie wheezed. "No, it's okay. I just think I might be hyperventilating a little bit."

Falcone rolled his eyes. "You couldn't do it with our usual trading goods. Our officials here know everything we've got for sale. But the supplies the surge teams receive aren't on those books." He eyed Jamie. "After a few months of this shell game, you must have run up quite a profit."

Jamie looked green. There was no sense denying it now. He mumbled something.

"What?"

"Forty percent," Jamie said. "On a hundred billion dollars in goods. Forty billion dollars."

"On a hundred billion dollars of company property that was never supposed to be out there." Falcone looked keenly at Jamie. "Wait. That's what you were expecting today instead of us, wasn't it? Your profits!"

The administrator was right, but Jamie didn't say anything. He simply stared at the desk.

"Jesus," Falcone said. He looked up at O'Herlihy. "Can you believe this guy?"

"I sure can, sir," O'Herlihy said, cracking his knuckles. "We've caught us a pirate in our home port."

Startled by the term, Jamie leaned forward and pointed at the manifest. "Wait, wait. I didn't *steal* anything! I traded the company's goods, sure. But you know how big the warehouses are for the security details. They *always* oversupply the grunts!"

"We're protecting the traders' asses!" Dinner snarled.

"And I'm sure you do a fine job. But there's excess capacity. With the billions we spend making you guys into walking death machines, nobody paid attention to me rotating in some goods that other civilizations actually wanted." He punched the desk beside the manifest. "But it's all back there, Falcone. I'm done. I put the principal into replacing all the goods in the warehouse. Go look. It's all there—and my profit is, too." He looked around, his lip curling. "Er...is that coming later, or what?"

Falcone laughed hard, setting off a coughing fit. Jamie's attempt at a smile vanished as Falcone caught his breath. "You need to see this for yourself," the administrator said. "We're taking you back to Altair."

"Altair?" Jamie laughed. "I'm going home soon!" He gulped, considering the prospect of the trip. "I'm a desk-trader. You guys can strap your asses into a shoebox and get shot across the galaxy if you want—"

"You don't get it, Sturm!" Falcone said. "You're slick, I'll grant you that. But something's happened you don't know about, and this thing is about to blow up on everyone, me included!" Falcone shook with anger. "I don't have time to explain. I have to check around here to see what the company already knows." He pointed angrily at Jamie. "But in the meantime I need to get you off this station, to where I can keep an eye on you. That means Altair!"

Altair! Jamie slipped in his chair. His expensive shoes suddenly interested him, and he took a closer look. It was nearly seventeen light-years to Altair, or about a forty-five-minute transit; whirlibang travel wasn't instantaneous for those in the passenger 'boxes. He doubted there was enough sedative on Ops to keep him from an embolism.

Falcone looked over the desk. "You all right, Sturm?"

"No, that would be me hyperventilating again," Jamie said. He looked up, green, as Dinner and O'Herlihy grabbed for his arms. "Can you get me a paper bag, or something?"

"To breathe into?" O'Herlihy asked.

"That'd be one reason."

4

"…and when the time comes," the solemn voice said, "remind yourself: nothing is more important than being right. They will tempt you, try to lure you away from the cause. But they will have nothing to offer you, my listeners—because you have all you need: the truth!"

The deep voice rose, talking faster into the communicator on the lectern. "Freedom? I'd rather have the truth. Power? I'd rather be right. Our people, the Xylanx, have been wrong for far too long. I will not add to their failings—and neither should you. We are the Severed. We live apart now, but we will lead our people back!"

Now, the speaker slowed again, his manner humble, his cadence respectful. "These are the words of Kolvax, descended from Forrah Glay. These are the words of truth. Speak the words, my followers—until next time."

Across the makeshift chapel, Kolvax's assistant gave the signal. "Message transmitted."

"Until next time, another waste dump out the airlock," Kolvax said. The hulking biped in black let loose with a ripping fart, audible even outside his high-tech environment suit. *That* was what his sniveling followers really deserved to hear. Kolvax turned toward his office and threw his parchment script over his shoulder. Tellmer scrambled to catch it. "Incinerate that," Kolvax snarled.

Tellmer blanched, horrified. "But it is a holy writ—"

"I wrote it on the commode. Send it back to from whence it came." Kolvax shook his head. Tellmer was still a believer. Were any of his listeners? He didn't know—or much care.

Members of the species known as the Xylanx, Kolvax and his band of followers had been exiled to the rotating space station by rulers with a cruel sense of humor. How else to explain it? The Severed stood for many things, but chief among them was disdain for the unclean. This end of the galaxy was a menagerie of creatures with strange forms; precious few had two arms, two legs, and a head like a being should. The Severed had sought to keep the Xylanx apart from all that.

So the members of the ruling body, the Dominium, must have thought it hilarious to banish Kolvax and his troublesome band to a run-down, strange-smelling station abandoned by the very filthy aliens they despised.

If so, their joke missed the mark in one respect they would never know about. Kolvax didn't believe his "truths" at all.

"Give me the spritzer," he said, leading Tellmer into the office.

"Yes, Great Kolvax." Awkward in his bulky space suit, slight Tellmer fumbled under the strangely shaped desk—the stars only knew what kind of creature it had been built for—and found a cylindrical container. Kolvax took it and began tending to his tree.

Sitting on the counter behind his lectern, it was the only personal effect they had let him bring: a puny, barely green cutting that had failed to thrive, no matter how much attention the Great Kolvax gave it. It would have done better in one of the great habitats back home, where the Xylanx did not wear their full armor; carbon dioxide and moisture circulated more freely there. But not wearing helmets here would run counter to the sanitary beliefs of the Severed. Kolvax had kicked himself for starting a movement with such views. *Next time*, he thought, *I'm going to start a religion based on public drunkenness.*

If anyone could pull it off, he could. Kolvax was a communicator, a politician, a general, a pontiff. Among the Xylanx, those could be the same things—but Kolvax was an unlikely candidate. He didn't have the right look for it. The face inside his helmet wasn't quite the same as the faces of the other members of his kind. His forehead was just a bit too high, his smeller just a bit too narrow. His fingers weren't as meaty as the others'. And while he loomed over Tellmer, he was short compared with other Xylanx. He still had just as much muscle in that more compact frame, as many of his enemies had learned. But he wasn't the perfect Xylanx specimen, by far.

They were small things, and in this would-be era of enlightenment, they had not impeded his rise. As all their people were required to, Kolvax had served with the Xylanx militia known as the Stalkers—and had fought well, rising to a generalship at a young age. But whether because of the old prejudices or his own mouth, he had gone no further. The Dominium was made up of people of lineage; no one else need apply. Kolvax had battered his bald dome against the wall long enough to realize that.

Fortunately, he had other talents. The booming voice that had driven his soldiers to fight with abandon was just as capable of moving minds. Ironically, his enemies in power had handed him the weapon. Media posts were just another sop to the military, sinecures to keep rivals at bay. Few Stalkers could form a sentence after a decade of being blasted and patched back together. But Kolvax was intact and intoxicating to his listeners—and with the eyes of a warrior, he'd found an unprotected flank.

No one was speaking for the purity of the species, so he did. He didn't look like the Xylanx ideal, but that simply inspired the thread about aliens and their diseases. In habitats across the region, Xylander veterans began wearing every day the armor they'd once saved for away missions. And why not? Behind their opaque face masks, *everyone* could be the ideal. That idea had been a huge draw. Kolvax sometimes had trouble restraining his laughter at some of the hideous uglies his cause attracted. He was doing the galaxy a service by keeping them out of sight!

But Kolvax couldn't earn his way into power, and he couldn't bargain for it, either. As soon as the Severed began setting themselves apart in serious numbers, the Dominium had moved against him. Kolvax was too popular to murder, but he could be neutered. First his followers were scattered to far-flung outposts—and finally, so was the self-titled Black Priest himself.

For two miserable years, it had been only Kolvax and his most loyal followers in this disgusting place. All alone, with a twig that seemed to respond to nothing. Kolvax drenched it again and gave up. He cast away the spritzer. "Cancel today's confessions, Tellmer. I'm going to take a—"

"Wait!" Tellmer stood in the doorway to the office, looking out into the so-called chapel. "You there!" Tellmer yelled out. "Guards! Stop them!"

Kolvax heard a scuffle—and then the electric whine of a shockpulse. *Now what?* He reached behind the counter for his ceremonial bludgeon, used with increasing frequency these days to settle doctrinal disputes. Arriving in the doorway, he saw fighting in the chapel. Half a dozen Xylanx believers charged in, overpowering his guards. All were armored, Kolvax's trademark golden collars ringing their necks beneath their helmets.

Tellmer rushed into the fray, armored arms waving. "The Black Priest is in contemplation! He cannot be—"

One of the intruders lashed out with a whirling fire-bolo that caught Tellmer just beneath the elbow. A sizzling flash later, and Tellmer was screaming on the ground, right next to his detached arm.

Kolvax looked not at his howling assistant but at the weapons he thought he'd hidden away. *So they've been into the armory.* It had amused the Xylanx rulers to supply the exiles with weapons; they expected exactly this.

"Pick up your arm," Kolvax said, stepping over Tellmer to enter the chapel. He could see the anger in the rebels' faces— which meant something all on its own. "What goes on here?" he yelled, slapping the rusty club against his gloved hand. "I can see your faces, adepts. You know facial screens should be set to opaque in this holy place!"

"Holy, my ass," the lead invader said. Kolvax recognized him as Gerrok, one of his more annoying pests. "This 'holy place' of yours was a counting room for a bunch of tentacle-heads," Gerrok snarled. "And it still reeks of it. I can't take off my helmet even in private—and we've been so long without a supply visit that our filters are clogged!"

"True cleanliness is in the—"

"Enough!" Gerrok shouted as he fired the shockpulse cannon in his hand. The blast struck the lectern just to Kolvax's left, blowing it into pieces.

Kolvax looked drily at it. "Fine. You have grievances?"

"We *live* in grievance," Gerrok's female companion said. "We've heard enough of your sermons! You're a prattling has-been. I can't believe we let you lead us into treason!"

"Into exile," another said. "Into prison!"

"*Into oblivion!*" Gerrok yelled.

Kolvax set his faceplate to transparent. It was better for them to see him now, his dark eyes. "Do you recall when you took the pledge to join my sect?" He pointed to the modest yellow ring at Gerrok's neck. "Do you recall when I affixed those collars to your uniforms?"

Gerrok moved menacingly closer. "If you're about to ask what the collars mean to us—forget it! We're loyal to the ideals, Kolvax. We have no attachment to you!"

"That's not what I was going to say." With his free hand, Kolvax touched a control on the wrist holding the bludgeon. "I was going to explain that they're not for decoration." He looked at the six rebels. "Right now, the emitters inside your collars are generating microscopic laser beams. That would be that stinging feeling you're experiencing."

Kolvax watched Gerrok's eyes freeze. One after another, the other intruders dropped their weapons and began pawing at their necks.

"Don't worry about the sensation," Kolvax said. "As the deflectors within the collars come online, an energy field develops, much like the ones we use in our prison doors—our *real* prisons, mind you. And that should be the end of your problems."

Eyes bulging, Gerrok raised his weapon high and began to move…

…and then his helmeted head tumbled off his shoulders. Around him, five more heads followed, bouncing on the floor of the holy chapel. The bodies followed, gushing geysers of vital fluids.

Kolvax looked down at Tellmer, writhing nearby. "Now they're *really* the Severed," he said, grinning.

Tellmer didn't laugh. He pawed anxiously at his own collar with his surviving hand. "Are all our collars like this?"

"Don't worry, Tellmer. If I didn't kill you over your cooking, you're immortal." Kolvax turned back to the office. He stopped by the doorway and picked up Tellmer's oozing left forearm.

"Here," he said, pitching the limb into his assistant's lap. "Take an hour off. See what the medic can do with that. But I want dinner on time. And it had better be good."

"Thank you, Great Kolvax," Tellmer said, beleaguered. Before his master stepped out of sight, he dared an addition. "There will be more."

"What's that?"

"There will be more," Tellmer said, looking back on the dead. "It's been too long. True Xylanx can't live like this—hidden away."

"Our forebears knew a lot about hiding," Kolvax said. "But don't worry. Something will happen. I have faith." With that, he returned inside for his overdue nap.

5

The human era of interstellar travel had started three years before Jamie was born, but he knew the story like everyone else. Observers had detected an oblong object hurtling into the Solar System on a wide arcing path. As it headed for the inner planets, many worried that an unknown Kuiper Belt body had been knocked sunward. Calculations of its size only worsened fears: 2103 BH$_7$ was the size of a railcar and twice as wide. As it continued its approach, however, it became clear the object posed no collision threat to Earth.

But it could have if it'd wanted to—and that was the new wrinkle. Because its trajectory changed not once, but twice, angling to catch up with Venus. Long before it began orbiting the cloudy planet, searchers for extraterrestrial life who'd buzzed for decades over unexplained signals knew they had their quarry.

Researchers quickly roused the nearest thing to the visitor, an Indian Venus probe inactive since the 2090s. Its cameras, used to looking downward, saw the alien craft—for it was one—unfold into a space platform. Two weeks later, one similarly sized box after another materialized at the Solar System's edge. All made their way to Venusian orbit, where they attached modules to the growing agglomeration.

The resulting contraption resembled an amusement park ride in space: a circular track half a kilometer in diameter, connected via several spokes to a central hub. When the structure was complete, a single boxy module began moving inside the track, accelerating as if in a centrifuge. And then the container simply vanished in a greenish flash. It all happened in silence, without explanation.

A hastily arranged manned international mission reached Venus in December, its arrival coincidentally timed two hundred years after the Wright Brothers' first flight. The investigators got there just in time to witness another flash and the appearance of a new vehicle, decelerating to a stop within the alien station's rings. This time, its occupants had something to say.

The Regulans' first words, once communication had been established, were of greetings and peace. Their second words were to offer the Earthlings a fine deal on Hordugan cheese tapestries. Oh, and, by the way, did humans have anything to sell?

Humanity learned the transit station—dubbed a "whirl-ibang" after a popular ride at Funworld Mumbai—exploited a loophole in physics permitting faster-than-light travel. The hub served a packet of matter to a twin device tuned to receive it, parsecs distant. Traveling without a receiving hub in place was possible but incredibly dangerous; hence, the unoccupied probe's arrival and the device's initial test run.

The first thing trailblazing merchants sent into an uncharted system was a way to get home.

Events moved swiftly. The first human voyage to Regulus was the following May, intentionally scheduled three centuries after the day Lewis and Clark left for the West. Finding the stellar neighborhood absolutely teeming with life, humanity responded with interest. More travelers followed by the hundreds—and then thousands. Jamie Sturm was born to an Earth with almost limitless horizons.

Sure, the mechanism of travel had disappointed those imagining colossal starships and tiny vessels warping through space. The universe accepted nothing larger than a 'box through its loopholes, and transporting anything smaller consumed prohibitive amounts of energy. Ships and stations had to be assembled from building blocks. But humanity was good at building, and container traffic was something Earth merchants understood. Whirlibangs paired with other stars were constructed. By 2138, the opportunity was open to most anyone who wanted to go.

Jamie had never wanted to go, but that didn't stop his escorts from shoving him into the 'box preparing to depart from Charlie. They'd manhandled him the whole way, sneaking him back into the transport Falcone had arrived in. They hadn't even let him pack a bag.

"I don't want to do this," Jamie said, grasping for a handhold in the zero gravity. "I'll just go home, like I was supposed to. Falcone can square things!"

"Forget it, man. You're going." O'Herlihy's frame blocked the exit—not that Jamie would have been able to get there if he tried. He was having enough trouble staying off the ceiling.

The interior of the passenger 'box was spare. Where the commercial modules the tugs took to and from Earth had dozens of seats, this one had only eleven—including one at the front, near a control panel. At the controls sat a brown-skinned woman in her sixties, dressed as his escorts were.

"This the guy?" golden-haired Geena Madaki asked, glancing back at Jamie for only a second.

"Yup," O'Herlihy said.

Madaki saw Jamie swimming against the ceiling, desperately trying to make it back to the seats. "Good God," she said. Observing that O'Herlihy and Dinner were casually strapping themselves in, she activated the door seal.

Jamie had recovered his bearings against a wall when a metallic clang reverberated through the compartment, sending him sideways. He'd seen it a hundred times from the outside: the container was in the queue and ready to be loaded onto the whirlibang's energized track. Nocked like an arrow. There wasn't much time!

Finding a surface to press against, Jamie shoved himself toward an empty chair just behind Madaki. Hurriedly strapping himself in, he glared back at Dinner. "Thanks for the help."

"My pleasure," Dinner said.

Jamie gulped as the 'box lurched again. A noisy clack, and the container began to move in the tracks. Slowly at first but quickly picking up speed. The trader felt the pull now, the floor of the cabin hugging the outside of the colossal wheel of rails. Gravity had been simulated centrifugally on Ops, but this was increasing swiftly. "How fast will this go?"

"Don't fear," Madaki said, punching a button. "As we speed up, the pulse generators rip us a nice hole through space—our angular momentum goes off into another dimension. Then it's smooth sailing."

Jamie looked back behind his guards. For the first time, he noticed their HardSHEL suits, secured in transparent lockers. But there were only two. "Shouldn't I have a space suit or something?"

"There's one under my seat if we need it," Madaki said. "Which we won't."

"What about me?"

"You're out of luck," she said. She glanced back at O'Herlihy. "This child fret all the time?"

"I can shut him up if you want," the bruiser replied.

"No problem," the pilot said. She looked back at Jamie. "We're already in the rift," she said. "Good and easy. You can breathe."

Jamie looked at his hands. His fingers had crushed indentations into the armrests. "Oh," he said.

But he didn't let go.

✳ ✳ ✳

Jamie knew the calculation by heart. In traversing twenty-four light-years, one day would pass in normal time—and one hour, for those aboard the 'box. Forty minutes passed in the cabin during transit, time in which the security guys snored. There was nothing to look at: for his benefit or not, Madaki had shuttered the forward viewport. They didn't need to see to travel anyway. A 'box was a speeding bullet while in transit—with just as much control.

The trader had almost begun to relax when the cabin shook with a noisy, crashing jolt. The breath went out of Jamie's lungs as the 'box returned to normal space—and a rocketing spin around the rings of another whirlibang. He choked a comment. "Good and easy?"

Madaki gave Jamie a sly look. "Didn't say anything about stopping. That's the 'bang' in whirlibang."

The Altair whirlibang rings drew energy from the 'box, slowing it to a gliding stop. The compartment detached from the tracks, and Jamie could feel the robotic arms attaching the engine mount, transforming their vessel into a small shuttle. Madaki triggered the forward viewpanel to open.

Staring through the filtered screen at Altair, Jamie looked on light from another sun. Only this one was twice Sol's size, with a spin so fast it had become a squashed tomato of energy. One of Earth's closer neighbors, in the G Cloud with Alpha Centauri, Altair had been one of the earlier outposts for Quaestor's merchants. Most had moved on to more lucrative territories; it was precisely why Jamie had chosen the system's base for his scheme. Overbuilt and underused. Who'd notice?

As the newly created shuttle soared toward Alabeyd, the asteroid home of the Altair expedition, Jamie felt his heart pounding. He'd told Falcone the truth: he'd restored all the merchandise he'd traded from here. And somewhere, in a warehouse on the other side of that massive rock, was his treasure. He was glad he'd come, now. Falcone would realize the best thing for his career was to feign ignorance—and Jamie would be able to send his profits home as planned.

He saw ASPEC first, a series of shabby concrete domes on the surface, with hangars sized to accept large tugs bearing 'boxes. He was surprised to see no tugs were here today. "You guys must be doing worse than I thought," he said aloud.

"They evacuated when it happened," Madaki said.

What? Curious, Jamie unhooked his harness and pushed himself toward the bulkhead. At the window, he looked past ASPEC to where the barracks should be—and saw the gouge in the surface of the asteroid. Fragments of a warehouse structure rose this way and that, buried in the tumble of rocks.

Jamie's muscles went limp, and had gravity been around to cooperate he would have sunk to his knees. He looked across the wreckage, straining to identify anything. "What—what happened?"

"The Spore happened," O'Herlihy said, waking up.

"That's your barracks, right?" Jamie felt faint. "*It ate the warehouse?*"

"Pretty much." The muscular man stretched in his seat. "We only saved one container out of the whole thing."

Jamie turned, eyes wide. "*What was in it?*" he blurted. Regaining his composure, he spoke more calmly. "I want to see it."

"Oh, you'll see it," O'Herlihy said, rubbing his knuckles against his chest. "I wouldn't miss this for the world!"

6

Bridget's mind went perversely back to a childhood rhyme before she took a second look at the floor. Yes, she had indeed stepped on a crack. The surface inside ASPEC station was smooth and gray, created from the same mixture of local aggregate and imported starcrete as the overhead dome. With Alabeyd's low gravity, it should have been close to invulnerable. And yet, right outside the entrance to the personnel receiving area there was a tiny fissure where one had not been before.

She punched the communicator at her collar before remembering no one was home in Structural Engineering. Falcone had evacuated everyone until the last Spore recon was complete, and only he could order them back. While Bridget waited, she and her teammates had gotten some time in on the power excavators working salvage. But as fun as those contraptions were—and Bridget loved machines more than anything—the work hadn't served to relax her at all. She'd have gone with Falcone in a heartbeat…if it hadn't involved going to the Solar System.

She wouldn't be ready for that for a while. Too many memories. Bad ones, of a terrible day eight years earlier—and all the terrible days that had followed. They had chased her out here, to the only outfit that would hire her. But while ASPEC was a marginal operation on the best of days, she wasn't about to let anything hurt it. Anything else, anyway.

A sound woke her to the present. In the next room, massive hinges turned. Bridget forgot about the floor and brushed herself off. *Okay*, she thought. *Let's see what they've brought me.*

The shuttle was in, the inner door closing behind it. Bridget walked in to see O'Herlihy and Dinner debarking. She thought for a second they were alone—until O'Herlihy stepped to the right. There, invisible in the soldier sandwich, walked a man roughly her age in a gray business suit. Slicked-back hair mussed from the ride, he looked around, surveying the area as if he owned the place.

Maybe he thought he did. After years with the security teams, Bridget had grown to loathe the pixel-pushers back home. But what this one had done put him in a whole new class. "This him?" she asked O'Herlihy.

"Chief Yang, I give you Jamison P. Sturm, Esq.," her teammate said, stepping out of the way.

The suit looked her over. "Call me Jamie," he said, somewhat wary. "I'd shake your hand but you're holding a very large gun. Is this normal?"

Bridget didn't look down at the rifle. She hadn't even remembered she was carrying it, but she already knew she didn't like his reedy voice. "You never know what'll come out of these containers," she said stiffly.

Jamie stepped off the ramp and looked around. "So, Chief, I saw there was some trouble here. I hear you saved a cargo unit?"

"Yes," she said icily. "This way."

Bridget led the trader and his escorts into another dome. In the middle of the round room, the battered 'box recovered from the crater sat beneath powerful lights. They'd patched the gash with sealant after finding it, but that had rendered its main door unusable. A gantry had been positioned next to it, with a stair-case leading to the container's flat topside.

Jamie studied it. "I can't make out an ID number."

"It's been through a lot," she said, leading him up the metal steps. "But we were able to save what was in it."

Eagerly, Jamie followed her up to the open top hatch. She stepped aside so he could look into the wide circular hole. Jamie squinted, puzzled. "It looks—green?" He pointed to the por-table lamp behind her on the roof. "Can you bring that closer? I want to get a better look."

"Certainly," Bridget said. She stepped back behind him— and delivered a solid roundhouse kick to the trader's backside. Jamie tumbled face-first into the opening and splashed into an emerald pool below.

"*Gah!*" Jamie said, surfacing in the goop. Exploded plastic con-tainers protruded from the morass beside him, and the ooze pul-sated like a living thing as he wallowed. Hair caked with green, Jamie looked up to see Bridget and her teammates above looking down the hatch and smiling. "Help me!" Jamie yelled. "*It's the Spore!*"

"Calm down, genius." Bridget laughed heartily for the first time in days. "Open your mouth and taste."

The financier had no intention of doing anything of the kind, Bridget saw. But struggling in the mass started him sinking again, and he got a mouthful anyway.

Jamie coughed, choking. "That's—that's—"

"Guacamole," Bridget said. Her teammates laughed. "Seven met-ric tons of it, to be precise—minus whatever vented to space earlier."

The trader gulped and gagged.

Bridget rolled her eyes and kicked a cable into the container. "You can haul yourself out," she said.

* * *

Jamie sat, verdant and pungent, at the foot of the 'box. Suit encrusted with green, he clawed clumps from his hair. Dinner and O'Herlihy stood guard over him, clearly amused. "What are *you* looking at?" Jamie said, aggravated.

"A dip," the Hawaiian said.

O'Herlihy laughed. "Yeah, too bad the Spore ate all the chips." He plucked a finger's worth of the stuff off Jamie's shoulder and tasted.

Arms crossed, Bridget scowled at Jamie. "I wish it was funny."

Jamie glared right back. "You pushed me in on purpose!" He raised his arms, sending dollops flying. "What *was* all that?"

"I told you," Bridget said. "Guacamole from a plant in Michoacán, Mexico—one of the exporters Quaestor deals with." She leaned against the 'box. "As for what it's doing here, Wall Street, you already know that. It was part of the cargo you requisitioned for my unit's supply house. You know, the building that's supposed to house machinery and tools to keep my team operating? Falcone says you were running an export store for aliens out of it!"

O'Herlihy nodded, mouth full. "Them aliens do love guacamole."

Jamie lowered his head. "I'm finished," he said.

Bridget stared at him. "Wait," she said. "You thought there was something else in there, didn't you?"

Jamie looked up at the woman through avocado-encrusted eyelashes. "Yeah," he said, resigned. "Forty billion dollars."

"*What?*"

"It was a 'box full of rhodium from the Regulan mines," he said. "It's what I consolidated the profits into after I was done with my trading orders." One of the rarest substances in the galaxy, it would've fetched forty billion easily on Earth. "Why couldn't *that* one have survived?"

"*Rhodium!*" Bridget yelled. Jamie saw the woman's eyebrows flare.

"Rhodium," Falcone said. The administrator walked into the facility, followed by a tall, slender, black-haired woman. He saw Jamie covered in green and smirked. "I see you've met already."

Bridget didn't look at Falcone. Instead she walked over and grabbed Jamie by the greasy collar. She shook him. "*Do you know what you've done?*"

Jamie's eyes widened. "What's the story, lady? You're just the hired guns! What do *you* care if—"

Bridget slammed him against the side of the 'box. Jamie's slick clothing sent him sliding off it and onto the floor. He looked up at her, astonished. Bridget turned to Falcone. "*Tell him!*"

Falcone started to speak—but the young woman who'd arrived with Falcone spoke first. "We don't know much about the Spore," the olive-skinned woman in her early twenties said. "But we know what it can't resist. Rhodium."

Falcone nodded. "Forgive my manners," he said. "This is Lissa Trovatelli, your new Q/A. She rode back with me."

Jamie looked up. "Q/A?"

"Quartermaster-Armorer," Bridget snarled. "She's my team's new tech." Their last junior genius had shipped out just after the Spore attack. Bridget barely looked at the new arrival. "Thanks to you, Wall Street, she's got no place to work."

"It doesn't matter," Falcone said, staring down at Jamie. "Our genius here has busted out the whole expedition."

Falcone quickly explained what he'd learned in his hours above Venus dealing with Corporate. The expedition was on the hook for all the cargo lost. "It was never insured, because we never knew it was there!" He looked gravely to Bridget. "You'll catch hell for this, too, Yang. For not protecting the goods—"

Bridget exploded. "We didn't know it was there!"

"It doesn't matter," Falcone repeated. He appeared older than she'd ever seen him. "We've got a hundred days before the Quaestor auditor will call it all due." He looked down at Jamie. "You got a hundred billion dollars on you, sport?"

"I had forty billion," Jamie said, sullen. "Something ate it." He smeared his hands on the floor—before realizing that everyone was staring at him again. He looked around, confused. "What? What's the problem?"

"You are, hotshot!" Bridget shook her fists. "What you've done to us. You don't see it, do you? Sitting back there on Venus, making your millions. You don't see where it comes from! To you, all the goods the expeditions send back just appear out of thin air. Magic through the wormhole! But somebody has to strike the deals, set up the warehouses, install the factories and keep the traders from getting killed by whatever's out there. That's *us*, you moron! Altair is...*was* Falcone's whole expedition. You didn't just wipe yourself out. You took us down, too!"

Jamie shook his head, chastened by the barrage. "Look, I know you've got a lot to write off. I'm sorry about that—"

"He's sorry!" Bridget said, laughing.

"—but you've got time, and this *is* a trading center. You may be able to square the books in a quarter, if your traders hustle—"

Falcone glared. "And you leave us holding the bag, right? I'll tell you, Sturm, I don't care if we all go down, but I'll sure as hell see you digging sewage lines in the Sahara if we do!"

The new Q/A spoke up. "We couldn't do it from here anyway," Trovatelli said, matter of factly. "This station's done for."

"We were discussing our careers just now," Falcone said, annoyed at the young woman he'd brought.

"That's not what I mean." Brown eyes scanned the ceiling. "I saw that crater out there," Trovatelli said. "Seven-Alpha must have gotten into the substrata."

Bridget stared. "You can tell that just by looking?"

Falcone waved his arms at Trovatelli. "No, no, no! We did a gravimetric analysis. The asteroid is still sound—"

A low thunderclap rumbled through the dome. Jamie looked up. "Don't tell me."

Bridget's eyes scanned the walls. In the shadows, a thin crack now traced from the floor up the inside of the dome.

Falcone saw it and shook his head. "That's nothing! We patch bigger than that all the time."

"No," Bridget said, walking to the wall. She traced the fissure with her gloved finger. "I saw another one, earlier."

The new Q/A flipped out her pocket isopanel. "This asteroid may have been just fine this morning," Trovatelli said. "But Altair's gas giants are coming around soon. There's enough mass intact to keep Alabeyd from breaking up, but they're perturbing this body just enough—"

"I'm already perturbed!" Falcone blanched. He looked off into the distance. "Will we decompress?" he asked, his throat dry.

"Not today," Lissa said. "But you'll have to reinforce every surface to keep the place airtight."

"That means emptying ASPEC," Falcone said. "We won't be able to trade out of here for months!"

"Then we're dead," Bridget said. She glared at Jamie.

"And you killed us."

7

His clothes sticking to his skin, Jamie followed Falcone and the surge team chief to the head office. There was nothing else for him to do now. Yes, the odds had been against the surviving 'box being the right container, but so much had gone wrong he'd clung to the slim hope that his treasure had survived. So much for that.

"I bet his horsing around is how we got the wrong armor," Chief Yang said accusingly.

Jamie staggered into the meeting room and collapsed in the nearest chair. The woman's latest accusation could be true, for all he knew; couriers had made all his trades, and something could have gone wrong. But there wasn't anything he could do about it now—not that it'd stopped the woman from haranguing him further.

He looked up, idly staring into the holographic star chart in the rotunda above the meeting table. Dots and lines, stars and connections. All his life, the network had meant money to him. Now, he wondered if the map held any place to escape to.

Could he run? It was a pointless thought. He wasn't a pilot. He couldn't get a 'box to the whirlibang, much less activate it.

Clearly, the chief cared about her team and the operation here: he knew intelligence and spirit when he saw them. Even now, she was imploring Falcone, trying to find a solution to their problems. "There's got to be a way," she said. "If they declare us insolvent, Quaestor will cut us all loose!"

Jamie knew it was wasted energy at this point. "What can I do?" Falcone said. "A hundred billion! You know we've never cleared a tenth of that in a quarter."

"There's always a way," Bridget said.

"I know how much it means to you, Bridget," Falcone said. "I know you kind of got stuck working here—and I appreciate your devotion. God knows you try harder than anyone else in this outfit. But I just can't see a way out."

Jamie's ears perked up. "*Bridget?*" He looked over at the dark-haired woman in disbelief. That face. He'd seen it in the news. She was the right age, too—around thirty-three. "You're Bridget Yang!"

Bridget looked at him coolly. "Yes."

"I know you," Jamie said, trying to recall the historical account of the infamous Overland disaster, years earlier. "You're Bridget Yang! You started the war!"

"Hey," Falcone said defensively. "It wasn't that simple."

Bridget wasn't looking at him. But Jamie kept on, remembering the events from eight years earlier. "The Arcturo-Solar War—the first interstellar war we ever got into. It all started because of you!" He looked probingly at her. "Quaestor hired *you?*"

The question sounded worse than he'd intended. But Bridget looked up at him, unruffled. "They hired *you*, too."

Jamie didn't know what to say to that. Finding Yang out here was certainly the capper. A lot of people died in that war, and rightly or not, Bridget had come in for some of the blame. He didn't know the company was into human reclamation projects—but if there was any place to hide someone like Yang, Altair was it. He slumped back down, and Bridget returned to her appeal.

For a place so full of opportunity, space certainly collected a lot of people on their last chance. His father had used all the money the family had—and some it didn't have—to buy a seat to the stars, back when it cost a fortune. Marty Sturm's trip, allegedly to clear his head, had ended with the man "going migrant," as so many had in the early 2110s. The family had never heard from him again.

Was Jamie's father running a falafel stand on Porrima—or had he perhaps become lunch for a Spore? Jamie had spent little time wondering about that over the years. All he knew was that he somehow inherited the black sheep status himself when his mother married into the politically powerful Keeler family. Since childhood, his ambition had been getting ahead on his own—far ahead of his mother and stepfamily.

The rhodium deal was supposed to do it. Instead, Jamie would be going home. Quaestor would have his hide, and others would want a piece of him as well. The Keelers would deny being aware of his existence. *The end.*

Falcone wasn't listening to Yang's pleas, Jamie saw. No, he was blowing his nose again and missing the handkerchief. Nauseated, Jamie turned his tired eyes back upward.

They saw something unexpected.

"What's that?" Jamie pointed at a line heading from Altair's whirlibang station in Aquila to a lonely point in Draco. "That hub, with all the links coming out of it?"

Falcone looked over his shoulder for a second before returning to his despair. "That's nothing. Sigma Draconis."

"Yeah, but it's in your color," Jamie said. "The whirlibang, the depot—it's your territory. Your expedition owns it."

The gruff administrator chortled. "It's useless. An old station—God knows who built it. Some white elephant that PraetorCorp picked up in a deal with the Regulans. Nobody else in Quaestor wanted it, so we got stuck. Mothballed. Nobody's even visited it in years."

Jamie stared. "But it links into a slew of inhabited systems," he said. From near the northern astronomical pole relative to Earth, the connections zigged and zagged outward, tracing through the section of the near sky that led toward Orion. "I've never heard of those places. Why haven't you gone prospecting?"

"Because we're not here to waste our time," Bridget said, irritated. "The biggest trading power in the Signatory Systems and the biggest conglomerate on Earth couldn't make a go of that area. Do you really think *we* could?"

Jamie looked around at the meeting room. "No, I guess not," he said. He didn't know whether Yang's surge team was good at its job or not, though Yang certainly seemed to like yelling at people. But he'd known from the financials that the traders of the Altair expedition were third-rate, and the shabby look of the boardroom confirmed it. This was a place to make deals?

Falcone stood, silent, staring into the images. "You know, it might work," he said.

Bridget looked up, seemingly startled to hear hope in that gravelly voice. "What?"

"He's right. Not one planet on that whole path has been opened," Falcone said. He looked at her, bloodshot eyes dead serious. "You know the deal. Any first-contact contracts the expedition writes go to *our* bottom line, not the corporation's. We find a hundred billion dollars in new business out there, and we erase what's just happened here." He fished for his pocket isopanel.

Falcone seemed interested, but the more Jamie thought about it, the more it felt like grasping at straws. The odds weighed against the idea; most trailblazing trips never earned a dollar. "I guess you could try," Jamie said, sensing Falcone was in the mood to try anything. "But it's no sure thing. It'd be a hundred-day sales offensive into a part of the Orion Arm humans have never visited—"

"'Orion Offensive.' Catchy. You'd better get to it," Falcone said.

"Me?" Jamie bolted upright.

"Your problem. Your solution," Falcone said. He started figuring.

"Hold on," Jamie said, flabbergasted. This wasn't what he'd intended at all. He stood. "I'm a commodities guy, not some… *traveling salesman!*"

Bridget glared at him, eyes steely. "Some of those salesmen die on this job," she said, voice dripping with disdain. "And their escorts."

"All the more reason I'm not going!" Jamie looked at her, flustered. "Besides, I thought your job was to protect these people. How many do you lose?"

"Don't you ever read your attrition reports? It's no trip to the beach out there!" She looked directly at him. "No," she said, reading his eyes. "You don't read the reports. We're just numbers to you. Color me shocked."

Jamie stepped around the table and pleaded with Falcone. "Leo. Really, you don't want me for this—"

"I don't," Falcone snapped. "But thanks to you, you're what I've got. My traders aren't here and my depot's falling apart. It'll take weeks to reposition product for Sigma Draconis. You're a great hustler when you're trading across the light-years, Sturm. Let's see how you do in person!"

Bridget laughed. "He'll be eaten alive by the first thing he pisses off," she said, smirking at Jamie. "If they can stomach him."

"I've taken that into account," Falcone said. He passed her the handheld data device. "Here's *your* new orders, Yang."

The chief gawked. "You don't mean—" "You're rebased. Surge Altair is now Surge Sigma Draconis," the administrator said. "I want you headed there to set up shop within the hour." Wiping his nose, Falcone walked past the stunned pair. He called back from the doorway. "You've had to take down some real menaces in this job, Bridget. Let's see if you can keep this menace alive… long enough to save us!"

✳ ✳ ✳

"Die, Black Priest!"

The shockpulse cannon fired, its deadly discharge enveloping one of Kolvax's true believers. The armored Xylander shook and fell, cooked inside his own armor. The mutineers weren't playing around. If not for the true believer heroically stepping in to protect his leader, it would have been Kolvax on the deck of the space station.

Simple fool, Kolvax thought, casting only a glance at the baked entity before dashing down the side hallway. His devotees had saved him again, but he was running out of them.

He'd made a mistake, ordering the heads and bodies of the heretics in the chapel attack marched through the commissary at dinnertime. True, that way led to the atomic furnace, and the Severed were too fastidious to allow a dead body to lie for any time at all. Even now, that fact was helping him as his attackers paused to dispense with his fallen protector. But the provocation had simply set up the next round. Rather than set an example, the sight of the heads had both angered the rest and tipped his hand about the traps in their collars. The devices weren't responding to his signals anymore. Kolvax didn't doubt that some smart person had deactivated them.

His followers weren't *all* incompetent.

Kolvax could always count on Tellmer, though, whom he now found fearfully cringing behind a metal staircase. The alien builders of the space station had crafted ways for many different kinds of creatures to go between decks, expecting traffic that never came. That was the saving grace of the place: lots of ways to flee.

But fewer ways now than there were. "Everything below the transit axis is blocked," Tellmer said, cradling his newly reattached hand. The surgeon hadn't done the work right, and this was the first time Kolvax had heard his mawkish aide speak of anything else.

"How many are we?"

Tellmer's helmeted head dipped. "Just you and I, Great Kolvax. Parrus and Jerroj never made it."

"Then that's it," Kolvax said. "Come on!" The black-armored leader scaled the steps quickly, Tellmer right behind. The transit rings atop the rotating station were the only escape. There was a passenger container loaded in the rings pointed at Xylanx space, where the Dominium's sentries would likely kill him the minute he arrived. However, there were other rings directed at unknown places. His fellow exiles had refused to use them for fear of emerging someplace unclean. Now, his movement shattered, Kolvax cared nothing for that. But he had to get to the rings quickly, and the long trip up to the hub would only be the start. Shifting a container from one track to another took time—

"*Hold!*"

Kolvax stopped dead—still alive, but maybe not for much longer. He saw his former followers blocking the way into the departure center. Behind, Tellmer turned to run—only to be struck from the side by a fire-bolo launched from cover. Tellmer screamed, his left arm sheared off at the elbow.

Weaponless, the Black Priest looked down at Tellmer's limb as the Xylanx moved to surround them. "Well, maybe you'll have a matched set now," he said sardonically. No one laughed. He looked at the leader of the insurgents. Rumber had become one of his high priestesses, back in the days when he'd felt like doling out titles. Now, she held a hand-cannon on him.

"Will you give me a weapon," he asked, "to make this fair?"

"No."

Kolvax smiled. "Neither would I." He stepped forward, hands outstretched, ready to make a good show of it when above, the crashing bang of an arriving container reverberated through the station. The rebels looked at one another, startled.

"It could be deliverance," Rumber said. "We've been pardoned!"

Promptly forgetting about Kolvax, Rumber turned toward the surveillance monitors behind them.

The leader looked back at Tellmer. "Pick up your arm," Kolvax said. He joined his former followers before the image.

"It's not the rings from home," Rumber said, astonished. "It's—it's one of the other portals!"

Inside his helmet, Kolvax's eyes narrowed. The image focused on the dimly lit receiving area in the hub, where arrivals made their weightless entry into the station. Several space-suited bipedal figures emerged through the airlock.

Two arms. Two limbs. And faces the Xylanx could see through transparent faceplates. The lead figure, checking something on a handheld device, nodded to the others, who began removing their helmets.

The Severed watched the newcomers in awe. Skin. Pale, yellow, brown. And hair, which even the most liberal Xylanx foreswore. Another figure joined the leader, speaking.

"Audio," Kolvax said, reasserting control. "Audio!"

It was all gibberish. "What are they saying?" Rumber said.

"Shut up," Kolvax said. "Listen!"

✳ ✳ ✳

"…two trips in one day," Bridget said, surveying the receiving area. "You're racking up the light-years, Wall Street."

"Coral Gables," Jamie mumbled, looking around fearfully.

"What?"

"I'm from Coral Gables," Jamie said. "Florida."

"Well, you're not there now. Welcome to Quaestor Center Sigma Draconis—also known as the Dragon's Depot." Bridget looked behind her. There were lots of shadows here, but it seemed as advertised—big, functional, and unoccupied, if cold. "Standard recons, people, but looks okay so far. Let's get moved in!"

✳✳✳

Kolvax gawked. They were humans. Humans! *Here!*

The others saw it, too. He turned from the monitor to the people who, moments before, had been trying to kill him. "You know what this means," he said.

"Yes." Rumber dipped her head, and the others followed. "Your message—your prophecy—it was right."

"*Humans,*" Tellmer said, the very word acidic to him. Every Xylander knew about humans. The mere presence of humanity threatened everything the Xylanx stood for.

Even if the humans themselves didn't know the Xylanx existed.

"We should never have doubted you, my priest." Rumber said. "You warned us. You were right."

Kolvax smiled. That wasn't all it meant. He wouldn't be the nuisance anymore, easily dismissed. After this the Dominium would have to contend with him. He was back in the big game.

He snatched the weapon out of Rumber's hand; she didn't protest. "Hurry," he said, heading for the staircase. "We're going hunting!"

EPISODE 2:

GOLDEN HANDSHAKE

8

Bridget heard the high-pitched voice in her headset. "Uh—this is Jamie. You know, the trader you're supposed to be protecting?"

As if I could forget. The security chief holstered her sidearm and rolled her eyes. "What do you want?" Bridget asked.

"I keep hearing things," Jamie said. "You said this station was unoccupied—"

"It *is* occupied. You're in it." *To the station's everlasting regret,* she thought. The Dragon's Depot hadn't seen visitors from Earth since Quaestor took ownership of it, years earlier. But today was moving day, with her newly retitled Surge Sigma team helping to move the trader in. Their security sweeps, like hers that had just ended, had turned up nothing. Not even much dust.

But the trader still had to be humored. "Why didn't you tell this to Welligan, Jamie? I sent his team with you."

A pause. "Yeah, they kind of got pissed at me...and left," Jamie said.

Bridget chuckled. Her opinion of Hiro Welligan was improving. "Just find them," she said.

Lissa Trovatelli slid out from beneath the alien-built console she was working on. "Was that five times?" she asked.

"Six," Bridget said, watching her frosty breath in the air. Trovatelli slid back underneath the console and returned to work. More lights were functioning here on the command deck now, but the biggest job lay ahead. Bridget's new base was two kilometers long, and she still hadn't seen a tenth of it.

Only one of the two giant habitation drums had been completed by the station's builders, and even this one—deemed "north" by her team—was full of exposed walls and half-finished work. The Regulans had seen the futility of trading in the region and given up.

Dubbed the Dragon's Depot by its purchasers, the station was a dumbbell of sorts: two giant rolling drums rotating in opposite directions around a fat central tube. The habitation cylinders turned slowly, generating one gee in the outermost decks without any of the Coriolis-induced dizziness of some of the smaller, Earth-built stations. One end of the station's spine was tipped with a circular collector dish with the same diameter as the station; it shielded occupants from Sigma Draconis's rays while harvesting necessary energy. And ringing the center between the "north" and "south" habitation bulbs were eight whirlibangs, connected to the axial cylinder by a spiraling network of tracks and girders.

The place was built for business, to be sure. Bangboxes by the thousands could pass through the depot, switching to other whirlibang tracks and going right out again. More still could be warehoused in the station itself. And eight transit rings were plenty. Bridget knew where five of the whirlibangs went, but the other three were still a mystery. One of them had a 'box loaded, ready to go.

She'd investigate that later—after Trovatelli got the climate controls fixed. The air was breathable but frigid. *Maybe they turned the heat down because nobody was home?* Bridget knew that was ridiculous, of course: the same elemental forces that powered the whirlibangs had made it possible to keep the place running, even when unoccupied. "I thought the Regulans left us an owner's manual," she said.

"They did," Trovatelli answered, hand tool sparking as she fused a connection. "Somebody's fooled with the controls. Odd—Regulans usually like it warmer."

The statement surprised Bridget. "You sound like you've been on the range before."

"Born out here," Trovatalli said with just the trace of an Italian accent. "Giotto Colony, Luyten's Star."

Bridget was glad to hear it. Jake Temmons, her last Q/A, had left abruptly and was probably settling in at his new university fellowship now. Bridget hadn't been too sorry to see him go. Baby-sitting precocious wunderkinds wasn't her idea of a good time. But Trovatelli's work had impressed so far, even as the young technician's appearance had caught many of her team-mates' eyes.

Bridget had wondered about something else. It was rare to find a woman in her twenties born on the other side of the whirlibang. Trovatelli belonged to what was still a small subset of humanity: the children of pioneers. The ease with which such people handled life on the range meant they were coveted by all the major corporations. What was she doing with such a hard-luck outfit? Bridget made a mental note to check into her record later.

Trovatelli closed the console's maintenance panel. "That's it," she said, wiping her hands on her flight suit. "Should be tunic weather in an hour or two."

As the chief started to offer congratulations her earpiece beeped. "Here we go again," she said, touching the device. "What is it now, Jamie?"

"I'm telling you, this time I saw something!" Jamie's voice had gone up an octave, if that were possible.

"I'm sure it's Welligan's people messing with you," she said. They *were* hiding from him if they were smart.

"I thought you hotshots were supposed to be pros," the trader replied. "Can't you—I don't know—scan for life-forms or something?"

"Yes, I'll check my vids archive for space opera and see how they did it." Bridget shook her head at Trovatelli. "Jamie, I'm working my way to your level. Hang in there." The broker started to say something else, but she muted the transmission.

Trovatelli gathered up her tools. "What's the story with him? I didn't catch all that back with Falcone—I was worried about the building falling apart."

"Idiot gambled with the expedition's money and lost it all, basically. Now we've got a few weeks to get it all back."

"How much?"

"A hundred billion dollars."

"Good luck with that," Trovatelli said. She looked at Bridget slyly. "Still, he's kind of cute…for an imbecile."

"I'm sure he thinks so," Bridget said. "He's gonna have to hope the judge back on Earth thinks so, too, if this doesn't work."

✳✳✳

This isn't going to work, Jamie thought. Here he was, 158 trillion kilometers from home and a hundred billion dollars in the hole. Well, more than that, actually—he hadn't told Falcone everything, and he hoped he wouldn't have to.

And he was freezing his ass off.

Alone on one of the rotating cargo decks, he sat in his space suit, helmet and gloves off. He only had the one suit he'd worn to Altair, and that still smelled like guacamole. He'd asked for more clothes, but they'd left Altair in such a hurry he could only get the space suit. He was in his jockey shorts underneath, and the suit's warmer wasn't doing its job.

The troopers had promised more clothing was packed in the gear they'd shipped. He hoped it was true: at this point, he was willing to make a turtleneck from one of Arbutus Dinner's socks. The entourage had brought a total of six 'boxes from Altair. That included two for personnel and two for shuttle conversion, plus one more for supplies they weren't likely to find stationside. He hoped something his size was in there.

And then there was the final container, jokingly known as the "general store," which had all any itinerant trader needed to open negotiations with new species. The store would be married to one or more of the personnel containers and an engine to make the trading vessel. The smaller items had been unloaded, and he had been spending his time studying up on his new job.

There was "the briefcase," a throwback to the traveling salesmen of the twentieth century. One side of the case contained the handheld menu that operated the large fabricator in the store. Up to a certain level of complexity, many products could be manufactured on the scene: it made a lot more sense than shipping one of everything by the 'boxful. So rather than bringing a sample of everything Quaestor had for sale, the trader could use the briefcase to produce a small number of items as examples, as long as all the component elements were in supply. After a sale, Quaestor would bring in an entire factory to produce the desired items in whatever quantity was demanded. Quaestor sold the fabricators, too, but in custom sizes suited for the consuming species—and loaded with whatever patented recipes the customers had bought licenses for. Jamie hoped someone had programmed it with some tailored shirts from Ascot Chang. The Dragon's Depot was a long way from Manhattan.

On the other side was the assayer, an isopanel that calculated market values back home for goods found on the frontier. It was the same system Jamie was working with on Ops and so the information was always a little out of date: its data could only be updated when another traveler arrived through the whirlibang with more recent commodity quotes. But at least it was a system he was familiar with.

And there was the badge, which identified him as a representative of Quaestor, a trading firm licensed by Earth, a member in good standing of the Signatory Systems. It was a golden, gaudy thing, festooned with pins and beads and clockwork that moved; Quaestor's designers had used a chelengk, a decoration from the Ottoman Empire, as a model. Jamie thought the tacky thing would have been rejected by even the flashiest of sultans.

The designers had crafted it to be noticeable by aliens of all species, whatever their sensory capabilities: they'd left nothing out. In addition to its garish looks, a jeweled section spun for the motion-sensitive and a small heater gave it a unique infrared signature. It made a little squawking sound every minute, as well as emitting signals beyond human hearing. It felt prickly, smelled like cinnamon, and tasted vaguely like lemon. Jamie could only imagine the alien who'd need to lick his badge to identify him. Oh, and the thing was slightly radioactive. Jamie thought if he tripped and fell with the badge on his chest, it would be the end of him.

He looked coldly at the badge before sighing and affixing it to his space suit for the hell of it. The thing's little widgets immediately began spinning and dancing. "My God," he said, thrilled the traders at Ops could not see him. Dear Selena would be laughing in the aisle.

Thump.

Jamie spun around. It was what he'd heard before. Someone else was out there!

"Welligan?"

Nothing.

He touched his earpiece. "Bridget, listen. Something's here—"

"I'm not talking to you anymore, Jamie," she replied in his ear. "I've got a job to do."

"Protecting me is your job," he said. "I tell you, I'm hearing something!"

"It's probably that toy on your chest," she said. It was peeping like a baby chick now. "I told you, I have things to tend to first. I'll see you when I see you." She ended the transmission.

Jamie fumed. He looked down at the badge and then around at the goods he was supposed to work with.

Screw this, he thought, pulling at the badge. But he couldn't get a good grip on it, and its moving and poky parts seemed to almost fight back against him. "Ouch!"

Aggravated, he gave up and let it remain on his suit. He opened his naked palm and triggered the interface to his EndoSys.

His personal supercomputer, the EndoSys resided on his left thumbnail, where it maintained a wireless interface with whatever knowglobes and other databases were around. The machine's readout appeared on his palm, the harmless work of resident pigment-stimulating nanoids injected into his system. EndoSys implants had already replaced tattoos in the twenty-second century, as humans eschewed static images in favor of becoming walking animation studios; now, EndoSys-enabled hands were replacing handheld isopanels. With a few words and a finger tap, Jamie saw on his palm the map leading back to the whirlibang. Then he requested instructions for activating the device. A reading of the details went to his earpiece.

The directions didn't sound too difficult. *I can do this*, he thought.

When a 'box was at a whirlibang station, it wasn't really a spaceship anymore. It was more like an elevator car, unable to go anywhere but where it was supposed to. Jamie knew which whirlibang loop was tuned to send 'boxes to Altair: the one he'd come in on.

Jamie wondered what would happen if he returned. Falcone might not have left any orders with the Altair whirlibang station crew regarding him. All Jamie would have to do is take one ride to Altair, and then the connecting link to Venus. He'd catch his shuttle home a few days late. And as for Quaestor's hundred billion dollars…

…well, he'd worry about that later. It wouldn't be his only problem back on Earth. Not by a long shot, not after his relatives found out. But back home, he'd at least have a chance of disappearing. He'd sell cheeseburgers to Czechs, lingerie in Lesotho. Anything would be better than this.

Badge peeping away, Jamie ran toward the exit. He heard the thump again, but this time he didn't stop to look. *Next stop, home!*

9

"Something's wrong with the security system," Trovatelli said, closing the panel. "We're locked out."

Bridget's eyes narrowed. "Falcone said the Regulans gave us all the codes in the sale."

"Well, they've changed," the technician said. "I think there's an access point one level up."

The chief nodded. Pulse weapon drawn, Bridget led the way. It didn't seem necessary, but their destination was a room she hadn't checked yet. Yellow rungs jutted from the wall ahead, the nearest route leading up.

"Mind if I ask a question, Chief?" Trovatelli asked the older woman.

Bridget looked back down the ladder. For the first time since Bridget had met her, the Q/A seemed less than self-assured. "Shoot."

"You were at Overland, weren't you?" Trovatelli followed her through the hatchway. "How—I mean, how—"

"How did I start Earth's first interstellar war?" Bridget didn't even flinch. Every new recruit to the team asked once they realized she was *that* Bridget Yang. Unless they were so clueless about the universe they lived in that they didn't know to ask…in which case she didn't want them on her team anyway. "A lot of things went wrong in a row."

"I know. I did a research assignment on it in school."

Great, Bridget thought. *I'm core curriculum now.*

"So I know *what* happened," the Q/A said. "I just don't know how you didn't...well, see it sooner. I mean, you seem to try to get to know all your recruits."

"Cause and effect," she said, knowing exactly what Trovatelli was referring to. "You're an engineer. You should understand that." She looked in a side door and pointed Trovatelli toward it. "That should be your spot, if the schematics are right. I'll check in later."

Bridget walked ahead in silence, alone. *Cause and effect, my ass,* she thought. *One big cause and all the rest, effect.*

That had been her life since Overland. The location in Nebraska was little more than a crossroads on the Platte River: a maintenance stop for the maglev line heading east. But everyone had heard about it after the events of 2030. Eight years ago—but yesterday, as far as Bridget was concerned. She lived through it all again every time someone brought it up...

In deep space the hot-tempered Gebrans had at last agreed to an exchange of trade representatives. However, being Gebran, the aliens had insisted on making their own way to Earth and landing in a remote area. But no place on Earth was truly remote anymore, and Bridget's special marine detachment had been just as capable of meeting the shuttle in the wheat fields as in the capital.

Hers had been an honor guard. But it was still a guard, and it had failed in that duty. Or rather, she had failed to spot until too late that two of her junior escorts had belonged to the radical Walled Garden movement, the last holdouts against Earth joining the interstellar community. Most of the members of the

Gebran delegation had died in the assassination attempt, and while Bridget's quick thinking had saved the ambassador, news of the event had touched off the war that threatened to undo the Signatory Pact.

Once humans began dying in battle, many people began grasping for someone to blame. Some faulted Bridget, who had initially been decorated for her role, for not having recognized Gardeners in her midst. There wasn't anything she *could* have done; the investigators had seen that, concluding that the turncoats had covered their pasts well. But Bridget had reflexively accepted responsibility anyway—in a public forum where no one could miss her admission of guilt. The flak that followed had cost her rank and commission, and ultimately she left the service after the muddle of a war ended.

She'd come to Quaestor for a job rather than redemption. Praetor, Lazarius, Osman, and the other trading firms had turned her down outright. Only a farseeing Quaestor expedition leader, realizing how much experience a small amount of money bought, had offered her a contract. Bridget had stayed ever since, running a crack surge team even as the fortunes of the expedition it was protecting faltered. Her past had convinced her that part of soldiering was making time to get to know all her new recruits and seeing what made them tick. There'd be no more Gardeners on her details.

And loyalty had demanded that she stick with the expedition now, even after bad years and Spore attacks. She'd even coped with the deteriorating quality of her new recruits, welcoming help by veterans like O'Herlihy and Dinner. This latest mission, however, had tested her loyalty to the limits.

It wasn't just that she didn't like Jamison Sturm—she hadn't been friends with most traders she'd protected. The job simply attracted a type of person she wasn't at ease with: show-offs. It made sense, of course, that sellers would have to talk themselves up, as well as their goods. It was part of making a sale. And yet show-offs in her line of work got killed. But that wasn't the issue.

No, her real problem was that she had no faith whatsoever that Jamie could do the job *at all*. There was an ocean of difference between issuing sell orders at a desk on Ops and trading with other civilizations. An ocean of plasma and void separated cultures that had few, if any, common understandings. Language wouldn't necessarily be the problem: they had the knowglobes for that, and they contained the facts learned by explorers who had gone before. It was the opposite that concerned her: that understanding Jamie might actually make anyone they met *more* hostile. And then the trouble would really begin.

People didn't understand that about surge teams—or about her. Her forces didn't cross light-years for a chance to shoot at bug-eyed uglies. Mindless organisms were one thing, sentient beings something else. Her job wasn't to start wars. It was to prevent them by keeping hostilities from breaking out in the first place.

Bridget had helped to start the Arcturo-Solar War. Now, she lived in terror of what trouble Jamie might start in the next few weeks.

Her earpiece buzzed again. This time she ignored it.

❋ ❋ ❋

From where he had been thrown to the deck, Jamie looked up in panic at the silver-clad figures looming over him. He'd never seen armor like theirs. Bulky and spiked, with two large shoulder fins rising on either side of a bulbous helmet. The faceplates were as dark as ink, but he didn't need to see faces to know their attitude. Each of his attackers held a frightening-looking weapon crackling with electricity or glowing with unreal fire.

For a moment Jamie thought Bridget had sent her goons to play a prank on him. There weren't any bipedal species in the Signatory Systems, nor any outside that he was aware of—and this crowd certainly had two arms and two legs. Except for the skinnier one he now saw through the crowd: he had only one arm attached and was cradling the other like he was carrying a loaf of bread. That one alone wore a golden collar.

"Welligan?" Jamie asked in a small voice. "O'Herlihy? Dinner?"

His assailants parted to allow the approach of another figure from the shadows. Powerfully built, this one wore black armor instead of silver. His faceplate was as opaque as the others'. Through his armor's public address system, the figure said something alien and unintelligible.

"Oh," Jamie said, reaching his knees. He pointed to the decoration, still clicking and tinkling idiotically on his chest. "Um… peace? See? I have a badge…"

***

The Black Priest of the Xylanx looked down on the simpering creature. "So this is a human," Kolvax said in his language. He glanced back at one-armed Tellmer. "Are you sure the surveillance imagers are off-line?"

"Yes, Great Kolvax. Old Liandro locked the intruders out of the system."

"Fine." It wouldn't do for the humans to find them here—not until he knew how many were coming. He'd seen a weapon in the hand of the dark-haired female that entered. He didn't expect the humans could defeat the Xylanx, but he wasn't ready to test that belief yet.

Instead, the Xylanx exiles spent the precious minutes after the humans arrived sweeping the station to hide evidence of their presence. If the dark-hair was bringing an army, Kolvax didn't want them to find any trace that would reveal the Xylanx's characteristics. Here, his followers' fastidiousness had come in handy: there wasn't as much as a dead cell to be found in areas they'd frequented. His chapel was the messiest of all the areas, owing to his own habits, but the mess, and the spatters from Tellmer's wound, had been hastily cleaned.

It was a lesson from Kolvax's training with the Stalkers, the Xylanx's ruthless paramilitary: "The longer your prey stands in ignorance of you, the mightier you become in their fears."

And then they had hidden using the warren of vents and service corridors to move about the station. When the humans left one of their number behind, Kolvax saw the chance to act—and to learn what they were up against.

Not much, Kolvax concluded as he studied the pale face of the human. Hair on his head the color of sand, with a narrow nose and chin. And thin. So thin! The Xylanx knew of humanity; from childhood on, every Xylander learned of the great existential threat that these creatures posed to their domain. But Kolvax wasn't impressed in the least. "His home must be a soft place for this thing to have lived," he said.

"It's repugnant," Rumber said. "We should kill it before it infects us with whatever makes them waste away like that."

"Later," Kolvax said. He slapped a powerful hand on the human male's shoulder and lifted him. The man howled, and Kolvax kneed him in the stomach. That stopped the howling but not the noise. The creature whimpered and mewled, clutching his midsection.

Kolvax's followers, clearly nauseated, held their captive's arms. Kolvax ripped the headset from the bewildered human and crushed it in his gloved hand. Then the badge caught his eye.

"I know this symbol," Kolvax said. "It's issued by the Signatory Systems. I gutted a few of their other members before the

Dominium withdrew us from the wider galaxy. Evidently, they've let the humans in." He stared at it. "They've advanced faster than I would have thought."

As Kolvax started to pull off the trader's badge, the eldest surviving member of his party spoke up. "It grows warmer," Liandro said, looking worriedly at a gauge. "They have control of the environmental systems again."

"We take him," Kolvax said. He looked to his followers. "The Xylanx have a destiny. We have all sought Forrah Glay, the great unknown. This human's coming is proof we were right—and a sign of the danger that awaits us all if we fail to act."

He grabbed the human by his slick and disgusting hair. "*You're* the sign," Kolvax snarled at the terrified being. "And I'm taking you back to our people—*now!*"

✳ ✳ ✳

Jamie was no xenobiologist. He wasn't even slightly interested in the subject. Documentarians had gone wild in the days after first contact, recording millions of hours about what existed out there; some people were really into it. Jamie thought it was all noise. The beings that were out there weren't anything he could relate to at all.

There were no humanoids with bumpy faces and extra arms, buxom females with exotic skin colors and odd-shaped ears. The old entertainment programs had lied to him. Sentient life ranged from the amorphous to the ethereal, and you could never read expressions or body language. How did the company's traders even have anything to work with? Jamie had no idea.

Jamie also had no idea what the armored beings that carried him were, but he was sure they weren't human. They had the requisite limbs—well, all but the little guy—but nothing about the powerful brutes or their odd barking language seemed familiar to him. If humanity ever opened up trade with these people, they'd need to shop from the big and tall section.

At the moment, that didn't seem a likely prospect. Following the black-clad warrior, who was evidently their leader, Jamie's captors dragged him through one darkened corridor after another. He could feel his limbs growing lighter as they ascended from level to level; even Jamie knew that meant they were heading toward the station's spine, where there was no gravity. Jamie hoped that might slow them down. But those hopes ended when his captors activated the jets in their backpacks. Small gimbaled engines fired, scooting the figures along higher and faster.

Jamie twisted to see where they were taking him. Bright yellow light shone down through an opening far above. He knew where it led. The security guys on the way in had called it the Shaft, joking that Quaestor had just given it all to them. A football field's width across and a kilometer from end to end, the Shaft was a vast cylindrical pressurized region within the station's axis, a weightless loading dock for materials shipped in from the whirlibangs outside. Grids of metal scaffolds extended from the rounded walls, providing places where 'boxes could be secured for unloading; hatchways back into the north habitation area could be seen on all sides. In the middle of the open space, Jamie saw the supply 'box the surge team had arrived with tethered to a metal scaffold. Nobody was here unpacking.

The alien leader grunted something as the entourage entered the Shaft, and Jamie now saw other silver-clad aliens joining the group from other places of hiding. This wasn't a small party, he realized: there were thirty or forty of the creatures here. Bridget's Surge Sigma team only had thirty-two people. One by one, all of the figures ignited their personal backpack rockets.

Propelled ahead with his kidnappers, Jamie squirmed. *They're taking me to the whirlibang! They're taking me away!*

Jamie began screaming again, indifferent to any threat. He saw the supply 'box tethered ahead and clawed for it—something familiar, something from home. Maybe some of his so-called bodyguards were inside!

The leader in black made a beeline for him, yanking him free from those holding him and slamming him against the side of the supply 'box. An ebon fist struck Jamie squarely in the nose, drawing blood.

"Stop!" a voice called out from behind. The brute turned his head to see what Jamie saw: Bridget in her environment suit, her magnetized boots holding her to the inside wall of the Shaft. "Don't be smacking our trader like that," Bridget yelled. "Not before I've had the chance!"

10

Kolvax looked back in surprise. It was the human woman from the airlock—and she wasn't alone. Other soldiers emerged from the hatchways, climbing out onto the skin of the vast tube, weapons drawn.

He didn't hesitate. Many of his followers had come from the Xylanx Stalker units he'd once led. The Severed could fight, he knew. He shoved his captive aside, the human's bright red blood still on Kolvax's glove.

"Stay here, stripling," he barked at the human. "Faithful, attack!"

✳✳✳

What the hell are these guys?

Bridget sidestepped as a burst of energy flashed past, striking the Shaft wall next to her booted feet. She'd thought her teammates were big, but Jamie had found himself a gorilla army—or they had found him.

She'd seen the massive silver-armored figures when Trovatelli got the station's surveillance system unlocked. Some tall, some beefy, all big—and whoever they were, they weren't worried about damaging the depot. On the black-clad puncher's command the flying people had opened up on her comrades with energy and missile weapons. Bridget hadn't understood their leader's words, but she had a good idea what he'd said.

Bridget figured the missile weapons weren't going to hurt the station this deep inside, but they could certainly do a number on her. She slid her legs back into the hatch she'd emerged from. Twisting, she snapped a tether from her suit to an anchor inside the hatchway. "Get back in the hatches and strafe with pulse weaponry," Bridget called into her mouthpiece.

It was the craziest combat setting she'd ever encountered: flying enemies in zero gee shooting at her people, who were attached like flies to the cylindrical wall. But the hatchways provided cover, enough to turn the tables and transform the place into a shooting gallery.

They only needed to give Geena Madaki time. And the pilot was already in motion.

❋❋❋

There was chaos all around. But Jamie only saw the blood from his nose, coalescing into droplets and bobbing in front of him. He had already felt sick from the weightlessness and panic. Now, he felt weak and disoriented. The armored bully had turned his back on him, but it didn't matter. Jamie couldn't see anywhere to go—and increasingly, he couldn't see at all.

Helmetless head lolling against the collar of his environment suit, Jamie thought he saw a metal monster coming toward him, its claws extending. Confused, he also thought he saw the face of Madaki, their shuttle pilot, in the mouth of the machine. A tug on his leg was the last thing he felt before he blacked out.

❋❋❋

Damnation!

Kolvax spun to avoid a shot from one side—and then from another. This was no good. By keeping her people in the holes like rodents, the dark-hair had put the Xylanx in a crossfire. He was sure his people could take the humans in close quarters, but that effort would take time—time in which more humans could arrive. But it cut to his spine to leave a fight unfinished.

Tellmer scrambled frantically around the corner of the tethered container he was using for cover. Kolvax's aide had parted from the company long enough to flash-freeze his severed limb at a prep station. Tellmer looked around, worried. "We should go, Great Kolvax!" He waggled his detached limb—hard as a rock. "You said we shouldn't leave anything for them to study. If any of us fall, that'd be something indeed!"

Damn it all again, Kolvax thought. Yes, the original plan was the right one. His captive would still be of use as a hostage, and then back home. He fired his backpack jets and darted around a floating cargo container.

The sniveling human was gone. An airborne cargo tender was backing away under its own power, a body slumped across two of its robotic arms. The station had several of them in this chamber—and evidently the humans knew it, too. Kolvax saw a human woman with a brown face at the controls inside the cab of the tender. The tender fired its thrusters, coasting away from him.

Rumber saw it, too. She looked at him. "Should we go after them?"

Kolvax started to say something…

Then he stopped and looked at his hand. "No. We go to the transit ring—all of us. Hurry!"

The Xylanx turned as one on Kolvax's transmitted command. Weaving in between the blasts, the silver behemoths rocketed toward the cylinder's center and the egress that led to the whirlibang. It took them out of range of the humans.

Kolvax saw through the tunnel the access leading to the passenger container. It had sat there for months, taunting them with the possibility of a return flight home. Now Rumber paused, not wanting to go further. "We don't have the human," she said, anger rising. "The Dominium will kill us if we return—you know that!"

"It's all right," Kolvax said. He looked at the back of his glove, encrusted with the human's blood. "I think we have our pardon right here!"

✳ ✳ ✳

Jamie opened his eyes to lights. He was on one of the middle decks, with just enough simulated gravity to keep him on the ground—but he wasn't going to be moving anywhere. Perhaps ever. "I'm…dying," he said, gasping. "Blood…loss. Help me…"

Kneeling over him, Bridget rolled her eyes. "Just breathe," she said, placing a mask over his mouth. "You've just got a bloodied nose."

"But…"

"The air along the center line of the Shaft cylinder isn't as dense as it is out where the station's rotating," she said. "The floors farthest from the axis have the most oxygen. I don't think the Regulans intended for humans to work in that area." Bridget stood. "Your new friends remembered their helmets."

Jamie sat up, throat dry. "They're not my friends," he said, coughing.

"Are you sure?" Bridget stepped to a counter in the medical clinic and pitched Jamie a water flask. "I thought maybe in all your scheming you hired a mercenary army to bring you home."

"Hardly! They weren't even human!" Jamie drank thirstily. Wiping his face, he glared at Bridget. "You saw them!"

"Armored guys, strange weapons? Check. They were just bigger than you. That's not a tall order." She turned to see O'Herlihy and Trovatelli sliding down the ladder from above. "What do you have?"

"Jack and squat," O'Herlihy said. "They took off in that one 'box that was loaded up in the Echo ring—wherever that goes."

Bridget looked to Trovatelli. "There's no record in the database of it," the young tech explained. "The logs say it made the handshake with the whirlibang wherever they were going. That's all."

"Shut it down," Bridget said.

"Already done." Their visitors wouldn't be able to return using the way they'd left.

Bridget ordered O'Herlihy to lead his squad on a sweep of everything—including the south bell of the station, which had never been occupied. "Give me everything," she said. "Fingerprints, eyelashes, the works. If these guys spit on the floor, I want to see it."

"Loogie patrol. Fun." O'Herlihy cracked a smile and went off.

"I'm telling you, they weren't human," Jamie groaned, lying back down on the floor. It was cool and comforting, and he appreciated the Regulans for putting it there. "Not human. Not. They were speaking gibberish!"

"You think every human speaks English?" Bridget glanced at her Q/A and clicked her tongue scornfully. "Yes, you probably do."

Jamie rubbed his nose. "Look, I can read a bottle of wine. But these guys weren't talking in anything I've ever heard."

"Wait. They were in environment suits?" Trovatelli asked.

Jamie rolled on his side and looked at the young woman, stunned that anyone was finally taking an interest. "Yeah. They had public address speakers or something—same as you guys in your armor."

Trovatelli looked at Bridget. "They're oxy breathers."

"How do you figure?"

"Because you heard the leader speak," the younger woman said. "If they couldn't breathe the air, why would they need public address systems to talk? They'd talk via their helmet mics, like we do when we're in space." She looked down at Jamie. "They must sometimes take them off."

"You see?" Bridget said, again impressed by her new recruit. "Oxygen breathers. Maybe one of the pirate outfits." While no one could make unauthorized use of the whirlibangs in the Solar System, there were other entry points across the Orion Arm and more than enough human settlements to generate a crime problem. Where there was commerce, there was piracy. "Maybe they grew up in low-grav and grew tall," she said. "But human enough."

"Maybe," Trovatelli said. "But maybe not. The database interfaces weren't set to Regulan or anything in our knowglobe. That's why I've had so much trouble with it. Do pirates have their own language?"

Bridget stared. Stepping over to a console, she took a look at the characters on the isopanel. "Huh."

"You see?" Jamie looked over at the Q/A. "Thank you—"

"Lissa," she said, nodding pleasantly.

"Lissa believes me."

"I didn't say that," Trovatelli said. "Just that all the evidence isn't in."

Bridget turned. "Okay," she said. "Check the security logs. Surveillance recordings. Everything."

Trovatelli rubbed her chin. "If they locked me out, they could easily have purged—"

"Which should be no problem for you," Bridget said as the tech walked out. "I have faith in my staff."

Seeing the man Trovatelli passed in the doorway, Bridget blanched. "On the other hand…"

"*You!*" Jamie turned to see the orange-haired Osakan in uniform. It was Hiro Welligan, the squad leader who had abandoned him—ultimately leaving him to the kidnappers. Jamie stormed toward him. "You nearly got me killed, you son of a—"

Welligan smiled broadly and held up his hands. "Hey, we did shoot at them for you." His eyes lit up. "Thanks for finding them for us."

"Thanks for…?" Infuriated, Jamie grabbed for the trooper.

Bridget interceded. Breaking them up, she glared at her underling. "You did leave him, Hiro."

"He called me a jackbooted thug!" Welligan said. He looked at Jamie. "Er…what's a jackboot?"

"It'll be the thing up your ass if you ditch him again," Bridget said.

Jamie thought she looked serious about it. The trader had watched the team long enough to know Welligan's role: he was the clown of the crew, right down to the spectral hair. Hiro had gone for the EndoSys follicular implants, which took the whole skin-printing thing a step beyond. The guy's hair went from orange to a cool and calming blue as he dipped his head and grinned in embarrassment before his boss. Jamie had known guys like Welligan on the bourse. They tried too hard, and their jocularity was usually covering up for an inability to make a sale. Jamie was glad to see that Bridget didn't seem to be buying it, either. The grin fled Hiro's face, and he seemed to wilt under his superior's scrutiny.

Duly chastened, Welligan passed Bridget a packet. "Bangbox just in from Altair," he said. "Falcone's gathered the logistical crews from ASPEC—they're heading here soon. He wants the first trading mission underway before he arrives."

"Trading mission?" Jamie goggled. "I just got kidnapped!"

Welligan's hair changed to an inspiring white with flowing, animated red stripes. "Got to save our jobs, ace."

"That," Jamie said, glaring, "presumes you were doing one in the first place."

Looking tired, Bridget just shrugged.

11

Alabeyd hadn't really felt like another world to Jamie. He hadn't ventured outside the ASPEC facility onto the asteroid's surface, and he already knew from the shuttle's approach run that there wasn't anything to see out there. Apart from the heap of debris that had once been his future, that was.

Stepping out of the transport onto Baghula, however, finally felt like the real deal. The red dwarf Struve 2398A loomed freakishly large overhead, a muted tangerine in the chlorine-rich haze. Baghula was closer to Struve than Mercury was to the Sun, but Struve was enough past its prime that it wasn't doing much, even with this face of the planet always toward the star.

Struve and Baghula were at the near edge of their expedition's sales territory, but Jamie already felt like it was the deep end. Survey reports shared with humanity by other Signatory members said there was an intelligent life-form on the planet, but it was so exotic that it had resisted all trading attempts. Jamie thought humanity's neighbor trading species were strange enough as it was. Anything too weird for them to handle was something he didn't want to mess with.

Mercifully, the trip in from Sigma Draconis had been his shortest hop yet. Struve's whirlibang station didn't require human attendants to run, but Falcone would send some anyway if it proved to be the hoped-for link in a logistical chain. Comprising two crew 'boxes, an engine, and the general store, the shuttle *Indispensable* had made the short trip from the Struve whirlibang to land at coordinates sent up by a local survey team. The explorers had sounded surprised to get their hail; it didn't seem like they got many visitors here.

Setting his briefcase down on Baghula's surface, Jamie understood why. He didn't know who or what had installed the whirlibang in the system, but it seemed a waste of effort. Bridget had said the place looked "pleasant and calm" just before she and her squad had left on their recon minutes earlier. "Calm" he agreed with—but he could hardly call the place "pleasant." Generated by the local life-forms and the briny lakes they lived in, the chlorine in the atmosphere contributed to a greenish-yellow fog that both limited visibility and made everything else look like a mirage.

Jamie checked the seals again on his SoftSHEL environment suit. Apart from the circulation pack, it wasn't much more than a jumpsuit, gloves, boots, and a fishbowl helmet. No wonder the traders needed guards if Quaestor dressed them like this. On the shuttle, Jamie had carped that Bridget's team got to be in its regular battle gear. She'd retorted that the trader needed to look nonthreatening—although she added that their particular trader probably didn't require the extra effort.

Jamie stood around for a minute before he looked back at Welligan. Hiro's squad had remained to form a safety perimeter around the shuttle, but Jamie still wasn't talking to him. But now he was growing impatient. He raised his arms. "What am I waiting for?"

Welligan pointed behind Jamie to a sloping rise leading off into the haze. Something was moving there, something big. Jamie started to turn, but Welligan wasn't looking alarmed.

Jamie didn't understand why. A giant wheel, three meters tall, rolled over the hill toward him. Through the haze, Jamie could see jagged, angry teeth around the wheel's circumference biting into the green-stained sand and propelling it along. Four robotic arms extended from either side of the wheel, helping to pull the contraption ahead. The rolling monstrosity rumbled toward Jamie.

"Stop!" Jamie yelled, unaware if the thing could hear him over his mic, since he had never tested his public address system. But before the trader could turn to run from the wheel, its robotic arms closest to the ground plunged into the muck, halting the vehicle's advance.

And it was a vehicle—for the unseen alien that rode inside the egg-like passenger compartment that was the wheel's hub. "I'm so sorry to have startled you, sir," a female voice cooed over his headset.

"Bridget!" Jamie yelled. "Bridget, I've got a native over here! And it's talking!"

Bridget stepped through the fog, rifle slung. She smiled. "That's not a native. That's our tour guide."

"Oh, dear," the wheel said, tilting left. Jamie could see the spongy alien peering through the egg's viewport now. It wasn't much more than a gray mass. "I'm sorry to have disturbed your friend, Chief Yang."

Jamie stared at the thing, startled. "Er…not a problem."

"Welcome to Baghula," the frothy voice said. "I hope you'll have a wonderful stay here, Mr."

"Sturm," Jamie said. He tugged at the ridiculous identification badge on his chest.

"Oh, a trader!" The wheel bounced up and down excitedly. "None have come for so long. I am just sure the Baghu will greet you warmly this time."

Jamie looked with concern. "What do they *usually* do?"

The wheel giggled—and Jamie took a step back, never having heard a wheel giggle before. "The Baghu are perfectly harmless, silly. They're just…particular about who they welcome into their community." The wheel pivoted back to face the hill, and the thing inside its hub gave something that sounded to Jamie like a sigh. "I've been here for years researching them—to little avail, I'm afraid. You can call me Lorraine."

Jamie stared. *The big alien wheel was named Lorraine.*

Bridget chuckled and walked past. Welligan's team was unloading the knowglobe from the shuttle. Hip-high and dodecahedral, the database held all the shared knowledge of the member Signatory Systems—including their languages. Every traveling party in the pact carried one, an all-purpose travelers' aid. And it was already aiding now, Jamie learned.

"Lorraine is a Sheoruk," Bridget explained. "Your suit's aural sensors are picking up Lorraine's words and putting them wirelessly back through the knowglobe. You're getting the translation in your headset." She patted the speaker outside Jamie's helmet. "And any alien who talks to you is getting your words translated, as well."

"Oh," Jamie said, realizing for the first time that when he spoke to the wheel, he was hearing a strange whispering echo that was not his voice. He was speaking Sheoruk; his uniform's system was doing its best to muffle it from his own hearing.

Bridget nodded to the knowglobe. "We'll be thankful for any help you can give," she said.

"Certainly." Lorraine wobbled toward it and wiggled a robotic arm. "There," she said. "Synchronization complete. You now have everything my mission has found about the Baghu—including their language. I do hope you find our research of use."

Jamie shook his head, flabbergasted. The alien sounded so chipper. "Okay," he said, still back on the name. "You're *Lorraine*?"

"You don't know *anything* about what we do here, do you?" Aggravated, Bridget gestured to the giant wheel. "The knowglobe has translated her name to a human cognate, and it's selected a speaking persona it believes is a good match for her." She stepped over and patted the metal frame of the alien's odd vehicle. "It appears the knowglobe has decided Lorraine would sound best as a nineteen-fifties flight attendant."

Jamie gawked. "Are you joking?"

"No, it's for real. The knowglobe has billions of bits of recorded human speech in it." Bridget checked a display in her helmet and continued with a smile. "Lorraine Buchwalder of Passaic, New Jersey, lives again as a Sheoruk xenobiologist on the planet Baghula."

"Whatever." Jamie rolled his eyes. He found his briefcase and picked it up by the handle. "Let's get to it."

"Thank you for flying Pan Am," Lorraine said. "Please step this way."

※ ※ ※

Flanked by O'Herlihy, Dinner, and Bridget's other troopers, Jamie and the chief followed the wheel through the green mist to a brown lagoon. The body of liquid was a soupy brine so dark nothing could be seen within it. The brown mud resolved into lighter, almost golden sands as the party approached the lakeside.

"Jesus!" Jamie yelled, dropping his case. Behind the troopers, a massive beast rose from the water. And then another, and another.

"The Baghu," Lorraine said.

"Uh-huh." Jamie stared, mystified—and glad that his space suit had ways of dealing with what had just been scared out of him. Because there were more now, rising from the nasty surf—and because the Baghu looked like nothing more than walking versions of the human stomach.

Bulbous two-meter-tall flesh bags waddling on pairs of gummy legs, the Baghu had large slimy tentacles extending from their midsections. And up top, instead of heads, the giant sacs tapered off to drooling nozzles.

One of the creatures tromped from the lagoon and onto the shore. "It's missing an esophagus," Jamie said, repulsed. "And everything else."

"Isn't it fascinating?" Lorraine chirped. "That upper valve handles sensory perception, eating, respiration, elimination—"

"Elimination?" Jamie asked. "It craps through its mouth?"

Lorraine tittered, amused by the slang. "I've never seen that, of course. But it breathes and sees through it, for sure. In fact, we've nicknamed them Breathers—I think you can hear why."

Jamie could. The Baghu leader—if that was what it was—expanded and contracted like a blood-pressure bulb. Its loud, wheezing respiration made Jamie glad he'd skipped lunch on the shuttle.

Lorraine prodded at Jamie with a robotic arm. "Speak," she said.

"I don't speak Baghu," Jamie said. But what came out of his uniform's public address system was something altogether different: a warbling series of gurgles and squawks.

"Splendid!" Lorraine said, rolling happy circles around Jamie. "You've just done it!"

Jamie looked back at Bridget. "The knowglobe, right?"

Bridget winked. "You're getting it. They have a rudimentary language. You have it now, too."

He shook his head. "I hope it's not making me sound like a Baghu fashion model or something."

"Just talk," she said, laughing.

Jamie picked his briefcase back up, faced the Breather, and took a deep breath. "Greetings," he said, trying to ignore the creepy echo from outside. "I'm Jamison Sturm, representing the Sigma Draconis expedition on behalf of Quaestor Corporation. Perhaps you've heard of us?" Instinctively, he put forward his gloved hand.

He immediately thought to pull it back—but astonishingly, the Baghu moved first, plopping a dripping tentacle onto his hand. "I am Baghu," the alien said in a breathy basso voice that Jamie suspected the knowglobe must have pulled from old recordings of sexual criminals.

Then Jamie realized the tentacle—and now his hand—was covered with a gooey slime. He quickly pulled his dripping hand back. "Ew!" he said, flicking his wrist madly.

"Mr. Sturm!" Lorraine called out, alarmed. The alien wheel ground its gear teeth into the sand. "Please, watch your behavior."

Jamie looked up at the Breather. If it was offended, he had no way of telling. He tried to restart. "You said your name is Baghu? Don't you have an individual name?"

"They do not," Lorraine said. "They know who they are."

"Maybe you'd like to buy a name?" Jamie said, finally overcome by the absurdity of it all. "Here's one for free. I'll call you Bob."

The Sheoruk tut-tutted. "So disrespectful!"

Jamie snapped back at the alien scientist. "You're a glob in a wheel named Lorraine! You're one to talk?"

"*Well!*"

With that icy response, the Sheoruk pivoted and rumbled away, heading over the hill to its survey vessel.

Bridget shook her head. "There goes our help."

Jamie took another look at the big Baghu wobbling indifferently on the beach before him. Then he looked back at Bridget. "Sorry," he said, chastened.

"No, you're off to a fine start," Bridget said, resigned. "I can't wait to see what happens next."

12

This Dominium session began as they all had, with the ruling body displaying a visual reminder of the dangers the Xylanx were up against. Kolvax, standing in the center of the circular assembly room, looked up at the suspended crystal imager and yawned.

There was the soundless monochrome image of a human woman, tromping up and down happily in a vat—dancing, the Xylanx presumed, in the blood of her enemies. A sure sign of a vicious people. And there she was again in another fragment: evidently a prisoner, she was forced, along with another slave, to stuff her mouth with dark morsels carried along by a conveyor. The segment ended there, but the Xylanx assumed that death had surely followed. A fiendish method of execution, showing that even the mightiest human could be brought low.

Kolvax looked away, annoyed. How many times could this thing be rerun? The seconds of video had no context now, nor had they ever: Kolvax even suspected that, viewed outside the martial lens of the Xylanx, they might be part of some human entertainment rather than a political message. There was something comic about the woman, in a curious way. No, *how* the images were transmitted was the key thing.

Xylander observers had found the signals decades earlier during a years-long focus on a nearby star believed to have no transit stations. Had the broadcast been meant for the originating planet itself, the Xylanx would never have found it: a signal directed around the horizon by a surface-based transmitter or down to the ground from a satellite would've leaked little into space and not been of sufficient power to span the vast distance. But these signals were directed outward, at a strength intended for reception off-world.

Had the humans colonized their star system? It seemed the most likely explanation to Kolvax. And it meant that a human presence in their neighborhood could be just around the corner—or even underway, by the time the Xylanx had received the signals.

Had Kolvax been alive then, he would have mobilized the Stalkers immediately to investigate. Instead, the Xylanx of that time decided to withdraw to within their borders, using the militia only to put down local rebellions. Rather than test themselves against the humans, the leaders chose the path of cowardice.

More images appeared now, some in color, depicting escalating violence. He had had enough. "You can stop showing this now," he said, his voice booming around the chamber. "I alone have seen them. Me and my followers!"

"The Great Kolvax," a voice echoed from above. "We had forgotten you were here."

Kolvax couldn't see the speaker's sneer, but he didn't need to. The Dominium's assembly room was structured to make anyone given an audience as ill at ease as possible. Kolvax stood in a tiny lighted circle beneath the crystal visualizer above. All around were the ranking Dominium members, silhouettes behind a hundred one-way partitions. It was a nod to egalitarianism: the guest, usually accused of some crime against the state, would have no notion of the identities of his judges and accusers. Kolvax knew, of course. "Well, Haarfat," he said, glaring at the shadow who'd spoken, "you won't forget me after this."

He turned and looked up to the display, which now showed, in vibrant color, scenes from the last hours of his exile: The arrival of the humans, recorded by the armor worn by him and his compatriots. The weakling captive chattering in fear. And the battle with the warrior female and her comrades, all of whom looked more formidable than the wide-eyed blood-stomper from the old transmission.

The Dominium members had seen the video, but he heard them gasp again from behind their protective screens. Kolvax smiled. He'd guessed correctly. The images alone wouldn't have been enough to save his skin; any talented Xylander could have doctored them. But he had something else: the coward's blood on his glove. He hadn't needed the hostage after all. Genetic analysis had already proven that the people he fought existed. And that, Kolvax hoped, would be enough to reverse his people's slide into irrelevance.

The Xylanx of his grandfather's time were the scourge of the region. Few species could match them for industry. The rivals who were more efficient did not long survive. The Xylanx made sure of that, laying waste to worlds, enslaving some species and eradicating others. The Stalker brigades, the Xylanx's high-tech armored special forces, were a tool of expansion and terror.

But thanks to the messages from humanity, Kolvax had been born into a flabby realm only interested in protecting territory already taken. Despite its public rumblings, the ruling body really had no interest in venturing forth against the humans, not when its members could use the threat to stoke fear at home and preserve their holdings. The status quo enriched the Dominium members, and opponents to the isolation policy were made to suffer.

Kolvax could have been one of those liquidated. He'd originally cursed his people's fear of and fixation on humanity: they limited their horizons, preventing conquests. But then he hit upon another way. He decided to outflank the ruling class with the creation of the Severed. If the Dominium wanted to protect what they had by sowing fear of another species, his people would *loathe* aliens, demanding that all contamination be purged.

Hewing to an even more xenophobic position had kept him alive and given him room to build his own power base—for a time.

And now he intended to pound the wedge in deeply.

"None of you believed the humans would ever leave their cradle," Kolvax said. "You showed the old images by rote, building up your boogeymen without the least interest in investigating the humans' challenge. Well, I have just reminded you. They are real!"

"You don't have to make a speech," Haarfat said. "Although we know that is what you most love to do." The Dominium member cleared his throat. "We've sequenced the genetic material you returned. It matches what we would've expected to see. We'll need to return to your place of exile in force to investigate."

Kolvax laughed derisively. *Some strategists these people are.* "All you'll do is alert them to us."

"And you didn't?" a female voice asked. It was Deeliah, Kolvax assumed, one of his harshest critics. "The humans saw you!"

"But we left no clue to follow—none that will be found before we have a chance to act," Kolvax said. "The Severed are meticulous and careful, even in exile. That buys us time. The humans were not on a military expedition—"

"They were armed!" Deeliah sputtered.

Kolvax waved his hand, and above, the image resolved to show the golden-haired coward, wearing his badge. "The human was a trader," Kolvax said. "He certainly wasn't a fighter. We saw them bringing goods into the station. They're leading a commercial—not military—expedition."

Silence above and around. The human accession into the Signatory Systems was by far the biggest shocker Kolvax had come back with. It was a fearsome development, portending the spread of humanity everywhere. It gave him the confidence to advance his plan.

"We need more information about their capabilities," he said. "I can get it." Kolvax gestured again. A twinkling display appeared in the crystal imager above, depicting stars as glowing red pulses. Eight pathways traced away from a flashing dot at the center, representing the transit connections from the Severed's place of exile. "A frontal assault on the station will mobilize them against us. But there's no reason to do that—not when there are alternate routes for us to reach places they're likely to go. We can find them where they're out trading. And I can take the information you want as easily as I took the trader's blood."

Haarfat said nothing for a moment. Finally, Kolvax heard a grudging question. "What do you want?"

"Command of a habitat. And control of a Stalker detachment, which I will direct from there."

"A habitat! You don't want much."

"I want to protect the Xylanx," Kolvax said. He raised a hairless eyebrow. "If the rest of our people knew who was lurking at the door, I'm sure they'd want you to advance me all that was needed." His lip curled. "Give me my license to speak to the masses again, and they'll know—"

"We're not making that mistake again," Deeliah said. The Dominium had withheld news of Kolvax's encounter from the general public. She sighed. "You will install your so-called followers in positions of power, we assume."

"Of course. You know the code," Kolvax said. "I claim this discovery. Rights assigned to it, and titles." He looked at the display and pointed. "I suggest Gharion Preserve—where I just came from. It's connected to the exile station, with transit links heading almost everywhere the trader can go." It also had thirty thousand Xylanders, he did not need to say, whose production would be under his command.

"Use discretion," Haarfat said. "If you know how to do that. The human traders may be accustomed to commercial rivals. Appear as one."

Kolvax would do more than that. The need to keep the humans from expanding was legitimate. "I will oppose them at every turn—until I have what I need." He looked up. "I mean, what *we* need."

Silence from above signaled the audience was over. Kolvax smirked and walked out into the receiving area. There, in the antiseptic atrium, Tellmer stood beneath the only color in the room: a great tree growing in a vast planter. Tellmer's other arm had been reconnected, he saw, and the aide was moving it around awkwardly.

"We got it," Kolvax said. "Everything I wanted." In less than a week, they'd gone from being exiled on an alien station to having control of the Xylanx fortress station next door.

Tellmer bowed his helmeted head. "Wonderful, Great Kolvax." Raising his head, Tellmer looked up. "I just remembered something, standing here."

"How to make a fist?" Kolvax laughed. Xylanx surgical science was remarkable, but Tellmer was still recovering.

Tellmer made a feeble attempt to point upward. "Remember back in your office, behind the chapel? You forgot your tree," he said.

Kolvax looked up. "Huh. So I did." But he was hungry and in the mood to celebrate, so he quickly forgot about it.

13

When he was eleven, Jamie Sturm had sold his little stepsister to the Regulans. Earth's first trading partner had taken a liking to Shetland ponies, which his mother's new in-laws bred: Jamie had opened their eyes to the prospect of shipping their excess animals off-world, taking advantage of a market that was, as yet, in its infancy. He had simply added one more name to the documentation: his stepsister's. Young Jamie had not gotten to keep the eighty thousand dollars, and to this day the sight of a live-animal shipping container still made Taffy Keeler cry.

Given how the adult Taffy had turned out, Jamie knew now he had been absolutely justified. The Keelers would drive anyone to extreme measures. But that early experience had put him on the road to thinking he could sell anything to anyone, anywhere. In truth, though, what Jamie had done at the bourse was much different from selling in the past. He'd conducted all his sales through an isopanel, only occasionally speaking to another human through a linkup. He'd never so much as had to sell a candy bar in person.

He'd tried selling candy bars and just about everything else to the Baghu in the hours since Lorraine left. The portable fabricator from the general store sat in the sand behind him, where Bridget's team had parked it earlier. Two and a half meters tall and twice as long, the tracked vehicle was in effect a vending machine capable of producing most anything small enough to emerge from its meter-cubed slot. It had worked as it was supposed to. But nothing it had produced had caught the Baghu's eye...or whatever the Baghu had.

His attempts had gone on for so long that Bridget's teammates had lost interest in making fun of him. Over by the beach, he saw the ludicrous sight of Dinner and a couple of his teammates building a castle out of blue sand. The Breathers paid them no mind. Nor did they seem to care that O'Herlihy was wading at the edge of the lagoon, tramping around and picking up rocks. "He's a collector," Bridget explained.

"More for his head." Jamie looked tiredly at the Baghu leader—and then behind him, at the heap of merchandise he'd manufactured. He'd gone through the routine a hundred times at least. Jamie would call up images on the menu isopanel. Something would catch the leader's interest. Jamie would order up a sample and wait for it to be manufactured. Finally, he would take the item to the Baghu—who would sniff at it indifferently and then turn away.

Jamie's pile of rejected junk was now almost as tall as he was. A trumpet. A brass ingot. A paper comic book. A surveillance bee. A wedge of Stilton cheese. A pink bow tie. A bowling ball. Cyclotron parts. A bottle of brandy. High-tech or low-tech, decorative or useful, the products failed to impress the Baghu leader, who had simply lost interest and waddled off. Bridget's main use had been to stand between the creature and the lake, and nudge him back into the sale. The Breather didn't seem to mind being detained; whatever duties he had scaring young children in their nightmares weren't pulling him away.

"This is pointless," Jamie finally said. "These things don't even have anything to trade!"

"Wait." Bridget walked up to him. "Hold out your hand. The one the Breather shook."

Jamie rolled his eyes. "This is a waste of time," he said, sticking his right hand out. Bridget turned it over and activated the sensor above her helmet's faceplate. A line of light swept past Jamie's hand.

"I was right," she said, checking a reading. "On your glove— and on the Baghu. Gold dust."

Jamie took his hand back. "What?" He eyed his glove. "I don't see anything."

"Microscopic, but it's there," Bridget said. "Maybe they *do* have something."

Jamie calculated. Gold was useful and desirable, even now. They hadn't been able to analyze the lake to any depth, but maybe the Breathers had something down there after all.

He tried to quiz the Baghu leader about it, but the thing simply hissed—a frightening sound that Jamie decided he never wanted to hear again, ever. "No deal?"

"We want first," the Baghu boomed. "Then we will trade you the things."

"The things."

"The things under the water," the alien said, its nozzle dripping ooze.

Jamie sighed. He turned back to look at the pile again. "What the hell do you guys want?"

Bridget walked back to the edge of the lagoon and kicked the liquid with her boot. "Why don't you hit the randomizer?" she asked. "Surprise them with something."

"I've been using it for an hour!" Disgusted, Jamie punched in the command again. Behind him, the fabricator returned to its work. Less than a minute later he heard the electronic chime in his helmet. Something fell from the slot and landed in the muck. Jamie didn't even try to catch it.

It was a teddy bear. Brown and fuzzy, the bear was a protected design licensed from the holders of the Zazzy the Zoobear intellectual property. It had been seventy years since any bears walked the Earth outside captivity, but the Zazzy entertainments had driven a generation of kids to fall in love with things ursine. The *previous* generation, Jamie knew: Zazzy was as dated as the animals that inspired him, and Quaestor had picked up the license for next to nothing.

Deflated, Jamie kneeled down to pick it up. But before his gloved hand touched it, a greasy tentacle snaked up and snatched the stuffed animal away.

Jamie turned to see the Baghu leader holding the fuzzy aloft and contemplating. Other Breathers took notice, somehow, and tromped out onto the beach. Then the lead creature flipped the toy up into the air and enveloped it with his snout. The Baghu swallowed the bear whole.

"*Okaaay...*," Jamie said.

Bridget's eyes widened with amusement. "Try another one!"

Another minute, another chime, another bear. Now the other Baghu pawed at the Zazzy® Brand Children's Bear Product with their tentacles. A sort of slap-fight broke out between the Breathers, and by the time it ended the toy had become a meal for another appreciative alien.

"Teddy bears?"

Standing in the lagoon, O'Herlihy laughed. "Maybe they like the way they go down."

All along the shoreline, Baghu beckoned, waving tentacles. More had appeared, and Jamie could barely see the surge team members through the crowd of aliens. "We will sell you the things under the water," came the call. "We want. We want!"

Jamie tried to shut out the cacophony. *Teddy bears!* As if this place wasn't weird enough. Jamie shook his head. "A sale's a sale, I guess." He looked to Bridget, still on the edge of the lagoon. "What now?"

"You're the trader—"

"A desk-trader, as you love to remind me," he said. "But you escort the traders all the time."

Bridget shook her head. "Once you settle on a price, someone takes the deal back to the Dragon's Depot. Falcone will send back Quaestor's factors to set up on-site production. The bears are easy enough to make locally."

"But what price?" He looked at the Baghu. "What's under the water?"

The lead Breather stood silent, and the end of its nozzle pinched. "Don't want to say," it finally said.

"Great." Jamie looked at Bridget. "Help?"

✳ ✳ ✳

Standing at the edge of the lake, Bridget grew nervous. There were fifty or more flailing Breathers now, some half in the lagoon, others on the shore. Jamie's random pick had put the walking stomachs into a consumer frenzy not seen since the Black Friday Riots on Earth brought out a military response a hundred years earlier.

"Chief?" O'Herlihy asked in her ear. She could barely see him over the aliens. The systems in her HardSHEL armor highlighted the locations of her other eight squad members up and down the shoreline; nobody was where they needed to be. She'd gotten complacent, been lulled into a false sense of security by the

Baghu's previously placid manner. Now, nobody was in position to protect Jamie, who was backing up farther from the beach, hemmed in against the fabricator.

Nearby, she could see Dinner trying to raise his rifle to protect the trader. The Breathers pushed and jostled right past, ignoring him.

"They don't know what our weapons are," she said.

"Shot in the air?" O'Herlihy asked, rattled.

"Hang on." Anywhere else, she'd consider it—but gunfire usually had a way of ending sales calls. Turning toward the lagoon, she slid between bouncing Breathers and waded into the brine. Maybe the answer was simple: they'd help the primitive Baghu complete the sale. *We will give you the things under the water!*

It wasn't really water, she saw as she tried her scanner again. Heavily laden with salts and chlorides at this level—and the body went much deeper than she'd imagined. Trovatelli had stayed aboard the depot to get the place running; Bridget could have used the Q/A's skills here now. "Inconclusive," she said. "Too murky." She turned and called back toward the beach, and Jamie. "Maybe we could—"

Bridget felt a chain snap around her neck. Reaching with her free hand, she felt it was no chain but rather the sinewy tentacle of a Baghu pulling at her. Every Breather on the beach and in the brine turned on the armored bodyguards, bullwhip tendrils snaking around limbs, chests, and rifles.

"Hostile, hostile!" she called. The fifty had become a hundred now, a mass of Baghu splashing up from beneath. *What the hell is happening?*

* * *

Jamie backed up against the fabricator. "Yang!"

The Baghu kept pressing toward him. Jamie stuck his foot in the delivery slot of the fabricator and scrambled on top of the big device. It rocked on its wheels, jostled by the pressure of the Breathers.

"We want," the Baghu leader said. "*We want!*"

Jamie didn't have the menu anymore; he'd dropped it. It was out there somewhere, pounded under the feet of the drooling stomachs. And out past them he couldn't see a single member of Surge Sigma. He'd seen two of his bodyguards go down into the lake with the Breathers—the creatures had lifted Arbutus Dinner like he was a child's toy.

"*We want! We want!*"

On his hands and knees atop a vending machine a hundred trillion kilometers from home, Jamie looked out over the sea of alien tentacles and tried to see Bridget—or any of the surge team members.

So much for my debut!

❋ ❋ ❋

Another tentacle and then another wrapped around Bridget's faceplate; she could see her companions being bound and hurried toward the lake. She heard a shot fire wildly as she fought to keep her balance. Her suit's internal armature held, keeping her in place. But the mucky soil beneath her boots did not hold, and the four Breathers holding her pushed out toward the center of the lagoon.

"Extract the trader," she called again to anyone who would listen.

Then they plunged, Bridget struggling all the way as the darkness devoured them.

EPISODE 3:

UNDERWATER HOLDINGS

14

All through grad school, Jamie Sturm had been plagued by the same nightmare. He was huddled on top of a pedestal, trying to avoid the clawing fingernails of people down on the ground who were crawling all over each other to unseat him. Ashamed of having a subconscious so embarrassingly on the nose, he'd never mentioned the dream to his therapist. Financial industry work came in two flavors: paranoia and panic. He'd known what was ahead.

Or so he thought. As faceless and frightening as the people in his dreams were, at least they'd never had tentacles for arms and drooling nozzles for mouths. The Baghu's slimy feelers slapped untiringly against the top edge of the fabricator. Twenty minutes had passed and the creatures' enthusiasm was unabated. Hunched atop the big machine, Jamie kept his hand pressed on the panic button of his sales badge. He'd already called out on the emergency channel and activated his suit's internal summons, but no one had seemed to notice.

"Welligan, where *are* you?" Jamie yelled again into his helmet mic.

Static.

The trader swore. He'd been abandoned. Was this Welligan's revenge for Jamie ratting on him back at the depot? Or was the idiot simply incompetent? Jamie didn't know. But he knew he hadn't heard anything from Bridget or any of the troopers swept into the lagoon, either.

And they were supposed to be protecting *him*?

On his hands and knees, Jamie desperately looked around. He couldn't see anything but the sea of tentacles; Baghu covered the entire beach. But he could still make out the lagoon, and he knew the landing site was back in the other direction. There weren't as many Breathers on that side yet. Maybe he could make a jump for it without being eaten or carried off himself.

Yeah, that's it, he thought. If the critters wanted the fabricator, maybe they'd ignore him. It was his only shot. He stood—

"*Sturm!*"

Jamie pulled back from the edge and yelled in response to the crackling voice over his headset. "Welligan! Dammit, man!"

"Sorry, friend. We're a little busy," Welligan said.

Jamie thought he could hear the sound of pulse blasts going off in the background of Hiro's transmission. *Well, at least someone's shooting.* "I need you to get busy over here, *friend*!"

"Can't," Welligan said. "But I'm sending somebody. Surge Three out."

"Wait! What?"

Nothing.

Jamie dropped again to his knees as a rumble shook the fabricator. Would the Baghu try to carry the machine into the lagoon, too, ignorantly assuming it was a boxful of teddy bears? And what would happen to him then?

"Welligan!" he yelled again. "Yang!"

"*Anyone!*"

❋ ❋ ❋

Bridget Yang looked at the time display projected on the inside of her faceplate. Thirty minutes. It felt like longer—and it was far too long to be helpless.

The Baghu who'd seized her had picked up speed as they plunged, carrying her down into the darkness of the alien lake. Her armor had registered the increased pressure and compensated; fortunately, the lagoon didn't seem that deep. They'd touched bottom after a little over a minute. She'd felt the creatures driving their legs into the muck at the bottom, adhering to the lake bed floor.

She'd struggled during the first few minutes, but she'd found it a futile effort. The Breathers' tentacles were wrapped around her in overlapping diagonal laces that tightened in response to any movement. It was like being stuck in a giant Chinese finger trap. Only eye movements, flexed fingertips, and spoken commands allowed her any control over her armor's internal functions at all.

There was no way to call up for help. Traditional radio waves couldn't penetrate the thick brine, and extremely low frequency communications of the kind used by submarines were a one-way affair from the land. Ginormous transmitters weren't part of the typical security squaddie's kit.

But the liquid proved a fine medium for ultrasound, and that was a capability her team's armor had. Her system's transducer raised her voice above the range where humans could hear and boomed her words straight through the Baghu tentacles surrounding her. If the act caused the Breathers any discomfort, she couldn't tell—but anyone nearby with similar equipment would be able to hear and decipher. She was a baby with a very noisy kick.

It only took a few minutes for her to determine that her whole squad was similarly trapped in the immediate vicinity. Some were still straining against the Baghu. She'd ordered them to stop and lie limp. The liquid pressure wouldn't crack the HardSHELs, but she didn't want to chance a test between the aliens' strength and their units' servos. One buckled plate could burst a seam, inviting disaster.

No, they needed to think on the problem. And they certainly had the time. Her onboard fresherpak, a bladder loaded with nanoids that drew on the armor's energy to mimic photosynthesis, would extend her suit's oxygen for quite some time. Power was the real limiting factor—and another reason not to struggle.

"They've got to eat sometime," Bridget said.

"So do we," called back Lopez-Herrera, the squad medic.

Bridget knew as soon as she'd mentioned food that it was a silly idea. Her suit's live datalink with the knowglobe was gone, but as a matter of course she and her team had downloaded everything known about the species to their personal systems. She'd reviewed it twice already—an impromptu study session at the bottom of an alien lake—and now she reviewed it again, searching the lines of text for anything helpful. Right now all she knew was that the Baghu could stay motionless down here indefinitely, absorbing whatever it was they ate through their trunks.

"Maybe we burn," Dinner said, referring to their last-ditch defense used sometimes against the Spore. "That'd make them let go."

"Then we'd be statues at the bottom of the lagoon," Bridget countered. Besides, she wasn't too sure how well the suits would handle the pressure afterward—or any retaliation by the Breathers.

More importantly, the act would likely kill their captors, and there were rules about that sort of thing. Lorraine's report said that no Baghu had ever been seen to act in a hostile manner before. There was a first time for everything, and this was certainly it—but mindless Spores aside, Bridget didn't cross trillions of miles to kill aliens.

If she could help it.

Bridget could hear O'Herlihy nonchalantly whistling a tune. *Just like him.* "Any ideas, Mike?"

"Just that old Phippsy must be laughing his ass off right now," he said.

And despite their circumstances, Bridget laughed. Years earlier, O'Herlihy and a friend had "borrowed" power armor units and carried a portable restroom to the top of Mount Everest. It was an old prank, but what was new was the fact that Coach Phipps, a lecher who'd harassed students for years, was welded inside. That, and a lifetime of other rash acts of chivalry, had led to O'Herlihy's unemployability outside Bridget's team. "So how long did it take for them to rescue Phipps?" she asked.

"Long enough for him to put the box to its intended use a few times," O'Herlihy answered.

"We may wind up with the opportunity ourselves. Just stay calm, everybody. We'll come up with something. And don't forget—Hiro's still out there."

A collective groan echoed over the ultrasound receiver. Bridget was half expecting that reaction, but she couldn't be heard to join in. Her verbal head count had determined that Welligan's troops weren't in the soup with her. Would he have the sense to do what he was trained to do in this situation? She hoped so, but she wasn't much more confident than her fellow prisoners.

She chewed on her lip. *Think, woman. There's got to be a way out!*

***

"Hey, guys! Knock it off!" The volume on Jamie's external speakers was set at maximum now, and he could easily hear his translated voice booming in the Baghu's language. But if they could hear him over the din of their own gabble, he couldn't tell. His interface with the knowglobe was still live, but there was nothing new to translate in the Baghu cacophony. Just the same "We trade, we trade, we trade." That was it. Talking to the Breathers was as useless as trying to talk to his own crew.

All at once the aliens' demeanor changed. Instead of waving their tentacles toward him, they windmilled their arms wildly. Squawks became shrieks, and the sea of Breathers around the fabricator heaved. A blaze of light cascaded across the aliens. Jamie looked up.

The *Indispensable*! The team's shuttle was in the air, descending through the billowing chlorine fog. Retro thrusters glowing, the massive vessel swung low over the crowd of aliens. Some dove back into the lagoon, but others simply ran in circles.

Its pilot evidently realizing the crowd wasn't going to disperse, the *Indispensable* moved in toward the fabricator instead. The door to one of the bangboxes that made up the shuttle opened. The ship descended to a point in midair just meters above and to the side of his metallic perch. For a moment, Jamie feared being roasted by the rockets—but instead the ship stopped its turn in exact alignment with the edge of the fabricator. It dipped gently, leaving a long leap between him and the hatchway.

"Come on over," he heard Geena Madaki say in his headset.

"Lower and closer," Jamie said.

"Not with those things on the ground," she said. "Jump for it!"

Jamie looked down. The Baghu were still there—and the arrival of the ship seemed to have agitated the braver ones. Breathers were climbing over each other now, clambering to reach him atop the device.

"Gah!" Jamie said as a tentacle wrapped around his booted foot. He leapt into the air, freeing himself from the creature. On touching down again, he made a bounding leap for the ship.

Jamie reached out for the open hatchway, even as Madaki chose that moment to bank *Indispensable* closer. Jamie's chest slammed against the bottom of the doorway, and his arms clawed for a handhold inside the vehicle.

"I've got you!" said an occupant from above. Lynn Stubek, one of the members of Welligan's squad, locked onto his wrists. "Madaki, we're clear!"

Jamie thought he heard the pilot say something then, but his mind was in no position to process information. *Indispensable* lurched back over the mass of Breathers and banked and rose, Jamie's body still hanging out of the vessel. He looked up at Stubek in panic. But the woman had him tight in her servo-assisted grasp. Within seconds, he was aboard—and panting for air on the floor of the shuttle.

"Welcome back," Madaki called back from the pilot's seat. "Seem to be making a habit of hauling you away from trouble."

Jamie looked at the monitor with the feed from the shuttle's underside. He thought the ground had vanished beneath the fog for a moment, but on closer inspection he realized that what he was looking at was a living carpet. It was as if the whole undersea population of Baghula had come up to see him off, both bobbing in the lagoon and writhing on the beach.

Stubek helped him to Madaki's side in the compartment. "Bridget's team," he said, wheezing. "Pulled under—"

"Chief's fine," the dark-skinned woman said. "I expect they're all having a nice rest down there." She looked back at Jamie. "But our Hiro isn't doing so well. Check channel seven."

Jamie had forgotten about Welligan. But he remembered quickly when he tuned his suit's receiver—and heard frantic, confused yelling and more of the blasts he'd heard before.

"That's not good," he said. His eyes widened—and a thought occurred. Jamie didn't want to be here: he'd made that plain at every turn to anyone who'd listen. The security guys, meanwhile, seemed to lap this stuff up—Bridget's leaderly reluctance notwithstanding. If Jamie hadn't brought them here, they would have been tussling with something somewhere. But Hiro Welligan hadn't seemed like the typical muscle-brained danger seeker. Was he here because he had to be, too?

Jamie looked again at the monitor depicting the tsunami of Baghu. He gulped. "I guess we should—"

"Already on my way," Madaki said. She put *Indispensable* into a roll, heading back toward the original landing site.

Jamie took a deep breath. "Thanks for the pickup, I guess."

"It's not personal." The pilot smiled primly. "You've got the badge."

15

Like most expeditionary spacecraft in the whirlibang era, *Indispensable* was a disappointment to model makers and others interested in indexing the starships of the galaxy. It could look like darn near anything, depending on the needs of the journey. While the current configuration linking the two troop 'boxes, the "general store," and the engine mount in a horizontal chain was standard for most sales missions, the crew could attach practically anything that came with them through the whirlibang.

In fact, Jamie had learned, the only thing that gave the collection of shipping units its name was his presence. Like an admiral transferring a flag, Jamie made any vessel he traded from *Indispensible*. It was a tough, positive-sounding name, and he'd been pleased to get it: most of the other Quaestor trading ships followed the corporate policy of reusing East India Company names, resulting in would-be professionals having to call *Constant Friend, Happy Entrance,* and *Trades Increase* home.

Then Bridget had told him why the name had survived on the list so long, unclaimed: the eighteenth-century *Indispensable* was a convict ship charged with carrying prisoners to Australia. That is, when it wasn't engaged in stabbing whales, a barbaric practice banned decades earlier. The name had been another joke on him by the members of Surge Sigma—but he hadn't objected. He'd felt like a prisoner during the whole ordeal since Venus.

Now, however, he was one of the few members of the crew who was free. And it had dawned on him that with Chief Yang out of contact, he might just be in charge. So why was *Indispensable* racing back toward the mass of crazy aliens?

"Slow down!" he yelled, clutching the back of Madaki's pilot seat. He couldn't see the Breathers through the fog below, but the ship's sensors had picked up no fewer than a thousand charging inland. They had engulfed *Indispensable*'s original landing site and were now pursuing Welligan's team into the uplands. And the shuttle was heading right back into the fight.

Looking out the forward viewport, he could make out the mass of aliens on the move. His stomach started to crawl up his throat. He could visualize how any landing might go: Baghu swarming over the vessel, just as they had the fabricator. Thoughts of Welligan, of rescue, of *anything*, fled from his mind. The blood drained from his face, and he felt his fingers going numb. "Put— put us back over the lagoon," he mumbled.

"What?" Concentrating, Madaki didn't look back.

Now he found his voice. "Put us back over the lagoon!" Jamie yelled.

"Calm down, Jamie," Madaki said. "If you're hyperventilating, your suit will add CO_2. Just breathe."

Jamie could only hear the creak of the shuttle descending. "Bridgie's team. We get them back—they'll deal with this!"

The pilot spoke in even tones. "We're out of contact with Bridgie's team. I've got to make a decision."

"I thought you said Yang's squad was fine!"

"I don't think a bunch of slimies can kill my Bridget," the older woman said. "But I've got one squad under assault and another underwater. We save the one under assault."

Jamie sat down on the shuttle floor as the ground below raced toward them. He tugged at his silly badge. "Does this count for anything?"

"Don't worry," she said, smiling. "My responsibility to you is to keep you clear of trouble, and I will." She put the vehicle into a steep decline.

Jamie cringed as *Indispensable* leveled off meters above the surface and then turned its nose upward to match the slope of the hillside. The shuttle was no helicopter or Coandǎcar: it was designed for short hops on-world, not aerobatics. Yet Madaki was neatly following the contours of the land, not even grazing the snouts of the ascending Baghu.

O'Herlihy had told him that Madaki was flying space missions before he was born: she, at least, had seemed competent. But Jamie had to wonder how typical these sorts of scrapes were if they needed an ace in the first place.

"Finally!" At the sound of Welligan's voice in his headset, Jamie looked up the members of Surge Three—Welligan's squad within Bridget's command—appeared as glowing figures on the shuttle's tactical display.

Behind Jamie, Stubek—still in her space suit, as he was— headed to the port hatchway and opened it. She looked back to Jamie. "Get by the other airlock!"

The notion of removing the metal barrier between him and Baghula's denizens didn't interest Jamie at all. But after a moment's hasty reflection, he decided he'd rather have the guys with the guns inside with him. Cycling the hatchway, he looked down at the windswept plateau.

Clinging to the inside of the starboard airlock's external doorway, Jamie saw Welligan and his other eight squad mates in a narrow circle facing outward and pointing their rifles at the ground around them. Baghu were charging up toward them, about to overrun their position.

"Ride's here, people," Welligan said, looking up at *Indispensable* and then back at the advancing wave of Breathers. "We're still on Regulation Three. Sonic bursts, ground sweep!"

At his command, the troopers fired at the surface meters in front of them. Unseen energy jackhammered against the ground sending wet dirt flying upward in clumps. The aliens skidded to a stop, evidently startled. As a group, Welligan and his companions began expanding their circle, clearing a Breather-free zone large enough to admit the *Indispensable*. The shuttle swung toward the surface. From her doorway, Stubek fired sonic blasts from a large shipboard weapon over her fellow troopers' heads. Her shots weren't even moving dust at that range, but the sound kept the Baghu from advancing as Welligan and his team backed toward the ship.

Five surge team members entered the airlock on Stubek's side, and Jamie helped three aboard on his. Welligan was the last to take Jamie's hand up. "I told you I'd send somebody." The soldier smiled, but his spectral hair was now white.

"Uh-huh." Jamie didn't even think about the head count and slammed the hatch closed. Before it finished cycling, Jamie felt *Indispensable* lurch heavenward.

"Take us to sea," Welligan called out to Madaki. Then he looked at Jamie and exhaled. "Enjoying your trip so far?"

Jamie gestured toward Welligan's rifle. "What was that sonic business down there? You guys have tougher settings—I expected to see bodies everywhere!"

"It's Quaestor's general orders for expedition security," Welligan said, undoing his helmet. "Regulation Three: *Don't kill the customers!*"

Jamie sputtered. "These guys aren't customers! They're trying to drown us!"

"It happens. I take it you've never made cold calls before?"

✳ ✳ ✳

"This is crazy," Dinner said in Bridget's ear. "I'm willing to let them have the armor and swim for it."

Bridget chuckled. True, Arbutus was a world-class swimmer—but that method of escape required getting free to start with. And they all knew that the brine wasn't that hospitable—nor was the air breathable once you got out of the lagoon.

Which made Bridget think of something. She was in intimate contact with the Baghu, after all, with the tentacles smashed against her helmet. She'd noted the residue from the leader's "handshake" with Jamie earlier; now, her visual and spectrographic sensors could get a really close look. And she really had nothing better to do other than watch her armor's power and oxygen waste away.

"Huh," she said, looking at the readout. There were concentrations she wasn't expecting. She struggled to remember her alien biochemistry lessons.

She was working her way through an onboard tutorial when she heard a faint whisper, not from any of the other prisoners. For a moment, she thought the Baghu had said something. But then it grew louder and clearer.

"Yeah, I heard it," Bridget said into the transducer. An extremely faint ultrasound signal was coming from somewhere above. A few minutes of adjustments on her part improved the signal. A buoy had been dropped into the lagoon above them, trailing a heavy sensor pack on a cable. Her team was out of contact no longer: *Indispensable* still existed.

"…okay down there?" Bridget could barely make out Madaki's voice.

"Just bumming around on the beach," Bridget replied. "Well, under the beach—and a ways out." The colleagues quickly compared notes on the situation topside and below. "How's the team?" Bridget asked.

"All secure, dear," Madaki said. "As is your trader."

"Hello," Bridget heard Jamie say.

"Hello." *Why does he have to be the one loud and clear?*

"This isn't my fault," Jamie said.

"Now, why would you think I would think that? No, I've always wanted to spend the day at the bottom of a lake getting hugged by aliens. Thank you."

A pause. "You're welcome."

Bridget would've given anything for enough range of motion to put her head in her hands. "Put Welligan on," she said.

Hiro recounted the evacuation for Bridget. They hadn't harmed any Baghu, but he didn't see how they'd be able to avoid doing so if they needed to forcibly enter the lagoon. "There's a good line of them six or eight deep on the shore—and more bobbing in the water. We were lucky we didn't clock one when we dropped the buoy."

"We've got a couple of hours' margin here," Bridget said. "See what the Sheoruk think. They're back at their camp, I'd bet. Maybe they know something about how the Baghu are acting. Maybe there was some etiquette we blew—something we did to set them off."

"And then?" Welligan asked. "I mean, what if that doesn't work?"

"Then you extract us however you have to. Just don't let them get close to you with those tentacles."

"Only one way to prevent that."

"I know," Bridget said somberly. "Surge One out." Then, having had a thought, she signed back on for a postscript. "And don't let Jamie piss off Lorraine again!"

16

Night never fell at this location on Baghula's surface, and it seemed to Jamie that the planet's natives never slept, either. Three hours had passed since the aliens went berserk, and their endurance seemed without limit.

Jamie had been known for his stamina on the trading desk. Sleeping was overrated when one market on Earth or another was always open. He'd driven brokers on the Ops floor to distraction by banging his cowbell at all hours, proclaiming his trading successes. Now all he wanted in life was to stay in the passenger seat of *Indispensable* and never move again.

But everyone else aboard was in motion. Madaki had parked the shuttle safely away from the stampeding Baghu hordes on a quiet mesa—and that had been the cue, evidently, for Welligan's team to begin rushing about the vessel. Some of the troopers were adjusting their weapons. Others were fiddling with crates from stowage holding metal tubes Jamie had never seen before. Some kind of ordnance, he imagined.

Boots off and helmet in his lap, Jamie felt like he was watching one of his immerse-goggle sitcoms. He was physically there, but he wasn't a participant. That was fine by him. He yawned.

"Glad to see you can keep a cool head," Lynn Stubek said from her seated position at the communications panel.

"Somebody has to." He opened his eyes and forced a smile. With buzz-cut red hair, Stubek was one of the youngest members of Surge Sigma—and one of the few that hadn't given him a hard time yet.

"I'll wake you up if I need the rest of my squad killed," she said.

"Roger." *Well, there goes that.* He directed his attention to her viewscreen, which was filled with static. "You still haven't raised the Sheoruk expedition?"

Stubek shook her head. "They're reporting the same crazy business we are. The Sheoruk rolled for their lives as soon as the Baghu started moving. They're locked in their compound now, but the Breathers have knocked down their external transmitter."

"I didn't think they were that intelligent," Jamie said.

"I didn't say they were. I think they're just running around and knocking stuff over." She worked a control. "Wait," she said. "I've got something."

A wave of revulsion gripped Jamie as he saw the image on the screen. Pulsating nodules of red and brown soaking in a blood-colored sauce. It looked like a close-up of someone's abdominal surgery. "Eww!" he said. "What the hell is *that*?"

"That's the biologist you met earlier," Stubek replied. "Lorraine."

"No, no," Jamie said, standing up before the monitor. Going in for a closer look was a mistake, and he immediately backed off. "Lorraine was a big wheel thing. That's just gross—"

"You've got your space suit, I've got mine," Lorraine said over the communication system's speakers. It was the same feminine voice he'd heard earlier—but now it was coming from a greasy blob, burbling pus from folds of flesh.

Jamie forced down a swallow. *That's our stewardess? No wonder Pan Am went under!*

Lorraine's voice had lost its lilt. "Really, I don't know why the humans decided to send such an insensitive being to work with other races." The mass on the screen quivered. "And I don't know what you said to those fine, peaceful creatures out—"

"Hey, those peaceful creatures were trying to kill me!" Jamie slapped his chest with his hand. It had been a long enough day already, and he wasn't going to take insults from something that looked like the middle of an oyster.

Lorraine's form rumbled back and forth, sacs quivering with what even Jamie could interpret as anger. "Now, listen here, you—you—*human*! I've been here for seven years. And never in that time have I seen the Baghu agitated in this manner!" Alien organs blushed a furious red. "They've been swarming our camp, looking for *you*! You must have done something!"

"I showed them a teddy bear," Jamie said, still not believing the episode. "They ate it."

Lorraine paused for several seconds—doubtless, Jamie thought, checking in with her knowglobe to see what a teddy bear was. Her next comment, a calmer one, confirmed it. "Interesting fellow, this Teddy Roosevelt," she said. "He seems to have had great respect for other species—unlike some humans. I should like to learn more about him."

"Whatever," Jamie said. "But before you get down to watching full episodes of *Zazzy the Zoobear*, tell me what they want. Our people are in trouble!"

The Sheoruk waggled in something like a shrug. "I've never known them to *want* anything. Their lagoon teems with food, although we've never studied their digestive cycle." Lorraine paused. "But they do seem to prefer some of the dried sponges on the beach. Perhaps your Zazzy bears are just the right composition for their palates."

"They offered to give me what was under the water," Jamie said. "What's down there?"

"Nothing. They've said as much before—they have nothing of value down there at all."

Lorraine paused again, apparently thinking. Jamie had had an easy time imagining a persona for Lorraine back when she was a mystery figure in a wheel, but now, strangely, he was becoming accustomed to talking to a picture of an appendectomy. *I've got to get out of this place*, he thought for the hundredth time.

"Things under the water!" Lorraine repeated. "It's a strange thing for them to say. Are you sure the Baghu said it?"

"Repeatedly!"

"And Chief Yang—has she seen anything down there?"

"She can't," Welligan said, snapping a power pack into his rifle as he walked up. "Look, we're about out of time. I need to know what's waiting for us down there."

"We don't have any idea about the Baghu community beneath the surface," Lorraine said. "They're protective of their privacy. They don't let anyone go farther out than wading on the shore. We haven't made any attempts to go down there."

"They're hiding something?" Welligan asked.

"More like they're—well, I don't know how to put it. Ashamed of something, is more like it."

"You're a research team," Jamie said. "Haven't you sent down a probe?"

The glob shook. "Would *you* like an alien probe poking around where you live?"

"No," Jamie said. That was an entirely different nightmare.

"But wait," Lorraine said. "Are you intending to enter the water yourselves?"

"Looks like we're going to have to," Welligan said. "We don't want to."

Lorraine paused. "No, I don't think you do," she said. "But be aware of this: I don't know how the Baghu will react to your incursion. And I don't know what level of force you can apply without harming one. No one has ever tried. We don't know what your weapons will do—and we don't know what they will do in response." The Sheoruk's strange form glistened with moisture. "You could bring on a calamity on a planetary scale."

Welligan nodded, his expression grave. It jolted Jamie, who had never seen the man looking serious before. "I'm aware of that," Welligan said. "But we don't have any other choice."

Lorraine seemed to go limp. "I—I understand. The Sheoruk cannot stop you. But I implore you, use mercy."

"Mercy," Jamie said. He snorted. "I don't think they understand that."

"That's just because you don't share the same frame of reference, trader," Lorraine said. "But every living being functions because of one thing: logic. *Something* makes their parts move. *Something* makes them behave as they do. If you don't understand what they're up to, it's not because they're illogical. It's because you're not thinking like a Baghu."

"Thanks for the help," Jamie said, not meaning it. He really didn't see any similarities between himself and a bunch of walking stomachs.

Unless, of course, they, too, were feeling nauseated right now.

17

In her years as part of the expedition's surge team, Geena
Madaki had been like a mother to Bridget. Or grandmother—
it was hard to tell any human's age anymore. All Bridget knew
was the soothing voice over the ultrasound receiver sounded
like home.

"We're coming for you, Bridget. You sit tight."

"That will not be a problem," Bridget said.

It had been for some of her comrades, some of whom had
wasted power trying to wrest free. Bridget hated feeling helpless,
too, but she seldom thought she actually *was* helpless—including
now. She'd been reviewing the Sheoruk researchers' notes on the
Baghu and their lagoon, and the tentacles before her face were
as good as a tissue sample for her armor's instruments. She just
needed time to put it all together.

And that time was running low. "Ten minutes," Dinner said.
His reserves were lowest.

"We'll be there," Madaki said. "I'm putting Surge Three on
the beach now."

Bridget inhaled deeply. *Here goes nothing*, she thought.

* * *

If Welligan was nervous about being all that was left to save his chief's squad, Jamie thought the man was doing a good job of hiding it. His hair was, too. Inside his helmet, Hiro's mop was a cool cinnamon, the EndoSys nanoids altering his follicles' pigment to reflect his mood.

Jamie's space suit was fully on again. The port and starboard airlocks on the two personnel 'boxes that were part of *Indispensable* were open. Two gunners were stationed in each one. Behind the troops in each doorway was a portable turbine the size of a suitcase.

"Pilot's going to bring us in at ten meters and do a three-hundred-sixty-degree turn," Welligan called out. "We hit the landing area with sonics—hit 'em directly if we have to. If they won't budge, switch to nitros and put some rounds into them. We've already seen the pulse weapons don't faze 'em."

Eyes wide, the trooper looked back at Jamie. "You're gonna want to stay inside, Jamie. We don't know what gases are in those Breathers. For all we know, they'll go up like grenades."

Jamie nodded. He wasn't planning on going near the exits— or even watching from the front. Welligan was going to open a landing spot on the beach and then tear a path down into the lagoon. *Indispensable*'s sensors had mapped enough of the body of liquid to reveal a sloping approach down into the undersea realm. Welligan's team would simply walk underwater toting the turbines. They would use them to reach the captives—and to help bring back anyone they freed.

There would likely be a big mess on the water afterward. Jamie didn't want to see it.

"Jamie Sturm!"

Jamie looked back. From the controls of *Indispensable*, Madaki looked urgently back to him. "I'm hearing Bridget through the buoy. She wants to talk to you!"

His eyes widened. "Me?"

"Patch into Channel five sixty!"

Jamie touched the number on his wrist. "Yang?" he asked.

"Jamie!" Bridget's voice was faint. "They *do* have something to trade!"

"What?" Jamie had forgotten all about the trading mission.

"I was right. They do have something to trade, but they don't think so. You have to talk to them again!"

Jamie's head swam. "But they did say they had something. You're not making any sense."

"Just shut up and listen! Remember—"

The connection went silent.

"Remember?" Jamie asked. "Remember what?"

Madaki looked back and shook her head, sadly. "Her suit power's too low. Either that or they've smashed the buoy."

From his position in the port airlock where he'd been listening, Welligan slapped the wall. "That's it, then. Bring us down, Geena. Weapons live!"

Bewildered, Jamie shook his head. His eyes searched the shuttle—and found the monitor showing the feed from below *Indispensable*. There was the throng of Baghu, bigger than ever. Stomping stomachs bustling all around the fabricator. But they hadn't destroyed it, he noticed. Much less moved it.

He had a thought. Quickly, he searched his suit's recorder for the encounter. "*We will trade you the things under the water,*" the Breather had said. It repeated it again more slowly, and the human voice it was translated into spoke with seeming passion. "*We will trade. We will!*"

Jamie cued it ahead—and listened to the Baghu calls from once he climbed atop the device. "*We trade. We trade. We trade!*"

He thought back on Lorraine's words about thinking like a Baghu.

Could it really be that simple?

Jamie bolted forward and grabbed Welligan's arm, stopping the trooper in mid-countdown. "Stop! You've got to get me to the fabricator!"

Welligan rolled his eyes. "I know you've got some money problems, but I think we're going to have to write this mission off."

"No, I mean it," Jamie said. He pulled again at his arm. "You get me down there!"

"Jamie, I can't—"

"Yes, you can," Jamie said, wedging himself into the narrow space remaining inside the airlock. He grabbed at his badge. "I'm the trader. While the trade mission's on, you work for me. And I say it's on!"

Hiro looked at him, amazed. Then he turned and called out to his teammates on the opposite side. "Stand down," he said. He looked back to Madaki. "Can you put us down on the fabricator?"

"It's where I picked him up from," the pilot said. "Round trips are my specialty."

Indispensable lifted away from the intended landing site and hovered above the fabricator. Welligan stepped inside the open airlock door with Jamie, who clutched the ship for dear life.

This is crazy, he thought, seeing the mad mass of aliens around. There was still time to change his mind, he thought—but instead he looked at Welligan and pointed down to where he needed to go. Welligan, hair flame red, nodded—and shoved.

Jamie's boots hit the roof of the fabricator with a thud. A tentacle from below lashed at him, and he slipped. Welligan landed on the other side of him, in perfect position to stop his fall. The trooper brought his rifle low and fired a sonic blast over the crowd closest to the fabricator's side. It scattered the creatures for only a moment—but that was all the time Jamie needed. He heaved himself off the fabricator and onto the muddy surface below. Seeing the Breathers starting to close in again, he turned and fell against the device.

It was the correct side. He found the manual override and punched the button.

A teddy bear, already manufactured earlier, popped from the slot at his side. In an instant, the alien wave halted.

"I trade," Jamie said, his announcement echoing in the Baghu language. He looked to the Breather closest to him. "I trade," he said again.

The alien sniffed at the stuffed animal with its snout. Was it the leader Jamie had talked to in the beginning? Who could tell? All the trader knew was at that moment, the creature barked something even Lorraine's vocabulary database couldn't translate.

And the mob fell still.

"Something's happening," Madaki said over the audio linkup. *Indispensable* was still hovering overhead. "Something's happening in the lagoon!"

The Baghu waddled away from the fabricator, leaving Jamie an open path to the shoreline. Jamie looked up at Welligan, still atop the device, covering him. Hiro nodded. "I think they want you to take a look," he said.

Mystified at the scene—and amazed that he might be right— Jamie walked with the stuffed Zazzy through a corridor of Breathers. At the lake's edge, he looked out to see a clear spot, free of bobbing Baghu, near where the buoy had been dropped.

And a moment later he saw Arbutus Dinner break the surface of the brine, propelled upward by his Baghu captors. Captors that now carried him gently to the shore, before releasing him.

The big man looked green. Jamie stepped up to him—and turned back to face the Baghu who'd made the sounds earlier.

"You gave me the thing under the water. So I trade." He passed the bear to the alien—and at once tentacles went up all across the beach. The Baghu whooped, jubilantly, as the leader thrust the stuffed toy high—before swallowing it, whole.

"We trade," said other Baghu, more calmly.

"Not yet," Jamie said, kneeling beside Dinner. "Welligan!"

The squad leader was already on the move, hopping off the fabricator. Welligan dashed over and cleared a landing area at the water's edge. The Breathers moved back, suddenly pliable. In moments, Dinner was back aboard the *Indispensable*, receiving emergency care.

Jamie ran back to the fabricator and cycled it again. Another bear—and another member of Bridgie's squad surfacing from below. He kept the machine operating at peak speed, worrying only that it would run out of whatever it made the bears from.

Welligan stood by Jamie, watching now in wonderment as the team members reunited. "Teddy bear ransom!"

"No," Jamie said. "Trading—Baghu style." He looked out at the aliens as his machine churned. "They didn't think they had anything to trade with—so they grabbed something they thought we wanted—our own people!" He recalled what he'd heard in the recording. "Before they grabbed our people, they were saying they were *willing* to trade. Once they had them, they said they were *ready*—but I didn't get it."

"Crazy!"

"Yeh." He pulled a final bear from the fabricator. "That's it," he said. "That's all we've got."

"That's all we need—Bridgie's the last one down there." Welligan opened a panel on the fabricator and turned a handle. With a whir, the sides of the massive device opened like petals, revealing its mechanical innards. The transformation seemed to puzzle the nearby Breathers. Welligan took the stuffed animal from Jamie and smiled. "If you don't mind, I'd like to be the one that saves the chief."

"If you feel you really must," Jamie said. He sat down on the sand and tried to remember how to breathe.

※ ※ ※

Walking up from the dark water, Bridget felt something like an ancient deity—only a goddess who'd lost her rifle. She saw what she expected when she emerged. With the fabricator cracked open, the Baghu had lost interest and dispersed. There were no more tasty bears inside.

She spied Jamie standing on the shore. He'd found his battered briefcase and menu and was receiving accolades from the troopers preparing to move the fabricator to the shuttle. Approaching him, she moved her gloved hand—and what it held—behind her back.

The trader looked at the dripping armored woman and smirked. "While you've been lounging around in the pool, I was saving the day." Jamie eagerly explained his theory, omitting any suggestion that he had gotten the idea from her. She let him.

"Oh, I don't doubt you were right," she said when he finished. "The Baghu didn't think they had anything to sell, so they stole us. They've never traded in the history of their race—they probably didn't get that stealing was wrong." She raised an eyebrow at Jamie. "There are some *civilized* races that don't get it."

"Hey!"

Bridget smiled curtly. "But you didn't get to hear what I figured out," she said. "Here." She pulled her hand from behind her back and presented Jamie what she had found in the water: a rocky mineral lump the size of a grapefruit.

"What's this?" Jamie said, looking it over.

"Breather dung."

"Gah!" Jamie dropped it immediately.

"I thought you loved money," she said. "That there is probably worth a hundred thousand dollars on its own." She reminded him of the gold flecks from the Breather's tentacle. "Between the water composition down there and the close look I got at the Baghu holding me, my onboard computer was able to make a guess at the species' body chemistry." She knelt and picked up the nodule. "Pseudofeces, just like a mollusk puts out. The brine at the bottom is thick with gold chloride, among other things. Highly soluble—and it winds up in the Baghu, where it turns into these."

She shook herself off. "Once they let me go, I stayed down long enough to see hundreds of the things all over the lake floor."

Bridget tossed the dripping ball back into Jamie's hands. He bobbled it but caught it this time. "Yecch!" he said. But he didn't drop it.

Bridget started walking toward *Indispensable*. "That's what I meant when I said they had something to trade—but they didn't *think* they did. To them these things are nothing—something to be ashamed of. I think maybe that's why they were so private about the lake. Hard to invite visitors in when you're living in your own filth." She stood in the doorway and looked back at him. "I think having all these down there was even making them sick. So they desperately want to trade."

Jamie looked back at the Breathers and nodded. "All right," he said. "I'll write a contract."

"You can clean up somebody else's mess for a change," Bridget said, stepping into the vessel. She thought for a moment about adding how one person's crap was another person's treasure—but, remembering how badly she wanted to pee somewhere other than in her armor, she decided to call it a day.

18

The Dragon's Depot was really taking shape, Bridget thought. She and her team had returned to Sigma Draconis from Baghula to find the cavernous Shaft at the station's center beginning to look like what it was supposed to be: a shipping terminus.

She'd once visited a century-old automobile delivery silo at Autostadt in Germany. This looked like a zero-gravity version of that: ring after ring of storage receptacles on the inside walls of the cylindrical Shaft. Bangboxes imported from the whirlibangs would stay here, plugged securely in, waiting for their next destinations.

The first batch of inventory was already in, relocated from ASPEC. It filled barely a twentieth of the storage space: the Dragon's Depot was that large. Some of it would be leaving soon. Now that the trail had been blazed and the deal had been brokered, Administrator Falcone's fulfillment crews would be taking material to Baghula to start Earth's first interstellar teddy bear factory. The trade would make a sizable profit for the expedition, and the Zazzy rights holders would surely wonder where all the sudden licensing money was coming from.

And the outer levels of the northern drum were beginning to look livable. Bridget complimented Trovatelli as their tour ended. "You've been busy," she said.

"Sounds like you had some excitement," the technician responded.

"Nothing we couldn't handle. But we could have used our Q/A. If you're done here, I want you on the next mission."

Trovatelli seemed apprehensive. "I was hoping to spend some more time studying our squatters."

Bridget shook her head. She hadn't forgotten about the armored intruders, but a surge team needed its engineer. "Bring the data you've collected—you can review it on the trip."

If Trovatelli was disappointed, she covered it well, giving Bridget a jaunty salute before heading off. Bridget turned and walked into the trading hall, beyond which Falcone's chosen office lay. Bridget slowed her approach as she heard raised voices inside.

"...how serious this is, Falcone. Everyone in the company is watching!"

"Relax, Bouchard. You'll have another heart attack," Falcone said from behind his desk. He spotted Bridget outside and waved her in. Bridget quietly found a wall to lean against.

"I can't relax," René Bouchard said. The balding auditor was just in from Quaestor's offices back home. "There's a hundred billion dollars in inventory that went to your surge team's warehouse. A hundred billion requisitioned—everything from accordions to zirconium!" The Quebecer's voice cracked with indignation. "What was it doing there?"

Falcone didn't answer. His eyes locked momentarily with Bridget's—and Bouchard noticed. "You!" he said, waving his handheld isopanel at her. "What the hell did you do with seven metric tons of guacamole?"

Bridget shrugged. "We were planning a party?"

Bouchard's white eyebrows shot up—and then he turned and slammed the isopanel on the desk. "We *told* you not to hire her! She's already a public relations disaster. And now—this!"

Falcone clasped his hands together. "I told you, René. There's just been a clerical error—"

"A damned big error! Your expedition is responsible for the return of that material." He looked around the office. "Does it even exist? We know the Spore struck the Altair barracks. The material's gone, isn't it? Digested!"

"Nonsense," Falcone said, wiping his nose. "The material went to us, yes—for whatever reason. But we shipped it all out again when the Spore threatened—"

"Where? He grabbed the isopanel back. "Tell me where the goods are, then."

"Other star systems. Other depots. I can't tell you just now— we're just settling in. But it'll all be accounted for at the end of the quarter, I guarantee." He pocketed his handkerchief and stood. "I don't know why we had all that merchandise—I'm still investigating that. But we got it all safely out, and we'll get it back here soon. Then you can have it." He raised an eyebrow. "Or you can let *us* sell it. Sigma Draconis is going to be a big earner for the company!"

Bouchard laughed. "A base on the edge of nothing! What kind of sales do you really expect to—"

"One of our new traders has just brought back a lucrative new contract," Falcone said. He stood by Bouchard's chair. "It's going to be a great quarter."

The auditor looked up at him, newly suspicious. "What new trader?" He touched a key on his isopanel. "What's his license number?"

"I don't have access to my files just yet—as I said, we're still settling in." Falcone forced a smile. "Really, René—one old goat to another. It'll be fine. Just let me get things sorted out here."

The auditor stood. "A hundred billion dollars, Leo."

"Fine, I tell you." Falcone slapped Bouchard's shoulder and guided him out the door.

When he turned back inside, alone, Bridget was standing near a counter. "That was close," she said.

"They'll get closer," Falcone grumbled. "We need to get your people moving again, pronto." He looked at her. "Does Sturm have the dossier on the next stop?"

"I gave it to him," she said. "I have no idea if he read it." The man made no sense to her. Jamie knew the stakes—he was the reason they were there, after all!—and yet as far as she could tell, he still hadn't bought in on the urgency of the mission. Yes, he'd crowed about his sales success on Baghula—naturally omitting mention of his panic attack on the shuttle, which Stubek had described for her. But when Bridget had told him another mission was coming up, Jamie had looked at her as if she'd put a bullet between his eyes.

Conniving *and* a coward. She didn't have any use for that.

And yet there was that report from Welligan that Jamie had acted to save the Baghu from being killed. Where did *that* fit in? *He probably only did it so he could make the sale,* she thought. Was doing the right thing accidentally still doing the right thing?

She wasn't going to figure it out now. She began walking out of the office, pausing only to gesture to a potted object on a counter. "Cute little tree," she said of the miniature sapling. "Looks like it needs water."

"It came with the office," Falcone said, shrugging. "Now let's find your trader before Bouchard does!"

* * *

Jamie sat on the stool at the bar and watched the world go by. The bartender and the manager were bickering again, and occasionally the curly-headed barmaid would amble past and sneer at him. They had never actually served him a drink, but he'd been going there to unwind since his midteens.

"Where the hell is he?" he heard Falcone say somewhere outside the front door.

"If anyone asks, I'm not here," he mumbled. No one at the bar took note, but then, they didn't exist. Jamie turned up the volume on his immerso unit, shutting the world out.

Holography outside a solid medium had never progressed very far, but isopanels were in use everywhere. Tiny processors inside them made still or moving images appear within transparent polymer sheets. When used in armor faceplates or eyeglasses, isopanels could insert images that appeared to the viewer's eyes as part of the real-world setting outside.

That was good enough for armor duty and the odd person-to-person call, but Hollywood had taken things a step farther with the immersos. Old two-dimensional entertainments had been converted into three-dimensional environments, with some programmed to integrate the viewer into the action. Jamie preferred the old classics. He'd been lucky to find a fully loaded immerso headset in his sales goods; it had most of the programs that helped him turn his mind off and relax. *Virtual unreality.*

Reality, sadly, returned. "Here he is," Bridget said, leading Falcone through the door. She saw Jamie wearing the goggles. "Oh, Lord. Where are you now?"

"I'm in a bar in Boston in the twentieth century," he said. "There's a mailman pontificating near where you're standing."

"Who are you?"

"I'm the wisecracking stockbroker."

"Creative casting," Falcone said. "Now get that thing off."

Jamie sighed. The immerso unit neatly integrated real and unreal things—you didn't want to trip over a real chair while lurking in a Korean War operating theater—and as he removed it, Bridget remained, but the actors disappeared. His bar was once again the food prep table in the back room of a space station's kitchen.

"How long have you been hiding out here?" Bridget asked, growing agitated.

"Not long enough. This was the only place with stools," he said. "Don't sit on that one," he warned, pointing. "Norm gets testy."

Bridget looked flustered. "We don't have time for this. You're supposed to be going over the briefing for the next mission!"

Jamie looked back at her blankly. "I read it." He looked at the digital display on his hand. "Took me—oh, eight minutes and a few seconds."

"The whole file?" Bridget sputtered. "And the financial data?"

"That was the few seconds," Jamie said. "Relax. Auction on Leel, got it. I've got all the angles memorized."

"You'd damn well better hope so, hotshot!" Falcone said.

"Nice to see you, too, Leo." Jamie slid off the stool and pocketed the headset and goggles. He hadn't seen Falcone since he returned. "I figured you'd want to congratulate me about Baghula."

"I've been too busy cleaning up the rest of your mess," the administrator said. "And one sale isn't going to get us anywhere."

"And you kind of blundered into that one," Bridget piped in.

Jamie glared. "You weren't exactly much help," he said. He turned on Falcone, remembering the list of grievances he'd compiled since Altair. After Baghula, he recalled his arrival on

Sigma Draconis. "She left me alone with Welligan when we got to the depot—and when *they* ditched me, that was when the aliens got me!"

"Aliens?" Falcone shook his head. "Your Q/A said they were humanoid. Squatters. I've seen the video—"

"I met them," Jamie said, flustered. "These things were brutes. I don't know what they were, but human they weren't." He spied Trovatelli passing through the hallway outside the door. Jamie pointed. "Hey, *she* believed me!"

"Don't drag me into this," the Q/A said, ducking past. A second later Michael O'Herlihy entered, making a beeline for a refrigeration unit and gathering up an armload of packaged food.

"I'm losing my bar," Jamie said, sadly.

"You're going to lose more than that." Falcone stuck a finger in his face. "I've got an auditor from Quaestor here. I can't keep this cover-up going unless you get us more cash flow—now!"

Jamie flinched. "I just got back!"

"And you're just about to leave again." Falcone turned on Bridget. "And you had better stow the disdain and help this guy out this time, or we're all done."

Bridget objected. "Leo, he's antagonizing everyone we meet! He's no salesman—"

"And you're no bodyguard," Jamie snapped. "Unless you call nearly getting yourself drowned protecting me."

"Drowned?" Slightly taller than the trader, Bridget glowered down at him. "I wasn't in any danger at all. And neither were you, if you'd kept your mouth—"

"*Enough!*" Falcone pointed to the exit. "I want you all off my station within the hour. You've just got time to make the auction at Mu Cassiopeiae—if you'll shut up and move!"

He turned and stormed out.

O'Herlihy leaned against the wall, chewing on a sausage stick. "Don't need an immerso around here with this floor show going on."

Bridget sighed in aggravation. "Fine. Mike, round everyone up. We've got a job to do." She turned toward the door.

"Try to actually do it this time, Yang!" Jamie yelled at the back of her head. "I'd like to actually get home one day!"

She stopped in the doorway and looked back, eyes frosty. "I can send you back to Earth at any time. In a body bag."

O'Herlihy guffawed as she vanished. "She got you!"

"Oh, shut up," Jamie growled. "Go back to stuffing your face. You'll need the energy when she screws up again. Maybe you'll *all* be buried alive this time."

The soldier chucked his garbage into the incinerator and sauntered back through the kitchen. He paused long enough to loom over Jamie. "I'd be careful there, Wall Street."

Jamie didn't budge. "What, are you gonna play big brother now?"

"No," O'Herlihy said, walking to the exit. "Bridgie can take care of herself." He paused in the doorway, looked down the hallway and smirked. "You know, she killed her last boyfriend."

"I'm sure he didn't die with a smile on his face," Jamie sputtered. "Or maybe he did—if it meant getting away from her!"

"I don't know about the smile," O'Herilhy said, his face serious. "They couldn't find the guy's face after the bullets went through."

Jamie blinked. O'Herlihy turned and left.

They're such liars, he thought, reaching for his goggles. *I'm going back to the bar.*

19

The being floated on the frigid air, looking not much more substantial than the plastic bags Jamie's dry cleaning came wrapped in. Only this plastic bag was intelligent, or so he'd been told. Another day, another system, another freak of evolution. It was becoming strangely routine for Jamie.

Mu Cassiopeiae was his fourth strange star since leaving Earth—fifth, if he counted the paired subdwarf wheezing its last in the distant reaches of the system. Leel was the only body of significance around the main star, and even that he found debatable. The almost-comet ice ball hurtled along on its oblong orbit, with its natives coming out to trade only when it approached perihelion.

And such natives! Looking more closely, Jamie could see a hint of color in the drifting pouch as it headed for the icy rostrum. Brain? Organs? What it ate for breakfast? He had no way of knowing. He'd consumed the financial data, just as he'd said. But his eyes always glazed over in exobiology class, and they'd done so again after they gave him the jacket on Leel. It was enough to know that the Signatory powers knew plenty about the Leelites and their proclivities—as compared to the Baghu, which they knew little about. The Leelites were regarded as possibly the most harmless species ever to achieve sentience. He'd hit that part in the dossier and gone back to his immerso.

Still, being in the actual place was just another in a series of strange experiences. Jamie shivered as he looked up in the ice cave. The system in his SoftSHEL space suit immediately responded, warming him. It didn't help. The place was enormous—almost a coliseum in crystal, with a massive star-shaped light fixture at the top. Wouldn't the place crack open like an egg once the body approached its sun?

Bridget and her teammates didn't seem worried. Her fellow troops were scattered across the frozen floor, admiring the architecture. They were in their lighter armor today, carrying their rifles but not expecting trouble. She'd brought the B team to guard the ship this time, led by Victor Gideon, a tall South African man who hadn't said a word to Jamie ever.

Also outside with *Indispensable* was the lovely Lissa Trovatelli. Jamie hated being here, but he was glad she was along.

But while the icy atrium seemed to be designed to host hundreds—or thousands, if you were a floating garbage bag—the humans were the only visitors here. "Didn't Falcone say this was an auction?"

"You don't read," Bridget said, shaking her head. "This is the Leel market. It opens only once a decade." She pointed to the aperture at the far wall, behind the rostrum. Several other Leelites floated from it into the big room. "Those are the dignitaries, I think. It's a big deal."

"It doesn't look like it." Jamie vaguely knew that the Leelites produced something, but he didn't know what.

"Just listen," Bridget said.

The first wispy being he'd seen, after consulting with the other creatures, floated up to a podium. A knowglobe sat next to it, identical to the one O'Herlihy and the humans had brought in.

"Greetings, gentle beings," the alien said. "I am Vremian, your auctioneer."

Jamie didn't hear the Leelite's words—while the place was pressurized, the aliens communicated through some other manner—but his audio system translated, giving Vremian the voice of a posh British butler.

Vremian waggled one of his hanging shreds in their direction. "I hope you've all had the chance to look around and enjoy Leel and its many amenities."

Jamie whispered. "It's an ice cave!"

"Hush," Bridget said. "He's proud of his home."

"And I'm so pleased to see the turnout for this season's auction," Vremian continued. "My people have spent a long time crafting wares for this event. I'm sure this will be our most successful market day ever!"

Jamie looked around, unsure if he was missing something. "It's just us!"

Bridget stomped on his foot. Jamie didn't feel it through his suit, but he got the message.

Vremian waited for a full minute, as if expecting someone else to arrive. When no one did, the Leelite's wispy streamers went into motion again, and the great light above grew dim.

"Look!" Bridget said, pointing to the floor.

Jamie looked at the image that was projected there. "Looks like a totem pole."

"That," Vremian said, "is Leel's specialty, for which we are known throughout the Orion Arm. In the rings of every transit station you'll find superconductor columns like these. And yet not like these—because Leelite columns are crafted by talented artisans, lovingly etched by our appendages. The work of an entire race, locked away from the outside world for all but one day each orbital cycle." His sales pitch reached its crescendo. "It's no wonder that so many other species wait for this date, traveling far to participate in the our famous auction!"

Jamie looked around. He was still the only buyer there.

From the stage, he heard what almost sounded like an uncomfortable cough from one of the other Leelites.

"This is nuts!" Jamie whispered.

"This is Leel," Bridget said. She rolled her eyes. "I actually read the report from the last people who participated. It gets stranger from here."

Vremian waited a long time before continuing. "All right, the big moment is here. We'll start with the eight-meter models. We have nineteen for sale. As always, bids are denominated in tons of bauxite."

"That, we've got," Bridget whispered. *Indispensable* was a two-by-two-by-two cube this time, including seven 'boxes of the stuff.

"They probably burn it for warmth," Jamie said.

"I'll start the bidding at one ton," Vremian said. "Please, all of you, speak clearly, and not all at once."

Jamie looked around again. Still no one else there—but Vremian seemed not to be aware of the fact at all. Did Leelites have eyes?

"One ton," Vremian said. "Anyone? Anyone?"

Apprehensively, Jamie raised his hand. "Uhh…one?"

"One ton is bid! One ton for these wonderful superconductor columns. Now am I bid two? Anyone? Anyone?"

Jamie looked around for a third time. Was this some kind of joke? "What the hell?"

For a full minute, Vremian held the auction open, asking in vain for help from nonexistent bidders.

"Is he expecting me to outbid myself?" Jamie asked.

"Just go with it," Bridget said. "Quaestor's building whirlibangs all the time, and the price is right. Just get them so we can go."

Vremian finally gave up on his calling. "Sold, to the—uh—*human being* there in the crowd." A polite murmur rose from the gathering behind him.

"Great," Jamie said. He looked again at the image of the totem pole–sized column. "Do you bring them out to us, or what?"

"Oh, dear, no." Vremian chortled—or at least, that was the sound that came from Jamie's earpiece. "We can't lift them. That's up to the buyer!" He flipped a shimmering shred in the direction of the big doorway. "All the merchandise is stored deep within our home."

"Cash and carry?" Jamie was flummoxed. "How big did you say those things were?"

"They are large," Vremian said, "but over the generations we've carved some nice stairs for beings of your kind. About five hundred of them. I hope they won't be too taxing!"

Bewildered, Jamie looked at Bridget. "Well, now we know why no one bothers with this place."

"I thought you read the briefing," Bridget said, annoyed.

"I did—this part, anyway. Whoever compiled it didn't say anything about carrying cargo by hand. I guess the other customers brought their own bearers." He looked back at her troops. "Er, are you guys up for…"

Rifle still slung over her shoulder, she raised her hands. "Oh, no! We're here to guard you. We're not manual labor!"

The light flickered again, and a new image appeared on the floor. Vremian was back at the podium. "Next, we have some of our fine ten-meter models. Very nice indeed. We'll start the bidding at three tons, shall we say?"

"I'll double whatever the human offers," boomed a deep voice from behind Jamie's party. "And if he offers more, I'll double that!"

Bridget turned, hands on her weapon. Jamie did, too—to see the figure in black armor who'd kidnapped him at the Dragon's Depot days earlier. And this time he was flanked by a dozen warriors outfitted just as he was. Massively built bipeds all toting hefty versions of the hand-cannons he'd seen them tote before.

"I am Kolvax of the Xylanx," the leader said. "And there's no way the humans will beat us—and live!"

2 0

"Fire team, star four!" Bridget yelled. At once, three of her armored companions were at her side, placing themselves and their weapons between Jamie and the new arrivals. At their various positions around the icy atrium, O'Herlihy, Dinner, and her two other troopers stood alert as well. She yelled into her mouthpiece. "Gideon, check in! Why didn't you tell me these people were coming?"

"Because he couldn't," Kolvax said, sauntering into the room. "Oh, he's all right—we didn't disturb your party at all. Our vessel began jamming your ship's communications on approach." His words dripped with malice. "I didn't want our meeting to be disturbed."

Jamie peeked out from behind his guardians. "How come we can understand you now?"

"It's not our intent," Kolvax said. "Our words aren't for such as you." He nodded to the stage and the Leelites' knowglobe. "But our people once attended this...event. Their device is patched in with yours. So you get our words—but that's all you get."

Bridget checked the audio stream. Sure enough, Kolvax's words were channeling through the Leelite database to their knowglobe. It had assigned him the voice of a scenery-chewing soap opera villain from more than a hundred years ago. It seemed to fit.

But the rest made no sense. "Your people?" Bridget's eyes narrowed. "You look pretty human to us!"

Several members of Kolvax's forces started forward, angrily snarling words foreign even to the Leelites' knowglobe. "You should be more careful," Kolvax said. "The Stalkers take offense easily. They aren't as patient as I am." He turned to calm his wary troops. "Easy. The little fool clearly doesn't know anything about us. And it's going to stay that way!"

Quiet until now, the Leelite auctioneer interceded from his podium. "I'm so pleased that you've arrived—Kolvax, did you say?" Vremian shook with excitement. "We've only just gotten underway, you know."

"I told you, *thing*, the auction is over!" Kolvax turned. "We will take all the superconductors you have, at whatever price you name. We will even pay you to keep them down there in your hole, as long as they are never sold to this species. This market— and *all* markets—are closed to them."

"Like hell," Jamie called out.

"Ah, the little trader," Kolvax said, his words dripping with malice as he stepped forward. Bridget raised her rifle as he approached. "We let you go last time. Continue your activities and we won't make the same mistake. And don't imagine these toy soldiers can save you. You're facing our finest warriors now."

Bridget shook her head. The idea of armed mercantile competitors was nothing new; the East Indies trading companies clashed all the time. But nothing like this had happened in years.

"Keep bidding, Jamie," she said, a defiant eye on Kolvax. "We've got as much right to be here as they do!"

* * *

The Leelite went through the motions of restarting the auction. Kolvax stood firm, watching the rattled humans through his darkened facemask. He smiled. He'd found them on the first try. And it was more than a good guess.

Mu Casseopeiae was one of the installed links from the now human-controlled depot station, and the exact timing of the Leelite auction was known by every race in the vicinity, even if most ignored the silly event. But given that the humans had mounted a trading mission from the depot, he'd wagered that this would be a likely early stop for them. Maybe they didn't know how bad an opportunity it was. Or maybe they'd assumed there wouldn't be any competition. Now, Kolvax was showing them the error of that judgment, aided by the crack Dominium-supplied team from Gharion Preserve.

He looked at the display in his helmet. The star their exiled station orbited was called Sigma Draconis, and the humans referred to the prison as the Dragon's Depot. He knew those words now from his radio link to the Leelite device. But its knowledge of humanity was limited to language—the information openly being supplied by the humans' knowglobe.

He couldn't hear the human merchant chattering with his bodyguards now; Kolvax's most recent outlandish bid for the superconductors had flummoxed them. *Good.* It was helpful to see how easily he could make them squirm. He'd meant what he said: there was no price at which they'd allow the humans to have the high-tech devices. The superconductors would simply help them build more whirlibangs—such a preposterous human word!—and the Xylanx would never allow that.

But in truth they were here for something else. He saw it now, right in front of him. This was their big chance.

Kolvax transmitted a signal to his forces parked outside. They'd hear it through their jamming of the human ship and would begin the countdown. His countdown was begun as well. "Get ready," Kolvax whispered to his warriors on the secure channel. "We move on my signal!"

* * *

Jamie had his briefcase open now, rechecking superconductor column prices on his assayer. The prices had risen to ridiculous levels for units they previously would've gotten at a song. Wasn't this crazy trip supposed to be about turning a profit?

He looked back warily at Kolvax, the brute who'd struck him at the Dragon's Depot. The guy didn't seem like a player. He wasn't thinking with his bids, wasn't using any strategy at all, so far as Jamie could tell.

Okay, let's see how big your wallet really is, he thought. They had seven cargo 'boxes with them, each bearing thirty tons of bauxite. Kolvax would be able to calculate that. But he might not have any idea how plentiful the substance was on Earth, and how easily it could be shipped here. He decided to take a chance on the second lot being offered. "Five hundred tons," Jamie said. "Two hundred now, three hundred later. It'll be waiting for you next time you…er, come out of your hole."

Vremian seemed to gurgle with glee—or at least, that was how Jamie interpreted the bizarre sound. "A fine offer. A wonderful offer! And you, Kolvax of the Xylanx?"

Jamie looked back to see Kolvax straightening. "I'll give you our answer," he snarled.

Booom! A thunderclap shook the atrium. Above, the crystal light source shattered, raining shards below. Bridget grabbed Jamie and slammed him to the icy floor. Above him, the chief and her companions shielded the lightly protected trader's body with their armored forms.

"Now!" the alien leader shouted. Through the legs of his protectors, Jamie saw Kolvax charging forward in the newly darkened atrium. His team of Stalkers did the same, firing their hand-cannons at the Earth team.

"*Unnhh!*" One of the blasts glanced off Bridget's armor, but she stood firm and returned fire. Jamie squirmed through an opening between his guardians, desperate to escape.

The only light now came from the energy weapons—and from the aperture leading down into the Leelites' lair. Ahead, on the rostrum, Jamie could see the flimsy form of Vremian, desperately trying to maintain order. "Please, gentle beings! Try to quiet down. I didn't hear that last bid!"

Jamie stumbled behind his team's knowglobe and looked back. With O'Herlihy and Dinner setting up a crossfire on the open floor, Bridget and her companions scrambled to regroup. Crouching, she switched to missile rounds and fired back. The slug hit Kolvax's chest dead center—and simply sparked off. Seemingly amused, the shadowy figure raised his weapon to return fire.

Kraa-aack! Another horrific sound rocked the atrium, and a mist of ice pellets fell from the ceiling. The weapons on both sides fell silent; from his cowering position, Jamie saw that Kolvax seemed puzzled. The black-clad leader looked back at his forces. "That wasn't—"

Another loud, shearing sound—this one from ground level. The floor shook. On the stage, the Leelite dignitaries fled for their underground haven. At the podium, Vremian followed it up with one last announcement. "This auction is suspended—*on account of early thaw!*"

Kolvax looked through the falling shards of ice—directly toward Jamie. "Hurry," Jamie heard the alien yell. "That's what we want!"

The Xylanx leader and his companions charged across the rumbling floor toward the trader. Off-balance, Bridget switched her weapon to use different ammunition and raised it to fire. But now the ground beneath her cleaved, sending the woman and her teammates tumbling backward against the rostrum.

Jamie struggled to see. Something was alive down there, coming up from the ice—something *huge*. With another sickening crack, a giant, clawed six-fingered hand shoved upward from the darkness, upending more of the ice floor and sending O'Herlihy and Dinner dashing away.

Above, the remaining Leelites in the room flocked toward the ceiling, terrified. Vremian screeched in horror. "*The jorvil! We've waited too long!*"

On his hands and knees behind Surge Sigma's knowglobe, Jamie looked up at Kolvax. His footing steady and momentary surprise past, the warrior regarded the mammoth reaching arm without fear and laughed. "I guess we know why the Leelite sales season is so short!" He turned and looked directly at Jamie once again. "But I think there's just enough time to finish what we started!"

Jamie gulped, remembering his nose's previous meeting with Kolvax's fist. *This was a long way to travel to relive seventh grade...*

EPISODE 4:
WINNER'S CURSE

21

As important as the discovery of extraterrestrial life had been for Earth's scientists, it had given the lawyers an even bigger thrill. The pact between the Signatory Systems had existed long before humanity reached the stars and had changed many times over the years. Around the globe, university departments opened to study the agreement. It would be several years before there would be much practical demand for anything taught in Interstellar Law 5010, but graduate students were used to that. The kindly aliens had supplied another way to postpone real life.

But while the pact had been amended many times, one thing was common to most iterations of the agreement: sanctioned merchants, whether they wore the official trader's badge or not, were not allowed to be armed. The agreement said nothing about their bodyguards, of course: that explained the small armies many merchants traveled with. But it somehow seemed important that sellers, who were often diplomats for their cultures, appeared unthreatening.

Jamie was certainly wishing for a change in the rules as he looked out from behind the knowglobe, the only solid thing in the room that wasn't moving. The giant creature the Leelites called the jorvil twisted and writhed as it bulged through another section of the ice floor, upending slabs in the middle of the room.

In the low light, the jorvil looked to Jamie like a great hand the size of an elephant, but it appeared the arm it was attached to had no end.

This would be a good time to have one of Bridget's fancy rifles, Jamie thought. *Or to have chosen law school instead.*

Kolvax didn't seem to care about the jorvil—or the rules regarding weapons in the hands of traders, if that was indeed what he was. Stepping deliberately up to the knowglobe, he tapped it with the barrel of his hand-cannon.

"Leave me alone!" Jamie called out, cringing behind the dodecahedron and remembering the kidnapping attempt aboard the Dragon's Depot. But there wasn't anywhere to run here, and his bodyguards were—where? Somewhere in the darkness, Jamie guessed, lost in the mass of ice or on the other side of the jorvil. *"Yang! Somebody!"*

It took a moment before Kolvax, face inscrutable behind his darkened faceplate, responded. "Pathetic," he said over Jamie. Then he turned to address his warriors, who were advancing across the quaking floor. "Take it!"

Jamie turned to run, but his right foot slipped on the ice. He slid sideways, landing in an awkward heap. He covered his head with his hands, imagining Kolvax grasping for him. But a second passed in which he felt nothing, apart from the rumbling of the floor and his throbbing ankle. Daring to move, he raised his head and looked back.

Beside Kolvax, one of his hulking crew members easily lifted Surge Sigma's knowglobe off the ground. "To the ship!" Kolvax ordered. The leader then turned to face Jamie. "Good-bye, idiot," he said.

Then Kolvax followed his troops, who were already making their way to the exit.

"Hey! That—that…" Jamie spluttered. "I was hiding behind that!"

He scrambled to his hands and knees. Where was Yang? Where was O'Herlihy? The shower of ice crystals from the ceiling had become a deluge, with clear shards falling from above even as the jorvil's gyrations tore at the floor below. More of the surface buckled, and Jamie saw what he thought was a rocky fin stab up from beneath. *Another monster?*

As it moved, Jamie realized what he was looking at. It was no arm that the six-fingered hand was attached to but a tremendous mineral-encrusted worm. The body shrank and stretched like an accordion-style air hose, snaking and grinding its way through the hard surface. Spellbound for a moment, Jamie gawked as the thing tore more of the floor apart.

That fascination ended when the six-fingered hand—which he only now understood to be the creature's head—twisted back toward him. The meter-wide talons opened, revealing a blood-red maw in the "palm." Violet tongues splayed outward from the hole and a gaseous breath hit Jamie full in his helmeted face, knocking him backward.

"*Yaaahhh!*" Jamie turned his stumble into a headlong run. He dashed for the exit to the surface, caring little that his would-be kidnappers had already gone that way.

✳ ✳ ✳

We wore the wrong outfits to this dance, Bridget thought in the blackness. The indoor avalanche had left hundreds of kilos of ice on top of her, and while the HardSHEL armor had taken the beating and kept her breathing, the internal armature wasn't strong enough to free her.

But unlike at Baghu, she'd held on to her rifle—or, rather, the armor had. The eruption from the floor had given her a split second to activate the death-grip feature. Any impact strong enough to separate her from the weapon would be strong enough to take her arm, too.

The weapon could fire from her verbal command, but she didn't know where it was pointing. This called for a different approach. "Switch sonics," she ordered. Seeing the confirmation that her rifle switched from impact ordnance, she continued. "Discharge, point-blank!"

Even her armor couldn't shield her ears from the shrill sound that followed. The sonic discharge was a ranged weapon, but here it was having a different effect. The weapon's vibrations rattled through her arm and entire body, and the outfit's exterior set the surrounding icy mass to quaking. Bridget went into motion then, as the crystal mass loosened enough for her to claw in the direction her sensors said was up.

Like a swimmer resurfacing after a plunge, Bridget punched up through material that was momentarily fluid, though not fully liquid. To add to her troubles, the rifle's functionality had been destroyed by her desperate maneuver, shaken apart by its own sonic vibrations, so she released it and clawed for a handhold amid the chunks of ice. The whole room seemed to be moving now, the ground rent to pieces by the massive creature.

She beheld the monster, rising and plunging. The chemical ice that made up the floor was still frozen—could liquids even exist on Leel?—but the thaw Vremian mentioned had evidently weakened its tensile strength, and the stony serpent was wending and crunching its way through it like a drill through balsa wood. At least it wasn't paying any attention to her—yet.

Bridget quickly checked her armor's team status display. All the members of Surge Team One were alive, she saw, but there had been several non-life-threatening injuries from the battle and the collapse. She suspected the Xylanx warriors had been doing as her team had: using lesser ordnance so as to avoid bringing down the atrium on everyone. But her team had been too near the place where the creature had erupted from the floor. She did an audio roll call, and everyone checked in.

"Those still armed use your sonics to get clear," she said. "It's a little busy up here."

Of all the members of her squad, only Arbutus Dinner was free from the icefall. At least she wasn't alone. He was crouched behind the onetime podium, firing explosive rounds at the beast to no noticeable effect.

"Dinner, where's Jamie?" Bridget asked.

"Outside," Dinner replied between shots. "He followed the Xylanx dudes."

A sign of intelligence on both their parts? she wondered. *Maybe.* Well, she still had people outside. "Gideon, come in," she said into her mic.

Static—but different from what she'd heard earlier, when the Xylanx leader boasted about jamming her second team's transmissions from *Indispensable.*

Jamie and the Xylanx would have to be Gideon's problem, she realized, as the monstrosity ceased its circular movements. The leading end of the beast rose in the air, towering like a cobra, heading for—what? Bridget trained her armor's spotlight above. Near the damaged top of the atrium, airborne Leelites swirled in panic, looking like bubbles circling a drain. Through the communications link, she could hear them screaming about the thing—the jorvil, they called it. So they knew what it was, she thought—and it certainly knew about them.

The upper section of the creature loomed over the erstwhile floor, grasping for the wispy aliens with its handlike head. The floating Leelites seemed an insubstantial meal for such a monster—*how did it get so big?*—but that didn't stop the thing from snatching and devouring every unfortunate creature that came near.

Her armor's interface alerted her to a nearby armament. Across the wreck of a room she spotted the oversized stock of a rifle, half-buried in the icy dust. She dashed for it, ducking underneath a moving section of the jorvil along the way. The rifle was O'Herlihy's, she realized on picking it up. All surge team members used signature weapons, useless in the hands of unauthorized personnel; in the chief's hands, though, it worked fine. She wondered what had happened to Mike even as she started firing explosive rounds at the jorvil's top section. She didn't want to bring the entire ice dome down—had it been weakened, too, by the thaw? But there really was no missing a target as big as the jorvil.

Nothing. She switched ammunition modes. It was the same story with electrical pulses—and with the sonic power that had freed her earlier. Almost too fat to be called a rifle, the Spraecher 300 had five ordnance settings—and not one of them seemed to even distract the jorvil from its prey.

"Vremian!" she called out into her helmet mic. "What is this thing?"

She heard the start of an answer from the Leelite, but it resolved into a scream as the jorvil lunged. The Leelite flitted out of the way, causing the monster's face to slap hard against the interior of the ice dome. The wall shook, and another shower of ice fell.

Worse, behind her the ceiling of the entrance tunnel gave way, closing off the exit and the last source of exterior light.

Inside her helmet, Bridget's visor switched to infrared tracking, allowing her to see Dinner again across the mess. "Party knowglobe connection lost," the computerized voice in her ear said.

"Terrific," she said, rolling her eyes. It was the end of her ability to tap the Leelites' knowledge base about the creature—not that she'd had a chance to even check. Her team had also been using it to boost their armor transmission signals from within the hall to make them audible to the team outside. Jamming or no jamming, they were truly cut off.

"What now?" Dinner radioed. He'd momentarily paused his waste of ammunition. "It's gonna run out of appetizers soon."

"Just don't tell it your name," she said.

Anxious, she tried again to reach the second team leader at the ship, to no avail. Where Hiro Welligan was her greenest squad leader, Victor Gideon had twenty years of experience battling strange things from beyond. That was more than anyone on her team had, Bridget included. But Welligan simply had trouble knowing the right thing to do. Getting Gideon to do the *sane* thing would be a triumph...

22

From a distance, Leel resembled a peeled apple: vaguely spherical, white, and featureless. The Black Butte, as the humans had named it on approach, was the solitary deviation: a half-kilometer-high mass of opaque ice, it housed the Leelites' auction hall. The surrounding area was said to resemble an empty Yukon mall parking lot—except during the once-a-decade superconductor auctions, when it looked like a *mostly* empty lot.

Today, however, it was a war zone—and dashing from the only entrance to the butte, Jamie found himself in a no-man's-land. A hundred meters ahead to his west sat *Indispensable*, towering and boxy in its current trading configuration. Between the ship and the butte, eight members of Surge Sigma's second team were in a chevron formation, kneeling and firing their weapons, seemingly at him.

Ducking back inside the passageway, Jamie quickly realized his teammates outside were shooting at the Xylanx. The black-suited warriors from the auction hall had emerged before he had and now were headed for their own vessel, which sat to the north. More Xylanx soldiers had fanned out in front of the ship, attempting to screen their compatriots' escape from the butte. Many meters separated them: Jamie thought the parties were using more serious ammunition, here outside the auction hall. It was keeping both groups well apart.

The Xylanx transport was a curious thing. Built from smaller modules, as all whirlibang-using craft had to be, the ship seemed to have cheese-shaped wedges for its basic building block. That gave the overall vehicle a spiky look, with sharp angles rising from a long, horizontal body. Two slender guns rotated atop the vehicle, firing green pulses at regular intervals to cover Kolvax's party's escape.

Behind Jamie, the ice mountain shook. He looked back to see the far end of the passage he'd emerged from collapsing. Afraid, he turned and charged into the snowfield…

…only to slip immediately and land faceplate first in the open.

"*Trader!*" a voice called out over Jamie's audio system. From the ground, Jamie looked across the dirty snow to see the husky form of Victor Gideon, second team squad leader, charging from the human forces' flank. "I've got him!" Gideon yelled.

Jamie scrambled to his hands and knees. Cave-in or not, the sight of Gideon charging toward him caused Jamie to think seriously about going back inside to face the monster again. Gideon had scared the hell out of him at every encounter. The man's HardSHEL armor looked as if he'd worn it through a fall from orbit: dented, banged, and pockmarked beyond belief. *Doesn't Quaestor spend billions outfitting these people?* Jamie had thought on meeting him. The guy could use a chamois and some touch-up paint.

And instead of the Spraecher 300s that Bridget's crew used, Gideon carried around a cluster of smaller weapons soldered and riveted together—presumably, Jamie imagined, so he could fire them all at the same time. And incongruously with the rest of his high-tech equipment, Gideon also had a shotgun slung over his shoulder. Or at least that was what Jamie thought it was: it looked like the thing Elmer Fudd had carried in the musical that won the Tony Award in 2136. He was surprised Gideon hadn't gone for a caveman club instead, to match his personality.

Xylander warriors happily took potshots as Gideon dashed across the open ground. A blast from the alien craft struck to his left, and then to his right. If Gideon paid any attention, he didn't show it. Between Leel's three-quarter-gee gravity and his outfit's sensors and servos, he dodged one snow-scattering blast after another.

Seeing the live fire chasing Gideon toward his own position made the decision for Jamie. He turned back and lunged toward the shelter of the still-standing exterior opening to the butte. But no sooner did he reach the icy stoop than he fell again.

"Trader down!" Gideon yelled as he neared the entrance. Throwing his body into a crunching roll, the forty-five-year-old tumbled to a stop. Squatting on top of Jamie's armored form, Gideon turned and pointed his gun cluster out at the Xylanx. The squad leader screamed a bloody oath and began firing a variety of things.

Jamie hated Gideon.

"Let me up, dammit!" the trader yelled, squirming.

"Nothing doing!" With a face cracked like Mars, Gideon set his teeth in an angry scowl and continued blasting. Return fire peppered the ground ahead of them until the rest of Surge Two's members shifted position to better protect them.

Gideon's silver-flecked brown eyes lit up as the Xylanx fire diminished. "That's right, that's right!" He laughed loudly and spoke into his helmet mic: "Gideon here, trader secure!"

"Is that even your real name?" Jamie asked from the ground. He'd heard a whisper that Gideon's real name was Eustace Clemmons.

Gideon grabbed at Jamie's space suit and hauled him up. "Is that your real ass I just saved?"

"They weren't shooting at me," Jamie said, pulling away. "They were shooting at *you*. When you came here, *then* they were shooting at me."

"Maybe you'd like to take them on alone!" Gideon elbowed Jamie hard, just beneath the merchant badge. Jamie stumbled a step back.

"Whatever."

As Gideon returned to blazing away at the Xylanx, Jamie dusted himself off, glad that his outfit had absorbed most of the blow. If Gideon was supposed to be one of his bodyguards, Jamie thought, he'd sure missed the class on not hurting his charge. Not to mention a couple of stages of human evolution.

Since he'd met the guy back on Altair, Jamie had found Gideon alternately terrifying and ludicrous. With close-cropped brown hair and no neck to speak of, the older man looked like a child's military toy. There was no mistaking why: everyone on the team knew what Gideon's problem was. Early experiments using nanoids to stimulate the adrenal glands had turned a whole cadre of human guinea pigs into rage machines. The microscopic robots inside Gideon weren't active any longer, but they'd messed with his sense of self-preservation, blackened his outlook on life, and tensed him tighter than a rubber band around a basketball.

"Dreadcases" who partook of the therapies were quite pleasant: Jamie's mother had a faithful bodyguard who played third flute in the National Philharmonic. He didn't know why Gideon hadn't gotten treatment, or why Bridget entrusted him with any authority. Perhaps he had once eaten a lion that had threatened her.

"These guys, these guys," Gideon said, blasting another armored Xylander at long range to no effect. The whole battle scene seemed bizarre to Jamie: combatants on both sides struck by projectiles would either shrug them off, or at most tumble backward, only to recover. Gideon's lower faceplate fogged and smeared, and Jamie couldn't tell from the man's expression whether he took his targets' refusal to die as a personal affront, or worthy of admiration.

"Who are these guys?" Gideon asked, to no one. "They won't go down!"

"They're called Xylanx," Jamie said.

"Lots of Xs. I like it. Sounds crunchy."

"These are the same people who got me on the depot."

"I know that, dishwhip. I was there," the squad leader said. "They came in here fast—jamming our transmissions before they landed. Set up a screen of fire so their people could reach the butte." He pointed to the top of the Xylanx ship, where Jamie saw the small cannons blasting away. "When their team left the auction hall, they stopped jamming, but I still can't raise Yang in there. What's going on?"

Jamie quickly described the scene inside the auction hall. Gideon's eyes narrowed when Jamie got to the part about the jorvil, and the squad leader actually seemed to growl a little.

"Big monster," Gideon said, seeming to consider the choice between saving Bridget's crew and continuing to shoot at enemies who could take what he had to deal out.

Jamie was doing some considering of his own: he was considering cowering in a corner to wait for a decision when Lissa Trovatelli's voice piped into his ear. "Q/A here," the quartermaster said from *Indispensable*. "Gideon, Unknown One is powering up to go," she said, referring to the Xylanx craft.

Gideon groaned audibly. "Yang's team's in trouble. Hate to leave this—"

"We need to grab one of these guys," Trovatelli said. "I want to know more about them."

"It's mutual," Jamie piped in. "They stole our knowglobe."

"I saw," Trovatelli said. "I've been trying to send a purge code to wipe the memory, but they've blocked that somehow."

"Stinkin' thieves!" Gideon said, firing faster.

Trovatelli spoke more firmly. "We need to stop them, Gideon. At the very least, capture one, so we know—"

"I've been trying!" Gideon snarled and spat angrily, the spittle striking the inside of his faceplate.

So that's what the smear is, Jamie thought. *Gross.*

"You guys were the ones who didn't want to arm the ship— you and your low-risk, low-reward mission," Gideon said. He slowed his rate of fire almost imperceptibly, seemingly having had a thought. "Hey, maybe we could ram their ship with ours. Or at least park on top of 'em—"

"Hell, no," Jamie said. The bauxite aboard wasn't that valuable on its own—except, for whatever reason, to the Leelites—but he was damned if he was going to be stranded here. "*Indispensable*'s my call, right? I say no!"

Gideon's jaw locked. "Puny, pissant trader..."

Jamie pointed back toward the collapsed tunnel. "Bridget! Monster! Remember?"

Gideon looked to Jamie as if he was struggling to concentrate.

"It would be easier if you stopped shooting at things," Jamie said.

"Shut up." But Gideon did stop firing—one of his guns, at least. He spoke in a calmer voice. "Scan Unknown One if you can, Q/A. Trader's safe and we can't take on their ship guns. We're going in after the monster!" He paused. "And—uh, to extract Surge One."

Trovatelli transmitted her disapproval. "We may not get this chance—"

"I'm in charge," Gideon said, glancing back at the cave-in. "Get me a reading on what's blocking the entrance. We're going in."

Jamie looked outside. The firing had ceased. "You can go in," he said, "and have all the monsters you want. I'm going back to the ship before my pulse rate needs a comma."

"You're not going anywhere. You're safer with me," Gideon said, turning into the darkness of the cavern.

"You haven't seen that thing down there," Jamie said.

"It hasn't seen *me*."

✳✳✳

I don't believe it, Kolvax thought as he reached the steps of the X-560. *They're going to let us go.*

Kolvax hadn't come here to wipe out the human expedition, as enjoyable as that might have been. But it was useful to take the humans' measure in battle, nonetheless. The trader's defenders on the surface were good, he had to admit. The forces outside the auction hall had exchanged fire with his team for a long time, with the humans taking only one casualty—and even that was just an injury.

Kolvax had seen the human's squad leader—"Gideon," the transmissions called him—carry the incapacitated soldier over his shoulder back to the cargo ship before resuming fighting. Later on he'd seen Gideon run across a field of fire to protect his trader. Foolhardy acts both, but the sort of defiant behavior he liked in a warrior. This Gideon had the heart of a Xylander.

He quickly dispelled the comparison from his mind. It was distasteful to think about the ways the Xylanx and the humans were similar. And he'd already discovered another likeness he didn't expect. The humans didn't have any ammunition that could pierce the Stalker armor of the Xylanx, but neither had the Xylanx brought any ammunition that could pierce the armor of the humans.

That'll change, he thought. He'd succeeded in his mission, despite things not going exactly as planned. His ship had fired the first shot at the butte, rocking the auction hall and giving him his advantage of surprise. He hadn't counted on the appearance of the jorvil, evidently awakened from its hibernation by the blast, but it had taken out the trader's defenders inside and made stealing the knowglobe simple.

With the Xylanx transport's engine rumbling, he watched as his underlings carried the human knowglobe up the steps. Some of the data would be instantly available: that which the team shared with everyone. But most Signatory Systems expeditions used their knowglobes for logistical assistance. There would be other information in the database ready for the taking. Useful facts about humanity—and about these humans in particular.

He had a lot of studying to do.

23

"Keep digging! I'll cover you!"

Bridget watched the jorvil warily as Dinner toiled below. The infrared visuals weren't much help to Bridget in seeing the cold-bodied jorvil, so her armor's motion-tracking sensors had pitched in to paint the creature into what she saw through her faceplate. Sadly, the darkness wasn't keeping the jorvil from chasing—and finding—the Leelites. With her connection to the Leelite know-globe gone, at least she was spared hearing the screams.

In the pit, Dinner, his helmet spotlight activated, shoveled away massive chunks of ice with his gloved hands. The big Hawaiian was throwing his back into it, she saw. The armature within their uniforms multiplied the wearer's strength; with Dinner, that hardly seemed necessary.

"I've buried a few buddies," he said. "Never had to dig any up!"

The good thing was that he wasn't alone in the work now. Cowling, Wu, and Lopez-Herrera had been unearthed—perhaps un-Leeled was the better term. Cowling was already down in another pit, digging. And while Lopez-Herrera was seeing to Wu and her hyperextended arm, she was using her armor's sensors to help locate the remaining four soldiers beneath the cold debris in the dark.

"I think I've got O'Herlihy," Leah Cowling said. "I need more light down here!"

"Star shells, embed mode," Bridget ordered. From wherever they stood, her troops above the ice adjusted their rifles. Together, they fired gleaming red shots toward the ceiling.

Driving into the frozen wall, the hissing munitions made like the ancient projectiles that were their namesake. The star shells glowed, blazing and crimson, giving the hall beneath an eerie cast. Now she saw more clearly the surviving Leelites, flitting past like insects around a bug zapper—and the jorvil, still after them.

Her armor did the counting. Just twelve Leelites left in the atrium. The rest had already closed and sealed the door leading down into their underground home. She'd joked about it before, but now needed to worry: What would the behemoth do when it finished off the hors d'oeuvres?

***

"I can't believe we just let them leave," Trovatelli said, standing in the broken-down passageway leading into the Black Butte. "Your Xylanx, I mean."

"Not *my* Xylanx," Jamie said, leaning against the wall as a load of snow went past. Surge Two had brought in the tracked cargo tenders *Indispensable* had transported to help deliver the bauxite with; now the soldier-driven vehicles were hauling away the debris blocking the entrance. Q/A had established that the tunnel was structurally sound and had concocted the plan to remove what had fallen. But nothing, it seemed to Jamie, could lift the woman's spirits.

"We really should have done something," she said, clearly unhappy. "They were in our depot. And now here?" She looked at Jamie. "Too coincidental. It doesn't feel right to you, does it?"

Jamie shrugged. "Don't ask me. I haven't felt right since I started eating cheese from a squeeze bag."

Trovatelli frowned. She was beautiful and smart, as he'd always known, but she hadn't seemed this worried before. The young woman he'd met on Altair had seemed very casually driven, certain her talents were up to any technical problem. Bridget had been the overserious one. Since the fight aboard the Dragon's Depot, however, the Xylanx had concerned her greatly.

Oh well, Jamie thought. Securing their base was partially Lissa's responsibility. *No one likes having their turf invaded.*

"Al…most…there!" Gideon called, rearing back with his arms to swing a great pick again. The squad leader was out ahead of the vehicles, chopping the hell out of the roadblock. Jamie imagined how happy Gideon must have been to find the heavy implement in with the freight.

"Think you'll start carrying one of those, Vic?" Trovatelli said, brightening with amusement.

"*Yeahhh,*" Gideon said lustily, smashing the pick into the ice. "I'll take two!"

Jamie rolled his eyes. The jorvil was about to have its turf invaded, too.

* * *

Michael O'Herlihy crawled out of the hole Cowling had dug. Seeing Bridget, he staggered toward her and pointed to the rifle in her hands. "I think that's mine," he said.

"Finders keepers," Bridget said, holding the weapon and watching above. "Mine blew up."

"So much for getting your deposit back." Arms sagging and clearly exhausted, O'Herlihy took a deep breath and straightened. "What'd I miss?" he said gamely.

Bridget stared into the space overhead. "I'm wondering what *I've* missed."

Near the ceiling, the count of Leelites had held steady in the last few minutes. And the jorvil had seemed increasingly agitated. Again and again, it facepalmed—an old slang expression that was exactly descriptive here—against the high wall of the atrium, missing its prey. The wispy aliens would appear a split second later, hovering close to the still-burning star shells. The jorvil would then twist and writhe, brushing the Leelites back into play with the ridged fins of its long "neck."

But the Leelites were tiring, she could tell, and the jorvil's movements were growing more frenetic. Was it hungry? Had it been above the surface for too long? Or...

The answer reached her literally in the form of rays from above. "It's the star shells!" she said. Nothing else they'd fired had hurt the jorvil. But it was moving in such a way that it did not expose its "face" too closely to the sizzling red-light sources. "Mike, what's in those things?"

O'Herlihy knew fireworks like no one else, having caused the evacuation of a chicken restaurant in his teens. "Basic tracer—strontium nitrate and magnesium. Burns redder than hell's own damnation," he said. "Give the old worm heartburn?"

"Maybe," Bridget said. She lifted her weapon—his weapon—and swore. "Out. Anybody else?"

"I fired all mine," Dinner said.

"My Spraecher's still under all that somewhere," Wu said, nodding to the ice pile from which Bridget's last team member had just been retrieved.

Another rumble shook the room. Bridget switched back to live ammo and spun—just in time to see a cargo tender punch through the darkened hole that had been the entrance. Against the faint light from outside the tunnel, she saw the tender's driver disembark.

"Surge Two reporting," Gideon said, standing outside the cab as his other troops filed in. He picked up his weapon from inside and looked up at the jorvil. He whistled. "Wow. The dink wasn't kidding."

Bridget clambered over a pile of ice to address him. "Gideon, do you still have any of your star shell charges?"

"I've got all of them," he said. "Never use 'em. They're non-combat items."

"Today's different. You've got four charges?"

"Eight," he said, pointing to the homebrew multi-rifle.

She turned back and looked up. "I think we can blind the thing if we can hit it in the face somehow," she said. But looking up, she realized that the jorvil's head was never lower than fifteen meters above, and there was no good angle on it from below. "How do we bring it down here?"

"Don't worry about that," Gideon said, slinging his rifle and pulling a pick from the cab. "I've got this."

As the man clambered over an icy obstacle, Bridget looked back to see Jamie and Trovatelli entering.

"He's crazy," Jamie said, face white. "Certifiable. A loon—"

"Careful, he'll hear you," Bridget said.

"I don't care. He nearly brought the cave down on us twice. He's twisted like a bag of bread!"

"I know," Bridget replied, grinning. She turned to see the leader of her second team charging up a large, slanting slab of upturned ice. Thanks to the internal servos, HardSHEL armor wasn't hard to run in, and the lower gravity was also working in Gideon's favor. But anyone else would have looked at the sheer ramp as forbidding—not to mention what awaited at the end: the enormous tubular trunk of the jorvil.

Not Gideon, who launched himself from the end of the makeshift ramp. Positioning the pick in front of him, he drove its head into the stone-encrusted body of the jorvil. Prying open a spot he could use as a handhold, he grabbed on with his free hand and swung the pick again.

"Stay ready," Bridget said to her team on the ground, most of whose guns were trained on the creature.

"Ready for what?" O'Herlihy said, weaponless.

Bridget blinked. "Well, I don't really know," she said as she watched Gideon chopping his own ladder up the massive free-standing spine. "But stay ready anyway."

Beside her, Trovatelli marveled. "It's like Jack and the Beanstalk," she said.

"Yeah," Jamie said, likewise spellbound. "Was Jack a homicidal maniac?"

Bridget chuckled—and then raised her rifle again as Gideon approached the top of the creature. "We've got to give him a second when he gets up there," she said. "Lasers, Spore nucleus package. Target the facial claws—and don't hit Gideon!"

Around her, the members of her team focused on the top of the jorvil. It might have sounded like a tall order, but this was a surgical-strike team accustomed to firing with pinpoint accuracy at tiny moving targets. The lasers were really only designed for slicing open Spore nuclei—they hadn't bothered using them against the Xylanx, whose armor's refractive coating would have diminished their power. Bridget didn't really expect them to do anything to the monster now either, but she hoped they might get its attention.

They watched as Gideon shimmied toward a gap between two of the six fingers splayed around the creature's facial orifice. Another moment and the pick fell from his hand. When the man reached the writhing creature's facial level, Bridget saw the facial talons begin to flex faster than any Venus flytrap ever moved for a kill.

"Fire!" Bridget yelled. A dozen beams appeared in unison, two targeting a finger each. That breakdown was just luck, but Bridget's hunch was correct. The claws stopped moving for a moment, short of the armored body of the man now crouching on the jorvil's face, gun pointed into its maw.

"Eat this, ugly!"

Gideon fired one star shell charge after another into the creature. A cavernous-sounding pop-pop-pop followed, resonating through the creature's mouth. Bridget imagined what was happening inside: as designed, the missiles were seeking walls to bury themselves in—and instead were finding themselves nice niches in the alimentary canal of a giant alien serpent. By the fourth popping sound, she could see Gideon wrapping his body around one of the facial fingers.

It was a necessary move, because in the next instant one of the final blasts went off deep within the jorvil—almost at Bridget's ground level. All around the circumference of the creature, the stony rings crackled and crisped, and chunks of its exterior started to fall off. When Bridget saw the jorvil swaying in her direction, she wasted no time in shoving Jamie and Trovatelli into motion.

"Go! Now!"

But the jorvil did not fall like a mighty tree. Rather, it crumbled from the base, sinking like an imploded building under demolition. A colossal din echoed through the atrium. From her position safely away, Bridget saw Gideon riding the corpse down, a man on the strangest elevator ride ever. When the last section tipped over a few meters from the ground, Gideon finally released the dead "hand" and dove away. He landed in a somersault that quickly ended in a chest-first splat on the soft but jagged ground.

The giant jorvil was now a pile of gigantic, ashen Christmas wreaths, the interiors of some still glowing with the blazing star shells. Whatever drove the body of the great worm, the surge team had found something it could not handle. From above, the surviving Leelites floated gently to the ground.

"Medic!" Bridget rushed around the debris to Gideon's side. "Don't try to move," she said, looking at his armor, even more banged up now.

"Ow," Gideon simply said. But she could see him smile.

2 4

Bridget shook her head as Lopez-Herrera helped maneuver Gideon's stretcher out of the auction hall. The other members of the team didn't know, but she had found Gideon in an Argentinean prison, serving life for his behavior at a football riot. He hadn't even known what teams were playing, a fact that had given him a wider range of targets. In eight months of confinement, he had brought the penal system to its knees. To settle complaints lodged by her guards, Gideon's final warden had agreed to give him over to Quaestor for deportation off-world.

It was a miracle that he'd survived as long as he had. Bridget had only put him in charge of the second team to make good on a threat two years earlier; she was trying to wake up a third-class, inattentive squad. It had worked pretty well. She'd convinced him to secretly agree to never order anyone else to do what he was going to do, but his squad mates didn't know that, and it had kept them on their toes ever since. It was hard to resent getting a dangerous job when the squad leader was taking all the rough assignments himself. *The things I have to work with*, she thought.

And now here's another, she thought, seeing Jamie approach through the disarray. He had recovered his briefcase, she saw, and was accompanied by one of the Leelites.

"We're back in business," Jamie said, pointing back to the Q/A, who was kneeling next to a pair of large dodecahedrons while another Leelite floated nearby. "Trovatelli brought in the spare knowglobe, and Vremian here's got us patched back into theirs so we can talk."

Bridget brightened as she heard the auctioneer's name. "I'm glad you made it," she said. "But I'm sorry about the others."

Vremian shimmered. "I am, too," he said, his voice again filtered and translated. "But this is why we always conduct our business here in a short window, to avoid the jorvil."

Bridget nodded. "If I can ask, why didn't you fly closer to the ground to get away from it?"

"Why," the Leelite said, "we were trying to keep it away from you. It may not have cared for the taste of humans, but you weren't having a good time of it when it was down there thrashing around." The creature expressed something that the knowglobe audibly interpreted as a sigh. "I know now that it was the act of those scurrilous competitors of yours, those Xylanx, in firing at our hall that awakened the brute. This kind of activity is simply unknown around here."

Trovatelli stepped up, accompanied by the other floating alien that had been helping her. "It looks like Jamie was right about our squatters," Trovatelli said.

"What?" Jamie gestured as if he was adjusting his helmet's audio volume. "Excuse me? Did someone say I was right?"

"Yeah," the Q/A said, smirking. Her expression didn't last long. "These Xylanx are definitely aliens," she said, her tone serious. "Vremian's aide was just showing me some things on their knowglobe's monitor. The Leelites encountered them more than sixty years before any humans went through the whirlibang. That's why they had a file on their language."

"Sixty years?" Bridget asked. "That means—"

"Yep," Trovatelli said. "Bipedal aliens. That pretty much settles it."

It was almost too incredible for Bridget to accept. For thirty-five years, humanity had been looking for anything that looked remotely similar to itself. And now they had not only encountered such a people, but fought with them?

"Who were they, Vremian?" she asked. "How come you haven't shared anything about them with anyone who's come around?"

The hovering jellyfish seemed to blush. "I'm...ashamed to say that nobody really ever comes around much anymore. You're the first bidders to arrive here since the last time the Xylanx appeared here. We've had no one to share the knowledge with."

Trovatelli interceded. "But who are they, Vremian? Your data over there doesn't say much."

"We don't know much," Vremian admitted. "Our encounters with anyone are necessarily brief. And they shared almost nothing about themselves—as they did this time." His tone changed. "Did they really do all this just to steal your knowglobe?"

"It looks like it," Bridget said. "But I can't understand why."

Behind Trovatelli, the Leelite who had assisted her chimed in. "Vremian, that sounds like the Luk'a."

"Don't be silly," Vremian replied.

Trovatelli's interest was piqued. "Wait. Who are the Luk'a?"

"The Luk'a were another bipedal species like yours," Vremian said. "Back even before my time. Forty thousand years ago, it must have been."

"They were thieves," his aide said.

"Don't be unkind, Torquin." Vremian's shreds wriggled. "It is true, though, that they had a poor grasp of how commerce worked." He gestured to the humans' knowglobe. "I've instructed my aide to provide you with all our information about the species we've encountered. I don't think we even have a language file on the Luk'a, but you can have what we do know on them—as well as our files on the Xylanx. The next time you encounter those reprehensible people, perhaps you can talk them into behaving better at public events."

Behind the alien, light appeared from the doorway leading downstairs. Vremian noticed it. "And now," he said, "we can conclude our business."

Bridget looked around the devastated atrium. "What business?"

"Did you forget?" Vremian said. "The auction. In fairness, I'm going to declare the Xylanx's bids null and void—so we'll accept your opening amount. Congratulations."

Jamie looked up. "Wait a minute. Our opening bids on everything? Every lot?"

"And more," Vremian said. "Remember, we haven't made any sales lately. There are quite a few superconductor columns in stock. More than will fit on your ship, to be sure."

Bridget and Jamie looked at each other. "Is there time to send another transport back?" Jamie asked.

"If you'll supply the forces to guard against another jorvil rising—"

"Another jorvil?" Jamie blurted.

Vremian seemed to shiver at the words. "Distasteful, I know. But you seem to have the answer for them. I was going to say, if your firm would be willing to put a trading post here with a garrison protecting us, we could trade year-round. And you would have the best terms in exchange, of course."

Jamie's eyes seemed to bulge. "Can we do that?" he asked Bridget.

"We do it all the time," Bridget said. "We can detach the bauxite 'boxes, encamp Surge Two here temporarily, and send another transport back with permanent staff from the depot."

"You really want to leave Gideon here? The building's still standing—barely."

"You really want him to come back with us?"

"Good point," Jamie said. Smiling, he turned and opened his briefcase before the Leelite. "If we can just step into anything you have resembling an office…"

25

Indispensable was a nub, now—a single bangbox transiting through the nonspace between whirlibangs. The passenger segment would have been the only piece of the ship the riders had access to in any event: vessels were dismantled into components small enough to fit in the rings. But while *Indispensable* had arrived at Mu Cassiopieae as an unconnected chain of many units, it was going back to the Dragon's Depot as a singleton shuttle. The other units remained back at Leel, along with Surge Two's living quarters.

For all his troubles in his earlier flights, Jamie felt he was getting the hang of interstellar travel. There wasn't gravity in the vessel whether inside the whirlibang or not, but he'd found a way to strap himself in so he could rest as he used to at his trading desk—sprawled across the chair, with his back against the armrest and his legs hanging over. If only he had his cowbell.

"This is starting to work out," Jamie said to Bridget, who was seated across from him and sipping from a food packet. He went over the figures on his hand. "This Leel contract is worth a lot—and it all goes to taking care of what we—"

"Of what *you*—" she interjected.

"Of what is *owed*," Jamie said. "And there's plenty of time until the end of the quarter."

"Not so much as you think," Bridget said. "Remember, while we're in the whirlibang, time outside is passing at a different rate. By the time we get back to Sigma Draconis, we'll have just over seven weeks left. And how much money do we need to make?"

"Tens of billions still," Jamie said. The air went out of him.

"I thought you knew the time calculations by heart," she said between sips. "Wasn't it part of your job?"

"Yeah. But I was never the one doing the traveling before." He sighed.

The whirlibang transit was a brief ride, but the flight from Leel to the jumping-off point was long enough that the rest of the crew was sacked out, with the exception of Trovatelli. Jamie had tried to engage her in conversations several times, but she seemed intent on studying the data she'd gotten from the Leelites.

"There's a lot here we should send home," Trovatelli said, hovering nearby.

Jamie liked what zero gee did to women's bodies. Her dark hair floated freely, and if he had never considered upside down to be a fetching pose before, now he was considering it. He watched her brow furrow. "I'm sorry," he said. "Were you saying something?"

She growled, aggravated. "About the Xylanx. We've got to alert the authorities back home."

"We will," Bridget said. "It's policy. All our encounter data gets uploaded to the knowglobe of the next 'box going home. You know that."

"I'm still very concerned," Trovatelli said. "Particularly about this Luk'a reference. Here's this ancient species—and yet the other Signatory races have told us precious little about them. And they're supposedly a bunch of interstellar thieves?"

"Thieves we know something about," Bridget said with a wink that Jamie easily saw. He groaned. "Get some rest, Lissa. We'll figure it out."

Reluctantly, Trovatelli returned forward and resumed her vigil over the knowglobe. Jamie leaned toward Bridget and whispered. "She seems more intense."

"New on the job, wants to do well," Bridget said. "And you're really one to say when someone's being intense."

Jamie gritted his teeth. "Will you lay off me? I'm playing the game here, aren't I?" He waved his hands in the air. "And what was that 'thief' stuff?"

"Oh, right. Just because you got us into all this trouble, putting the whole expedition at risk, why should we pick on you?"

"I get it," he said. "Kick me. All of you do. But I'm here."

"Yes, you are." Bridget crumpled the food bag and stored it. She studied him. "Look, maybe it would be easier for us all to accept you if we knew why you wanted all this money in the first place. I mean, a hundred billion dollars—"

Jamie pointed his finger in the air. "My cut was only forty."

"Still!"

Jamie stared at her for a moment, trying to decide whether to explain. "Okay," he said, finally. "When did you last live on Earth?"

"Seven years ago or so," she said.

"Oh, that's right," Jamie said, scratching his head. "I forgot. You left after things got too hot after Overland."

"Yes, and thanks for bringing it up. But you were saying?"

"Well, if you lived any time in the US—"

"Canada, mostly," she said.

"You would have known Senator Keeler," he finished.

"Elaine Keeler?" Bridget said. Her eyes widened. "Yeah, I know her." Her voice grew cold. "She was on the Overland committee. She made my life a living hell."

"Mine, too," Jamie said. "She's my mother."

✳✳✳

Jamie was back in his favorite bar again. Only he didn't have the immerso goggles on, and his bar was a kitchen—and Bridget was sitting in the accountant's spot. *Norm would be horrified,* Jamie thought, pouring her a drink.

They'd both changed to casual clothes since arriving back aboard the Dragon's Depot, and Bridget had completely changed her treatment of him since his admission back aboard *Indispensable.* For the last hour, she'd been positively human—and completely amazed at the story of his life.

"So what you're telling me," she said, "is that you embezzled all this money so you can get rich and shove it in your family's faces?"

Jamie took another swig of his drink. "Oh, not just my family. There are plenty of other faces to consider. But the Keelers are right up there in front."

The Keelers. He'd taken to thinking of them just like that, as a collection, a species. For a century, they'd been the power brokers of the southeast: Boca Brahmins with too much money and a sense of noblesse oblige. Only their noblesse had *obliged* them to meddle in other people's lives everywhere.

US Transportation Secretary Jacob Keeler had upended an industry, issuing the regulations requiring all Coandăcars to be retrofitted onto existing auto chassis to conserve metal. Supreme Court Justice Loren Swenk-Keeler had cast the deciding vote prohibiting humans from interfacing cybernetically with data systems. And European Union Vice-President Olivia Keeler had run the commission that decided, ultimately, how the whole world would respond to the Regulan gestures at the dawn of the interstellar age.

The Keelers had sided with no one political party in their sixty years of public life. Their primary loyalty was to the family, and to the goal of making it richer and more powerful. If they had not yet added president or prime minister to the family résumé, it was only because it had served them better at the time to work from someplace else in the system. They just liked messing with things to show they could. If there had been a movement to legislate the spelling of *ketchup* as *catsup*, a Keeler would have been somewhere nearby.

It was an old goat of a Keeler that married his mother not long after Marty Sturm flipped out and went into space. The aging senator had never adopted Jamie, nor made the slightest move to make the boy feel welcome. After a few of his antics, Jamie was buried in boarding school and forgotten. Elaine Sturm—Elaine *Keeler*—did little to intervene, as Jamie saw it. By the time the old man finally kicked off and his mother took over his senate seat, Jamie's relationship with her was as dead as the old man.

Jamie refilled his glass. "It would take," he said, "ten billion dollars to get a Keeler to recognize you as a life-form. Twenty to really get their attention."

"And forty billion?" she asked.

"Think thousand-dollar pants with piss stains." He clinked his glass against hers. "Cheers."

Bridget shook her head. "This is just dizzying. Your family, these numbers?" She chuckled. "I grew up in a town of three hundred people on the tundra."

"Until my mother hauled you before her committee and ran you off the planet."

"Yeah," Bridget said. She shook her head. "I don't care. They were going to find someone to hang."

"I guess we're both refugees from Elaine."

She emptied her drink and set her glass down. "Still, this is all crazy, Jamie. Jealousy? Sibling rivalry? This is not exactly what I was expecting you were going to tell me."

"What, you thought I was going to open a children's hospital with the money?" He shook his head. "Buy a few billion boxes of

Girl Scout Cookies? That's not me." He chuckled. "Unless doing so would annoy my family."

Bridget smiled a little. She started to say something when her earpiece beeped. Jamie watched her as she listened.

"It's Leo," she said. "The high-grav suits are loaded for Xi Boötes," she said, getting up. "Yours, too."

Jamie looked back at her weakly. "Mine, too?"

"Well, you'd better have one, or you won't be able to move there."

"Xi Boötes," he said, groaning. "I don't go to stars with umlauts. Sorry."

She stowed her glass and walked toward the exit. "I'll see you at the loading tube."

"Wait, wait," Jamie said, head buzzing. "Oh, so I share everything and you walk out?" He laughed. "Little town in Canada is all I get?"

"Nothing to know," she said, shrugging.

"Oh, really?" He looked at her and smirked. "O'Herlihy told me you killed your boyfriend."

She stopped in the doorway. "He did?" she asked, her back to him.

"Yeah," Jamie said. He stared at her as she stood there in silence. "Wait. You mean he was serious?"

"We go in an hour," she said. "You'd better shower and change. And it's better to throw up here than in zero gee, if you're going to."

She closed the door.

26

Kolvax sat beneath the great tree, immersed in the whole of human history. Like most Xylanx space stations, Gharion Preserve had a sizable greenhouse ring. His armor shed, Kolvax luxuriated in his underclothes near an artificial brook, studying from a small crystal display.

Texts and videos translated into the Xylanx language had taken him far away to Earth, which was what the humans called their homeworld. He had followed Homo sapiens from the days of caves and darkness to the discovery of agriculture, through the births of religion and writing to the splitting of the atom. He saw the species become a silly people in the previous century, obsessed with entertainment and squabbling over irrelevancies. And he saw the arrival of the busybody Regulans, and the great awakening that followed.

It was all in the knowglobe, there for anyone to find. The second he returned from Mu Cassiopieae with the humans' device, his followers within the Severed had gone to work analyzing the information inside. There were so many details to sift through. The humans even had a name for the star the Gharion Preserve station orbited: Pi3 Orionis. Couldn't they come up with a better name than that?

Humans had no marketing sense at all.

The most shocking thing, however, was that none of what Kolvax had already learned had required any decryption at all. The humans put it all out there for the taking, like something they were proud of. He hadn't imagined that possible. The Xylanx were champions of obfuscation and self-censorship when it came to their own origins. The grand traditions the Dominium sought to protect were whatever things served its politicos at the moment: the true past was always kept out of sight.

But any time humanity's representatives met another mercantile species and linked knowglobes, they passed on their complete profile. It was a deranged practice. Slavery, biological warfare, dancing contests—no horror was so shameful the humans would not share it. Kolvax was surprised anyone traded with them at all.

Most tantalizing was the information from the last few years, since the people of Earth reached out to the stars. The speed with which they had integrated into the local commercial scene was truly amazing. And yet there were counterforces at work on Earth. The humans were concerned about contaminating their planet with alien biomaterial: it helped that the whirlibangs were all millions of miles away, in the orbital neighborhood of a planet called Venus. Bangboxes sent through the transit stations underwent standard inspections before being carted to the blue planet.

And then there were the assassinations at Overland carried out by the Walled Garden movement. The Xylanx had heard the filthy Gebrans were involved in a war some eight years earlier, but they didn't know with whom they'd fought it. The news explained a lot.

The existence of an isolationist movement on Earth was unsurprising: xenophobia was a powerful sentiment among Kolvax's own people, who had been in space far longer. He himself had done a lot to milk it. But there was no mistaking which side of the argument had the upper hand on Earth: humans would continue to migrate any place they were allowed to go. That was part of why they had to be stopped.

Still, a fifth column of humanity, willing to take extreme measures to cut off their world from the galaxy? *That could be useful,* Kolvax thought. Fellow travelers to his own silly excuse for a movement. If not usable in his current plans, then maybe such a human group could come in handy some day in the future.

He was sure about one thing, however: the influx of information was certain to feed the Xylanx's paranoia about the species, and while that served him well, it had its downside. He was reluctant to even visit the scriptorium where his Severed disciples were boiling down the salient points to send back to the Dominium. The flood of facts must be sending his dear fearmongers into overdrive.

And there was one now, Kolvax saw, looking up. An armored figure quivered behind a nearby bush.

Kolvax sighed. "Tellmer, get out here."

"I'm sorry, sir," his aide said, barely visible through the branches. "You're naked—"

"No, I'm not," Kolvax said. *Stupid movement.* "If it makes you feel any better, adjust your visor's settings so my unholy kneecaps will not offend you."

Tellmer stepped out into the open. "That's better," the relieved Xylander said.

"You're talking to a shrub, you idiot," Kolvax said. "I'm to your right."

"Sorry. I can't see very well." Sheepishly, Tellmer turned toward him, face-mask darkened. Of all Kolvax's followers from his Sigma Draconis exile, only Tellmer had kept on wearing the deadly golden collar. The others had removed the booby-trapped devices, but Tellmer had decided to continue to allow Kolvax to have the ability to kill him on a whim.

Of course, Kolvax had that ability in any event: Tellmer was a weakling. Maybe Tellmer was just making things convenient for him. That was an aide's job, after all. And maybe, after losing and regaining two limbs in the last weeks, the imbecile figured the medics could do the same with his head, should it go astray.

"You have news from Liandro?" Kolvax asked.

"The elder believer has broken the code," Tellmer said. "The operational data you wished is now yours."

Kolvax looked at his display. Yes, the information was feeding to it. "You've read it all?" he asked.

"Yes," Tellmer said. "Full profiles on all the members of the trader's team. Biometric information, principally—they monitor each other's well-being while in armor."

"How touching," Kolvax said, scowling as he scanned. He was more interested in the histories. "What does this mean? About the merchant?"

"Ah. That was the most difficult encryption to break," Tellmer said. "Evidently, the trader—one Jamison Philip Sturm—had among his mission dossiers record-keeping about his own goals. As near as we can figure, he is obligated to obtain what is apparently a vast sum of riches in the next few weeks."

"Or what?" Kolvax said.

"I would imagine they'd kill him. Or perhaps they would simply mutilate him in some way." He flexed his gloved hands, uncomfortably. "It's what we'd do."

"Hmm." Kolvax hadn't studied up enough yet on what the human sanctions were for poor job performance. But in examining the file Tellmer was referring to, Kolvax observed that the trader certainly seemed motivated. A breakneck trading schedule had been plotted out, human visits to several destinations emanating from the Sigma Draconis station that had once been their place of exile.

"This Sturm is in a real hurry," he concluded. "You're right. It must be pretty bad, what he's facing. You've seen him, Tellmer: he's almost as big a coward as you are."

And now Kolvax had his itinerary.

The Xylander went silent for a moment, contemplating. Yes, he had the resources now for one of his more ambitious plans—and the knowglobe had given him more than enough information to pull it off. He spoke his thoughts out loud. "What—what if we could really take care of the human problem once and for all?"

Tellmer straightened. "I thought the Dominium advocated going slowly on the human matter, Great Kolvax. They just wanted you to investigate."

"So I've investigated," he said. He waved the crystal display in his hand. "What more do they want me to find out?" He licked his cracked lips. "No, this is perfect. The next time we see Jamison Philip Sturm, his whole world is going to change." He looked up. "And so will ours."

27

"Can we please stop giving cute names to things that can kill us?" Jamie asked.

Bridget laughed. It was true; the Moogles were more than a little frightening. They resembled mammoth muffins: each on three legs, each leg the size of an elephant. Ten slender arms were evenly spaced around their wide muffin-top midsections, and giant mouths appeared as sphincters on the top of their "heads."

"Just stay out of traffic and you'll be okay," she said. The Moogles walked by twirling around on one giant foot, and if they had a way of seeing what was underneath them, she didn't know what it was. The dossier on the Moogles suggested the arms, which seemed to be constantly in motion, might provide some kind of optical or motion-sensory input, but nobody really knew. All that the Signatory Systems knew was that Moog, the planet the Moogles lived on, was a commercial dead zone. And a heavy one, at that.

Xi Boötes A was a G-type star more similar in size, color, and age to Earth's sun than any they had visited recently. Of course, it wasn't the only star in its system, and its main inhabited planet was a dense iron ball twice the size of the Earth. Landing on Moog had caused Bridget's weight to more than double instantly: they probably wouldn't be putting in any spas for the weight-conscious here. And breast implants wouldn't be too popular either. They would not be founding New California on Moog.

All the members of Surge Three wore their high-gravity HardSHEL armor units, with armatures specially designed to provide movement—and inside, exerting pressure to keep blood flowing back upward. Nonetheless, they couldn't stay here long, on account of Jamie. The others were in peak physical condition, but Jamie was already nursing a sore leg from a fall on Leel, and she didn't take him for a workout nut. He had also had the usual sea-legs difficulties getting around.

"I feel like I'm drunk," Jamie said, staggering on the yellow stone surface.

"You were. Now you're just heavy. Let the servos do their job," she said. "When you fall down, you're falling almost three times as fast."

"Every day's a thrill ride," Jamie said, resigned.

"You'll be an old hand soon," she said. "Like me."

"Dear God, don't let that happen."

Bridget grinned. After their conversation in the kitchen, she'd come to appreciate his situation a little better—if not to approve of his actions. Jamie wasn't whining nearly as much after the sales coup on Leel—it really was a big deal—and it seemed to Bridget as if Jamie was finally beginning to understand just how diverse and exotic life in the galaxy was.

From a desktop, she thought, it was probably easy to imagine that the creatures of the universe were just like you. Dealing solely with names and numbers, you never imagined just how unfamiliar your trading partners really looked. The Sheoruk, the Baghu, the Leelites—these had to tell Jamie that the universe was a lot more complicated than he imagined.

That great variety, however, also made the bipedal Xylanx—who were shaped like humans—of definite interest. But they were of interest for different reasons than they would have been even half a century earlier.

Intelligent life was everywhere in the cosmos, humanity had found: that Big Question had been answered, but good. As the possible configurations that sentience took grew and grew, though, Earth's travelers noted a disappointing lack of locations that humans could live in without space suits or mechanical assistance.

Earthlings could live and work, of course, quite comfortably in those other places: the revolutionary Supralight Hygienic Environment Layer, the innermost skin of a HardSHEL or SoftSHEL suit, made that possible. But many humans longed for a place where they could kick back outside, lounging beneath a tree in a nitrogen-oxygen atmosphere, protected by an ozone layer at twenty-four degrees Celsius. And while potential Earthlike planets had been catalogued by researchers since the late twentieth century, no actual Terra-twins had been found. Shafted by the final frontier, real estate brokers everywhere had gone into therapy.

So the Xylanx were of interest on their own, but also because of what their existence suggested. Weighing eighty kilos, having long limbs, and owning opposable thumbs made sense only on a certain kind of planet. The Xylanx seemed a little more massive than the baseline human, but their general shape was still close enough. Did they breathe air in those helmets? What was their sun like? Did they have more than one home?

Moog's sun was nice and familiar, but no humans would be moving here. And it didn't seem as if there was any trading to do, either. The Moogles were allegedly intelligent, and their stomping grounds had great mineral riches. But they protected the ground just by walking around.

"Porriman trader approaching," Hiro Welligan said from his watch point. "Hold on to your wallet."

Jamie and Bridget turned to see a tracked vehicle crawling slowly toward them, giving the herd of tromping Moogles a wide berth.

Natives of Porrima were chubby lumps. About the same height as humans, Porrimans propelled themselves along, slug-like, on a sheen of internally generated ooze. With their four arms, minds for deal making, and home conveniently located near several other Signatory Systems worlds, the Porrimans had inveigled a position for themselves as the premier warehouse keepers for the stellar neighborhood. Granted, they seldom got shipments right, but that only attracted foreign advisers by the 'boxload there to work as observers—while spending money in Porriman establishments. Bridget thought it was a pretty good scheme.

The trader's vehicle trundled up. Bridget could see clearly the Porriman's pudgy body mechanically—and, she imagined, uncomfortably—suspended inside his vehicle. Robotic arms hung limply outside the carriage. The Porriman's dark eyes stared at them. "More victims here, I see," a jolly but sarcastic male voice said over the airwaves.

Jamie did a double take at the words.

"Victims?" Bridget asked.

"To try the impossible—selling to the Moogles." The Porriman gestured back with one of his hands toward the milling field of giants. "Humans, aren't you?" he said. "Well, Frocky of Porrima welcomes you. Even as he's about to leave!"

"Now come on!" Jamie said, looking back at the team's know-globe. "That's Phil Silvers!"

Bridget blinked. "Who?"

"Television comic from the twentieth century," Jamie said.

"Oh, that again," she said, dismissively. "You have a strange hobby." She understood nostalgia: remembering things you were exposed to in your youth is good for your synapses. Nostalgia for things before you were born, on the other hand, made no sense to her.

Jamie shook his head. "I'm just imagining how much licensing money the knowglobe people must pay out. Personality rights are descendible, you know. That started with Elvis."

"Who…?" Bridget shook her head. "Never mind. You'll just tell me."

Frocky wheeled toward Jamie. "What's the matter, my friend? You sound troubled. As if trust is missing from our relationship. Tragic, given how long we've known each other. Why, it must be two minutes we've known each other. You're breaking poor Frocky's circulatory organs."

"Well, it's not you," Jamie said. "Or maybe it is. Our knowglobe has selected for your voice a human who was famous for portraying a con artist."

"Portraying?" Frocky said, sounding mildly interested. "Was he one?"

"I don't think so. But listening to you, I can't take you seriously."

"Well, it's a two-way street, young man—to use an expression which is completely meaningless to me. Because *my* knowglobe, back at the ship that you've so thoughtfully double-parked, has chosen a communications profile for you that I wouldn't wish on my worst enemy."

Jamie's interest was piqued. "Who is it?"

"Weren't you listening? It's my worst enemy. Supervisor Vangwoo. The mere sound of your voice makes me want to crawl back into the egg."

Bridget smiled. "You were saying about the Moogles?"

Frocky waved his arms. "Hopeless! Completely hopeless. No one can sell to these things. Better people have tried. I just have. It's useless to ask. They're living on a field we know holds wealth beyond measure—and if you poke a stick into the ground, they stomp you to death! You can't trade them anything, because there's nothing they want!"

"Maybe it's all in your approach," Jamie said. "Have you tried teddy bears?"

"A comedian! Funny, this kid is." Frocky shook his head. "Well, you can do the floor show without me, because I give up. Good old Frocky is through!" With that, he started rolling toward his spacecraft.

Bridget looked back at the Moogles. There *were* hundreds of them, wandering aimlessly like cattle—only cows that gesticulated constantly with ten hands. "I think we'll give it a try anyway, Frocky."

"'A try,' she says!" Frocky waved with four arms to the brilliant blue sky. "Well, young lady, I'm sure you will do wonderfully well in my absence. Just don't come to Frocky after you've been flattened. I can't stand the sight of anything that's been inside anyone else, regardless of species or creed!"

"Wait," Bridget said. "You said you talked with them. We don't have a language file—"

"You wouldn't." Frocky stopped and looked them over. "Sure," he said. "Why not. I've got nothing to lose. It's a sign language. They're always moving their arms, right? Astonishingly, it means something. I've spent a month learning it. Here." He touched a control inside his compartment. "I'm transmitting it to you now. I hope you enjoy all the time it'll take for you to learn it!"

At that, he rumbled off to his ship.

"It takes all kinds," Bridget said.

"Then we're in luck, because it looks like the universe has them all," Jamie replied. "And it keeps sending them all to me."

***

Simply walking out onto the yellow plain had been a challenge for Jamie. He'd fallen twice and would have broken his arms if it weren't for the power-assist his outfit was providing. This time, he'd been given a high-grav HardSHEL suit like the other troops had, although without the armament. *Stupid regulation.*

But the internal armature had come in handy on another front. As always, Jamie marveled at what Trovatelli was able to accomplish. She hadn't wanted to come along, as she was still absorbed in her studies of the data on the Xylanx. But even from *Indispensable*, she'd been able to help Jamie accomplish something in hours that had taken Frocky a month.

Under the watchful eyes of Bridget and her companions, Jamie stood before a single Moogle that had wandered away from its herd.

"Hello," the trader said. As he did so, the servos caused his arms to flap up and down.

"You're a seagull," Welligan said, laughing.

"I'm talking here," Jamie replied—and that statement, too, caused his arms to gesticulate wildly.

It got the Moogle's attention. It twirled backward on one leg and then returned to its original position.

Jamie read the readout projected inside his helmet. His cameras, interfacing with the language database Frocky had provided, interpreted the response as an acknowledgment. Nothing more.

I feel like a marionette playing charades, Jamie thought.

"I have much to sell," Jamie said. He started to point back to the ship, where the fabricator had been rolled out, but his arms began moving in a wild sequence of gestures that sent the briefcase tumbling from his hand.

He felt like a football referee on a bender. Now all his bodyguards were chuckling. Bridget picked up the briefcase and held it for him. "Try again," she said, smiling.

"I will trade for mining rights," Jamie said, trying to use as few words as possible so as to protect his poor arms. "We will not damage your land. You must tell me what you want."

As soon as Jamie's arms finished their sequence of moves, the Moogle raised its hands in the air and thundered off to the west, running away from him and toward the herd, far away.

"What the hell?" Jamie asked. He regretted he'd opened his mouth. "Interface off," he snarled.

Bridget stared into the distance. "Something rattled that guy," she said. It had reached its companions in an amazingly short time for something so massive.

Jamie heard a chime in his ear. It was Trovatelli calling in. "You guys had better wait," she said, her voice sounding urgent.

"What is it?" Jamie asked. He stared at the Moogles. Something was going on out there, half a kilometer away.

"We forgot something with the sign language," she said. "The Porrimans' language required four arms."

"Yeah," Bridget said. "But we allotted for that. We built a vocab using just the words that required his, er, top arms."

"That's what I thought," Trovatelli said. "But I was just rechecking—and I think we misread 'dominant arm' for 'top arm.'"

Bridget's eyes narrowed. "You mean Frocky was left-handed?"

"Bottom-handed," the Q/A said.

Jamie saw the huge herd beginning to move. "So what did I just tell them? I asked what they wanted!"

"No," Trovatelli said. "You told them you wanted to eat their young!"

Bridget took a step back. "That's…no good." The herd was moving now, stampeding on all threes toward them.

The entire team turned, struggling to run in the high gravity.

"Well, I think we know what they want now," Jamie yelled, huffing. "They want to stomp us to death!"

EPISODE 5:
TIP FROM A DIP

28

Jamie was sixteen the first time he pretended to run a four-minute mile. He was desperately looking for a way to improve his grade in gym class, and his jock friend owed him money. So to settle the debt, Sven Torgaard switched pedometers with Jamie. Sitting at home watching the readouts, their absentee coach had no idea Jamie wasn't the fastest kid in the state. Things had snowballed from there, with Jamie receiving three track scholarship offers before finally being found out.

On Moog, Jamie wasn't doing all his own running either. The serious efforts were coming from the armature inside his high-gravity space suit, servos powerfully raising and stomping his feet. But while Jamie had taken fewer steps than he had in his past fraudulent efforts, it already felt to him as if he'd run a marathon. And hundreds of meters behind charged the great mass of angry Moogles, sounding louder than ever. Thundering monsters, all after Jamie—the guy who'd accidentally demanded their young for dinner.

Where's my ringer when I need him?

"Go, daddy, go!" Hiro Welligan called out to him from a few steps behind. The Surge Three squad leader and a trio of his companions had encircled the trader, hurrying Jamie away from the stampede. But they could go no faster than he could, and he was already feeling the pain. Muscles being mechanically flexed for him were still being flexed. And even if he wasn't feeling the full burden of moving two and a half times his own weight due to the increased gravity, his suit's shock absorbers couldn't prevent him from feeling his boots slamming violently against the compacted rock surface.

"I don't think we're supposed to run in these!" he yelled.

"Forget running," Bridget said, looking backward from up ahead. "I'll be happy when you approach *walking*! Now move it!"

She pointed the way to sanctuary further along the plain. Configured for a high-gravity landing, *Indispensable* today was more engine than vessel: six bangbox-sized thrusters surrounded the habitation and general store modules. The nine members of Surge Sigma's first team were on the ground in front of *Indispensable*, fanning out in Jamie's direction to cover his approach.

But while the ship squatted only half a kilometer away, it might as well have been light-years. Jamie looked back in panic. Behind Welligan, he could now make out individual Moogles in the mob: footstools the size of dinosaurs, spinning and stomping ahead on their trios of legs. The creatures' limbs whipped furiously around their midsections, a fleshy hula skirt from hell.

"Hurry," Bridget said, waving along the trader's guardians from twenty meters ahead. "Come on—and don't look back!"

Thoom! Thoom! Jamie looked back. Several of the Moogles had closed the distance with the humans in astonishingly little time, pulverizing the world beneath with each crushing clomp. Terrified, Jamie turned his head to return his focus to the ship…

…and saw the rubble-strewn ground rocketing upward toward him. He'd fallen while walking on Moog enough times; now, while running, he slammed breastplate first into the rocky surface, as if thrown.

"Terrific!" Bridget said. "Hiro, get Jamie!"

"On it," Welligan said, scrambling over the stony surface. "Stubek! Abaza!"

Forcing himself to roll over, Jamie saw the squad leader leaning above him. Welligan's spectral hair was shot white, as if all the color-stimulating nanoids in his follicles had decided they had something better to do. Two of the troopers who'd been running alongside Jamie joined him.

"Heave!" Welligan said. The two bodyguards—Jamie recognized Lynn Stubek from Baghula—hefted him from the ground, their more powerful armor seemingly untaxed by his weight. Their arms under his, they began to run again, carting Jamie along, his boots dragging as he faced backward.

From his awkward dangling position, Jamie saw Welligan starting to stand up amid the rocks—and an enormous figure racing toward the man. "Hiro, look out!" Jamie shouted.

THOOM! The leader of Surge Three cried out as he vanished beneath the massive foot of a Moogle. The mushroom-shaped monster twisted on one leg, grinding—and then hopped to another foot, landing again. And again.

"*Hiro!*" Jamie heard Bridget yell.

An instant later, he heard gunfire—and could see rounds of something sparking off the Moogle's hide, fired from the troops behind him. Then Jamie began to fall again, as Stubek released his right arm and reached for her weapon. The trooper hanging on to his left arm, a coffee-skinned male, yelled at her. "Lynn, don't! We have to get—"

Jamie didn't hear the rest. Supported now by only one soldier, the trader saw flashes go past his face. Stubek fired recklessly—pointlessly, it seemed to Jamie—as the wave of Moogles broke past and around Welligan's assailant. Stubek charged them. Within a second, she was gone, too, lost somewhere in the flurry of alien feet.

Jamie could feel his remaining rescuer shoving him forward. Stumbling again, Jamie landed hard. Ahead, he saw Bridget running toward him, her rifle slung. "Come on," she said, reaching out for him. Jamie put his arm out—

THOOM! Another elephant-sized Moogle foot slammed down just behind Jamie. The impact lifted the merchant's body from the ground in defiance of the heavy gravity. Landing on his side, Jamie looked back in vain for the bodyguard who had been escorting him. There was nothing to see. Nothing but a jumping behemoth—and a bloodcurdling screech resonating through Jamie's communications system.

Bridget reached him. Half-astride Jamie's fallen form, she drew her rifle and switched settings on the weapon. She showered the Moogle with sonic energy—an act that seemed to confuse the beast more than harm it. As Jamie started to crawl forward, the other surviving members of Surge Three appeared at either side of Bridget.

More troops arrived from behind. Jamie looked back to see O'Herlihy and Dinner chugging toward them, leading the members of Bridget's first team. There was no screening their approach to *Indispensable* now, Jamie saw as he looked past them. The Moogles had outflanked them, cutting off access to the ship. It was guard *Indispensable* or guard the trader—and the Moogles weren't showing any interest in the ship.

"Lay down sonics," Bridget ordered as the line of reinforcements reshaped to surround the breathless Surge Three members and Jamie. The members of the circular firing squad pointed their weapons outward, bathing the Moogles in shrieking sound.

"This ain't working," O'Herlihy said after a few minutes. "I think it's just pissing them off!"

Jamie could tell. Their sonic pulses on Baghula had kept the Breathers at bay. Here, the intense sounds seemed to simply annoy the natives. Moogles reaching their perimeter twirled angrily and backed off, to be replaced by others. The tactic was keeping them alive but only while their weapons' power held out.

Jamie called into his helmet microphone over the whine of the weaponry. "Madoka! We need the ship! Do something!"

He couldn't hear the pilot's remote response. Still firing, Bridget looked back at Jamie and shook her head. She looked as worried as he had ever seen her.

Jamie swallowed. And for no reason, he remembered he had lost his briefcase again.

2 9

Three troops down, Bridget thought. She thought; she didn't know. Welligan had yellowlined—unconscious—and both his and Stubek's armor were reporting systems failures. Bridget wasn't getting any reading from John Abaza's unit at all.

She cursed herself for not having insisted on outfitting *Indispensable* with a munitions package. It had been too much weight, and there wasn't time to make the modifications. There'd been no time to do anything right since Jamie Sturm entered their lives.

"Alternate fire," she said. "Pattern Eagle, to the ship." Her forces did as asked, trying to reshape their circle into a wedge leading toward *Indispensable*. But there were as many Moogles ahead as there were behind, now. The humans had gotten as far as a little hill: not much more than a pitcher's mound, it was a mountain for Kansas-flat Moog. It was clear they were going no further.

Jamie looked down, rattled, from the top of the mound. She'd had to tell him there was no way Madoka could simply fly over and pick them up as she had on Baghula. *Indispensable* handled like a warthog in its current configuration and could well crush or roast them by accident.

She wasn't as concerned about the Moogles. She opened the channel to *Indispensable.* "Hover as low as you can, Madoka. East side of our position. Torch 'em, scare 'em. Whatever!"

"Six minutes minimum to lift-off," the pilot voice replied.

Exactly as suspected. "Do what you can," she said. "Yang out."

Jamie, who'd heard the answer, looked back down at her from the mound. His eyes were wild, his arms shaking. He was scared out of his wits. He'd seen Welligan and Abaza go down, she figured. She stepped up to him and grabbed his wrist. "Jamie!"

He blinked. "Yeah, I'm here."

"Not for long," she said. "We're going to move you." She turned him to the east, where the rumbling of *Indispensable's* revving engines could only barely be heard over the commotion. "Madoka's going to pass over the Moogles and then clear off. We're going to open up and you have to run then—into the gap she leaves."

"H-h-how do you know she'll leave a gap? Will the thrusters kill them?"

"No idea," Bridget said, her eyes locking on his. "But it'll be better than standing here. Do you need me to slave your suit? I can match your armature's movements to mine. You'll run that way." *Not well,* she didn't add as she called up the command screen in her helmet interface.

"I'll be okay," Jamie said.

"Look out!" O'Herlihy called. To the west, a particularly angry Moogle had reacted differently to the sonics, charging forward and rolling on its side. The gargantuan being crashed through Bridget's orderly lines, and soldiers dove to avoid being crushed.

Jamie jumped, too. Bridget looked back to see him turning east and bolting, way too soon. "Jamie, not yet!"

He took a couple of steps forward, only to have Bridget quickly seize control of his armor, as she'd been preparing to do earlier. Only she hadn't had time to link it to her own motions. So Jamie's arms, which had been flailing birdlike in his excuse for high-gravity running, suddenly locked in position. He fell over like a toppled statue, with his outstretched right hand striking the surface at the foot of the mound like a knife. That position held for half a second, until he toppled over and landed on his back with his arm sticking up saluting the sky.

Bridget turned back to the Moogle that had infiltrated their ranks. She raised her weapon…

…and paused. Because the Moogle, having reached its feet again, stopped, too. Ten knobby arms went into the air.

And all around, the Moogles stopped moving.

It took Bridget a moment to register what had happened, and another to order the ceasefire. The sonic blasts ending, only the roar of the ship's rockets remained. The Moogles' attention—as best as she could tell—was on Jamie, who was still frozen in his position.

Jamie spoke quietly and slowly at first. "Will…somebody… please…*help me!*"

Bridget looked at the Moogles, and then back at him. "Override off," she said.

Freed from his mechanical rigor mortis, Jamie groaned and struggled to get to his feet. He looked around dizzily. Seeing the Moogles motionless, he glanced back at Bridget. "Whoa," he said.

"Yeah." She watched as the infiltrator Moogle tromped toward Jamie. It was slow, now, unthreatening—and its arms went into motion again.

"*Merchant*," said a low, mysterious-sounding voice.

Bridget blinked. "It's the sign-language interface!" she said. She patched into *Indispensable*'s channel. "Belay attack until ordered, Gina. Things have changed…maybe." Thinking again, she called for Q/A. "Do we have the *right* language package now,

Trovatelli?" she said, more than a hint of aggravation in her voice.

"This time, yeah," came the engineer's guilty response.

"Do your thing," Bridget said to Jamie.

"What?"

"You heard the Moogle. It wants the trader."

"I thought that was the whole problem." Bewildered, Jamie tromped back up the mound. It put him at less than half the height of the creature. "I'm the merchant," he said, his arms moving automatically, another series of gestures dictated by their knowglobe's translator program.

"*What merchant said—is of value,*" the translation came.

"I haven't said anything," Jamie replied.

"*Your motion,*" the Moogle said. "*I would…buy…your motion.*"

"Excuse me?"

"*Your motion. What do you want for it?*"

Jamie looked up blankly at the looming giant. "I—uh…"

"Wait," Bridget said, suddenly having a thought. "Wait a minute."

Jamie jerked his head toward her. The other Moogles were starting to stomp impatiently. "I don't think we have a minute."

"Ask him for a minute, then!" Bridget quickly accessed the data interface on her helmet's faceplate.

Looking back at her with worry, Jamie shrugged and turned to the Moogle. "I need a few minutes," he said. Robotically, his arms went into motion, signaling the message.

"*Sold,*" the Moogle signaled with its limbs. Rocking left and right on its mighty hooves, the creature in the clearing raised and lowered its arms. The translated words came through Bridget's audio system. "*I have traded them respite,*" the Moogle said to its brethren. "*You will obey.*"

All around, Moogle feet pounded the surface angrily.

"I don't think this guy speaks for everyone," Jamie said nervously.

But the Moogle was no longer speaking—if that was even the right term. The mammoth alien was moving now, scaling the mound. Seeing the giant heading up, Jamie rushed to get out of the way.

"He's not after you," Bridget said.

"Prove it!"

From the top of the rise, the Moogle started to bolt forward on one leg, as if to run again. Only this time, it froze—stretching two of its arms into space before it. It wobbled there precariously for a moment, until gravity won out. The Moogle tumbled down, just as Jamie had. Its impact nearly knocked Bridget and her soldiers off their feet.

"What the—?" Jamie said.

Bridget cut him off. "Watch."

The Moogle came to rest on its back like a giant overturned ladybug. A single one of its arms pointed defiantly upward. On all sides of the group of humans, Moogles stomped in place and waved their limbs frenetically.

"Jeez!" Jamie said, struggling to pick himself up again. "What the hell was that?"

"I think it was your fall earlier," Bridget said. "When I took control of your armor." It wasn't graceful looking, but it was unique. Her eyes widened with excitement.

Could it be that easy?

As their interlocutor rolled over and recovered, Bridget stepped up onto the mound. Facing the large Moogle in the center of the clearing—she'd come to think of it as the Grand Moogle—she gestured. "Watch this," she said. In the next second, the heavily armored woman threw her hands to the air and kicked her boots together, her body twirling as she did so.

Internal servos whined, and she came to ground with a noisy thud.

O'Herlihy looked at her, astonished. "You crazy, Chief?"

She shook her head. "No. Look!"

The Grand Moogle's limbs were in motion again—as were those of many others in the crowd. "Tell him that one was for free," she said to Jamie.

Befuddled, the trader repeated her line—and his arms did the rest. Seconds later, Moogles all about were in motion, leaping with their arms to the air. Each kicked two of their three ginormous hooves as they came down hard. The whole world seemed to quake as they landed.

Jamie looked around, stunned. "What the hell are they doing?"

"What I just did."

"What did you just do?"

"A grand jeté," Bridget said. "Two years of dance classes in grade school. I hated them." *But I remembered them*, she thought.

"I don't get it," Jamie said.

"The Moogles' entire culture is based on kinesics. Manual communications, gestures. But it's more than their language. I think maybe it's their whole economy, too!"

The Grand Moogle's limbs went into motion again. Bridget's onboard systems saw the movements and interpreted them. "*More.*"

"You see?" she said. Bridget quickly triggered her armor's interface with the knowglobe. "O'Herlihy. Dinner. Sling your weapons."

Arbutus Dinner looked back at her, startled. "What? Why?" he asked, even as he did as ordered.

"You'll see." Her eyes found the file she was looking for on her helmet menu. "Surge Sigma Draconis, Yang, commanding units Dinner and O'Herlihy. Load tactical systems, motion pattern tango."

"I've never heard of that one," O'Herlihy said. As soon as he finished the sentence, his armored body lurched toward Dinner's.

"Not tango the call letter," she said, watching the two massive soldiers robotically join hands. "Tango the dance!"

Metallic chests came together with a clang and the two faced outward. O'Herlihy was leading—but really, it was the knowglobe leading him, forcing his outfit's armature through motions that had originated in South America more than three hundred years earlier. Startled soldiers stepped out of the way as the two figures struck a pose and shifted weight, heading in the opposite direction.

"Someone shoot me," Dinner said.

The lead Moogle shuffled excitedly. "*Yes. More*," it said.

Within seconds, Bridget had sent Joe Cowling and Cathe Wu into a sequence of automated t'ai chi poses, her medic into a disco hustle, and three other soldiers into a Russian troika dance. All were moves programmed into the team's knowglobe—along with a lot of other rarely accessed information from humanity's past. And all the time, the Moogles surrounding them waved their arms and stomped.

O'Herlihy looked frantically at Jamie as he reached the end of a turn. "Make her stop before she puts us in a kick line!"

Jamie looked at Bridget. "You know what happened earlier. How do we know that all this moving around isn't telling them we want to fillet their grandmothers?"

"We don't," Bridget said. "But I think we'd know that by now."

The Grand Moogle confirmed her guess. "*The motions of our limbs…are all we own. Original clusters of movements denote status. That is important here. Many will bid for your movements.*"

"Can't others just copy your motions once you, er, perform them?" Jamie asked.

"*Not without sanction,*" the Grand Moogle said. "*Such rights must be purchased. Those who would steal the motions of others are banished to starve on the Blasted Plain of Tarchos for a hundred cycles.*"

Bridget and Jamie looked at each other. It was certainly a novel intellectual property regime. "But wait," Jamie said to the Moogle. "What do you *pay* for these movements?"

"*Other movements.*"

Jamie looked at Bridget and rolled his eyes. "We won't get rich learning how to stampede from these guys."

"Hey!" O'Herlihy called out. "Over here. Remember us?"

Bridget looked to see O'Herlihy and Dinner faceplate to faceplate as the bodyguards leaned into a dip. On the bottom of the move, Dinner looked at her plaintively. "For the love of God, let us go! Or let me lead!"

"I think that's got it," Bridget said. Her demonstration done, she released the coordinated control of her troops. The sighs of relief were many and enthusiastic. Triggering her own armor's interface with the Moogle language, she turned to address the Grand Moogle. "You exchanged us time for my movement, earlier. Will you give us access to our ship and companions for what you've just seen?"

Before her arms had even finished moving, pathways began to open between the giant creatures. "*Those that have seen will give access.*"

Jamie snapped his fingers. "If you'll do that, will you give us access to the grounds beneath your feet?"

"*For what purpose?*" the Grand Moogle asked.

"There are materials there we want," Jamie said, his arms flapping. "Underground. We can remove them without damaging the surface you live on. In return we can provide you with a vast library of movements—whatever you want."

Moogle arms all around went into motion. After a few moments, the Grand Moogle conveyed the will of his people. "We agree with your terms." At that, living corridors appeared between the giants.

Once she was sure the way was safe, Bridget directed her troops to rush out in search of her missing teammates. "Protect Jamie," she told Dinner as she started to follow the others.

Jamie looked at her excitedly as she went past. "Full mineral rights for a song—or dance, rather. This could be huge!"

She looked back at him grimly. "Thank Abaza."

"Thank *who*?"

"That's what I figured," she said. Then she dashed between the Moogles and was gone.

3 0

Jamie had never spoken a word to Walter John Abaza before. He had seen the guy around the depot and during the Baghu incident weeks earlier, but that was it. Abaza was a second-year man, Jamie had learned: a demolitions specialist with two small children back in Cairo.

And he had been crushed to death saving Jamie from the Moogle stampede.

"I didn't know him," Jamie had said when Bridget had returned, ashen-faced, from visiting the crater that had been a man.

"He knew you," Bridget had simply said as she handed him his battered briefcase.

And she had certainly known Abaza, Jamie could tell. The others in the party who'd heard the news first had filled him in on the basic details of the man's bio, but Bridget knew everything else. He'd heard it all on the way back to the ship after he closed the deal. She'd made sure of it.

Bridget knew Abaza had enjoyed skiing, that his older daughter loved zebras, and that he visited Mecca every year. She knew he had once rappelled from the Millau Viaduct in France, that he was a seven handicap at golf, and that he had a talent for barbecuing. And she knew he had never been solely responsible for securing the life of a trader until today.

A trader that had never spoken a word to him.

Now, aboard *Indispensable* in orbit over Moog, Jamie found more than the air chilly. Bridget had seemed enthused earlier on the plain when she figured out what the Moogles wanted, but that moment felt long past, now. Abaza had been found since then. And she had helped conduct Hiro Welligan on board, a delicate process.

The man still lived but was a mess of splintered composite materials from the inside of his HardSHEL armor. He'd been fortunate, if it could be called that, to have been pummeled in a rubble-strewn region of the plain where stones absorbed part of the blows. His interior cocoon had remained sealed against the vacuum, but many of his bones had been crushed. He was also paralyzed from the waist down.

Jamie saw Welligan now, half-lucid and fighting off the sedative, safely secured and enveloped in the team's bioblanket. Every suit of armor and many articles of clothing used in space included Supralight Hygienic Environment Layers, whose microscopic nanoids infiltrated wearers' bodies to provide diagnostic information, perform minor medical tasks, and regulate temperature; Jamie wished he'd had one when he first arrived on the Dragon's Depot. The bulky bioblanket was the field medical version. Its nanoids were inside the man's body, working to stabilize his condition and repair what little internal damage they could until he could reach a hospital. One of outer space's first hit products on Earth, the coverings had already cured cancer and put old age on the defensive.

But massive trauma was something else again.

And somehow, Hiro was awake now and trying to smile behind his oxygen mask. "Jus' lemme sleep it off," the squad leader said, "an' I'll kick some Moogle ass." He looked around woozily. "Do they have asses?"

Laughter went up from the soldiers surrounding Welligan. Jamie wasn't about to go back over there. Hiro was well liked, a favorite of nearly everyone; exactly the opposite of Jamie. And if any members of Surge Team Sigma had come to value the trader's presence in recent episodes, that was all gone now. Fault was being assigned, and as always, he was first in line.

Lynn Stubek floated away from the gathering besides Welligan, both her broken arms in shrouds. She glared at Jamie. "Hiro will be all right," she said.

"I'm glad," Jamie said, meaning it.

"No thanks to you," Stubek said. She put her arms in front of him for the eleventh time. She had miraculously survived by grabbing one of the attacking Moogles' arms and executing her armor's death grip; clamped on, she had gone for a devil of a ride. The Moogle hadn't been able to shake her off, but it had slammed her around a lot.

Jamie mumbled that he hadn't done anything wrong—and that happened to be the truth. But it was also, he immediately knew, a mistake to say anything.

"You started the stampede!" Stubek said.

"That was a screw-up. We got the translation wrong!"

"Whatever. We wouldn't be out here at all if not for you."

Jamie sank back into his chair, hoping for anywhere else to go. That was a problem he had noticed with zero gee: when you were strapped in, it was tough to get out of uncomfortable conversations.

Stubek left him alone finally, but he knew it wouldn't be long until someone else took up the cause of berating him. It was natural to lash out, he understood. But there was no thought of vengeance against the Moogles: the aliens' hostility had been earned by the faulty translation.

That left only him. Him, and the Q/A. Jamie saw Lissa Trovatelli now, floating out of the small private room in the back of the passenger bangbox. It was Chief Yang's conference area—and, for this trip, the morgue. Bridget's first act on reaching orbit had been to summon the young engineer back to see what had been recovered of Abaza. Trovatelli looked white. She had been crying, Jamie realized—and arguing.

And the argument wasn't over. "How many times can I say I'm sorry?" the dark-haired woman asked, not seeming to care that the soldiers were now watching. "I didn't mean to—"

"I didn't say you *meant* to," Bridget said, following her out.

"It was an honest mistake," Trovatelli said of the translation error that had started the stampede. "It never occurred to me that Porrimans could be bottom-handed versus left-handed. Who has four hands?"

"Things out here do. If you want to make it out here, Lissa, you have to start thinking like an alien!"

Jamie had heard that one before. He unsnapped his harness and drifted in between the chief and the quartermaster. "Lay off. She's new. Why can't you cut her some slack?"

Bridget scowled at him. "I really don't think *you* want to get involved in a question of responsibility—"

"Don't give me that," Jamie said, fully between Bridget and Trovatelli now. "I thought you soldier types were all about leaving no one behind. I didn't see you running back to save Hiro, or Abaya—"

"*Abaza!*" Bridget's eyes were alight with anger.

The room went silent, apart from Hiro's labored breathing. All eyes were on them now, and Jamie found himself wishing there were nasty aliens surrounding him instead.

But Bridget closed her eyes and took a breath. "You still don't understand," she said when she finally spoke. "We're not soldiers, Jamie. We're bodyguards. *You're* the one we don't leave behind. Hiro lost sight of you back on the depot, and we nearly all paid for it. But Hiro saved you on Moog, just like Abaza did."

She looked back at Stubek, who had floated to a corner. "But not like *you* did," Bridget said to the short-haired woman. "I saw your actions, Lynn. It's in the video my helmet cam took. You were ordered to get Jamie to the ship. Instead, you let go of him to fire at the Moogles—and left Abaza to try to move him alone."

Stubek looked up, stricken. "They were attacking my squad leader!"

"And if he'd escaped thanks to you, I'd want him ripping your ass now, too," Bridget said. "You are a bodyguard. Do your damn job."

Rattled, the injured woman put her broken arms in front of her. "Nobody here signed up to go around battling walking tanks. Sturm's the only reason we're out here in this crazy place—"

"Yes. He is the only reason we're in trouble. But he's also the only reason we have a job. He's the trader. We protect the trader!"

"I don't *want* to protect him!"

"Then quit!"

Stubek seemed to shrink. Jamie's eyes goggled as Bridget floated close to the ceiling. Her hands on it, she spoke down to the seated and hovering troops like a sage from on high. "We don't get to decide where we go. We don't get to choose whether we like the trader or not. This is a business, and the business is the trader. Do you all understand?"

No one said anything. But everyone watched.

She spoke more calmly. "We have a few more weeks to this thing. I'm going to protect the trader because that's my job—and yes, I'm going to try not to lose anybody. But I can't protect everyone at once. I've got to trust that all of you want to be here—and that you know what you're doing."

"Got it, Chief," O'Herlihy said forcefully, making it clear to anyone listening that he spoke for the whole squad.

"All right." With that, Bridget looked past Jamie to the front of the cabin. "How long to the whirlibang?"

"Sixteen minutes," Madaki said.

"Hurry it up." Bridget shot a cold look to Jamie, pushed off the ceiling, and glided back to the private room. No one said anything as she passed. Nor did they say anything to Jamie when they began talking again.

Jamie watched the door as it closed. Contemplating, he understood the depth of Bridget's problem. Despite her pep talk, it was clear that a lot of Surge Sigma members clearly did *not* want to be there, and she had to know that. Some, he had seen, like Victor Gideon, were unemployable elsewhere. Others, like Stubek, must have been unable to make it with the better expeditions. Jamie had never expected nor intended to win them over, but he now wondered whether that would ever have been possible at all.

And he found himself wondering about Abaza. Bridget had known so much about him, and yet she'd allowed him to die. It didn't make sense. If you cared enough about your people to get to know them personally, how could you ever just let them die without doing anything?

Something didn't add up.

He spied Trovatelli, alone with her thoughts now, sitting with her hands folded in her lap. Seeing her needing a friend—and desperately needing one himself—Jamie floated over to where she sat. Kneeling in air, he spoke, covering his mouth. "Don't sweat it," he told her. "These military people can be jerks. I live with it every day."

"It's okay," Lissa said, dark eyes looking up at him. "I made the mistake. I owned up to it."

She looked back coldly at the doorway Bridget had gone through. "And it's not like I started an interstellar war that killed millions, you know?"

3 1

Kolvax fired his weapon and watched another alien pop like a balloon full of goo. It was wonderful how thick the Porrimans built the walls in their space stations; it had allowed him and his troops to break out the hand-cannons without fear of explosive decompression. The only explosions here were the Porrimans, nasty four-armed sacks of ooze and attitude. The Severed members among his troops had been dainty about it, fearful of getting any fluids on them. Kolvax hadn't cared. Reducing a rival species back to protoplasm was what life was all about. In the survival-of-the-fittest sense, sure—but it was also a joy.

The Stalkers were, at last, doing what they were trained to do: what their order was named for. The armored warriors were rampaging through the interstellar way station, hunting down every last Porriman. They'd mostly succeeded: their sensors were acute. Now, Kolvax suspected he might have found the last holdout.

Kolvax kicked the door open. The Porriman quivered in fear inside. From the strange fixtures, Kolvax imagined the room was some kind of toilet facility.

The Porriman seemed to blush. "Ah," he said, translated voice resounding inside Kolvax's helmet. "You were looking for me, weren't you? I'm sorry, there should have been someone at the information desk."

"Are you the director of this station?" Kolvax asked impatiently.

"Me? No," the creature said, his innards visibly wiggling within his transparent form. "I mean, yes. I was. But I retired. Stepped down, yes. Ten minutes ago, just before you arrived. I wanted to spend more time with my family. My successor has already been appointed. I'm sure she's around here some—"

"Shut up," Kolvax said. He fired his hand-cannon at close range. Colorful liquids spattered against his armored form.

He stepped out from the puddle and back into the hallway. Old Liandro approached. Armor spotless, Liandro looked at Kolvax with unease.

"What is it?" Kolvax said.

"We've...infiltrated the filthy aliens' systems, as you asked. We've gotten the information you requested."

Kolvax nodded. He needed to know everything about how commerce moved in the Signatory Systems, and how Earth was involved. The humans' knowglobe had some information, but the Porriman depot was certain to have more. "I want every surveillance system purged," he ordered.

He saw Tellmer appear behind Liandro. "What about the other thing?" Kolvax asked.

Tellmer bowed. "We found just what you were looking for, Great Kolvax. A container—a bangbox—of human construct, waiting in the warehouse area to be filled."

"Ship it back to the preserve," Kolvax said. He pointed to Liandro. "You're going to enter in the system that this container was sent away before what happened here. A good while before. Do you understand?"

Liandro nodded and turned to depart. Another figure replaced him in the hallway: Borranz, Kolvax's new least favorite person.

"Here I was thinking you were going to screw this up," Borranz said. "Congratulations." The observer sent by the Dominium, she had insisted on going along with the strike team to make sure that the operation didn't expose the Xylanx. That was just how Kolvax wanted it, though: her in his sight at all times. Left back at the Gharion Preserve, Borranz would be free to snoop around and contact her masters. Kolvax expected there were other spies in his midst, but she was the one with the official title.

"The Dominium said I could make the raid if no one found out," Kolvax said. "No one will find out."

"You should rig the station to blow up after we leave," Borranz said. "The Signatory species will investigate—"

"Let them. We leave no trace of ourselves, as always. Maybe they'll blame each other. That'd be fun." He glared at her. "Am I going to get the strategic stockpiles released to me?"

"It's an expensive request. I wish you'd explain to me what you have in mind."

"Will I get what I need?"

Borranz looked around at the mess Kolvax's team had made of the Porrimans. "I think so. You tend to get what you want, I've noticed."

"Damn right." Kolvax stood as Borranz turned away, heading up the hallway to the transit rings. He nodded to himself. It was unbelievable, given where he was in life just weeks earlier—but they would give him what he wanted. He would let Borranz watch, and report back. And by the time she—and they—realized what he had in mind, the future of the entire Orion Arm would be transformed.

"We should go now, too," Tellmer said, looking with distaste at the mess on the floor.

"Just a minute," Kolvax said. "I need to use the facilities." He jabbed a thumb at the open doorway—and the exploded Porriman within. "You think you can clean up in there a bit, first?"

He couldn't see through Tellmer's faceplate, but he could guess what his expression was.

∃ 2

"Sergeant Yang, how long have you been part of the Visitor Contact Group?"

"Four years," the young woman at the table said.

"And with a land/air regiment before that?" the senator asked from the long desks at the front of the hearing room.

"Three years with the Queen's Own Rifles of Canada. I was a master corporal when I came over," Bridget said.

"But like everyone else in the Contact Group, you have dual citizenship in your operational theater."

"Correct."

Sitting in the front row, Jamie watched his mother and tried not to smirk. He didn't know why: she couldn't see him. He was never at this historic event: he was a ghost, an electronic voyeur from the present day. But it was just like his mother to ask a question she already knew the answer to. Elaine Keeler was in her second year filling her late husband's shoes and Senate seat, and he could tell she was just getting warmed up.

"Then you are subject to our laws, Sergeant—and you were protecting your own soil," the blonde woman in her midforties said. "You accept that?"

227

"I think that's obvious," Bridget replied. "I'm here talking to you." There was some laughter from the crowd.

Bridget was in her dress uniform, Jamie saw. She cleaned up nicely. Her hair was much shorter in 2131 than it was today, to be sure. But she had the same sharp eyes that he already knew, and she was holding her ground so far against a force of nature he knew too well.

That couldn't last long, he thought.

"So, Sergeant," Senator Keeler said, "you would regard, as any American would, any incompetent act that damaged the United States as criminal? Tantamount, even, to treason?"

Bridget's adviser whispered quietly with her before she responded. "I don't think I accept your characterization, Senator—"

"There are a hundred and eighteen senators, Miss Yang. And I can assure you every one of them would resign and more, had we been culpable of an error on this scale. And yet no one—not with the Contact Group, or anyone involved in the wretched matter—seems to want to take the blame. The others have asked you before. I will ask you again. Six hundred thousand are now dead, including many of your fellow citizens. Will you now take responsibility? Or do we have to keep you here all—"

Someone knocked on Jamie's forehead. He slipped off the immerso goggles and saw Bridget standing in the Dragon's Depot kitchen before him, eight years older than she'd been in the recording he was watching. "So what am I saying now?" Bridget asked.

Jamie tensed up. "What do you mean?"

"I mean, you're not back in one of your sitcoms," she said. She yanked at the goggles.

"Hey!" Jamie said, feeling the elastic band snap against his ears as she pulled. Within seconds, Bridget was wearing the set.

"Ah," she said, cuing up the file name. "Committee on Foreign Relations, United States Senate, One Hundred Seventy-Second Congress, May 10, 2131. Hearing on Security Oversights in the Overland Disaster." She frowned. "Never seen it from this angle. It wasn't a good hair day."

Jamie looked away. "How did you know?"

Bridget switched off the goggles and removed them. "Trovatelli said you were asking about Overland. She seems to be an authority on it herself."

Sheepishly, Jamie took the goggles back. *No, I'd better not put them on again*, he thought, watching her head to the refrigeration unit.

"Sorry," he said as she leaned against the counter. She'd found a sandwich. "I've been watching a lot of stuff. This is the longest stretch I've had when we weren't running anywhere."

"I don't care what you watch," she said, starting to eat.

The pause after Xi Boötes had been necessary to make the proper arrangements to complete the Moogle deal. Directing mining operators to the planet wasn't difficult, but finding experts in dance and martial arts to send back was definitely off the menu. Through Falcone's efforts, Quaestor was grabbing anyone in the stellar neighborhood with skills to fulfill the contract. A part-time football referee would be one of the first to go in. The Moogles would soon learn a new way to express unnecessary roughness.

It had also given the Sigmas time to memorialize Abaza. The ceremony was brief and modest and while Jamie was not unwelcome, neither did he stay long. What had started back on *Indispensable* had continued. The first mission casualty had turned a grudging forbearance into a simple grudge, where many of his bodyguards were concerned. Most of them knew the kitchen he haunted and had chosen to use one of the other six in the north end.

"I'm surprised to see you here," he said.

"It's lunch," she said, disposing of the wrapping. "And I had a message for you anyway. There's a chain of 'boxes coming in right now. From Earth, via Altair. Your assayer's been updated."

"Yes!" Jamie said, reaching next to the counter for his dented briefcase. The thing had survived a Moogle stampede. He'd thought better of asking why everyone's armor wasn't made of the same stuff. He pulled out the assayer and studied a stream of numbers.

"This…this isn't good," he said.

"What?"

"Quaestor's valuations of the deals. Baghula, Leel, Moog. It's only thirty billion."

She stared at him. "You thought it'd be more?"

"It *should* be more," he said, angrily punching digits into the display. "My unit used to help do the preliminary valuations." He could see the sneering faces in the room at Ops, now. "They're screwing me!"

"Nobody knows you're here."

Jamie flipped the assayer back into the case. "We've got less than six weeks left. We're not going to make it!"

Bridget sighed. "That settles it, then. We've got to do Kano."

Jamie groaned. Kano was a world orbiting 37 Geminorum. It was farther than any place they'd yet visited: more than two hours would pass for them while they were in transit, and more than two days in real space. It was a lot of time to waste getting around. But the bigger danger was what awaited them there. Bridget had already declared she would bring all three of her teams—even decimated Surge Three—if they got the go order.

"An Oklahoma land rush against giant killer robots," Jamie said, remembering Falcone's briefing. "Joy."

"Maybe they'll want to learn to dance," Bridget said. She threw her trash away and walked out.

Jamie sat and stared at the assayer, and then back at the goggles. "I don't think it's worth it," he mumbled.

"What was that?" Bridget asked. She was back in the doorway.

"I didn't say anything," Jamie said, closing the briefcase.

"No. You said something."

He inhaled. "I said I didn't think it was worth me going. It's a long shot. I don't do long shots."

"Oh. I thought you meant something else." She turned, ready to go again.

"I don't think it's worth it for your guys, either," Jamie said. He turned and looked at her. "It's too dangerous. Risk/reward is just silly on this one."

Bridget looked back at Jamie. She nodded. "I agree."

Jamie chuckled. "That's a new one." He turned back to leaning over the counter. He put his finger inside the band of the goggles and pushed them idly around on the countertop.

Bridget stepped behind his bar stool. "What—what did you want to know?"

"What's that?" he asked, not looking up.

"About Overland," she said. "About me."

Surprised, Jamie looked back. "I guess I don't get it. How you got stuck out here when it turns out you're good at what you do."

"So it turns out." She grinned.

He paused. "And I don't get how you try to know everything about your troops—my bodyguards—but don't flinch when ordering them to do stuff that might get them killed."

"I explained that back on the ship."

"Well, I didn't get it. I change people's lives with a push of a button in my world—but I don't see them. I don't know if I could do what you do."

Bridget watched him for a moment. Then she pulled up a stool.

"You know the Visitor Contact Group was the task force that handled all alien visits to Earth."

"Before Mom and her cronies got the visits banned, yes."

Bridget nodded. "Well, I was there for the last one—and a few before that. It was a great job, working with some great people. We were doing what I do now with you, only we were escorting creatures who were seeing our world for the first time."

Jamie remembered seeing videos of the trips. High pomp—and even heavier preparation. It wouldn't have done for the alien creatures to pick up an Earthly disease, or to transmit a disease of their own.

"The last year and a half," she continued, "I had my best team ever. The best of them was a guy we called Skinner. He'd come in from Quantico, former FBI. Strong, tough—and smart. He was an operator, like you—only not. Nobody ever wanted to break his neck just on general principle."

Jamie chuckled. "Sounds like he got the world tour, too."

Bridget smirked. "Not quite. Well—not immediately." She rolled her eyes. "But yeah."

Jamie could sense the tragedy coming. "Was he at Overland?"

"We all were. The Gebran ambassador's shuttle had been scheduled to land at Lucerne. They picked Nebraska instead. They're Gebrans—go figure. It was no problem for us. We had a maglev train meet us."

"Only you didn't know it had already been hijacked by the Walled Garden crazies." Jamie knew that part of the story.

"Because there were crazies in my own ranks," she said, sounding sickened. "But I didn't know that either. I found out when the power went out on the line right at the Overland crossing. They'd been found out, and the route had been taken offline. That's when they started killing Gebran representatives in the other cars."

Jamie had seen the immerso docudrama once. He wasn't much for action shows, but he remembered some of what she was describing.

"My team and I tried to get forward," Bridget said. "We took some of the kidnappers out," she added, a little proudly. "But it came down to me—and Skinner. I'd reconnected with him, trying to get to the Gebran ambassador's compartment. He'd lost his gun somewhere. I was down to my nine," she said, patting her shoulder holster. "We had to move, though. I could hear on my headset they were talking about blowing the train up. We were out of time. But we found him—the ambassador."

"In the dining car, right?"

"That was for the immerso. He was hiding in a bathroom. Skinner found him first. And I found Skinner—with his knife already in the ambassador's gut." Bridget looked away. "The ambassador was still alive, but Skinner pulled it out and was going in for another. That's when I shot him. Twice, to the back of the head."

Jamie gawked as he put the pieces together. "Wait. Your Skinner guy—he was Lucas Baines?"

Bridget didn't say anything.

"And the two of you were an item together?" Jamie looked back at the goggles. "I never heard that part."

"Nobody knew it. I was doing a job and he was one of my squad. I didn't want word getting around—and he was fine with keeping it quiet. I should've realized that meant he had a talent for keeping things secret."

"Yeah," Jamie said. "Like the fact that he was a crazy nut job that wanted to lock off the Earth from the rest of the universe."

He looked up at her. "Sorry. I guess he was important to you, all the same."

"It's all right. You could have simply asked the obvious question: whether he was playing me."

Jamie raised his hands. "Hey, I didn't—"

"The answer is, I don't know. Obviously I had a lot of time to think about it afterward, during the investigation. And since." She looked at the wall. "I finally came to the conclusion that it didn't really matter how he got everyone's confidence. I screwed up by not realizing who he was."

"But if people had known that you and he were—"

"It'd matter to them," Bridget said, turning to face him. "It wouldn't matter to *me*. There were two conspirators in the guard unit. I was involved with one. It was my job to field a security detail that would faithfully execute its job—not the people it was protecting." She pointed to the goggles. "That's why I finally broke in that hearing, with your mother. I'd been cleared, but I wasn't innocent. I took the blame all on myself. And it was all downhill from there."

Jamie shook his head. "A lot of us down here at the bottom of the hill."

Bridget nodded. "So you see, I have to get to know all my troops well. If I don't, I could be risking a lot more than my own life—or yours. And yet I can't care what happens to them, because that's not my job. I'm here to protect you, not them."

She stood up. "That's where we're the same, actually. Your job isn't to care about them, either. If you start to, you become a less effective trader."

Jamie's shoulders sank. "I bet I'm the most effective trader you've ever seen, then."

"And that's what pisses me off about all this. I was mad at you when you came here because we weren't anybody to you. You'd ruined us with the push of a button. But the truth is, that's how you're paid to act. And that's where I envy you. Because you have the luxury to let someone whose name you've never heard of die for you. I have to know who they are. And I have to let them die."

She walked out.

Jamie pocketed the goggles and sat for several moments, thinking about what he'd heard. But his contemplation was broken by noises in the hall. Jamie slid off the bar stool and stepped out.

"There you are," Leonid Falcone said, looking as if he'd swallowed a bottle of caffeine pills. The administrator's clothing was more rumpled than usual, and he was out of breath. Bridget stood near him in the hallway, in stunned silence. Falcone reached out for Jamie. "You've got to go!"

Jamie pulled back his arms. "What? Where?"

"Kano!" Falcone said, pushing Jamie back into the kitchen.

Stumbling backward, Jamie shook his head. "The Kano event doesn't start for a couple of days! We're not even—"

"Shut up!" Spying the briefcase, Falcone slammed it into Jamie's hands.

Bridget entered the kitchen, speaking frantically into her headset. "Scramble everyone to the whirlibang, Mike!" she called out. "We're heading out!"

"Send them the back way," Falcone said, pointing at her. "They can't be seen!"

"It's thirty people!" Bridget said.

"There's thirty back ways around here!" Falcone grabbed Jamie by the collar and shoved him and his briefcase toward a side door. "Take Sturm and go!"

Bridget hustled out, pushing a befuddled Jamie ahead of her. Falcone stood in the doorway and called out after them. *"And watch out for Saint Peter!"*

33

People on Earth had many reasons to hate the Gebrans after the Arcturo-Solar War, but one was almost a point of etiquette. A human splinter group had ambushed the Gebran diplomats, yes, and killed most of the contingent. But it was also humans—Bridget in particular—who had saved the ambassador from death. Despite that, the Gebrans had retaliated anyway, starting the war. Scientists, traders, settlers—all had been targeted, from Proxima Centauri to Luyten's Star. The sheer ingratitude was galling.

Bridget didn't consider them ungrateful. She'd seen the attacks at Overland, of course, and knew how touchy the Gebrans were. She also understood, as most of Earth's strategic thinkers were now coming to accept, that the war had offered the Gebrans a chance to brush back a newcomer on the commercial scene. That move certainly hadn't worked, but Bridget understood the motive. She didn't hate the Gebrans.

But she didn't need to like them, and it was hard to when they did incredibly stupid things. Kano was a case in point. Orbiting 37 Geminorum, another star quite similar to Earth's sun, Kano was one of the Gebrans' early claims on the Orion Arm. Slightly smaller than Earth, Kano had twice the land area thanks to its lack of oceans. The Gebrans had taken a liking to the hilly world, planning to flatten it and use its entire surface to raise a particular cactus they found tasty.

The problem was that the Gebrans had automated the planetary renovation project. Factories had been landed from orbit to crank out titanic land-smashers, missile-firing ridge-blasters, clawed scour-bots, and a variety of other demolition machines. But, typically, the Gebrans had neglected an off switch. And the nuclear-powered machines—being produced in ever increasing numbers by the unmanaged factories—went on a tear, working to flatten not just Kano, but every Gebran settlement on its surface.

The Gebrans had bombed the factories out of commission, but the horde of "reshapers" remained, stomping and rolling around the globe, evading all the Gebrans' attempts to destroy them. Finally, they had given up, deciding to outsource the work—this time, to any species that wanted to assume the risk.

Thanks to Falcone giving them the bum's rush, Surge Sigma had arrived more than a day early for the Great Kano Clearing. Dozens of shelters had been set up in the start zone, and representatives from a dozen species had arrived to vie for a piece of real estate. Because for every two districts a participant cleared, the Gebrans would award a lease for one of them: it was a decent deal for a planet that had substantial resources underground.

And Kano had something else:

Air.

Unlike the races gathered under the other tents, humans could breathe here for short periods. The pressure and oxygen content were similar to what existed at five kilometers above sea level on Earth. Many wouldn't be able to acclimatize to such an environment, but neither would it mean death to open one's mask and take a breath. It was no Twin Earth, to be sure: it lacked water in significant quantities, and while its atmosphere did screen out the more harmful rays, its sun was blinding. But it felt good to Bridget to be walking about on a world with only a dark visor covering her face.

The other Sigmas were enjoying the day, too, she saw. Everyone definitely needed a break, if only this short one. O'Herlihy had the football out, unwinding with the other men and women of the team. A guy who'd climbed Everest for a joke wasn't minding the thin air. As for Gideon, he had joined the Gebran patrol responsible for keeping the start zone clear of reshapers. It was just as well, she thought: he didn't behave well at sporting events.

She hadn't seen Jamie, who had been stone silent on the trip in. They'd had a good talk earlier, but Falcone's directive as they'd left was clearly bothering him. "*Watch out for Saint Peter*"? It was hardly necessary to say that to the trader. He'd spent every second of their odyssey worrying about reaching the pearly gates—or someplace else—prematurely.

Bridget switched modes on her visor and scanned the horizon beyond the barricades the Gebrans had set up. There were the reshapers, large and small, running amok: blasting, carving, and chopping the crust of Kano again and again. Between their nuclear-power packs at night and plentiful solar power by day, the machines could well run for all eternity.

The Q/A wandered up, looking with disbelief out at the chaos. "This place is insane," Trovatelli said.

"So I've noticed," Bridget said. She changed her visor settings and smiled at the young woman. Trovatelli wore a baseball cap over her own shades. "I haven't seen you much. Been having fun?"

"Working," Trovatelli said. She looked at Bridget. "I thought you were still mad at me. The engineer had been on edge around her since the trip back from Moog.

"Everyone gets one mistake," Bridget replied. "In this outfit, six or seven. What's up?"

Trovatelli shifted from one foot to the other. "Well, I was hoping I could go back to the depot. There's supposed to be another shuttle coming in with more munitions for you."

"And miss the fun?" Bridget said, her voice barely audible over a crash from beyond the horizon.

"I want to look some more at the data we got on the Xylanx—and their connection to the Luk'a."

Bridget remembered. "You think they probably *are* the Luk'a."

"I'm not sure. But that's why I want to be at the Dragon's Depot. The Xylanx lived there for however long. There's got to be some traces of them, some DNA or something, that we missed."

Bridget nodded. "Laudable. But we've got the contact response people at the depot now, looking for exactly that. And I need you here. I'm hoping you can get us a tech solution to these monstrosities." She gestured out to the mountains of debris. "We find a way to take them all out at once and we've got the planet to ourselves."

"Not to ourselves," Trovatelli said, leering in the direction of the Gebran rule-giver. Turning back to Bridget, she saluted—unnecessarily—and traipsed off.

Bridget remembered studying Trovatelli's file earlier. Lissa had come from Giotto Colony on Luyten's Star, but she and her family had left the planet two years before the Gebrans attacked. She didn't have any ties to the people who suffered there—and while she'd shown a clear distrust of aliens while in Bridget's company, that wasn't too unusual. Anyone who'd had such a close call would be wary.

"Help!"

Bridget reached for her sidearm at the familiar cry—and then put it back in her shoulder holster when she saw Jamie dashing through the camp. Buzzing along behind him was one of the smaller reshapers, a camera stalk rising over a wide, studded cylinder. It looked as if Jamie were being pursued by an evil paint roller.

Jamie stumbled and fell. Before Bridget could intervene, Victor Gideon pounced from behind a stack of crates. Fully recovered from his exertions on Leel, he dove onto the whirling device, grabbing the vertical stalk with his bare hands. Snapping off the top module, Gideon rode the rumbling drum to a stop and began clubbing the remains with the robot's erstwhile head.

Gideon looked at Bridget and smiled toothily. "I like this place!"

On his hands and knees, Jamie panted. "I think...we've found...Victor's vacation spot."

"Which makes it nirvana for you, I'm sure," Bridget said, helping him up. She looked at Gideon and sighed. "Where was Jamie's security escort *this* time?"

"I told them to leave me alone," Jamie said, brushing himself off and adjusting his visor. He took a breath from the small oxygen tank in his backpack. "They're being jerks to me again."

"They're not supposed to leave you alone even then," she said. Who else could she chew out that she hadn't already?

Jamie looked back at the smoking ruins of the reshaper, currently being ground beneath Gideon's boots. "I don't need to be here."

"I've been hearing that a lot lately," Bridget replied. "Forget it. Quaestor was never going to play in this crazy game until you came along. You'll identify the highest-value patches for us to secure, and we'll do it for you." She crossed her arms. "I don't need to tell you how much it's not our job."

"No, I already hear that plenty," he said, looking out past the barricades.

Bridget had felt from first hearing about the event that Kano really required a professional army, as some species had sent: the odds against twenty-plus bodyguards, even in the heavy combat armor they'd brought along, winning an appreciable slice were high. But they were where they were. She would do what she could, for whatever good it did.

She looked up. "Hey, there it is," she said, pointing up at the shuttle.

Jamie gawked. "That's one of ours."

Bridget nodded. Her teams had left Sigma Draconis quickly, assembling *Indispensable* out of three crew 'boxes and a fourth for equipment. But it had always been her intent to send more munitions along. "Looks like Falcone's shipped us a goody box," she said. Her eyebrows arched as she looked. "But there's a passenger unit, too. I wonder what's up."

Jamie looked at the landing vehicle making its approach to the camp. "I've got to go," he said.

"What?" she asked. "What is it?"

Frantically, he looked around. "Which tent's ours?" Gideon pointed, and Jamie started running.

Gideon stepped up beside her. "What's going on now?"

"I'm almost afraid to ask," she said.

34

The shelter was more of a lean-to, a large fabric roof covering all the Sigmas' gear. Crouching between cases, Jamie looked quickly from label to label. As usual, he couldn't make out what anything was. A short container that he assumed held helmets instead held a boot. A single, half-million-dollar boot. He had no idea where the other one was, or who it fit.

All he knew was that he had to hide. Going back to *Indispensable* was out: he'd be found quickly there, and certainly he didn't know how to fly the thing. That left going to another species camp. He'd need more than the backpack with oxygen; he'd want a headset and public address system so he could speak other languages. When hiding in a Regulan's closet, it helped to be able to offer an explanation.

It's come to this, Jamie thought as he rummaged. Since Abaza's death, he'd felt all his chances dwindling. The impossible task was proving impossible, after all. Making a hundred billion dollars in a hundred days was a crazy, insurmountable goal from the beginning: he'd been desperate to agree to try. It was only after a couple of successes that he'd begun to think he could actually do this. But Quaestor's valuations of his deals made in the field, while astronomical, were too far short of his estimates. And he'd seen the list of planets within reach, following Kano. Unless there was a big surprise waiting, he doubted any of them had enough wealth to trade to help him close the gap.

But all of that was meaningless, now, if the shuttle held who he thought it did.

He tried to open another massive container, only to send it tumbling off the pile. The weighty 'box slammed to the ground. Jamie stumbled backward to protect his feet from being crushed.

"Freeze!" someone said from the end of the aisle.

Jamie looked back to see Trovatelli standing like a guard squaring off against an intruder, holding something aimed at him.

"Don't shoot," Jamie said, picking himself up. "It's me!"

"It's just an atmosphere tester," Trovatelli said. She lifted her visor, as the sun-filter was unnecessary beneath the shelter. The Q/A approached him. "What's going on? What are you doing here?"

"Get down," Jamie said, sliding down beneath the stack of containers. The dark-haired woman did as he said, though her expression was quizzical. In the shadows, he looked urgently at her. "I need your help, Trovatelli."

"Lissa," she said, smiling gently. "What can I do?"

"I've got to get out of here."

Her brow furrowed. "What's going on? Did the Gebrans do something?"

"I haven't even seen one," he said, shaking his head. "It's something else."

"What?"

"I didn't tell Bridget and Falcone everything."

"About your big scheme? The one that went wrong?"

"Sort of. Connected to it. It affects what happens to me if I go home. I think my problem has followed me here."

Lissa stood partway up. There were voices outside. Jamie started to scramble. "I can't let them see me!"

"Wait," she said, finding the case that Jamie had dislodged and opening it. "Hang on!"

* * *

The man had brought his own dark glasses to Kano. They matched his elegantly tailored black suit and neatly trimmed hair. A tanned hand reached out for a handshake.

"I saw you all coming in," Bridget said, noticing the man's firm grip. "Do you want an oxygen unit?"

"I've lived in the Andes," the visitor said in an authoritative voice. "But my associates might want something."

Jamie stood sheepishly to one side, looking through the faceplate of the helmet Trovatelli had found for him. There were five newcomers in all: all as officious looking as their leader. As Bridget vanished to look for oxygen packs, the athletic man noticed Jamie standing in the combat armor.

The man smirked. "What are you supposed to be?" he asked.

"What do I look like?" Jamie said, glad his voice was being filtered through the public address system. Trovatelli had given him a rifle and set the faceplate to opaque, so Jamie looked like any other armored sentry.

Well, any other terrified armored sentry.

"The trader has a team of bodyguards," the visitor's older female companion said.

"He'll need them." The newcomer turned to see Bridget approach with the gear.

"Here you go," Bridget said, passing the items out. "I'm sorry. I didn't catch your names earlier."

"I'm Peter Santos," he said. "Special investigator for the US Securities and Exchange Commission." He looked around. "I'm looking for a trader named Jamison Sturm."

"*Saint Peter,*" Jamie whispered inside his helmet, remembering the nickname he'd learned on the trading floor. And whispers were about the only way he'd heard the name. The traders at Ops were millions of miles away from Earth—and they quaked at the thought of the crusading policeman of interstellar finance.

Santos introduced his companions. "This is Theda Dalrymple, of the Commodities Futures Trading Commission. And these gentlemen are United States marshals. We have a warrant for the arrest of Mr. Sturm."

Jamie dropped his rifle. It clattered against the compacted dirt floor, and Jamie fumbled for it. Bridget, noticing him for the first time, stepped over to pick up the weapon. Lifting it, she looked him over.

She rolled her eyes—and in an instant, Jamie knew she'd recognized him. She stared into his faceplate as she asked Santos a question. "What did he—I mean, what did this guy do?"

"Possible violations of SEC Rule 10b-5," the agent said. "We're concerned by a large number of irregular trades he executed."

"Trades—on Altair?" Bridget asked, still staring at Jamie. "I didn't know your jurisdiction went so far."

"It extends as far as the United States wants it to go, Miss Yang." Santos reached into his vest pocket and produced a small isopanel. "But, no. The trades in question took place on Earth."

"*Earth?*" Bridget turned.

Santos handed the electronic ledger to Bridget. Her eyes scanned across the information. "As you can see," Santos said, studying everything as he walked around the tent, "Mr. Sturm made efforts through a large number of margin accounts to short the world's rhodium markets. It's as if he was expecting a large shipment to arrive from space, to destabilize the price."

"Expeditions do that as a matter of course," Bridget said. "Quaestor has traders who do exactly that." She hastened to add: "Or so I've heard."

"That's true. But everyone on the Venus bourse has equal access to information about what's being shipped in from deep space. Mr. Sturm in this matter was not trading for the company but for himself, based on information no one else on the trading floor seemed to have. Not even his own firm." Santos clasped his hands together. "We're suspicious."

Jamie gulped. It was the thing he hadn't told Falcone about. He'd planned to sell the forty billion dollars in rhodium he was shipping back from Altair, yes. But he'd also placed a number of smaller bets on the side, using his own money—and that of some others—to hedge against what his own shipment would do to the markets.

It was a vainglorious attempt to tack on a little extra to what was already going to be an enormous score. Now, the rhodium no longer existed, having been eaten by the Spore. But his contracts were still out there and must have come due. He wondered if Bridget understood what he had done.

He soon found out. Santos took the ledger back from Bridget. "Administrator Falcone told us—eventually—that Sturm arrived here with you." He looked keenly at her. "Can we count on your cooperation?"

Bridget glared in Jamie's direction. "As far as I'm concerned," she said, "if you find him, you can have him!"

EPISODE 6:

TENDER OFFER

3 5

Once the immerso age of entertainment began, an action game finally passed the test of being indistinguishable from the reality it was trying to simulate. But virtual bloodbaths like *Hell's Hunter 15* had never interested Jamie Sturm, who sought simpler pleasures bankrupting opponents in classics like *Slumlord: The Next Generation*.

Now, with an alien scour-bot rumbling across Kano toward him, Jamie found himself wishing he'd played more than the demo for *HH15*. It would've helped. The game's programmers had been invited to design the interfaces for the first human HardSHEL battlesuits: any gamer would've found the combat armor a cinch to control. Jamie couldn't even figure out how to fire the gun—a gun he, as a trader, wasn't supposed to have.

But he didn't have any choice. He'd been pretending to be one of his own bodyguards for days, trying to avoid being arrested by Agent Santos back in camp. Since the Great Kano Clearing began, most of Kano had become a battlefield: it was only a matter of time before he found himself crouched behind the remains of a ruined wall, trying to figure out how to defend himself.

The rifle in his gloved hands wasn't doing anything. Not when he pulled the trigger, nor when he gave the verbal command. That hadn't stopped him from trying as the scour-bot advanced. "Shoot it! Shoot it!"

"Shooting not authorized," the computerized voice in his ear said.

"Dammit!"

"Damning not authorized."

He looked up to see the scour-bot just meters away, backlit by Kano's bright morning sun. A bizarre metal crustacean the size of a double garage, the robot ripped up the ground beneath it with a dozen spiral rotors. How many monstrosities did it take to turn a once-mountainous world into a perfectly flat plain? Jamie didn't want to know. He just knew the scour-bot had ground half the onetime Gebran settlement into rubble and that now it was heading straight for him.

Jamie fled back into the ruins. A single door frame still stood in what had been the rear wall of the hut. The trader was to the doorway when the scour-bot reached the spot he'd been using for cover. The floor quaked beneath his boots, and Jamie stumbled forward. He fell clear from the building, landing flat on the surface of Kano. Behind him, the shattered building disappeared, overrun by the mad machine. Claws and gears tore at the structure, pulverizing it.

Jamie heard but didn't see it. Getting back to his feet, he clutched the rifle and ran without looking back. At least the suit moved when he did. The armor had been Hiro Welligan's; there had been no time for the team to remove the injured man's gear from the shuttle before the trip to Kano. He and Hiro were about the same size. He was glad he hadn't tried to hide in an outfit belonging to Arbutus Dinner.

The mindless devices were everywhere. Raising hell off to the left were the ridge-blasters. The tracked vehicles, designed to level hills, were targeting the tallest things they could find in the area. Far to Jamie's right lumbered the land-smashers, stomping around on their six hexagonal pile-driver feet. Jamie felt as if he'd wandered into a planet-sized demolition yard.

And here and there he saw people trying to stop the devices. Not people as he understood the term; the members of Surge Sigma were out there, of course, but he hadn't seen them lately. No, the combatants he could see were aliens, members of other Signatory species vying for cheap land in exchange for their help in the Great Kano Clearing. He recognized a quartet of giant rolling wheels—Sheoruk, as he'd seen on Baghula—circling a land-smasher, pummeling it with rockets. Evidently the Sheoruk weren't all as peaceful as Lorraine, Jamie realized. There were armored members of at least three other species in the field, all engaged in the same mission.

Most of the reshapers seemed to have little notion that the combatants were there: the machines simply treated the aliens they encountered as one more obstacle to be leveled. The main exceptions were the robo-hunters—or as Jamie thought of them, the Derricks of Death. The towers galloped horselike on long metal legs, spitting chemical fire from some kind of tub mounted high above. Jamie had heard the Gebrans had originally deployed the robo-hunters to exterminate all the local wildlife on Kano. *True princes, the Gebrans.*

At the moment, the robo-hunters were fighting a rearguard action, belching blazing streams at the contestants attacking the demolition machines. It was a confused mess. *The* Hell's Hunter *designers could find inspiration for their next hit here,* Jamie thought. They could have it. He found a hiding spot behind the smoking corpse of a land-smasher.

He lifted the rifle again and carefully peered back at the robo-hunter blocking his way to camp. He'd seen other fighters destroy the machines with a single well-placed shot to their upper regions; the robo-hunters' designers weren't expecting the wildlife to fight back. As he looked, the targeting system inside his helmet activated, as it had earlier. His armor's systems projected glowing blue crosshairs on the inside of Jamie's faceplate, superimposed over the distant target.

And once again, the rifle—which his armor said was fully operational—was a dead weight in his hands.

"Come on! Let me fire! You know you want to!" He pounded the butt of the weapon against the body of the dead land-smasher and swore. "Do it!"

"Command not understood."

"*You* don't understand, you stupid machine!" Jamie said. "I'm in trouble! *You're* in trouble!"

"Urine trouble acknowledged," the system chirped. "Deploying catheter."

Jamie jumped in the air and squealed as he felt a small mechanical arm from his armor's interior fishing rudely inside his shorts. "Jesus, no!" He dropped the rifle and clawed at his groin. "Stop! Halt! Cease! Desist!"

"Process suspended."

"I should say so!" Jamie gasped for breath. "What the hell is wrong with—"

Before Jamie could finish, the world around him started to move. It was at this moment that he understood that the land-smasher—which towered above him, even fallen—was merely dazed. Enormous pistons activated, bringing the metal monster woozily back to its full height.

"*Gah!*" Jamie yelled. He scrambled to get clear as the thing began tromping in place, shaking off whatever had happened to it. The land-smasher was bigger than a Moog, with twice the number of legs, and industrial presses for feet.

Jamie had no interest in being anywhere near it.

But the act of moving brought him into the view of the robo-hunter he'd been targeting—which Jamie learned as the machine began targeting *him*. The cannon mounted high on the walking tower flashed, and a blaze of fire erupted from it. There was no escaping the high-pressure chemical stream. Bathed by a hydrant from hell, Jamie writhed like one aflame. He wasn't on fire—and his armor wasn't, either—but the alarms screaming in his ear told him it was just a matter of time.

Instinctively, he dropped, intending to roll. But the move deposited the still-blazing-hot trader directly between the stomping feet of the land-smasher. Jangling proximity alarms joined the din—and so did Jamie.

"*Help!*"

At once Jamie felt his body go stiff. As on Moog, he felt his suit's internal armature engage, whipping his body back and forth, fishlike, between the crushing footfalls of the land-smasher. A second later, the bright sky outside returned—and Jamie found himself lying faceup and smoking in a trail of rubble in the contraption's wake. Miraculously, it seemed to Jamie, it had walked right over him.

Control of his motions returned to him. Jamie sat up. The land-smasher had moved away and was now tromping toward the robo-hunter. The two machines would not intentionally collide, Jamie had been told—they were at least *that* smart—but something was forcing the issue.

Or someone:

Bridget!

With solar filters set on high, he couldn't see her well—but as he knelt, the Surge Sigma leader's ID appeared in his helmet, superimposed over her silhouette. Somehow, while Jamie was literally underfoot with the land-smasher, she had grabbed on to one of the robo-hunter's big legs and was riding along with it, firing one round after another into its hip joints. One finally gave way. Bridget leapt free as the 'hunter tipped over—its lofty drum of infernal liquid slamming squarely onto the passing land-smasher. Another flash trumped anything Jamie's filters could handle, and the shockwave that followed sent him somersaulting.

Recovering, Jamie looked out to see the land-smasher kaput for real this time—its massive form blown in half by the force of the explosion. He couldn't see any sign of the robo-hunter at all. Or the woman who had been its temporary passenger.

"Bridgie!" he yelled, struggling to get to his feet.

"Present," Bridget said. He turned to see her standing behind him. "Welcome to the battlefield." She was holding her weapon—and another: his, recovered from the ground nearby. "It's a good thing you're not really one of my troopers. I'd bust you for losing your rifle."

Jamie looked at her. "I guess it's a good thing I'm the trader instead. You're obligated to protect me this way."

"I am?" She gestured to his chest. "I don't see a badge on there."

Jamie looked down, suddenly feeling naked without the garish symbol.

"Forget it," Bridget said, passing him the rifle. "This way!"

36

Bridget led Jamie to a shady spot behind another battered building. The fighting had moved away, as her troops and those of other species chased the reshapers into the distance. Able to see her face, Jamie asked, "Did you take control of my armor earlier? To keep me from getting crushed?"

"Not this time. You're in the regular-gravity suit. The system will reflexively respond to a threat if it sees you're not responding yourself. But you can't always count on it—as you found back on Moog."

She did not mention Abaza and Welligan. He was glad. "But what's with this?" he said, raising the rifle. "I can't fire the damn thing!"

"Watch where you point that," Bridget said.

"What difference does it make? I told you, I can't fire it!"

Bridget nodded. "You're not authorized to fire it." She took the rifle from him. "You're in Hiro Welligan's armor. Trovatelli may have fixed it so you could wear and operate the suit, but the rifle's another matter."

Jamie blinked. "I can't believe she'd have forgotten that!"

"Lissa was just looking to hide you from Agent Santos," Bridget said, fiddling with a control on the rifle. "She probably didn't think you'd go into battle."

"Neither did I!"

"Then what are you doing out here?" In the shade, he could see her glaring at him.

Jamie shrugged. "Saint Peter—I mean, Santos—kept nosing around the camp, looking for me. He can't tell who I am in this suit, but I can't keep being the only soldier you leave behind. I took the rifle as a prop. And it was about as useful," he said ruefully.

"Then you need to hide somewhere."

"I was trying to! Those monsters ate my hidey-hole!"

"Sounds painful." Bridget finished making her adjustments on the weapon. "There. I've authorized you to use it." She passed the rifle back to him. "Congratulations, Jamie. You're now in violation of the Signatory Pact, in addition to all the other laws you've broken."

Jamie slung his rifle and sighed. Bridget had been riding his ass ever since Santos arrived. "Look, I told you I was sorry—"

Bridget laughed derisively. "Another apology for the collection!" She started counting on her fingers. "You were sorry when you defrauded the expedition. Sorry when you got my barracks eaten by the Spore. Sorry when you nearly got us all fired. Sorry when you dragged us out on a crazy hunt for a hundred billion dollars. Sorry when not everyone survived. And sorry that your mother ruined my life."

Jamie's brow furrowed. "Hey, I'm not responsible for that!"

"Something you're not responsible for—that's a first!" She raised her hands to the heavens, theatrically. "But you made up for that. A forty-billion dollar profit from your scheme wasn't enough. You had enormous side bets on the rhodium market! Isn't anything enough for you?"

"It wasn't that big a deal," Jamie said. He corrected himself. "It wasn't *as* big a deal. I was just covering my bases, if I didn't earn what I thought I would from the 'box from Altair."

"It's insider trading!"

"That's debatable."

"Santos says so!"

Jamie waved his arms. "Santos is a hack from an executive branch that hates my mother. Why else would he chase me out here? He's out to get me!"

Bridget shook her head. "He doesn't seem like that kind of person to me."

"Well, we know what kind of a judge of character you are when it comes to—"

Bridget froze. "Watch it, Jamie," she said coolly.

Too late, Jamie realized what he'd said. "No, no," he said, stepping backward. "I just meant when it comes to political types like my mother."

"I know what you meant. And you do, too." She looked at him for a moment and then away. Her arms sagged. "I don't know why I even try," she said to no one in particular. "Impossible man."

Jamie found a remnant of wall and slouched against it. "Look, I didn't mean it. I'm just tired. Tired of all the running around—tired of the Surge Three people snarling at me…"

"You're pretending to be their injured squad leader."

"I didn't choose the suit," Jamie said, gesturing to Welligan's name imprinted on his shoulder guard.

Bridget turned away. "Well, I didn't choose any of this." She began to walk off, before pausing.

"What is it?" Jamie asked.

"I'm getting a call." Jamie watched her as she listened for several seconds to something in her earpiece. At last she looked back. "Well, we're a little closer. The Gebran Clearing Command says we get credit for securing this district with those kills back there. We get half the territory."

The trader stepped out from the shelter and looked up. After his filter activated, he could just make out the Gebran vessels descending from orbit with the pulse generators. Positioned along the district's perimeter, they would discourage—though not entirely prevent—any further reshapers from entering the area. The menaces would be corralled into a smaller region now.

"What district is this?" he asked.

"Two Eleven."

"That's good," Jamie said. He'd kept a mental estimate of what each parcel was worth. "If your other teams keep clearing at this rate, we might reach twenty billion dollars on this trip."

"Which only gets us halfway to the goal," Bridget said, indifferent.

"Unless they open up District Two Eighty," Jamie said, still figuring. "That's the big one." The vast low-lying parcel was the territory most desired by humanity, for its more substantial air pressure and resources underground. But it was also the land that had been most heavily settled by the Gebran colonists, and therefore the most heavily infested with reshapers run amuck. "That could be a ten-billion-dollar score all on its own."

"Which still doesn't get us there," Bridget said. "We've got less than a month left."

Jamie sagged. "Are you giving up?"

Bridget stared at him. "No. But I'm no longer sure you're worth helping." Obviously tired, she pointed to the west. "Surge Three is coming back to escort you to Staging Area Bravo. You'll come back to camp with them on the hovercraft. Stick with them this time, and try not to get hurt."

"Where are you going?" he asked.

"I have to collect your money—from people who hate my guts." She walked away into the blinding noon light.

✳ ✳ ✳

The Gebran's head was an oval festooned with a hundred orange eyeballs. That, plus the sloping, vaselike curve of his midsection made him look a bit like a tulip bloom in a two-meter-tall vase.

The first humans to encounter a Gebran had reacted with that unthreatening image in mind. Of course, it had only taken one conversation to realize just how far from flowery the Gebrans were. There was no race in the Signatory Systems more incendiary—or more aggravating. Bridget knew that only too well.

"I can't believe I have to do this," Fieldmaster Wo-grump said. Several long, leaflike tendrils from his carapace curled up in front of his eye-cluster in an expression of disgust—or so Bridget interpreted it. The grating voice came from a translator device worn around his neck. There was no way to turn it down. "The stink," he cried. "I can't handle the stink!"

"I'm wearing armor," Bridget said as the creature slithered into Surge Sigma's tent. "And you don't have a nose."

"*Silence!*" Wo-grump screeched, rising to his full towering height. Gebrans moved around on six large, curled tendrils. They could reach three meters by standing on tippy-tentacles when irritated, which was often. "I know who you are, Bridget-yang. And I am offended—*offended!*—that your people would send *you* here—here to *our* planet!"

Bridget simply stared, annoyed with herself for removing her helmet. At least she could have controlled the decibels that way.

"But then what should I expect?" Wo-grump asked, shortening himself and gesturing to the others in the shelter. "You live to insult us. You love to insult us. You want a piece of this planet, do you? Well, I'll tell you what you deserve, human. *War!*"

Bridget glanced back at Peter Santos, who was lingering nearby. He seemed startled by the plant-thing's declaration. "Don't worry," she said. "This is just their way of saying hello."

Santos nodded and smiled politely while Wo-grump ranted on. The investigator had removed his glasses, revealing his watchful brown eyes—and had donned a flight jacket with a US government seal on the front. Bridget knew Santos was still hunting—in vain, so far—for any trace of Jamie, but she also knew the agent had taken an interest in the proceedings on Kano. There was an enormous amount of money pumping into Earth's economy and that of the United States from outer space. Here, Santos had a chance to see interstellar commerce up close—not to mention what Earth's envoys had to deal with.

He had a nice smile, she thought. He was certainly more polite than another recent arrival from the Solar System she could name. And he definitely beat the newest visitor to their tent. Wo-grump was quivering with rage and overflowing with invective.

"…you certainly deserve war, death, and destruction," the Gebran railed. "You deserve to have your cells ruptured, your genetic material corrupted, and your breathing sacs inflated to bursting! I, for one, would love to be the agent of your demise!" His frond-arms shook with fury…

…and then went limp. "However, I have an office to perform," he said grudgingly. "I have been dispatched to this disgusting pit of filth to carry out a most heinous act. Something that fills my petioles with ichor. Something that makes me wish my ancestors had died screaming in agony before continuing the line. An act so dire that…"

Bridget mentally tuned out the next section. Human know-globes had nailed the Gebran character right from the first meeting. Almost all Gebrans' voices were translated into the shrill screeches of Paymer Bosch, a 2050s-era shock comic popular with the mostly deaf. Bosch's abuse of his vocal cords had eventually destroyed them; there had been a movement by a thankful British people to award a knighthood to the doctor who performed the laryngectomy. The reproduced voice was far from pleasant to listen to now, but anything more tolerable simply didn't seem right for the aliens—and the Gebrans had embraced the choice themselves, using it in their own devices. *Horrible things should sound horrible*, Bridget thought.

"...and so," Wo-grump continued, "bound by some utterly foolish rules clearly devised by someone too stupid to be allowed to reproduce, I must award fifty percent—*and no more!*—of District Two Eleven to the representatives of..." The Gebran looked down at her. "What do you things call yourselves, again?"

Bridget rolled her eyes. "We're the Quaestor expedition, from Earth."

"Aha! Earth! Earth, where your scurrilous cowards murdered our delegation. Earth, which we defeated so soundly in response!"

Behind Santos, O'Herlihy looked up from his lunch. "That's not how it went, partner."

Bridget winced at the interruption—with good reason. "*Heresy!*" the Gebran screeched. Wo-grump began chattering, speaking almost too quickly to be understood. The listeners caught a phrase here and there about humanity's wretchedness and inferiority at combat.

Bridget glowered at O'Herlihy. "Now you've done it." She looked at Santos and rolled her eyes. "This should take about an hour," she said.

Santos merely smirked. He clasped his hands, sat down, and settled in for the Gebran's version of history. Bridget imagined as a law enforcement agent he'd heard his share of tall tales before. The poor man hadn't heard anything yet.

37

Six hours later, Santos stood in the opening of the tent with Bridget and watched Fieldmaster Wo-grump slither back to his hovercraft. The creature continued to swear the whole way.

"I've heard some crazy stories before in my line of work," Santos said as the Gebran puttered off, "but that one's a marvel. It's one long delusion. It's as if they're not even aware they lost the war."

"They're not," Bridget said. "That was the beauty of the peace deal the Signatory powers brokered. Call it face-saving for people with no faces."

He shook his head. "I'm amazed a deal could be made at all."

"That's just your first encounter," Bridget said. "Wait until you deal with them as often as I have. The Gebrans think they were the first sentient species of the universe, and that all the rest of us evolved from the mites and other pests that infest them. We're nothing but parasites to them."

"I thought plants needed insects for pollination and such."

"They're not plants, really," she said. "Is 'incorrigible' a species?"

Santos laughed. 37 Geminorum was setting now, and he could step outside without his dark glasses. He inhaled deeply.

"A new world," he said. He looked to the horizon admiringly. "Despite the craziness, it's a nice place. It's like the Atacama."

Bridget walked up beside him. "I was thinking the same thing. The sun's too bright here in the day, and it's too cold out at night. But if humans could live here only at twilight, the place would be perfect."

"It'll still be a popular destination," Santos said, "regardless. Everywhere else we've found in space, exposure to the outside is catastrophic. Companies will shave millions off anything they do here."

She laughed. "I forget I'm dealing with a money guy."

"I just arrest the money guys," he said, smiling. He was about to say something else when something to the left caught his eye. "What's that over there?"

"The returning heroes," she said. With the competition called on account of darkness—the reshapers tended not to expand into new areas in the dark—the other members of Surge Sigma approached. She already knew everyone had made it. Gideon's squad had taken three tracts today, with the man nearly giddy at the many opportunities for action that surrounded him; she needed to remember to give his teammates extra rest.

And there, in the rear, was the remaining Surge Three team returning from Staging Area Bravo. They were leading the dark-helmeted Jamie—and if he wanted to avoid calling attention to himself, he was failing miserably.

"Shut it off," he said amid laughter from the other troopers. "Help me shut it off!" His arms were a mechanical blur, his hands violently jabbing this way and that.

Santos squinted. "What's going on with your trooper there? He looks like a traffic cop on devil dust."

"I haven't got the slightest idea," she said. "Excuse me."

She stepped across the dirt into the crowd of bodyguards. Two of them were doubled over from laughing so hard. Jamie was helpless in their midst, his arms flapping like the wings of a metal bird.

"What's going on?" she asked him.

"Don't make me say anything," Jamie pleaded, as his limbs went into overdrive.

Bridget sighted. Behind her, she could see the members of Surge One were emerging from the tent to join the fun. "All right, who did this?"

Several could barely stifle their laughter in their chief's presence. No one confessed.

"I don't get it," Jamie said. "It's like I'm talking to the Moogles again, and the armor's moving me!"

"That's because you've activated the sign-language subroutine," she said. Since the team had gone to Moog, the knowglobe had added the language capability to all their armors. Not that they needed it here. "Didn't you get someone to help you?"

"I did. But it got worse—and no one will help now!"

Bridget stepped up and opened a hidden flap on Jamie's breastplate. She studied the display. "Well, I see someone did try to help you once, because they locked the program in and set it for high-data transfer. It's translating into Moogle sign language all the words you're saying—and also the constitution of every nation on Earth. It looks like you're up to Senegambia." She deactivated the subroutine and shot an acidic look to her comrades. "Very funny."

Jamie sagged. Bridget walked around him, kicking at the other troopers. "Get out of here. You don't have anything better to do after fighting all day?" She turned her glare on Victor Gideon. "And you didn't stop this?"

Gideon looked down at her and scowled. "Not a lot of folks like him pretending to be one of us."

"Least of all, pretending to be Hiro," Lynn Stubek said.

Bridget knew. Her teammates' treatment of Jamie had been getting worse. "Go eat. And nothing to the cops," she said, sneaking a look back at Santos. He was still outside the tent, watching with interest.

Bridget spotted Trovatelli walking some equipment past. She got the Q/A's attention with a wave and pointed Jamie toward her. "Go with her," Bridget said. "And try to stay out of trouble."

Wearily, Jamie wandered toward the engineer.

Bridget turned and walked back to Santos, who lingered even as the other troops went past him into the tent to dine. "Rookie problems," she said.

Santos looked at a glowing name on his exposed palm. "That's odd," he said, reading from the EndoSys display. "I thought that guy was Hiro Welligan, one of your squad leaders."

"Er—yes," Bridget said nervously. "His problems are with the rookies. He likes to clown around like that, and I think he's setting a bad example for them." She pursed her lips and looked away. *Another smooth recovery like that,* she thought, *and Jamie will be doing a perp walk from the whirlibang.*

She looked back to Santos—only to see two of his oxygen-masked investigators approaching him. "No sign of Sturm at the other camps," she heard one of them say.

"Keep at it," Santos said. "He's here." The officers walked past into the tent.

The treasury agent looked at the setting sun and then back at her. "You know," he said, "I was hoping we'd have your cooperation." He removed a pair of leather gloves from his suit pocket and put them on. "I'm well aware of who you are, Miss Yang."

She was sure he was. Who wasn't? She shrugged.

He looked keenly at her and continued. "If I might say, I think you got a raw deal in your hearing. My office has definitely had its share of run-ins with Congress. There are a few people who care about justice there, but more who simply care about scoring political points." He clasped his hands behind his back and looked to the sunset. "I think you're someone who cares about integrity."

Bridget was startled by the expression. "Er—thanks."

"And that's why I'm not asking you to give up a friend, or one of your troops, even now. You have your mission; I have mine. But I will suggest this to you. If you do know where Jamie is, you can tell him things will go a lot easier on him if he'll come and talk with us."

"Surrender, you mean."

He looked back at her and smiled gently. "I don't like to put it like that. But he can only help himself."

She looked at him, puzzled. "Are you...aware of who Jamie's mother is?"

"Senator Keeler?" He nodded. "Their connection is hardly popular knowledge, and after what I've learned about Jamie Sturm, I can understand why she'd want to keep it that way. It doesn't look like they've spoken in years. But their link means nothing to me, Miss Yang. We still have a separation of powers in the United States, and I have a job to do."

Bridget marveled. No wonder they called him Saint Peter. She chuckled. "Have you ever fought in a suit of armor?"

"Excuse me?"

"Never mind," she said. "And call me Bridget."

✳ ✳ ✳

Jamie sat slumped in the darkness at the foot of a tall stack of 'boxes. It wasn't Surge Sigma's tent but one belonging to a

Regulan team; Trovatelli had thought it best for him to hide here. He could slip in and out underneath the unsecured canvas, and there was enough of a gap between the crates for two people to hide. The cops had already checked the location once during the daylight, she said.

The place had provided Jamie with his only opportunity to remove his helmet in days. Here, and the latrine his teammates had set up—but he sure wasn't going to remove his helmet there. Whatever was wrong with Victor Gideon's body, it had extended to his digestive tract.

He sat in a stupor for several minutes before Lissa slipped lithely beneath the canvas to join him. She was in a parka, he saw; she had brought him a warm drink. He took it gratefully.

Lissa sat on the floor beside him. She looked up at him cautiously as he downed it all. "Are you going to be all right?"

He looked at her weakly as he put down the cup. "I only want to die every other minute. I'll be okay."

"I don't know about that," she said, looking in the dim light at his armor. "How long can you stay in that thing?"

"Until Santos leaves, or we do," Jamie said. He shook his head wearily. "I can't believe he hasn't left yet."

"He's not going to," she said. The Q/A looked away. "I heard him. He's staying until he finds you—or until we leave."

"That's what I was afraid of." Jamie sighed. His goose was cooked.

She looked back at him. "I can't believe *you're* still here, to be honest."

"Huh?"

Trovatelli huddled closer to his armored form. "This crazy contest. Everything you've been doing. Baghula, Leel, Moog…"

"I remember," he said. "I've been trying to forget."

"But that's just it. You don't really think this is the best thing, do you? Turning over rocks all over the galaxy, looking for spare change?"

Jamie laughed. "You forget who you're dealing with. I'd eat my briefcase whole if it got me home."

"Then why don't you leave?" Lissa said.

Jamie blinked—and looked directly into two of the warmest brown eyes he could remember seeing. "I can't just leave," he said at last. "I don't know how to fly a shuttle."

Lissa pulled herself closer. "I do," she said, looking around. "I know how to activate the whirlibangs. Here—and at Altair. It's two hops and home. And there are shuttles all over the place here," she said. "We have one. The Feds came in one—though it left the other day. I think they just moved it. The other teams—"

"Slow down," Jamie said. "I've thought about going home. Believe me. But I can't just go. It's more complicated than that."

"You think you owe these people something?"

"They think I owe them something. A hundred billion some-things!" Jamie chuckled deliriously. "Well, not quite that much now. But we're still at least fifty billion short."

"But you weren't caring about that before," Lissa said, "when you were playing with their money. You knew this expedition was already on the ropes. Quaestor was going to pull their franchise regardless. They were already going to be broken up and sent wherever. If you go now, you'll just let that happen naturally." She paused. "And you can do it before you discover even worse trouble someplace."

"We've already found that," Jamie said.

"I'm serious. There's *always* something worse out here. Something that could follow us back to Earth," she said. "Like your Xylanx."

"Look, even if you taught me how to escape, I'd never remember—"

"I'd go with you, silly."

He stared at her. "You're serious."

She nodded.

Jamie broke her gaze and shook his head. "You make sense for me—but you don't make sense for you. You've got a career here."

"That won't last much longer. I just told you that."

"But I won't last much longer either," he said. "You can still get another job. I'm in debt—and probably a fugitive. You don't have any reason to tie yourself to—"

She interrupted him with a kiss. It went on for twenty seconds, and for five of them all Jamie could think about was that while it was a hell of a long way to travel to find romance, Lissa Trovatelli might just be worth it.

"Huh," he said when she pulled away.

"That wasn't the response I was expecting," she said, an eyebrow raised.

"Sorry, just processing new information," he said, looking into her smiling eyes. "It's not like patching into a knowglobe."

"We'll go," she said. "You're smart. I'm smart. We'll go. We'll find a way back to Earth and start normal lives again. It'll be good, I promise. I'm very fond of you, Jamie. I think you've gotten a raw deal."

"No, I'm just…" Jamie stopped.

She pulled him close again. "Don't take too much time. I just heard they're doing District Two Eighty tomorrow."

"That's the best one!"

"That's the *last* one. The other teams had a field day today. The Kano Clearing ends tomorrow—and then we'll have to go. All of us."

"I'll never get past Santos. I'll have to take off this outfit when I board the shuttle, and he'll be standing in the door." Jamie fretted. "If I stay until the end, I'm going to prison."

She kissed him again. "Or we can get out of here. During the battle tomorrow—it'll be the perfect time. No one will be watching the shuttles."

"I'll think about it," Jamie said.

"Don't take too much time," she repeated, before ducking back out into the night.

Jamie thought about it.

38

Jamie looked up at the morning Kano sky. With the filter in place, there wasn't much to it. But it didn't hurt his neck quite so badly to look up.

He'd slept with the helmet on all the previous nights, just in case Santos or one of his investigators stumbled over him. With Trovatelli's help, he had figured out how to adjust the suit to induce sleep—but it was a horrible, wretched sleep, and he always awoke feeling like his spine could snap like a pretzel at any moment. He didn't know what was different today. Except, perhaps, that it was the last day, for better or worse...

...and then, of course, there was Lissa. He didn't think of her as Trovatelli the Tech anymore. She'd always been the least abusive to him, and they both had suffered the ire of the grunts. It still didn't make sense to him that she was getting interested while he was on the decline, but at the moment he'd take any solace he could find.

Because as good as he felt now, he knew the day was going to be a nightmare. Even Trovatelli's crazy idea to escape together depended, she'd said that morning, on using the chaos of battle for a distraction. Whether he stayed or left, he had to go through the motions.

The whole camp had been dismantled and taken to the final staging area on hovercraft. Madaki had relocated *Indispensable* to the busy parking area nearby; Jamie didn't know where the Feds' shuttle was. There would be no hiding from Santos today. He knew Two Eighty was the biggest prize on the board, and he was expecting to see the entire Sigma detachment ready to head out—"Hiro Welligan" included. He could tell that the agent had ordered his people to keep a close eye on him. And if they had not yet ordered him to unmask—he wondered if they lacked the authority somehow—he would not be able to keep up the masquerade much longer.

Danger loomed nearby—and depression lay ahead. A topographical one. District 280 was an enormous basin, as dry as the rest of Kano. All the remaining death-machines had wound up here, whirling and chopping at the pitiful remains of a onetime Gebran city. There would be some damage deposits owed, he was sure.

At the edge of the enormous pothole, armored warriors from a dozen species stood poised and ready to go on command. In the Quaestor sector, the Sigmas lined up in three groups. He could hear Stubek and the others lined up behind him carping about their "dear leader." They mostly hated him now, and he felt about the same way toward them…and himself. At least he was only playing the leadership role for the moment. Bridget had agreed to run Surge Three for real today, understanding that they needed the help and that he wouldn't be able to do anything of use.

She was with Santos now. He was wearing his silly designer turban and sunglasses, standing in a three-piece suit on an alien planet amid armored warriors. Jamie didn't get it. He would be self-conscious doing the same thing. But Saint Peter stood there looking like he was the toughest guy at the dance, speaking every so often into his little headset. He seemed to be waiting on something—or someone.

Santos noticed Jamie's gaze and looked directly at him. Jamie shifted nervously and turned to face the murderbots again. It felt safer.

Bridget sidled up next to Jamie. "I think you're in trouble," she said over her private channel.

"Did you tell him who I was?"

"No," Bridget said, sounding miffed. "I'm about out of reasons not to, though. And I can't make any guarantees of what will happen after today."

Jamie gritted his teeth. "Your people hate me. I'm surprised they haven't ratted on me."

"I can't make any guarantees they haven't, but I've done what I can."

"Fine."

A hovercraft sailed past, and Fieldmaster Wo-grump delivered a speech that was broadcast to all the participants. In their knowglobe-connected armors, they all heard the screed in their own languages—except for those who muted it. Jamie figured at least 95 percent of those in attendance had chosen that option.

Bridget looked at him. "Ten billion dollars, you think?"

Jamie patted the small armored pack on his back. "I've got the assayer from the briefcase in here. I checked the soil samples their probes brought up. Between mineral rights and real estate—yeah, this place will earn about that."

"Too bad there's not four more patches like it."

"Yeah." There was time left but no question of any more sales trips with Santos here. It was over. "We tried. It was fun while it lasted."

She chuckled. "Really?"

"No."

Jamie stood poised and ready for the signal flare that would start the final Kano Clearing. He would run down with the rest of Surge Three, get lost in the tumult, and hide behind the first building they secured. Even with binoculars, Santos would not be able to see where he was. What happened after the fight was anyone's guess. He tensed to go...

"Wait," Bridget said. "Something's wrong."

Jamie looked at the Gebran on the hovercraft. He was gesticulating angrily at something above. Jamie looked up toward the blinding sun...

...and saw a spacecraft descending from the sky. His armor recognized it before he did.

The notation "*Unknown One*" appeared superimposed over the ship in his faceplate. The ship the Xylanx had taken to Leel!

The vessel settled in the near end of the basin, well away from the reshapers in the distance, but definitely over the starting line for the competition. The other teams rumbled with confusion and indignation. And Fieldmaster Wo-grump, whom Jamie had never seen in less than a tizzy, was positively apoplectic.

The ramp dropped, and Kolvax strode confidently down the steps. The black figure's polished armor gleamed under the sun as he led a crew of similarly clad Xylanx down onto the surface.

The Gebran hovercraft floated up to them. "What's this about?" Wo-grump sputtered. "Who are you? You're upsetting my schedule!"

"Deal with it," Kolvax said, his voice amplified. Jamie's systems indicated he was speaking in Gebran. "There's a new player in the game."

"You can't just show up like this! We don't even know who you are!"

"What difference does it make?" He pointed at the human squad, higher on the ridge. "They went to war with you, and you're letting them compete. My people demand the same rights the humans have." His fingers curled into a fist. "And you can bet we'll beat them!"

* * *

It had worked out better than Kolvax had ever imagined it would.

He'd known from Jamie Sturm's agenda on the human knowglobe that the so-called Clearing was his next stop, but Kolvax had no idea how long it would last. It had also required a couple of transits to reach 37 Geminorum; in each case, he had left warriors to secure the whirlibang stations, guaranteeing his return trip would be possible. Kano was easily the farthest any Xylander had traveled outside the home territory since his days as a cadet.

But he had arrived in time—and better yet, on the last day. The Gebrans had delayed today's start to give the Xylanx time to take positions with everyone else. He looked along the ridge to the human contingent. He was sure the trader was over there somewhere. With so many greedy aliens in one place, where else could he be?

Borranz appeared next to him. She was armored, as were the others, with her faceplate darkened—but she was ostentatious in bright green. The Dominium didn't want him to ignore her, as if he could. He hoped one of the Gebran's demolition machines would take a liking to her.

"This is insane," Borranz said. "You know very well the Dominium has a long-standing policy against interaction with neighboring species!"

"You weren't complaining when we hit the Porriman station."

"That's because you killed everyone there. You can't possibly do that here!" She looked around the ridge of the depression. There were hundreds of warriors present, if not thousands. "And what do we care about winning a patch of land here? Are you planning to settle, Kolvax? Raise a house and live here amongst the vermin?" She chortled. "Perhaps you'll find something to mate with—if it'll have you!"

"Don't be obscene," Kolvax said. "I swore to the Dominium I would get them everything they needed to properly defend against human encroachment, and I will do exactly that. I just need one more thing."

"It's here?"

"Oh, yes," Kolvax said. He could feel it.

The fool Gebran was on his hovercraft again, starting some foolish speech over from the start. The Xylanx had the language thanks to the human knowglobe; he regretted that fact now. He muted the feed and walked to the edge to survey the battlefield.

This was where he belonged: on a strange world, about to head into violent conflict. It reminded him of his youth—and his one brief taste of what it truly meant to be Xylanx. It had been over too soon, but he had remembered it vividly his entire life.

When Kolvax was still just a new recruit for the Stalkers, the prefect of the territory he was serving in ordered his brigade to invade an unoccupied region. It hadn't been *completely* unoccupied; there were some natives. But they, of course, didn't matter. That was also when Kolvax had first met Signatory members—some merchants too far out for their own good—and tested them in battle. He had seen his first trader badges and murdered his first true aliens.

It had been exhilarating: a glorious year of doing what Xylanx *should* do.

The Dominium had put a stop to it—and a stop to the heartbeat of the renegade prefect. She had threatened the decadent stability of the political class and had to pay. But that year on the frontier had inspired young Kolvax and convinced him that the rulers of the Xylanx were weak-minded fools. What good was it to proclaim racial superiority when there were no inferiors about? Serving as a basis for comparison was the only function their captive slave races performed anymore.

They needed to start moving again. Everything Kolvax had done since then sprang from that experience. And he knew the humans were key to unlocking the gates that held his people back.

No, check that. One human.

The Gebran raised his silly-looking arms. It was time to begin. Kolvax didn't need to look back at Borranz; he knew the spy would stay within five meters of him at all times.

That was fine. In fact he was counting on it.

The flare shot into the air. Kolvax smiled.

Charge!

39

Everything that had come before on Kano was just the appetizer, Bridget thought. District Two Eighty was the nine-course meal. She led Surge Three forward in a wedge, trying to keep Jamie safely behind her. But the sector was thick with ridge-blasters expending their seemingly endless supply of missiles at the very buildings she was hoping to secure. Another shot impacted nearby, sending two of her flankers tumbling away. *So much for an orderly approach!*

"We're gonna have to take these things down," she yelled. She looked back to see Jamie jostled by the explosion and leaning against Lynn Stubek. "Watch him," Bridget ordered. To her companions: "Explosive rounds. Aim for the base of the rocket launchers. Let's go!"

A line reformed, and Bridget charged into the smoke and flames. This was going to be messy work. She prayed they had enough ammunition.

***

Jamie ducked—or his armor did—as a ridge-blaster rocket went screaming over his head. Another struck just ahead, showering him with dirt and stones as he hit the ground.

He looked in panic to Stubek, crouching beside him. Her arm, still on the mend since Moog, had been immobilized in her armor casing; the most she was supposed to do was provide supporting fire from the rear. She didn't look any too happy to have drawn the job protecting him.

Jamie crouched and looked through the haze. Bridgie and the Surge Three members were engaged in battle up ahead. Unable to deal with opponents in close quarters, the ridge-blasters were firing wildly. "We've got to get out of here," Jamie said, rising. He saw Stubek rise to follow.

There was a pit up ahead; a crater left by a previous blast. Jamie paused before it, wondering if the reshapers would target it again. But before he could give it much consideration, he felt a shove from behind.

Jamie landed hard. Twisting, he looked up to see Stubek standing at the pit's edge, unslinging her weapon with her good arm. "Stay there," the woman said. "I've got fighting to do."

"Don't leave me!" Jamie felt the ground rumble. He knew the land-smashers were out there. "You *can't* leave me. I'm the trader!"

"Funny. You seem to be wearing my squad leader's suit," she said. Then Stubek turned and dashed off.

✳ ✳ ✳

The Xylanx surged forward, weapons blazing at the Gebran demolition machines. Kolvax cackled. "That's it. Enjoy yourselves!"

The Gebrans' rules forbade the combatants from different teams from attacking each other. Kolvax hadn't bothered to share that with his troops, though; he really didn't care. But he wasn't surprised that his compatriots were focusing on the big industrial terrors first. Who'd give up on such fun?

Sadly, he had to—but he knew he had an excellent reason. Kolvax activated his armor's tracking program, which Liandro's engineers had developed using information from the human knowglobe. Each Sigma soldier's armor broadcast a signal indicating his or her condition and location to the rest of the team. Standing back from the fray, Kolvax looked carefully at the display.

"There you are, little man," Kolvax said. One of the troopers was motionless, despite being uninjured. And his blood pressure was sky high. "That's our target," he said. "Come on!"

Armed with his hand-cannon, Kolvax began moving. Four of his companions turned to follow. Puzzled, Borranz followed as well.

Your mistake, Kolvax thought.

＊＊＊

Bridget vaguely heard Jamie screaming something over her earpiece. But he was still in one piece, or so her systems said—and she was worried about herself at the moment. Holding on to the side of the ridge-blaster with one hand, she used her other to jam a broken girder into the area where the missile battery pivoted.

The gears seized up, and the ridge-blaster—almost as if in some kind of machine anguish—fired all its missiles at once, directly impacting the land-smasher bearing down on her crew.

Bridget tumbled free and landed hard in the dirt. Her head turned to the side, and she saw scour-bots on the way. *No rest today!*

＊＊＊

Jamie called and called into his microphone. No one answered. The normally bright sky was gray now, and he saw flak bursts in the air over the pit.

OVERDRAFT: THE ORION OFFENSIVE

Rocks tumbled from his prison, and the area above went dark. A scour-bot trundled partially over the hole, not stopping. Jamie saw its twisting claws snapping open and shut as it went. And it did go: on its way, evidently not noticing the pit and its prisoner below.

"The hell with this," Jamie said. He changed to the private channel Trovatelli had given him. "I'm ready to go," he said. "Let's get out of here!"

✴✴✴

Borranz was at Kolvax's heels. "Where are you going? What's this all about?"

Kolvax shook his head. "Don't you ever shut up?" It wasn't far now, he knew. The humans' battle had moved away from the trader, his tracking program said. There weren't even many demolition machines still working here. This would be easy.

Or not. Borranz stormed ahead of Kolvax, turned around, and pointed her hand-cannon at him. "That's far enough," she said. "This madness stops now!"

✴✴✴

Lissa arrived at the edge of the pit above Jamie. She was in her regular gear as Q/A—partially armored, with her face visible. She lifted her goggles and looked down at him. "Ready to travel?"

"You'd better believe it." Jamie smiled. He clawed at the pit, but the gravel kept giving way. "I think I'll need a rope."

"I'll get something," she said.

Then she looked to the east. From below, Jamie saw her eyes narrow. "What? What is it?"

281

"It's the Xylanx," she said, voice serious. "Something's happening." She looked down at Jamie. "I want to check this out. I'll be back!"

"Wait! What?" Jamie yelped. "*Lissa!*"

✳ ✳ ✳

"Your authority is hereby rescinded," Borranz said. "Under the powers given me by the Dominium, I'm taking control of this force and returning us to Gharion Preserve." The Stalkers who had been at Kolvax's side quickly left him and lined up, flanking the Dominium observer. They pointed their weapons at Kolvax.

The Black Priest simply laughed. "Is that all?"

"You'll be returned to the Dominium—along with my full account of your activities here. I don't suspect you'll be looking at exile this time." Lowering her weapon, Borranz shook her head. "I have no idea why the Dominium chose to give you the power they did. It was obviously a mistake."

"I can tell you another mistake," Kolvax said, hearing rumbling from the north. "Not keeping tabs on who's behind these helmets. Because there are Stalkers loyal to the Dominium—and then there are Severed loyal to me." He nodded, and the troopers beside Borranz grabbed the startled female. Her hand-cannon fell to the ground.

"Wait! What are you doing?"

"Ah," Kolvax said, spying a scour-bot trundling toward them. It was in bad shape—afire from a rocket blast—but it was still knifing and clawing its way blindly along the surface. "There," he said.

"Don't!" Borranz screamed. "Don't…"

Kolvax's loyalists heaved, and the observer's armored body landed right in the scour-bot's path. A scream followed and then a series of noisy cracks as rotating gears beneath the robot jammed, one after another. The scour-bot ground to a halt.

Kolvax smiled. He pointed to the west. "Keep going," he said to his companions. "You know the coordinates."

As they ran into the smoke, Kolvax looked back at the scour-bot. It was dying but still trying to gnaw whatever was beneath to bits. He was committed now. But he couldn't have anyone with the Dominium knowing his true next steps…

He saw something out of the corner of his eye. Someone was watching from behind a debris pile. *A human!*

Kolvax bounded, drawing his hand-cannon on the woman. Unarmed, she stood, terrified.

"Who are you?" Kolvax said, grabbing her hand. At first he thought she was the trader's bodyguard. But he soon changed his mind. "You're not the leader."

"N-no," the human woman said. "I'm the quartermaster." She glared at him—frightened but defiant.

Kolvax held her arm for a moment. She had dark hair but wasn't Bridget Yang. The eyes, cheeks, and skin tone weren't what he remembered from Leel—or from the knowglobe personnel files. And he thought he remembered seeing this woman's image there, too: Trova-something?

No, the woman was telling the truth. *I can't believe I'm starting to be able to tell them apart,* he thought. She was even almost attractive for a human, if such a thing was possible. "I thought you were someone else," he said, releasing her. "Get out of here."

She studied him for a moment, looked back at the scour-bot, and then ran away.

The human had seen him kill Borranz, but it didn't matter to him in the slightest, seeing how she would have no context for the action. Besides, he had someone else to find. And when he did, the maneuverings of the Dominium and its minions wouldn't matter anymore, either. He tromped off into the haze.

4 0

Jamie was beside himself, wanting to be rescued. "I'll be there soon, babe," Lissa Trovatelli said, speaking into her headset mic. "There's one more thing I need to get."

She switched off the private channel and looked at the demolished scour-bot. Somewhere underneath the twisted mass of metal was the body—dead, she hoped—of one of the Xylanx warriors. She didn't know why the Xylanx had thrown one of their own underneath, yet the behavior seemed to be typical for them. Regardless, she wanted to examine the body, and it was just a matter of cutting her way down to it. Safety visor on, she ignited the laser torch from her pack and began cutting.

O'Herlihy's voice came over Lissa Trovatelli's headset. The first team was looking for her, worried whether she was all right. She wasn't supposed to be on the battlefield, unless to quickly repair armor. The Q/A sent a single tone back, indicating she was okay but busy with something delicate. That would get rid of them for a while, she thought, and it happened to be the truth.

Unlike almost everything else they knew about her.

Fact was, she was not twenty-three but a young-looking twenty-eight. And while she *was* from Giotto Colony on Luyten's Star, she had not emigrated with her family in 2128, two years before the Gebrans attacked. She had been present—and her family and fiancé had been killed. She had nearly died herself, enduring eight agonizing months while waiting for rescue.

She knew, as all did, that agents from the isolationist Walled Garden movement had precipitated the Arcturo-Solar War. Reaching Earth in 2132, she had sought the organization out, seeking revenge. Instead, they found her first and offered her an explanation—and a path.

Conflict with the Gebrans was inevitable, the members contended; anyone who had ever met the creatures could see that. It was better to get it over with, to show the world how dangerous space was. The Gardeners had hoped that in seeing stories like hers, humanity would turn its back on the stars. It had not happened: rather, after the war, Earthlings moved back into space with renewed fervor. They clearly didn't know what was good for them. But the Garden, too, would grow, drawing upon the newly displaced and disaffected. People like her. By working with the Garden, they said, she could prevent any further outrages.

She could not easily shake the identity of Lissa Trovatelli— her name had been recorded when she came to Earth. But few records from Giotto Colony survived, so the Gardeners decided to simply reconstruct her past. Now she was no longer on Earth as a refugee but as someone who had safely escaped the carnage. Her "parents" had entered her into one of Europe's best technical colleges, a favorite feeder for the trading corporations. Since she had already graduated college once on Luyten's Star, it guaranteed "young Lissa's" marks were genuine and impressive.

Upon graduation, Lissa found that her technical skills and background as a child of pioneers put her in demand by the major corporations; the Gardeners saw that she got the right interviews. Three months ago, her real job began. She had infiltrated the commercial system at what she saw as its weakest point: Quaestor.

Quaestor wasn't that successful anymore and had several expeditions that were on their last legs. Leonid Falcone's Altair expedition was one. Her assignment had been to put it out of its misery. It wouldn't be traceable to her, of course; it was why she was starting with the most marginal operation. It would fail, and they would move her to a better expedition, and she would undermine it as well. Between her—and others similarly minded and placed—the profit would go out of interstellar trade. And that profit was all most Earthlings cared about.

At Altair she had found her first opportunity for mischief—as well as justification for all her beliefs. Seeing the destruction the Spore had wrought on Alabeyd had confirmed every fear she'd ever had about alien contamination. Why didn't anyone else understand the danger? It didn't matter. What did matter was that the event provided her with a chance to shut the place down by exaggerating the physical defects in ASPEC's facility. She got them to abandon the trading center, and Garden agents with the cleanup team were going to come in and make sure the place never became operational again.

What she didn't expect was Jamie Sturm, and Falcone's decision to move operations to Sigma Draconis. That had put her off-balance. She hadn't fully understood at first what Jamie had done to the expedition, or how he had done it. And Bridget Yang had given her precious little time to find out, ordering her to assist in moving the team to the Dragon's Depot and then tasking her with getting the station into usable shape. Seeing how many links there were to other worlds from Sigma Draconis, Trovatelli had strongly considered using her position to sabotage the station.

However, something had stopped her. The Xylanx were a group that no one had ever seen, and the Walled Garden took a strong interest in being aware of all threats to Earth. While it would have been better for humanity to simply stay in the Solar

System and ignore the rest of the galaxy—that was, in fact, the Walled Garden's goal—they weren't so narrow-minded as to ignore the fact that there *were* other species out there. The more the Garden and Earth knew about an alien species, the easier it would be to oppose them if push came to shove. And they were very ready to shove.

As the Walled Garden saw it, friendly creatures interested in trade were as big a threat as bug-eyed monsters intent on invasion. The latter could be defeated and eradicated. The former would tie humanity ever more tightly into the galactic community.

So she had stayed her hand at Sigma Draconis in part so that she could study the scant evidence the Xylanx had left about themselves on the Dragon's Depot. Were they aliens? Were they a threat? She would have found out—if Yang hadn't insisted on dragging her out on these senseless trading missions. Of course, Trovatelli had encountered the Xylanx again at Leel, but the buffoonish Gideon had prevented her from finding out anything more then. Now, burning away one sheet of metal after another from the scour-bot, she hoped to get her answers. Nothing could stop her now.

Except, maybe, the one other thing that had stopped her from taking decisive action earlier.

Jamie.

Trovatelli had learned, from the other members of Surge Sigma and from Falcone's files foolishly stored in the team knowglobe, exactly what it was Jamie had done to get drafted by the expedition as trader. She'd understood that he was some kind of crook; when she found out how he'd accomplished his deed, her perspective on him changed. He could be useful.

The biggest challenge to the Walled Garden was moving agents and information around the Orion Arm. All the movement's members hated space travel and encounters with alien cultures. Those born on foreign worlds, like Trovatelli, felt no different. But travel was a necessary evil to achieve the organization's goals—and it was often very difficult. Single agents could move using the commercial passenger lines, but those trips were often indirect, involving multiple hops. And forget moving heavy equipment from world to world, which the Garden's dreamier plots required. Cargo 'boxes were coded with identification tags that cleared them through whirlibangs in multiple systems; the expeditions that ran or rented space on off-world transit systems kept a close eye on what was moving where. They had simply never found anyone with the position and skills to make it happen.

But Jamie Sturm had done it all on his own. He had figured out angles to the shipping system no one had ever considered, moving around billions of dollars in off-the-books material—all from a trading station near Venus. He seemed to have the knack for getting merchants and shipping agents light-years away to do his bidding. And he seemed to keep most of the incredibly complicated network in his head. Amazing!

It hadn't taken Trovatelli long to realize that Jamie could be a valuable recruit to the Walled Garden—probably more important than she was. He seemed to dislike aliens with a passion, and the fact that he was estranged from a powerful family could only help. Ambition was useful in the movement; it had certainly served Lissa well so far. Thwarted ambition could be an even better motivator.

So while she had secretly worked to end Jamie's bid to put the expedition back in the black—purposefully fouling up the translations on Moog was a step too far, nearly exposing her—she had also considered how she might deliver him to her organization. The Walled Garden could give Jamie a new name and appearance, placing him with one of the better-funded trading firms.

From a desktop working at a place like PraetorCorp, Jamie could become the maestro for the whole movement.

It would be good for all of them, she thought—and it might even be good for the man himself. Once she got past his whining, Lissa had been pleasantly surprised by Jamie's resilience over the past weeks. He alone had tried to reach out to her—not counting Bridget's ham-handed attempts to get to know her troops. With a cause other than greed, Jamie Sturm might actually turn into someone she could admire.

Their arrival on Kano earlier in the week had felt like a decision point. The Gebrans had killed her family in their attack on Luyten's Star; falsified records had hidden that fact from Quaestor and Bridget. The sight of the disgusting Gebrans made her want to vomit. The appearance of Treasury Agent Santos was a welcome surprise, and she'd happily helped Jamie to hide.

It was perfect. As an outlaw, Jamie would definitely go with her. It would even be worth her shedding her current identity to recruit him into the Garden. They could always forge her another, and in Jamie's departure, any chance of the expedition recouping its funds would vanish. Falcone would lose his charter and Yang would be sent to the street. Trovatelli thought the chief deserved no better. The only reason Bridget was at Overland was because she was playing guardian to the Gebrans. *Maybe next time she'll defend her own people*, Trovatelli thought.

The engineer had just finished making the preparations for her escape with Jamie when the Xylanx returned. Elated, she'd taken the chance to find out who they were once and for all. She realized it was a risk, but in learning more about them all her objectives and more would be achieved in a single hour. She was already going places within the movement; this episode would grant her power indeed. With a flash she burned away the last chunk of metal trapping the Xylanx beneath. She set down the laser torch and heaved away the final plate.

The Xylander was definitely dead, whoever she was. Bright green for armor—why? It didn't matter: it was spattered with dark red now. One of the scour-bot's claws had come down hard, piercing the midsection of the alien woman—if she was female at all. Trovatelli didn't know. She'd theorized that the Xylanx were really the Luk'a, the race of interstellar thieves active in humanity's ancient times. But the limited evidence said the Luk'a were frail. Not like the bulky body beneath her at all. *I guess they've been working out.*

She reached for the oxygen mask around her neck and put it on, fearful of infection. The corpse's helmet was loose. With a gloved hand, Trovatelli removed it…

And instantly knew who the Xylanx really were.

Trovatelli reached inside her utility belt for the syringe she'd stolen from the medic. That had been her plan all along, to extract DNA for later study. She jabbed the needle into the Xylander's neck. In seconds the sequencer in the handle had done its work. She looked at the results…

…and fell to her knees, stupefied. Of course. *Of course!*

Everything had changed—everything! Quaestor and its expedition were no longer important. Jamie Sturm was no longer important. What remained was an almost unimaginable threat to humanity. But it was real. She knew what she had to do, and she knew the Walled Garden would approve of it wholeheartedly.

And if it meant killing Bridget Yang, the murderer of Lucas Baines, martyr of Overland—well, that was just a wonderful bonus.

She stood and covered the body with one of the plates she had cut away. There was more work to do.

41

"Lissa! Lissa!" Bridget called out into her helmet mic. "Jamie!" She looked out at the other Sigmas. "I can't get anybody!"

The bodyguards stood amid a mountain of debris. The team had won District Two Eighty quite by surprise. The Xylanx had been making headway when they suddenly all retreated to their ship and left. Their departure had opened the field for Surge Sigma, and the Gebrans had—with extreme reluctance—just declared them the winners.

Bridget didn't care. She had two missing people. Jamie's locator signal wasn't broadcasting at all, and Trovatelli never had one. The chief found O'Herlihy and Stubek standing by the edge of an empty pit.

"Got tracks leading away," O'Herlihy said. "Looks like he was dragged."

Bridget glared at Stubek. "I told you to guard him."

The young woman blanched. "There was a war going on! I couldn't just stand here!"

"You weren't going to do us much good with your arm," Bridget said. "You had one job. You should've stayed—even if it meant climbing down in there with him!"

"He isn't a trader, Chief! You know that." Stubek said. "I don't see any badge on his—"

"You're fired," Bridget barked. "Go back to the staging area and shed your gear." She turned to her teammates. "Sweeps, everyone! Find them!"

The ground rumbled as more shuttles took to the air: disappointed teams leaving the Kano Clearing.

She saw some figures approaching through the haze. "Jamie!" she called out, walking around a downed land-smasher. She walked right into Santos, who had his full contingent with him again. The agent looked grim.

"Looking for someone?" Santos said.

Bridget smiled sheepishly. "Well, I—"

"Never mind. I haven't been sitting around on my hands while you've been out there having fun," he said. He took a sheaf of documents from the CFTC agent beside him. "Theda took our shuttle out a few days ago—and just came back with these."

Bridget looked down blankly at the documents. "Papers?"

"I can get them to you in whatever format you'd like to read. You're looking at a search warrant that we got from the Third District Court."

"Kano's in their jurisdiction?"

"Quaestor is. They're incorporated in Delaware. The Sigma Draconis station, your base while here—it's all Quaestor's. Our agents served a similar warrant several days ago at the Dragon's Depot—and we found surveillance-camera evidence of Jamie Sturm. In your facility. Boarding the *Indispensable*—with you. And Leonid Falcone is now talking about what Sturm did and why he's with you." He crossed his arms. "You're in an incredible amount of trouble, Miss Yang."

We're back to "Miss Yang" again, she thought.

"I'm going to have to ask you to come back to our shuttle," he said. His earpiece beeped. "Wait a moment."

For the first time Bridget saw Santos looking flustered. He whipped out his isopanel from his breast pocket and brought up an image. "What the devil?"

Bridget looked puzzled. "What?"

"This person," Santos said, turning the isopanel toward her. "Your quartermaster, right?"

Bridget looked at a crackling video image of Trovatelli. It looked like she was sitting at a control panel. "That's her. Where is she?"

"Heading for orbit," Santos said. He pointed to the air. "She just stole our shuttle!"

Bridget's jaw dropped. Santos's officers went into motion, running back for the landing pad as the officer barked commands. He looked back at Bridget accusingly. "My fugitive just ran away with your engineer!"

Bridget fumbled for words, stupefied. How did Jamie ever talk Lissa into something like that? "Jamie—running off with the Q/A? In a stolen government shuttle? I can't believe it!"

"That's because it isn't true," she heard a deep voice say. Victor Gideon staggered into the clearing. His helmet was off, and his armor was once again a battered mess. He'd taken out more reshapers singlehandedly than anyone on Kano, and it showed. "Couldn't call in because my transceiver was busted," he said. "But I saw 'em take the trader."

"Who?" Bridget and Santos said in unison.

"Those Xylanx freaks. They dragged him out of a hole and back to their ship. I tried to chase them down myself, but I had a robo-hunter wrapped around my leg."

Bridget gawked at Gideon and then looked up at the sky. "What in the hell is going on?"

***

Jamie was out of the armor at last. Unfortunately, he was half-naked—and shivering in the cold hold of an alien spacecraft. They'd stripped him and placed the few items he had in his armor's compartments—assayer unit, immerso goggles, badge—in a sealed container nearby.

He'd felt the launch; much more abrupt than any trip he'd every taken off-world. He was in orbit now but couldn't float around much while strapped to the wall.

Trovatelli had never come back for him: the Xylanx had found him instead. Had they done something to her? Was she here in the ship? The Xylanx had repeatedly denied it, for whatever that was worth. He couldn't imagine that she'd abandon him.

The black-armored figure reentered the hold. It was Kolvax, whom he'd seen twice before—and then earlier in the day on Kano. Jamie had no headset or knowglobe around, but Kolvax's armor seemed to translate his barking speech into English just fine. "We're headed to a transit station," Kolvax said. "What is it you call it? A whirlibang." He chortled. "Silly name for an important thing."

"What do you want?" Jamie said. "Why won't you leave me alone?"

"Relax," Kolvax said, floating up to where Jamie was bound. "You see, I know all about you, Jamison Sturm. You're an outsider with that expedition. You're no merchant—and you're certainly no warrior. I know you were pressed into service to resolve a debt. A considerable one from the sound of it: some one hundred billion units of your currency."

"How would you..." Jamie blinked. He realized something. "You—you got all that from our knowglobe! The one you stole!"

"That much was there, yes." Kolvax nodded. "We learned a lot about you. You—and your people. And I think it's time you learned something about us." Kolvax's gloved hands reached up and worked the seal on the helmet. He removed it…

…and Jamie gawked. It was the fleshy face of a man—sort of. Kolvax was bald, with sunken eyes, a large forehead and a big overbite. Jamie thought he was looking at a character from a horror movie. But he wasn't an alien character. "You're—you're *human*," Jamie stammered.

Hairless eyebrows flared upward. Kolvax spoke again, words now translated by a public address system in the room. "Human? Don't insult me."

"Sorry. I didn't want to say—"

"What? What do I look like to you?" He clutched the straps binding Jamie, pulling his floating body closer to the trader. "What do you *imagine* I look like?"

"I don't know," Jamie said, trying to look away.

Kolvax shook with anger, and Jamie shook, too. "Say it!" Kolvax yelled.

"*A Neanderthal!*" Jamie said. Guiltily, he lowered his voice. "I mean, you look like a Neanderthal. No offense."

"None taken," Kolvax said, smiling toothily. "I'm proud of what I am."

Jamie stared, speechless.

"And you don't know your own language," Kolvax said. "The 'thal' is pronounced 'tal.'" He sniffed. "It's kind of a lousy name. Do you always name people after where you find their bones? It's morbid."

Jamie heard the words and shook his head. It didn't make sense—and it couldn't be! "You—you can't be…"

Kolvax laughed and released Jamie. Kolvax floated over to retrieve his helmet. "You'd like answers. Well, we both need something the other has."

"We do?"

"You're the trader. You should understand that." He loomed over Jamie. "So listen closely, little man. Because I'm about to offer you the biggest deal in the history of your people—or mine!"

EPISODE 7:

STRIKE PRICE

4 2

Jamie tumbled violently through space. He wasn't really in space, he knew. He was standing on the floor in a room aboard an alien space station—or wherever it was the Xylanx had brought him to. The room had normal Earth gravity, or the simulated effect of it; he wasn't moving at all. But his stomach didn't know that, and it was doing the talking right now.

The Xylanx had found his immerso glasses and somehow loaded the device with the program he was watching. They had also enabled the unit's balance affect feature, something Jamie never usually turned on. He'd never understood why others wanted to feel the gyrations of the camera in the shows they were watching; some immerso directors were known primarily for their ability to make viewers nauseated. It was not an experience he needed to have. With his hands bound behind his back, though, Jamie had no way of adjusting the controls.

He'd asked his captors again and again to switch the feature off. No one had answered. His breaths came in a hurried rush inside the strange oxygen mask they'd given him. What if he threw up in the mask? Would that get their attention? Would they care?

The motion sensations matched the sights. Through the glasses he saw a star flash past and then a whirlibang. And a big yellow globe—was that Venus? If it had ever moved that fast outside the window at Ops, it would have sent the whole trading floor running for the bathrooms.

Which was exactly what he wanted to do now.

He crammed his eyes shut and felt his innards moving. It didn't help that the Xylanx had finally fed him an hour earlier. Some sort of glazed cubes with the consistency of diced apples and no taste whatsoever. He'd survived the fieriest Thai foods—how could anything so bland burn so much? Were they *trying* to make him sick? After the whirlibang trip on the Xylanx shuttle—he was well traveled enough to recognize *that* sensation by now—they'd brought him to this featureless white room. Was it some kind of lab, to test his tolerance?

"Open your eyes and quit squirming!"

Jamie felt a smack to his head, and Kolvax's face slid into view, a phantom in the stars.

"I want you to see something," the Xylander said.

"Unless you want to see something really awful, you'll switch this thing off!"

Jamie gritted his teeth and tried breathing through his nose. The tumbling slowed now, and a small blue dot appeared in the distance before his eyes. It grew steadily, and Jamie realized he was watching a recording of an approach to Earth. It wasn't one of the programs he'd loaded on the unit, so he assumed it was a simulated journey. The Xylanx had never been to Earth that he—or anyone else—knew of.

If it was really the view from a spaceship, the vessel was entering orbit now. Recognizing geographic features below, Jamie wondered if the Xylanx had somehow gotten into his itinerary. Because it was almost like the trip he was scheduled to have taken weeks earlier. Whoever recorded the images seemed to be heading for Ibiza, skipping Jamie's intended flight to Barcelona and the ferry. Jamie almost chuckled at that, but it made his gut hurt.

The Mediterranean grew massive and black in front of him, and the trader felt himself tumbling again. The vessel bypassed the island and headed for the Iberian mainland, itself as dark as night. Jamie strained to find any point of reference on the shore. *Where are the city lights?*

The image lurched, and Jamie had the feeling of a quick descent. There was a forest below. Another wobble, and he fell into a clearing. More darkness.

"I don't know what you want me to see, but you'd better turn on the lights."

"Just wait," he heard Kolvax say.

The "flight" was over. Jamie looked out onto a forest glade illuminated by a full moon. It was Earth all right. From Jamie's point of view behind a clump of trees, he looked out upon a small gathering. Beneath a star-filled sky, a low fire burned in the open. Shadowy bipedal figures huddled around it.

It didn't take long for him to realize it wasn't a Boy Scout troop.

A cracking sound came from the other side of the glen—and in that second, the people around the fire bolted for the trees. Only one figure remained: Kolvax, bareheaded and walking toward him.

"They're pretty skittish," Kolvax said, backlit by the flames. He didn't try to conceal his sneer. "Give them a minute."

The Xylanx had figured out another setting on his immerso goggles, Jamie realized. For while Kolvax was in the white room with Jamie in real life, he'd insinuated his presence in the Earthly scene. The goggles had a safety feature that allowed them to integrate real-life objects (and obstacles) into what they were displaying for the wearer. So Jamie saw Kolvax among the—what were they? A dark figure skulked past the trader, creeping back out cautiously from the woods.

It was a man—of sorts. Burly, bowed over, with an elongated face—and eyes that glinted as he looked up into the light.

"Now *that's* a Neanderthal," Kolvax said, walking up to the oblivious figure from the past. Jamie saw their differences now. Kolvax stood taller and had at least forty kilograms on the crouching figure. The Xylander's nose was narrower, his forehead higher. The Neanderthal was much hairier. But otherwise, Jamie thought, the two could be related.

Of course, the Neanderthal was fur-clad, while Kolvax was wearing his black suit of high-tech armor, minus helmet. A minor quibble.

"What am I looking at?" Jamie asked. "When is this?"

"Thirty-seven thousand years ago by Earth time." Kolvax stepped to the side as the fearful Neanderthal headed back to the fire. Slowly, others joined him. "They prefer to do their cooking in caves. But most of the good spots are gone. Now they take their chances wherever they can."

Jamie shook his head. *Okay, fine. The aliens have kidnapped me to show me an anthropological documentary. Why not?* It tracked with everything else he'd experienced.

And if anything, the production values were a little off. He craned his neck. "It's hard to see anything. Did your people produce this?"

"It's not an entertainment for your benefit, Sturm. It's real."

Jamie chortled. "Right. You visited Earth with a camera crew."

"No. Shut up and you'll see."

Jamie heard a bird squawk—and saw another mass exodus from the fireside. It took long moments for the group to reassemble. Males, females, children—Jamie saw them more clearly this time. All wide-eyed, all terrified.

"What are they so afraid of?"

"You," Kolvax said.

"They can't see me!"

"Not you personally, idiot. I suspect they'd happily bludgeon any sniveling merchants who came to visit. No, I meant your kind. Homo sapiens."

"They're here?" Jamie looked around. "Where are they?"

"Where aren't they right now? They've infiltrated this continent—and now the Neanderthals are down to this last peninsula."

"I always heard it was interbreeding and such that took out the Neanderthals."

"Don't let any of my followers hear you say that. You'll offend them." Walking around the fire, Kolvax looked down at the Neanderthals. "Besides, it doesn't matter what happened to the rest of the species. What matters is *what happens next.*"

Kolvax ambled casually away from the heedless gathering. Jamie shook his head. "I don't get it. What's about—"

Before he could finish his sentence, the fire and everyone around it disappeared, as if swallowed by the jaws of an enormous monster. Neanderthals nearby fled, screaming, and Jamie saw another great maw reaching down. Big, black, mechanical—much like one of the clam-shell excavators he'd seen working on Earth as a kid. Only these metal mouths weren't attached to big machines. They were flying on their own. And they were larger—the size of bangboxes.

In terror, a young Neanderthal couple ran past Jamie. He saw the thing that had devoured the fireside lift up into the air, powered by jet thrusters. The woman near Jamie screamed. He looked behind him to see the cause: other people had arrived on foot. Bipedal and armored in black, like Kolvax and his Stalkers, the creatures advanced from the woods, herding the savages back toward the clearing with electronic prods. But they were skinnier than the Xylanx, and the Neanderthals, too. It didn't matter. The violent flashes from their weapons were all the convincing the natives needed to move.

Kolvax watched them pass and smiled. "There's your imaging crew, as you call them. The Luk'a."

Jamie remembered the name. It was the group of interstellar thieves the Leelites had warned Surge Sigma about. Jamie didn't know why they'd want to steal cavemen, but they were certainly doing that, taking a big chunk of the local foliage as well. Dozens of the flying claws were in the air. Some arriving, some departing.

"Nice of them to record it, wasn't it?" Kolvax said. "What you've been watching was recorded by one of their scouts on the ground." He was standing next to Jamie now, looking on the chaos with what the trader almost interpreted as admiration. Kolvax clapped an armored hand on Jamie's shoulder. "Hold on to your intestines. We're about to move."

Jamie felt the image shift and shift again. He was moving, no longer seeing the sights from the ground but rather from the point of view of a vessel leaving ancient Earth. A veritable fleet of the enclosed metal claws were already in the air ahead.

"It's moving day," Kolvax said. "They hit spots all over the continent."

Jamie saw the journey thereafter in fast-forward. The component pieces assembled into a larger vessel, which then made for Venus—and a whirlibang.

"I don't get it! There wasn't any whirlibang in the Solar System until the Regulans showed up thirty-five years ago!"

"The Luk'a constructed their own. And when they left, they activated a thruster to carry it into your sun." Kolvax laughed. "We don't have images of that, naturally. Be fun to see, though."

Jamie rubbed his hands together behind his back. The Xylanx liked their space station cold—like the Dragon's Depot had been when he arrived. They seemed to like crazy stories, too. Jamie couldn't see the sense in Kolvax's bizarre tale. "What's the point of all this? Where did they take them?"

"You'll see it now," Kolvax said.

Jamie did—in blinding fashion. The place before his eyes was as bright as prehistoric Spain was dark. When his pupils adjusted, he saw an antiseptic place with shined white tiles on the floor, walls, and ceiling; much like the room the Xylanx had brought him to. Only this place had environment-suited Luk'a leading drugged Neanderthals around on automated stretchers.

"The Luk'a were dying as a species," Kolvax said. "They were doing what they had to do."

The scene around Jamie shifted to reveal an operating theater—and theater was an apt term. The room was cavernous. As sterile as the one he'd first seen, and populated only by row after row of examination tables. Neanderthals were strapped to many of them, looking up blankly as laser- and saw-wielding Luk'a probed at them. In the light, Jamie could now see the Luk'a's resemblance to humans was limited to the number of limbs. Their heads were flattened, like coins, and their gloved hands each had four fingers pointed like devils' tails. That didn't seem to handicap the armored surgeons, who were doing their work with ease.

And such horrific work. Jamie felt his last meal starting to move again. "They're dissecting them alive," Jamie managed to say.

"Just some," Kolvax said, walking between the tables. "And you'll see it's not just Neanderthals around here." He gestured to the rest of the chamber. "They should be slicing up some Porrimans over there."

Jamie put his hands over his glasses. "I don't need to see that."

"Good choice," he said, almost smiling. He quickly turned serious again. "As I mentioned, the Luk'a were driven to this—that's important. They'd stolen some genetic engineering technology a few centuries earlier and had engineered themselves an improvement or two. Problem was, one of those improvements generated a lovely little retrovirus that threatened to wipe out their entire species."

Jamie studied the Luk'a surgeon ahead of him, moving seemingly without emotion as he—if it was a he—did his work.

"They were sure the fix they needed existed in the DNA of another race somewhere," Kolvax said. "But no one else would help them, because of their past acts of piracy. So they decided to take up the part once again, resorting to what they knew best: theft."

"They stole *people*?"

Standing between two operating tables, Kolvax raised his arms. "Any beings they could find—particularly specimens of young, hardy races. They thought by experimenting with all of us, they'd find their magic solution."

"*All* of us? With humans, too?"

Kolvax rolled his eyes. "So self-centered. Yes, they stole Homo sapiens, too. But those didn't last very long here. Not hardy enough, I guess." He smirked.

Kolvax walked to the side of a prone Neanderthal. It was the same male that Jamie had seen him standing next to on Earth. Here, the man was in a stupor, staring upward.

"They did a lot of work on this fellow's kinfolk," Kolvax said. "The Luk'a bred them in captivity—while engineering some tweaks into their genome to augment their mental capacities. They were pretty sure the Forest Glade people, as they called them, were the solution to their problems. That somewhere, in these people's minds and bodies, there was something that would end their misery once and for all."

"Why would they think that?"

"No one knows." Kolvax shot him a smarmy grin. "We think it's because we're so wonderful."

Jamie rolled his eyes. "Were they right? Did they find what they were looking for?"

"In a way." Kolvax stared closely at the catatonic Neanderthal. "Because one day these simple oafs all woke up and decided they'd had enough. They killed all the Luk'a and claimed their technology. They weren't refugees from Earth anymore, weren't savages in need of places to hide." He stepped up to Jamie and switched off the immerso unit. "They had become us. And we were the Xylanx!"

43

"Geena, I think I'm losing my mind," Bridget said. "Nothing makes sense anymore."

Madaki looked back at her from the pilot's seat of *Indispensable* and smiled weakly. "That, girl, means things are just about to get better."

"Is that some West African aphorism?"

"No. But I don't know what else to say. I've been hauling crews like yours for years, and I've never seen a trader kidnapped by aliens and a Q/A go AWOL on the same mission. You're kind of off the map, sweetie."

Bridget nodded and sighed. They *had* lost the trader. Really, physically lost him. They'd seen the feed from the camera in Gideon's armor: sure enough, the Xylanx had hauled Jamie off, kicking and screaming, to their shuttle. She'd saved him from being kidnapped by them once, weeks earlier. After they'd left him alone on Leel, she'd doubted they were interested in him any longer—and she'd assumed they wouldn't be able to locate him in Hiro Welligan's armor.

Another wrong bet.

Her responsibility to the expedition was to go after him. There were ten different whirlibang rings in orbit around 37 Geminorum: the Xylanx had taken one of them to get to Kano.

Surely she'd be able to find out if they'd used one to go back. Then, if the link was still live, she'd be able to take her full force to follow.

The problem was, she was no longer in command of her own forces. Santos had reluctantly placed her under arrest following the confusion; he hadn't any other choice, given how she had been hiding Jamie's presence. Of course, she had to assume Santos was right—he usually was—that a Quaestor encampment was still United States territory for jurisdictional purposes. Whether he was right or not, corporate protocol was for her to cooperate; they'd let the lawyers sort it out.

On the other hand, Trovatelli's theft of the Feds' shuttle had complicated things immensely—logistically as well as legally. It had made their young Q/A a fugitive, too, while stranding the law enforcement officers on an alien planet. There was no question of the cops chasing after an armed force like the Xylanx on a hunch, so Santos and the marshals had commandeered *Indispensable* to take them all back to the Dragon's Depot.

He had been polite about it, but it had been an awkward ride nonetheless. She had told her team members not to lie anymore about Jamie's masquerade; she would be taking the full responsibility on herself. Santos had agreed to those conditions in order to get everyone to talk. Taking the rap for something she was only partially responsible for was something she was familiar with, and she slipped into the feelings easily. But she also knew it was her fault for not rejecting Jamie's wild scheme from the start.

Besides, she liked Santos. He was as straight a shooter as Jamie was crooked, and while she had learned from hardship to distrust first impressions, he had seemed genuine. Enough so that it felt bad to disappoint him.

The man floated back to the front of the compartment, leaving the marshals interviewing her troopers behind. He looked grim. "We're about finished. Will we be there soon?"

"Five minutes," Bridget said. She reached for a seat and pulled herself to it. Santos found one across from her and did the same. She didn't look up as she strapped herself in.

When he finally spoke, he did so quietly. "Bridget, do you have any idea why Trovatelli would leave the way she did?"

"None." Bridget was relieved—and a little surprised—to be asked about something other than Jamie. "I've told you. I've only known her for a few weeks. Her CV checked out and her recommendations were stellar. Her psych eval was fine. She's seemed a little antsy about aliens, but that's about it."

"And you think these Xylanx are aliens? The ones that took Jamie? I thought one theory was that they were human outlaws."

"They still could be. We've gone back and forth."

"If there's never been a two-legged, two-armed race encountered in thirty-five years, wouldn't it make more sense that they *are* humans and maybe in league with Jamie? You said his end of the warehouse trading scheme alone was forty billion dollars—not counting what he would have gained from the market trades I'm investigating. That could buy an awful lot of help. A man who could run such a trading scheme from a desktop could certainly enlist allies across the—"

"No. I'm sorry, but that just doesn't make sense—it's crazy."

"But you said that it was Jamie's idea to start trading from the Sigma Draconis station. Think about it. He deliberately steers you to a place where he knows his associates—or henchmen, or whatever—are based. You interrupted them taking him away."

"They were manhandling him!"

"Because they'd learned his moneymaking scheme had failed," he said matter-of-factly. He spoke slowly and evenly, seemingly reluctant to call her out for not being more suspicious. Was it because he was a good agent, she wondered, or because he didn't want to accuse her of being too trusting?

"When they encountered him a second time, he was earning money again. Maybe they left him alone, then, so he could finish. Perhaps he had cut a deal for more time. And then, on Kano, they learned from him that I had arrived. And so they took him away—to deliver their own brand of justice."

Bridget felt herself getting dizzy. "That's some pretty serious chess you're playing there."

Santos templed his fingers. "It's what I'm paid to do."

Bridget took a deep breath. True, Jamie fancied himself a mastermind. But she'd seen him up close and in action. It was hard to picture a grand player, capable of schemes within schemes, nearly wetting himself on encountering something with more than two eyes. And how many evil criminal impresarios spent their free time at imaginary twentieth-century bars listening to trivia about the postal service? Shouldn't they be sitting at pipe organs, petting their ravens and cackling about their plans for world domination?

She shook her head—she just wasn't seeing it the same way as Santos. "We'll see. But there's just one piece missing from your board, Peter: Trovatelli."

"From your board, too, Bridget." He raised a black eyebrow. "But which color piece is she?"

"I'm not sure," Bridget said, glad to no longer be Miss Yang. After a moment, she added: "I think maybe she's playing her own side."

"So maybe it's not chess at all but Chinese checkers," he suggested. "With multiple players and multiple goals."

Bridget looked away and wondered. The possibilities were staggering—and Saint Peter was something, too. She wasn't sure what game the two of them were playing, either.

A loud bang signaled their arrival, interrupting their discussion. The passengers felt the jerky return of rotational motion and heard the rattling of the 'box around the tracks of the transit rings. Bridget assumed she'd brought her last expedition back to the Dragon's Depot. Whatever happened to her, Quaestor would be closing up shop here altogether. She was carrying the land contracts from the Great Kano Clearing, but they wouldn't be enough. Falcone's charter would be terminated in two weeks. Legal troubles aside, she would be out of work—and so would all the members of her team. Usually, she worried more for them than for herself. At the moment, she was too tired to feel quite that noble.

Their container's motion slowed. The 'box had switched to a spiraling side track, leading it from the whirlibang and inside the Shaft. She looked at Santos. "Do you guys cuff me or what?"

He chuckled. "I think I can keep an eye on you."

Bridget unsnapped her seatbelt and floated toward the exit. With a whoosh, the door opened, and pressurized air exited. She took a deep breath and pushed out, ready to face whatever her new life was going to be like.

"Why is it so cold in here?"

Trovatelli watched her breath coalesce before her face as she worked. She had been moving nonstop since leaving the battlefield, Jamie, and her old job behind on Kano. Stealing the Feds' shuttle, flying to the whirlibang, and returning to the Dragon's Depot had been difficult—but it was also only the first step. Her real mission was here, at Sigma Draconis, the first place the Xylanx had been spotted. And it was necessary, because what her analysis tool had seen in the DNA of the fallen Xylanx warrior was as stunning as it was indisputable.

The Xylanx were Neanderthals. The tool had determined that with great precision. There had been some modest alterations to their genome, but there was no way that the Xylander she examined could have descended from anything other than a Neanderthal. Earth's scientists had fully sequenced an intact specimen long before. The evidence was overwhelming.

And under no circumstances could humanity learn of the fact.

Within seconds on Kano, the likely progression of future events had flashed through her mind. Someone—with Falcone's feeble expedition or otherwise—would find out the same thing she just had: that humans and Xylanx were related. And instead of slowing humanity's race to space, the discovery would send it into overdrive.

How much of early space exploration had been focused on finding life in the great beyond? The actual discovery of life, when it happened, had at least been muted a little by how strange the other species were. But once people knew they had ancestral cousins living in the stars? That would be it. Forget it. No barriers, no movement could ever contain the curiosity it would engender.

After rushing off to see the so-called relatives, many humans would start finding kinship with every bit of genetic flotsam they uncovered. The Earth would be one more cage in a galactic menagerie, one more stop on the freak show.

One more chance for humanity to be wiped out forever.

It didn't matter to Lissa how the Neanderthals had gotten to space, but some of the possibilities there gave her even further cause for concern. Many already believed the nonsense that humans were planted on the world by an alien race. Nothing would stop that foolishness now. There would be a rush to find the Xylanx, to trade with them, to learn from them, to integrate with them.

And it wasn't at all clear that was a wise thing—or what the Xylanx wanted either, given the behavior they'd exhibited. Hostility. Blind, unthinking hostility. Was this what humanity wanted in a neighbor it sought to embrace? What if the Xylanx were jealous of humanity? More importantly: What if they coveted Earth?

No, that was the prospect, more than any other, that drove Trovatelli to quickly abandon her plotting against Quaestor. In comparison, undermining an expedition on its last legs was of no importance. Neither was delivering Jamie to the Walled Garden. She had encountered an Alpha Threat—one of a number of special situations that every movement member memorized and understood. In the face of an Alpha Threat, operational security was meaningless. So were the lives of agents responding to them.

Still, she had no intention of dying.

She pulled the hood tight around her neck. That had been her first act on arriving: getting out of her lightly armored outfit from Kano and donning a standard-issue hooded jumpsuit. She needed to move around more freely now, and the high-tech garment would keep her warm as she worked to make the space station inhospitable. There was no easy way to vent the station to space, or to blow it up: intelligent builders rarely installed self-destruct buttons in their multi-billion-dollar creations. But she knew from her first visit how to alter the temperature, and that would be a good start for the work she had ahead.

"Who's there? Let me out!" Falcone squawked again in her ear. She could see the poor fool on the surveillance monitor feed; she'd affixed the portable isopanel to the back of her wrist. He seemed to be having an embolism. The sudden and unexpected arrival of the Feds' shuttle had been followed first by the drop in temperature and then Trovatelli's security-sealing of every door on the station—including the one to his office. Lissa smirked at the image. The pudgy old thing was cold and going nowhere.

She, meanwhile, was just getting warmed up. The passenger 'boxes from Kano had arrived. *Bridget.* She hadn't had time to prevent their arrival: taking a whirlibang offline was a serious undertaking, requiring more than the press of a button. But she had a welcome prepared.

"Lunch is ready," she murmured, watching the image from another camera as Bridget and company emerged from their vessel. "Come and get it!"

44

"Is it ready?"

"We're working on it," Liandro said, standing on the deck of Gharion Station's shipping floor. "You have to give us more time."

"You've had plenty of time." Kolvax rolled his eyes. He knew the old man was tired and frustrated, having spent many days working with the technology of aliens he found offensive. And not just any offensive aliens, either. Well, he didn't have time for that. He pointed at the shipping container they'd stolen from the Porriman station. "All your skill, and you've gotten nowhere with it."

"We made the most important modifications, of course. And we confirmed what we learned from the humans' knowglobe about their shipping protocols," Liandro said. "This bangbox, as they call it, requires a special code to be passed through other Signatory depots on the way to Earth. Without it, it can go no further than a single port of call—wherever our transit station is linked to."

And of course they weren't linked with Earth. The closest connection went through the Sigma Draconis station, their old prison—and then to Altair, before reaching the Solar System. He certainly wasn't going to employ that route.

"Fine. We need the codes for the transceiver, like I thought all along. I'm on it." He jabbed his finger in Liandro's helmeted face. "I need you to be ready with your part."

Rumber approached holding a metal case with a handle. "Borranz's people came through with the request," she said. "Will this container work?"

Kolvax took the case and tested its weight in his hand. It looked similar, but not identical, to the briefcase Jamie had carried on Leel. "It'll suffice."

As he turned to leave, Rumber reached for his arm. "The Dominium is inquiring after Borranz. They'll want a report from her."

"Fake one. We're almost there. Everything's ready—I just have to finish speaking with the trader."

"Where's the alien now?"

"With Tellmer," Kolvax said, heading for the exit. "I'd better go quick, before Tellmer tries to convert him. Or bore him to death!"

***

Outer space lay beyond the thick walls of the Shaft—and yet it was darker inside now. Every light in the Dragon's Depot had gone out mere moments after the last member of Bridget's team disembarked. Bridget had put on her headset then, to hear Falcone and the other permanent staffers on the station engaged in one big audio freak-out. Whatever was happening, it wasn't a malfunction.

Cold was how the Xylanx liked the station, Bridget remembered. Dark was new. She didn't want to take chances. But then, she wasn't sure if she was in charge anymore.

The forward lights on the 'box still worked, and her team dressed quickly. Santos floated beside them, half cast in shadow.

He was just as concerned as she was. The agent saw Bridget looking fretfully at him. "What are you waiting for, permission?" he asked. "This is your turf. Go."

Bridget chuckled. She directed Surge Three back aboard the container to distribute arms and armor. Whoever was messing with them would have to hit them with more than darkness and cold.

Someone handed Bridget her armor leg plates. Looking up, she saw it was Stubek handing out the gear. She nodded to the woman. "Watch the Feds," she said, starting to strap on the plates.

Sheepishly, Stubek saluted.

Before Bridget was halfway done dressing, she heard shouts from the area up ahead. O'Herlihy and Dinner were out first, as always, flooding the cavernous shipping center with their high-intensity lights. Something was on the move. "Look out!"

A massive monstrous shape barreled through the darkness, knocking Dinner away with a clang and drawing fire from O'Herlihy. It slammed hard into the passenger container, sending it careening into the wall.

"The cargo tenders! It's the damn cargo tenders!"

Bridget looked out in surprise to see more of the jet-powered vehicles on the move, charging through the void. "Scatter!" she yelled.

Her team was already doing that—to the extent that she could see, which was not very well at all. They were all suddenly pedestrians on an icy highway with construction vehicles screaming toward them and vehicles swirling behind. Another crash, and another. The passenger 'box was now spinning wildly, its searchlights strobing past the chaos. An armored figure lost hold and went hurtling away.

This is the worst discotheque ever, she thought.

Victor Gideon didn't seem to agree: he'd eagerly grabbed on to one of the machines and was ripping at its reaching claws with his bare hands. He and it were in a dance of destruction now, bouncing together against cargo pods and off into the darkness. It was then that she saw that no one was driving the tenders—they were on automatic. And the air was a maelstrom of metal debris from cargo collisions. Ducking a dark chunk of something, Bridget reached for the door of a control station. Naturally, it didn't open.

"There!" O'Herlihy said, pointing off toward the southern end of the cylinder. "Someone's moving by the Echo ring! Not one of us!"

"Be careful," Bridget said, struggling in the weightless night to find a helmet, a rifle, a glove, anything she could use. "We don't know that's not a friendly!"

They knew an instant later when the bullets flew.

"*Get back!*" Bridget swam in space, desperately squirming for cover. There was plenty of that, at least, given how much the tenders had knocked around. Live rounds were coming from the far end of the Shaft, pelting noisily off everything. Bridget didn't think mere bullets could decompress a Regulan-built station, but they could certainly mess up any one of the half-dressed troopers. Grabbing a loose metal plate, she put it between herself and the flashes as best she could, trying to keep her own gyrations to a minimum. She heard screams of pain from the darkness around her and the cracks of return fire.

Then it was only the incoming fire she heard. Casting aside the makeshift shield to cling to a somewhat stationary module, Bridget called out over her headset. "What's wrong?"

"Our rifles!" O'Herlihy said. "They've been de-authorized!"

"And that's not all," said a new voice on the channel. "Programmer One, commanding Surge Sigma, entire team. *Burn! Burn!*"

No! All around, Bridget watched in horror as one by one her teammates' armored frames lit up with megawatts of energy. It was the last-ditch protocol used for Spore attacks—but it also turned her people into motionless dummies. It wasn't supposed to activate without the wearer's initiative—or the chief's directive. It would take the skills of a quartermaster/armorer to hack that...

Oh, no...

"Why don't you guys just hang out there for a while," the confident female voice said. "Your Q/A has things to do."

Bridget gawked. It *was* Trovatelli—and she had immobilized two-thirds of Bridget's team in an instant!

"Lissa?" Bridget asked. "Whatever's going on, you don't have to do this—"

"I'm already doing it. And I'll be done in a few minutes. Ciao." Silence followed.

Bridget wasn't wearing armor, but she seethed anyway. She slapped angrily at her shin plating. If she'd finished dressing, she'd have been immobilized, too. But she couldn't see what else she could do now, especially when she couldn't see.

A hand grabbed her. It was Santos. She could see black droplets seeping from his shoulder in the half-light. "You're hurt!"

"Winged," he said. He handed her his service weapon. "Take this. If it's your Q/A, the weapon's not on her system."

"Thanks. Now I just need to be able to see her—"

"Try these," he said, pulling the expensive sunglasses from his pocket.

"It's a little dark for those."

"They're not for style."

Bridget saw why when she put them on. "Thermal imaging in a fashion accessory?"

"The investigator's friend," he said. He pivoted back to tend to his wounded companion. "Stay safe!"

***

Every possibility ran through Bridget's mind as she made her way through the murk to the loading tracks for the Echo Ring. Industrial sabotage, terrorism, insanity—any one could have driven her young Q/A to this craziness. But while the acts were mad, they were also certainly planned—and the plan wasn't done.

Bridget knew that when she saw the munitions bangbox loaded on the tracks. The shape was unmistakable, even in the dark. It was used for rare missions where demolitions capabilities were needed.

She saw motion. Someone was atop it, shutting a hatch. Trovatelli's form had a cool, regulated temperature that Bridget recognized; she was wearing one of the outfits from the depot.

"Don't move, Lissa!"

Trovatelli spun—and Bridget felt the painful screech of a sonic pulse weapon. The force of the sound waves sent her tumbling.

When she could hear again, Trovatelli's voice returned. "I'd love to stay and kill you personally," she said. "Especially after what you did to Lucas Baines."

Baines—the Walled Garden assassin? Is that what this is about? Bridget didn't have time to dwell on it. Instead, she looked desperately for a handhold. Something to shoot at. Anything!

"But I think this will take you out all the same," Lissa Trovatelli continued. "In a minute I'll have this 'box loaded in the E Ring. I'm setting it to go off seconds after I'm out of here on the other whirlibang. With any luck, that'll take you out, too."

"Lissa—if that 'box is moving, you could split the station in half!"

"Better yet. Casualties of war, and all."

"You're the only casualty I can see," Bridget called out into the darkness. Even with the glasses, she still couldn't find her bearings. "It doesn't have to be like this. I'm giving you one last chance."

"Shut up," Trovatelli said. "I'm busy."

Right. Bridget tapped her earpiece. "Falcone?"

The gruff voice resounded in her ear. "Yeah, I hear you."

"I think it's time."

"You're damn right." She heard a beep, and he continued. "This is Falcone, Leonid, expedition administrator. Authorize Overland Option One."

"Yang, Bridget," she said into her mic. She shook her head, saying the words she never expected she would have to say. "All SoftSHELs in location Five South. Overland Execute!"

45

Trovatelli had no idea what nonsense Bridget was going on about, and didn't care. Huddled over the detonation controls, she redirected her portable light as she continued her work. Just a few more wires to go, and her bomb would be ready to put into the chute.

Bridget's earlier words, though, had excited her. She was only hoping to destroy the link to the Xylanx's realm. Taking out the entire station, on the other hand, would be a bonus. She knew the civilians would likely be safe, up in the habitation portion; only the paid thugs of the corporation would be blown apart or vented to space.

Murder would have been alien to her before the massacre at Giotto Colony. Now, murder was what any friend to aliens deserved. At long last she would become a soldier herself. She felt giddy as she reached for the next-to-last wire.

Then she felt woozy.

Then she threw up.

***

Bridget Yang had trained and lived in armor. And what her Overland Option used was the thing that was innermost in every one of those suits of armor.

323

In the early twenty-second century, the nations of Earth had taken a cautious approach to the new goods from beyond. It was important to protect humanity itself first and then its industries. Commodities markets had to reckon with new supplies of elements and compounds not available in abundance in the Solar System. Manufacturers concerned themselves with possible obsolescence, as disruptive technologies came in from beyond. In the early years, the list of allowed imports was kept deliberately small.

But one product proved so useful that neither concerns about its safety, nor outcry from earthbound stakeholders could slow its spread. Superlight Hygienic Environment Layers were already in wide use among the Signatories when the Avallorenes, a race specializing in nanotechnology, introduced them to humanity in 2110. The first SHEL variant to reach Earth, a cozy footed pajama with hood, proved more than a luxury fashion item. Much more. For when the opening to the hood was zipped shut, it cured several kinds of cancer. And diabetes. And heart disease. Programmed to understand the optimal operational characteristics for a human being, the SHEL released within its air circulatory system a host of nanoids: microscopic robots tasked with repairing and restoring the wearer. Minutes inside a SHEL strengthened cell structures and repaired genetic damage; an hour nearly brought to a halt the effects of aging altogether.

Authorities withheld the devices for testing, but there seemed nothing amiss with them. All the Signatory powers were using SHELs in one way or another. As the outfits were already radiation-proof environment suits, they only needed transparent areas for sighted species to see through; humans found they needed little else for outer-space work. The garments already regulated for ideal air pressure and temperature, and the nanoids even allowed wearers to stay hydrated without drinking and carried out waste products, within the narrow limits prescribed by the SHEL's attached supply reservoirs.

Naturally, the linings formed the basis for the new generation of human space suits, including the weaponized HardSHEL units that the Surge Team members wore. Those incorporated weapons technologies so advanced that the Signatory powers had restricted their production to a single governing body. On Earth, however, the variety of SoftSHEL units ballooned. The first wave of units available for public use appeared at the hospitals' and doctors' offices; the medical industry understood a disruptive technology when it saw one but could hardly reject the advance.

The simplest of the SHEL variants could be found in articles of light clothing. Such things were expensive, of course, but workers off-world found them invaluable. The jumpsuits, in particular, became standard issue for most expeditions. There were safety reasons as well: the operators of off-world colonies could instantly act to prevent the spread of an antigen simply by communicating its presence via radio linkages with SHEL garments.

Interference with the proper workings of SHEL nanoids was regarded as a heinous crime. It was important enough to be the subject of a major section of the Signatory Pact. It was in the obvious interest of the Avallorenes to do everything possible to prevent their creations from being abused, and they did. Bridget fully understood, and agreed with, the rules.

But after Overland she had determined never to lead others again without something else backing up her once-faulty judgment. She had to have a Plan B, a fallback, an insurance policy.

It was part of why she worked so cheap. No one else but Falcone was willing to offer her the kind of control she wanted. There was no one else she would even dare to ask. Falcone knew about Overland—had really *gotten* what had happened to her—and understood. Only he had agreed to her terms, and a black ops technician of her acquaintance had provided the know-how.

It was a power she had never used before and never intended on using. Not even to save one of her teammate's lives. But she used it now.

She could never have another Lucas Baines on her watch.

Bridget kicked off against a container as she followed the sound of retching. "That'd be the nausea," she said. "Your balance should be gone, too."

A cough. "What—what have you done?"

"What I had to do," Bridget said. She wouldn't tell Trovatelli, but the Dragon's Depot—via a system Falcone had quietly had installed while the Q/A was away at Leel—had advised every SoftSHEL garment in this end of the Shaft of the presence of the Arcturan Plague.

The nanoids would most obviously react by expelling stomach contents. Bridget felt for anyone else who was nearby; at least none of her troopers were down here. She, of course, wore garments that were "off the grid." But the emergency nanoids, before going inert and dissolving harmlessly, would make some more emergency moves.

"You should be getting sleepy about now," Bridget said, raising her weapon. She'd spotted the munitions container again. "And I'd expect some other...*less pleasant* effects."

"This—this is criminal!" she heard Trovatelli say. She'd figured it out.

"Great! The opinion of an expert. But you'd better think fast—if you can."

Bridget popped over the top of the 'box and saw the portable light, abandoned and still burning over unfinished wiring. It didn't smell very good over there. She scanned the area from left to right. Off to one side, she heard a noisy clack—the sound of another 'box heading onto the tracks to leave on Ring F.

"This isn't finished," Trovatelli said over her earpiece.

"No, but you *are* fired."

4 6

Not long after Jamie's mother married Old Man Keeler, the senator had dragged the family out on a vacation to Europe, presumably to drum some culture into Martin Sturm's young son. The trip had included a visit to La Oliva, a Trappist monastery in Spain—coincidentally, not too far from where Jamie's recent ancient video ride had taken him. The only things he remembered from the tour were that the old buildings had a retail shop that sold tasty cheese—and that everyone was wearing robes and hoods as if they'd missed a millennium's worth of fashion.

Jamie felt like a monk now. The Xylanx had given him a long pinkish cloak that covered him from head to toe. And the fellow leading him, he gathered, was something of a monk on his own. Tellmer, an assistant of sorts to Kolvax, had been charged with giving Jamie a tour of Gharion Preserve—and also with protecting the sensibilities of his fellow neo-Neanderthals.

"Your appearance may disturb the others here," Tellmer had said. Wearing silvery armor with a yellow band around his neck, the aide kept his own face hidden from the Xylanders they passed; Jamie wondered just how ugly the assistant had to be. In addition, Tellmer certainly was having trouble doing anything that involved his hands. They'd stood at one door for a minute while Tellmer had tried to get his fingers to work right. Finally,

Jamie had punched the entry button himself. The guards behind him hadn't liked that.

As the group passed from one long hallway to another, Jamie realized just how numerous the Xylanx were. Xylander men and women passed by, paying the group little mind as they went busily about whatever their jobs were. They didn't seem like mindless automata, but neither did they seem particularly cheerful. There were only a few of the black-armored Stalkers here; everyone else was wearing identically tailored outfits, differentiated only by varying colors. Were the suits made of leather? Rubber? Jamie couldn't tell—but he wasn't going to reach out to learn. Bald seemed to be the operative fashion, genetically engineered or otherwise—and many of the Xylanders were heavier set and taller than Kolvax was.

Jamie didn't have to see inside the Tellmer's armor to guess that the guy was probably the last pick for the Gharion Preserve soccer team. Tellmer was the slightest of any of the Xylanders that he'd seen, and he seemed to be an endless trove of stories about the Xylanx and their struggles.

"...and despite having been cast adrift from their garden mother, the Xylanx created their own Forray Glay, in the shadows of night. We are the trees plucked from the ground, rising to reach the stars. And one of the branches of our greatness can be found in the next wing, devoted to fungal geomycology..."

Jamie tuned it out and listened to his own breathing instead. He could breathe well enough without the strange air mask, but the locals on the station were worried about his contaminating them. Since it also worked with his earpiece to translate, he kept it on.

It also kept him from smelling the place—and something there plucked at his subconscious. The Xylanx were, above all things, a clean people. Their space station had to be enormous, given how much curved floor he had traversed with one gee of simulated gravity. And yet every meter he'd seen had been spotless. And yet, for some reason, he had what he could only classify as a preternatural response every time he saw an unmasked Xylander pass. He scrunched his nose, as if fearful to smell. Was there some ancient revulsion to the species—or subspecies, or whatever they were—that humans still carried? How fragrant could his own ancestors have been? It was bizarre. He made a mental note to ask someone back home about it—if he ever saw home again.

"...and as you will see here," Tellmer said, "these teenagers are hard at work crafting the next generation of tympanostomy tubes, which provide many of our people with a constant audio interface with our rulers in the Dominium. Regard the custom shaping of the grommets, designed for easy and comfortable insertion by—"

Jamie cleared his throat.

Tellmer turned. "Did you have a question?"

"Tellmer, do they send you for beer and move to different seats while you're gone?"

The guide stood dumbfounded.

"Sorry," Jamie said. "Look, the tour's great. I'm sure your stockholders are thrilled. I guess I was just wondering if this place is *all* like this."

Tellmer seemed to understand. "Ah. No, there's our final destination. Perhaps that will impress you," he said acidly.

They left the laboratory for an elevator. A very short ride later, Tellmer led Jamie into a place as colorful as the rest of the station was colorless.

It was a garden stretching nearly out of sight. The floor was long and curved; they were inside a huge rotating cylinder, Jamie presumed. Exotic bushes, flowers, and trees climbed improbably high, reaching for a gleaming light source near the center of the drum.

Jamie marveled. He'd seen hydroponic gardens in space before, but they always looked…fake. Transplanted. Florist shop-window. This was different. Oranges, golds, reds—and so many greens. It had been a year and a half since he'd been on Earth—and he felt it here.

This *was* Earth. But taller, bigger. And, well, rounder.

"This is how we remember Forrah Glay, the place from which we came."

Jamie nodded. "It's amazing." He slipped his hand inside his cowl for a moment and pushed away the breathing mask. Yes, that was air, but fresher than he'd ever experienced on his homeworld—and with a light sprinkling of moisture. There were fountains about and waterfalls. There were Xylanx tenders here, he saw, and also some others who seemed to be simply enjoying being in the place. They were higher-ranking figures, he imagined; they were better dressed than the worker bees he'd seen.

His first impulse was to offer Tellmer a deal. Surely they could do with some tourism dollars, no? In exchange for the exclusive concession, Quaestor could ship tour groups here by the 'box. Then Jamie realized in swift succession that he probably didn't represent Quaestor anymore and that with their xenophobia, the Xylanx probably wouldn't be too thrilled anyway.

He also realized that Kolvax was approaching from the forest.

Kolvax was out of the black armor now, wearing loose cinnamon-colored robes and seeming almost contemplative and serene here. He held a shiny briefcase. Tellmer saw him and bowed.

"So, human," Kolvax said to Jamie, "have they been making you comfortable?"

"You're kidding, right? Uncomfortable for me is cutting all my fingernails but one, and then having to live with it all day.

I've been kidnapped by Neanderthals in space. You do the math."
Jamie exhaled. "But this place really is something. These plants
are all from Earth?"

"From Forrah Glay, yes. Everything in this biome is descended from the other materials the Luk'a stole."

"Forrah Glay? Forest Glade!"

"A smart one, this trader is." Kolvax grinned. He passed the
case to Tellmer and gestured for the guards to depart. "Nice day
for a walk, isn't it, human? Come on."

47

Kolvax led Jamie along a winding path through the woods, with Tellmer following a respectful distance behind. "This is one of many such preserves. They're very much at the heart of our culture."

Jamie looked up and around. Only now, in Kolvax's presence, did he contemplate the creepiness of Neanderthals keeping a colossal shrine to a world long since lost. "You—you don't want the planet back, do you?"

"No," Kolvax said.

"But you've been hassling us. Kidnapping me, stealing our knowglobe!"

"And now you know to what end," Kolvax said. "Since we met, I've been working toward one thing: making sure that our meeting, when it did finally happen, would disrupt neither of our civilizations." He snorted. "Well, my civilization. I don't that much care about yours."

"I gather."

"Look, I'm going to lay it on the line, here." Kolvax turned, his hands clasped. "I want your people to keep out of our territory and our lives forever. No selling, no exploring, no nothing. Tellmer brought you up to speed on our history?"

"As much as I could keep awake for, yes."

Kolvax gave Jamie a hard look but then glanced back at Tellmer and shook his head ruefully, as if to commiserate with the human. "Then you know the Xylanx have quite a complex when it comes to you people. The Xylanx conquered the Luk'a—but they've still got the knowledge that before that, they were savages, hiding in trees from humans. Since we're advanced now, a lot of my people assume you must be even further advanced. And they assume, by default, that you're aggressive."

"But you have the knowglobe! You should be able to tell that we're not—"

"Yes, *I* can tell. But it serves the people who rule us to see shadows everywhere and to keep our explorations bottled up as a consequence. It's been that way ever since we got the first messages from Earth."

Jamie laughed—the first good laugh he'd had in the whole ordeal. Yes, he'd been shown the historic recordings by Tellmer. "That thing with the stomping was a comedy show!"

"You don't say."

"Lucille Ball, she's great. I need to start you on *Gilligan's Island* next. Did I mention I once owned a stake in a band called The Mournful Howells?"

Kolvax stared blankly at him for a moment. "The recording—it really was an entertainment?" Kolvax seemed startled but not completely surprised. "But it was aimed directly at one of our star systems—like a warning."

Jamie explained about the mostly insane twenty-first-century billionaire Kayman Weber, who thought that peace with the life in the universe—at that time, completely undiscovered—could be guaranteed by transmitting humanity's most innocuous entertainments at random stars by orbital transmitters using high-powered lasers. Jamie reached for his immerso goggles in the folds of his cloak. "I can get you the rest of the series if you want—"

"Never mind." Kolvax waved his hand. "It's all too complicated. The Dominium won't turn us back out to space again with you lurking out there. Luckily, there's a swath of whirlibang routes we have access to that neither you nor any of the Signatory Systems have entered yet. We need you to go back and tell them to stay away from our routes."

"Exclusive territory?"

"Just that. But we're willing to strike a bargain to make it happen. We know from your knowglobe that you broker exclusive trading deals with alien races, and that your corporations use your laws to protect those rights. Is that accurate?"

"Sure."

"Then I am naming you the Xylanx's official and sole broker of trade to the Earth. You will return to Earth and run an auction in our name. Your product: the exclusive right to trade for a set number of wares each year from this station—all materials to be shipped from here, with no further contact permitted." He looked up at Jamie. "Would your people honor such an agreement?"

Jamie's eyes widened. "If they knew what you had here—and believed I spoke for you, yes."

"They'll believe you—especially since we'll be sending you back with your old knowglobe. We've added our own information to it—what we want to share, that is. The knowledge will answer your culture's questions, and its authenticity will be irrefutable. It will detail the scope of the agreement, and the routes to be avoided. It will also adequately communicate the cost to the whole galaxy if we don't reach this agreement."

"I already work for a corporation," Jamie said. "Quaestor."

"Not in this you don't. I want the auction on Earth, with all your major players participating. They'll respect the result that way."

Franchise agent for Neanderthals! Jamie contemplated the angles. Yes, Kolvax had come up with the one construct most humans would respect: a contractual one. The auction would effectively put whatever buyer Jamie found in the position of protecting the entryways into Xylanx space, with all legal and physical means. Kolvax was going to get his own border guards—and get paid handsomely in the process!

But there was something Jamie didn't understand. "I don't understand why you just don't take a flight to Earth yourself."

"The Dominium will not allow me to serve as an emissary to Earth. I am politically unpopular here—and we have seen from your history how visitors are treated. Besides, we can see that the most likely incursions from your people will be commercial in nature, not military. We can't have those either. But you can speak in the language of these people. You're a salesman."

Jamie shook his head, bewildered. Here he was, in an alien Eden, negotiating with a Neanderthal like a salesman on a golf course. "So what's in it for me?"

Kolvax grinned. "Your freedom and a ride home aren't enough?"

"No."

Kolvax snapped his fingers. Tellmer stepped forward and passed the case to Kolvax. "Your knowglobe suggested you were in dire straits. How much of your currency do you need to square things for your expedition?"

"I'm not sure. Did Surge Sigma win District Two Eighty?"

"We believe so. We saw what happened as we lifted off from Kano."

"Then about forty billion dollars. Give or take."

"Here. Take," Kolvax said, working the latch. He passed the cracked-open case to Jamie.

"It's heavy." Jamie opened the lid and looked inside. He was momentarily blinded, as the light from above reflected off the ingots inside. "It's platinum."

"Not just any platinum. Use your device."

Jamie sat the case on the path and reached for his assayer in another pocket of the cloak. As he had on Kano, he used its spectral analysis tool on the substance. The results boggled his mind. "It's Platinum-190!"

"An isotope. The rarest material known on your world or in all the Signatory Systems. No more portable storehouse of value exists."

"It's impossible," Jamie said, waving the device around. "This thing's been tampered with. You messed with my immerso goggles—"

"We never touched it. Look, we have labs all over the station. Any one could confirm what I'm saying." He looked at the figure on Jamie's assayer. "I'm correct that it's valued at forty billion points?"

"Dollars."

"Dollars, yes. It's hard to sort out of all the ways you humans keep score."

Jamie nodded. "The true value's really speculative. No one's ever seen a fraction of this much in one place. And if you've got this much, it can't really be that rare, can it?"

"If we never bring what we have to market, though, how would it affect you?"

"Just the knowledge that it exists, that you might—"

"We won't. And we'll never meet each other again anyway, will we? Not after you've made our deal on Earth." Kolvax took back the case and closed it. "I've got to think the simple existence of the Platinum-190 will go a long way to selling your story—regardless of what you actually decide to do with it. Save your expedition, take it for yourself—I don't care. Just deliver our message."

Jamie nodded. The platinum might be enough to put fear into the corporations, fear that the Xylanx had the productive capacity to wreck human markets at will. A contractual, managed flow of goods from the Xylanx would be in everyone's interests, no matter who won the contract. Any race that could produce ridiculous amounts of rarities, like pulling rabbits from hats, could devastate another's economy if it really wanted to.

And Kolvax didn't seem to want to. "Consider it a price we pay for peace."

Jamie nodded. "Okay. What do I do next?"

✳ ✳ ✳

Back on Kano, Santos had suggested that he'd left behind more investigators aboard the Dragon's Depot. Hours after Trovatelli's escape, Bridget still hadn't seen them all. There were at least as many federal agents aboard the station as there were Surge Sigma members. All of them were hard at work, looking for clues or any other surprises Trovatelli might have left behind.

It wasn't a simple financial case anymore. It was a terror investigation.

But none of it was her concern. The expedition had been ordered halted; their trader was gone. So she'd spent her morning in sick bay, looking after four of her companions injured in Trovatelli's escape. Until things got sorted out—if they ever did—she had nothing to do.

Santos had made a brief appearance in sick bay to check on his injured marshals. She was worried about him. The man had ignored anything but the most basic first aid for his own wound. She greatly respected the agent's drive and devotion—she'd seen precious little of those things during some years. But it was possible to push oneself too far.

And there was no sense in deciding to care too much, she decided. She'd noticed some chemistry, yes. But as a federal agent and an accused accomplice, she and Santos were hardly a match. *Better to forget about it,* she thought as she left sick bay for the elevator.

Feeling the full gravity of the outermost layer of the station, her shoulders sagged as she walked the halls to Falcone's office. There were agents aplenty here and there, going over personnel documents and shipping manifests. Trovatelli had gone out on the whirlibang that went to Regulus, but of course no word could be sent there before she arrived. Messages had to be physically carried through the whirlibang, and everything traveled at the same speed.

She was likely long gone.

Falcone stood in his office doorway. He looked white. "Yang," he said, when he could finally speak, "what in the world could she have wanted?"

"She really seemed to want to destroy the Echo ring," Bridget said. "That was the one the Xylanx used to escape weeks back."

"Escape to where?"

"We don't know. Their home?"

Falcone's gray eyebrows raised. "She was going to bomb them!"

"No, we can tell she intended it to detonate here. Destroying our link to them so we could never use it."

"Walled Garden," Falcone grumbled. He slouched back into his office. Bridget followed. "You know, I didn't think we rated infiltration by those people."

"Neither did I," Bridget said quietly. It was another reason the expedition had felt like home. And now she'd used up her one trick, the enemy would know it. It was just as well. As much as she wished she'd had the same power eight years earlier, actually using the Overland Option didn't make her feel very good. It wasn't a fair way to fight—even *if* Trovatelli had pulled a similar trick first.

She stood by the wall looking sad and staring at Falcone's plant. It was a nice little tree, if a little peaked. It had perked up since the first time she'd seen it.

Wait.

"Leo," Bridget said. "You said the tree came with the office?"

Falcone looked back at it, harried. "What?"

"The tree. You said it was here when you moved in."

"Yeah," he said. "Out behind the lectern. I brought the counter in here. Who cares?"

Bridget's fingers hovered over it. She was almost afraid to touch it, for some reason. "Leo, the Regulans built this station. The PraetorCorp people bought it and sold it to us. Did they ever occupy the station?"

"No. The only visits here were by acquisitions people and then auditors…"

"And the Xylanx! This is their plant!"

Falcone stared at her. "What difference does that make?"

"None. But maybe lots. Wait here!"

The room outside Falcone's office had originally been for Regulan financial managers—and then it had served as some sort of gathering place, some chapel, for the Xylanx. Now it held a strange assortment of mercenary bodyguards and Treasury and Justice Department officials, all seated on the benches and waiting for a briefing. Arm patched, Peter Santos stood by Falcone at the lectern and watched Bridget emerge from the office. One of her female troopers followed, carefully carrying the potted tree.

"You said you had something for me," Santos said. "I didn't think it was a housewarming gift!"

Muffled laughter came from the listeners seated in the room.

"I don't know if I introduced you to Cathe Wu," Bridget said. "She's on Surge One. She's also a budding horticulturalist."

"No pun intended," Wu said. She gestured to the tree. "What you've got here is something special—really special. *Betula szaferi*. The szaferi birch."

Falcone shrugged. "So it's from Earth after all. Who would bonsai a birch?"

"You can stunt just about anything," Wu replied. "That's not the important thing. What *is* important is that the szaferi birch has been extinct in the wild since the twentieth century. Your Xylanx were growing a tree that's been dead since before we went to the stars."

"Are you sure?"

"There's a live specimen growing in the Kraków Botanical Garden, and it's been sequenced. Unless they visited Poland recently to steal it, you'd have to say they got this at an earlier time. *Much* earlier."

Santos blinked. "The Xylanx visited Earth in ancient times to steal a tree?"

Bridget stepped back up. "I don't think so. The thing made us take a look at the rest of the office again. The rest of the station was spotless when we got here; the office was probably the messiest, by comparison. So we hit it again, with your forensics guys."

She turned to face Falcone. "Leo, we found fingernail cuttings under your desk—"

"Not from me!"

"—and things you don't want to know about in your bathroom. And typing that material led us in a crazy direction indeed..."

48

Falcone sat back in the chair beside the lectern, looking green. "There's been a Neanderthal crapping in my bathroom. Well, that explains a lot."

The revelation that the Xylanx had mostly identical genetic material with Neanderthals had kept the room alive for an hour. Neither Santos's people nor hers were inclined to believe fabulous theories in the absence of more reasonable alternatives. But the fantastic seemed to fit the facts.

"Neanderthals left for space and took some trees with 'em," O'Herlihy said. "I can buy it. You should see ol' Dinner's work with floral arrangements."

His pal grunted.

"We still don't know what we're really dealing with," Bridget said, speaking loud to be heard over the buzzing room. "But whatever it is, *that's* what Trovatelli was afraid of." She faced Santos. "And there's something else. We know they wanted our trader."

Santos leaned against the wall, thinking.

"Look, you can't think Jamie Sturm would have Neanderthals for henchmen," Bridget implored him. "He nearly ruined his spacesuit when he met a Sheoruk."

"You're right," Santos said, clasping his hands. "So what do you propose to do?"

"I want to go get our trader back."

"You want to do it because you think it'll answer something?"

"No. I want to do it because it's our job."

More noise now from both sides of the aisle. Falcone shook his head. "How would you know where to look?"

"We take a 'box out in Echo Ring—the same route they were going to use to get Jamie out the first time." Bridget pointed to the status display on the wall. "We know the link's still live—"

"But," O'Herlihy said, "we have no idea if they're immediately chucking incoming 'boxes into a garbage-smasher."

"That risk bother you, Mike?"

"Not at all. If I stay here you'll just make me clean Falcone's toilet." He looked back to his companions before turning back to face Bridget. "I'd say we're all in."

Santos's proper companion from the CFTC spoke up. "I hate to remind you that Miss Yang is still under arrest," Theda Dalrymple said, sounding to Bridget as if she'd like nothing more than to remind him of the fact.

"Not anymore." Santos drew an isopanel from his pocket and began making notations. "I'm asking the marshals to deputize you," he said to Bridget, "and anyone who follows you into a Fugitive Task Force. You are directed to find Jamison P. Sturm and return him here."

"We can't use soldiers for law enforcement under the Posse Comitatus Act," Theda said.

"I'm not a soldier," Bridget said. "I'm a bodyguard."

"You hear that?" Santos said. "She's a bodyguard." He turned to face the Sigmas. "Well, what are you waiting for? There's a wanted man out there. Go get him!"

✳✳✳

For a man who'd traversed dozens of light-years in just a few weeks, Jamie only now imagined himself a pioneering astronaut. He had a coterie waiting to see him off, and all his supplies for the voyage were prepared and ready to go. He only lacked the space suit, and he didn't mind that at all. The Xylanx had somehow tailored for him a smart gray double-breasted suit in just his size. Evidently what he'd seen the workers of the production colony wearing was not the only way to go. If the Xylanx ever got tired of being cranky hermits, they could open a store on Savile Row.

But he was flabbergasted at how much the bangbox the Xylanx were preparing for him looked like a legitimate shipping module from Earth—right down to the faded manufacturer's logo. Forty-billion-dollar briefcase in hand, Jamie floated around the vessel in the weightlessness of the loading area. It was, in fact, *too* good a likeness.

"Hey," he said. "You didn't mock this up. This container is real!"

"We...*found* it," Kolvax said. The Xylanx leader was watching carefully from his handhold near the doorway to the 'box.

Jamie ran his finger over the number on the nameplate and gasped. It was one of the hundreds of 'boxes spread across the Signatory Systems that he'd employed in his trading scheme. He laughed nervously.

"Is there a problem?"

"Just something ironic."

"Does it matter?"

"It won't to my trip." Jamie shook his head. The Xylanx weren't so far from the Luk'a in the theft department.

The Gharion Preserve, he now knew, was shaped like a colossal top. Above and beneath the massive drum that held the terrarium and industrial floors, the tubular spindle he was in connected to a variety of whirlibang rings. One went to a Signatory depot, his first destination.

Jamie crawled around to Kolvax's position. His associates were carting the knowglobe into the ship now. "Give them a minute to secure it to the floor," Kolvax said, intent on overseeing the operation.

Jamie studied the unmasked leader. Kolvax seemed more willing to show his face than his followers, he'd noticed. He couldn't tell whether Kolvax was a military leader, a politician, or a flim-flam man. Some of the silver-clad Xylanx had called him their priest. Whatever. People in power were the same everywhere, Jamie knew. They made deals in their best interest.

Just like he did. "You know, I could be a *lot* more convincing if you sent me with *two* briefcases of the platinum."

"You think we have them just sitting around?" Kolvax snorted. "It took all my pull with the Dominium to provide me with that. I'm not even sure I trust you not to run off."

Jamie waved his hand. "We've been through that." They'd spent four hours discussing the safeguards to the deal. Jamie would enter the clearance codes from inside the 'box only after the container was racked up and ready for transit. He could clear them easily, should the Xylanx pull a fast one. And Kolvax had placed some kind of sensor on the briefcase lock that only triggered under the particular light from Earth's sun, as filtered by the planet's atmosphere. He'd have to make the trip regardless, if he ever wanted to actually see the platinum again.

He could understand some apprehension where forty billion dollars was concerned. Was that figure even correct? His mind reeled. The amount of money he'd intended to clear in a year's scheming—in ingots that fit in a briefcase! It was enough to wipe out his debts—and if he couldn't make the Feds go away, he could at least afford to tie them up for years.

And yes, he thought, Kolvax was probably right. *It's even enough to save my expedition.*

Jamie caught himself. *My expedition?*

Huh. Well, even if he couldn't save it, he could find a way to help out the people who'd been less hateful to him. That nice Geena Madaki for sure. Bridget? Maybe. He'd have to think about that one. And he definitely had the funds now to buy Lissa Trovatelli a night on any town she wanted.

After a word or two over her abandoning him, of course.

"It's time," Kolvax said as his aides exited the 'box.

"Hold on," Jamie said. He was upside down and having trouble finding his way inside the container one-handed.

"Oh, for..." Kolvax muttered. "The more advanced species, my ass!" He snatched the case from Jamie's hand, twirled him, and pushed him inside the 'box. Jamie looked back to see Kolvax pitching him the weightless briefcase. "Here."

"Thanks." Jamie cycled the outer airlock door shut. It hissed and locked loudly.

Well, this is it. He closed the inner door and tugged at his collar. The room was just like the passenger 'box he'd first ridden in: a single pilot's seat with some empty chairs behind. Secured to the floor behind that was the meter-high knowglobe dodecahedron, lights blinking on its various panels. He reached the pilot's seat and called up the code menu on the display isopanel. He'd sent codes like these across the Orion Arm in the past year but had never entered one personally. It was quick.

Jamie found Kolvax on one of the exterior monitors. The trader spoke into his headset. "All right. With this I'm cleared through two different Signatory transit stations and then to Venus. Then I'll get an express hookup to Earth. It's like I told your planners: I should be there in six days." He looked back on the bulging satchels of supplies, leashed to the floor. "I'm glad you packed me a lunch." *Such as it is*, he did not say.

"You're sure your code will work?" Kolvax asked. "The 'box will be cleared through to Earth?"

"Yes—the code's the one I was going to use for my rhodium shipment. It's all automatic. Next stop: Johannesburg."

"Excellent."

Above the ceiling Jamie heard some thumping around. He looked at the monitor. "Is that part of departure prep?"

Kolvax looked back mildly. "For you, yes."

"What do you mean, *for me?*"

"I mean we're severing your transmitter so you can't call out when you get where you're going—or do something to change your destination. You might as well sit back and enjoy the ride."

"Why would I do that?" Jamie said. He lifted the briefcase in front of the 'box's internal camera. "You already said this thing won't open until I get to Earth." He gave the clasp a try for show.

It snapped open.

Inside: dull gray bars.

Jamie's breath caught in his throat. He reached for his breast pocket and found the assayer. A sweep of the device confirmed it. Iron.

Jamie lifted one of the bulky ingots before the camera. "What's the big idea? You switched cases on me?"

Kolvax smiled toothily. "Like I said, evolution has a sense of humor." He flashed an identical case in front of him.

Angered, Jamie punched at the isopanel to erase the clearance codes. Nothing happened. He pushed the button to abort the departure. Again nothing. Same for triggering the door.

"Like I said," Kolvax said, "we've done some work."

Oh, yeah? Jamie wasn't about to let anyone cheat on a deal so blatantly. Even as he heard more preflight knocking about above, he pushed his way back to the knowglobe. If he was indeed inside a genuine standard-model Ballistodyne bangbox—and the knowglobe was the one Kolvax had stolen on Leel—there should be some operational instructions in the device.

But its displays, again, didn't respond to Jamie's words or touch. Agitated, Jamie pounded on one side of it with his fist. "Work, dammit!"

Startlingly to Jamie, the knowglobe responded to his attempts by—*blooming?* The panels mechanically folded back like petals, revealing at the center of the macabre blossom a glass-like orb suspended on five small struts. In the sphere glowed a pulsating, green, living luminescence.

"*The Spore?*" Jamie shrieked. He pushed himself backward from the thing as fast as he could. "You're shipping me to Earth with a batch of Spore? Are you nuts?"

Kolvax responded from the monitor. "It's in a protective encasement that it can't eat through."

"Are you crazy? There's nothing the Spore can't eat through!"

"Hey, we should know," Kolvax said. "Who do you think designed the thing to begin with? We wouldn't invent something we couldn't contain!"

Jamie's eyes bulged. "You engineered the Spore? Set it loose?"

"The last time we wanted to deal with annoying neighbors, yes. Hardy little bugger, though—it tends to stick around and multiply. Based it off something the Luk'a scraped up from one of your streams, in fact. We're just sending it back home."

"B-b-back home? With *me?*"

"Yes. But you should be safe. The encasement will remain secured until the door to the bangbox is opened. And we've made modifications to that, too—it only works from the outside. So you see, there's no way out. For you—or your misbegotten species. At least not until it's too late."

Sweating, Jamie shook his head. He could feel the 'box beginning to move. Any moment it would be outside in the transit rings and starting its departure circuit. "Kolvax, this is insane! I thought you didn't want a fight with us!"

"And there won't be one. Not now," Kolvax said. "I told you right. The Dominium *needs* the Earth. It's been a scary fairy tale to keep people with true ambition in line. Now that we've found out more about you, they're working out ways now to modify their myth—to keep themselves in power. Well, I'm going to free my people—by destroying yours!"

EPISODE 8:
POISON PILL

4 9

Over the years, academia on Earth had seen countless branches of study rise and fall. But job insurance had always gone to those in each field who studied worst-case scenarios. Flights of fatalism covering everything from solar flares to viral outbreaks had launched and maintained millions of careers. So many that by the middle of the twenty-first century, there was enough business in doomsaying that one university, St. Theobald's at Brooklyn, launched an interdisciplinary program devoted just to disaster.

It was a fitting topic for an institution named for the patron saint of panic attacks. The school's researchers did pioneering work on the fertility scare of the 2070s, the economic deflation of the 2080s, and the disco revival of the 2090s. The discovery of Formation Seven-Alpha—the Spore—however, was enough to drive even Theobald's most stoic sages to the chapel to pray for deliverance.

One STBU study after another modeled what would happen should the Spore get loose on Earth. Microscopic amounts might fail to thrive; thimble-sized portions might be contained after they reduced a city to a crater. Beyond that, the papers offered a parade of cataclysms. Replicating virally, the Spore would devour everything in its path; clumsy attempts to destroy it would only spread it further. The oceans would drain into the

Spore basin, only to disappear. Within eight weeks, the most frightening estimates said, the crust of the Earth would be consumed.

St. Theobald's scientists differed as to what would happen after that. With nothing left to eat but superheated iron, would the colony reach some kind of stasis, ceasing its replication? Some said yes. Others said no. Still others observed that it was the very definition of a purely academic question, and that it was time to go to the bar. But the researchers' findings had one effect. They were key in driving the nations and corporations of Earth to agree to the Signatory Pact, the primary thrust of which was simply this: Formation Seven-Alpha could never be allowed to reach the homeworld.

Jamie knew about the studies. He also knew the fact that the organism tended to devour infected containers so quickly had kept the Spore from being more than a theoretical danger to Earth. But something *could* contain the Spore for transport. He was looking at it!

Clinging to the headrest of a nearby seat, Jamie gaped at the orb atop the pylon. The substance containing the Spore seemed like nothing more than glass with a slight bluish tint. But his assayer drew a blank when he waved the device past. *No wonder,* he thought. The device only responded to known compounds.

At least the five struts attaching the globe to the floor appeared sturdy. He waved his assayer past them, hoping to find them made of the sturdiest titanium.

Rhodium.

Jamie blinked and looked at the display again. "Oh, no!" His mind flashed back to Alabeyd and his hard lesson about Seven-Alpha. There was no substance the Spore devoured more greedily. Looking as closely as he dared into the container, he could see little injector ports through the translucent shape. That would be how the Xylanx would trigger their disaster, Jamie realized. The struts were more than supports: they were syringes, ready to inject rhodium needles into the goo like control rods in a nuclear reactor. The Spore would devour them, then the struts, and then the 'box itself. The whole compartment he was traveling in was a biological bomb waiting to go off when someone opened the door...

...if the flying briefcase didn't smash the Spore's prison open first. Jamie saw it out of the corner of his eye. *"Gah!"*

Jamie pushed off against the nearby seat and soared through the air toward the case. The Xylanx's preflight routine had set the 'box to rocking, buffeting around the contents; Jamie had forgotten about the briefcase, weightless yet bulky. Jamie's legs just cleared the top of the ominous orb as he swatted the case away. Of course, the abrupt move dislodged the assayer from his pocket, now sending *it* tumbling threateningly toward the sphere. Contorting himself, Jamie slapped the metal device away—only to see it carom off the ceiling and back toward the orb.

He was playing handball against himself...and losing.

Unthinkingly, Jamie placed a bare hand on the glass ball and shifted his weight, protecting the globe with his body. The assayer dinked off his back—and now the briefcase made its return visit. The 'box was in some kind of elevator now, jostling all the contents. Even Jamie's lunch cooler was on the move.

"Ayeee!" Realizing he was bear-hugging the burbling bubble, Jamie drew his hands and arms back frantically. The Spore didn't seem to care. Jamie pushed off against the ceiling and coasted about, gathering the loose items.

Jamming the case beneath the armrest of the pilot's seat, Jamie heard another clang. The indicators on the forward panel lit up: the 'box was outside the pressurized confines of the Gharion Preserve now, moving on tracks toward the acceleration rings. Metal girders and darkness went past on the displays.

Jamie scanned the walls. He had to get out! But there were no space suits to be seen. He looked in anguish at his swanky business suit. The Xylanx had dressed him well for his trip—and his funeral!

✳ ✳ ✳

"The time has come," Kolvax said, standing unmasked before the podium. The scene was carefully prepared, the speech long in coming. "For years I have preached the truth. The humans of Earth—which we call Forrah Glay—have long existed in our people's imaginations as great horrors. Rivals, who once nearly wiped us out—and who might some day rise to follow us, finishing the job."

He spoke forcefully but calmly, a departure from his energetic exhortations as Black Priest. The focus groups on Gharion Preserve had found this approach stately. He wanted to educate, to prepare them for what was coming. "We did not know where Forrah Glay was. We did not know how far the Luk'a had taken us from Earth until we saw the broadcast years ago. We should have acted then. But the half-hearts of the Dominium held us back, choosing instead to shape the humans into their own bogeymen. The humans became unwitting accomplices in a power grab from you, the people!"

He revealed what he had learned from Jamie and the know-globe—that Lucy, the strange woman from the broadcast, was not an evil redheaded executioner gleefully stomping the life out of sentient beings. It had come as surprising news earlier to the members of the Severed in his live audience—some of them gasped again now—and it would certainly shock his listeners across the stars when they heard the recorded broadcast.

"The Dominium made a human clown into a tool for their own oppression—and in so doing made fools of all of us!" He turned on the measured indignation. He was every Xylander's best friend, rightfully offended at how his brothers and sisters had been lied to. "If the humans really were a threat—and I think they do have that potential—we'd never know, because the Dominium would never act. Why, when the humans' continued existence has served them so well? Our whole generation has been restrained, kept from the cosmos by fraud!"

Kolvax slapped his hands on the lectern. "The humans have an expression that is apt here: *a monkey on one's back*. And that is what they have been. We've had a rival primate weighing us down for too long. Forrah Glay is no heaven taken from us: it is rather the hell from which we were delivered. You've seen the information from their knowglobe; you know all that was good on Earth we've cultivated in our own preserves.

"So I have put an end to the charade once and for all!" His voice grew louder and more forceful. This had been tested before an audience, too. "Today, I have seen us *severed*—and yes, now you understand the real meaning of the name of my movement— from our ancestral manacles. The Earth is destroyed, using one of the tools we held in abeyance for too long. The humans who survive will do so as a vagabond race, dispossessed from their home just as we once were. Only we have grown during our time away. They will wither and fall, leaves from the tree.

"Was their threat real or imagined? It no longer matters. I have ended it—and now declare a new age for the Xylanx. As you hear this, my followers are rising across the empire. Join them, and throw down the Dominium members who lorded over you. You will find it is not as difficult as you thought. You have the truth—and you will now have the power." Kolvax raised his fist before him. "Heed the words of Kolvax—warrior, exile, patriot. You have been prisoners too long—paralyzed by trumped-up fears of a belligerent Earth. I came to destroy that prison. No one will ever use the nightmares of Earth against us again. I came to set you free on the galaxy, now and forever!"

All around his supporters cheered. It was the opposite of the pious and morose reception the Severed members had previously given his speeches during their exile together. The members of the Severed had been reactionaries, bonded together against the human threat; now, he had made them revolutionaries. Kolvax liked this response better. His listeners had even removed their helmets for the occasion. Liandro, Rumber, and the others all looked pasty and white-faced; Tellmer looked a ghost. *I did this just in time*, Kolvax thought. *I've probably saved them from suffocating!*

Tellmer was in tears. "A good message, Great Kolvax. A great message. And cleansing the galaxy of the humans—it's right, no matter what. They're just so—so *dirty...*"

"Whatever makes you happy, Tellmer." The xenophobia would certainly stick with some of his followers, Kolvax knew. "Release the video as soon as we've got confirmation the 'box has done its job," Kolvax said, stepping out from behind the podium.

Rumber looked confused. "How will we know?"

"I've got scouts undercover in one of the Regulan bazaars. Anything that happens to Earth will be known there shortly afterward. They'll get word back to us right away. By that time we'll already be in place everywhere in the realm. We make our announcement—and then we move." He looked out at the assembled listeners. "We'll be the ones in power then. You won't have to hide your faces again." *Even though some of you probably should*, he thought, taking another look at Tellmer. *Is that a growth or just your nose?*

OVERDRAFT: THE ORION OFFENSIVE

Kolvax looked up at the display. They had retreated to the rotating section of the station, not far from the loading area, to record the message. But the container holding his precious bio-bomb was still moving to the rings. "What's the damn holdup?"

Liandro looked down guiltily. "It's the humans' shipping container—it wasn't sized perfectly for our tracks within the station. It's taken some encouragement to get it out to the rings."

Kolvax snorted. "I'm sure Jamie Sturm has already locked himself in the toilet." He took the goblet Rumber offered him and raised it. "Relax, little trader," he called out to the 'box. "It won't be long now!"

359

5 0

"Light armor! Fresh weapons!" Bridget floated by the doorway to the passenger 'box, passing out gear as her troops entered. "Propulsion packs—we don't know if there's gravity over there. Don't wait out here—dress when you're aboard! Load up!"

There had been nothing organized about the departure. The lighting in the Shaft had been restored since Trovatelli's chaotic escape, but there was no time to remove the munitions 'box their traitorous former Q/A had loaded onto the exit tracks of the Echo Ring. They would simply have to take the pod with them, along with their single passenger container and their thruster unit. Bridget's teammates would need fresh weapons and equipment from the stores; Trovatelli had done a number on the gear they brought back from Kano, and Yang didn't want to use anything that the woman might have touched recently. Bridget had assembled a melded crew from her three teams to take with her. *But to where?*

Arbutus Dinner looked at her with furrowed brow as he approached, helmet in hand. "You sure about this, Chief? We've never jumped blind before."

"You know how it works. If there's no connection, we won't go anywhere." A whirlibang could transport a 'box without a partner station on the other side—that was how transit stations were inserted in systems—but the power required was beyond the capacity of the Dragon's Depot to supply.

Victor Gideon grunted, shotgun in hand, as he passed her.

"How long has it been since you slept, Victor?"

"Not long. A week?"

"Good man."

O'Herlihy was last to board. She looked up at him—game for anything, as always. "Thanks for this, Mike. I was afraid you guys wouldn't go across the street for Jamie, much less the galaxy."

"We're not doing it for him. We're doing it for you." The muscular man patted her shoulder. "I don't know if this guy is worth saving or not. But none of us have exactly stellar résumés, and you've taken chances on each of us. We figure if you'd hire Arbutus after the Funworld incident, you'd go out on a limb for anyone."

The corners of Bridget's mouth lifted as she remembered. On a hot Florida day years earlier, Dinner had infamously reached the end of his normally boundless patience while wearing a cartoon dolphin suit. Three of the teenagers taunting him had to be rescued from the lake, and a great-grandmother near his rampage had required resuscitation. Dinner had recorded his video application for Quaestor from the holding cell that night, still half-dressed as the aquatic mascot—the bottom half. Bridget chuckled. "I guess you're right. I hear what people say— the primary qualification for serving on my team is having nothing left to lose."

O'Herlihy winked. "No sense wasting all that desperation on a job we could survive."

"Load up."

Finally inside the container herself, Bridget looked back out as she started to close the door. Across the Shaft, Peter Santos clung to a railing and watched. Seeing her facing him, he gave a salute.

He's come to see me off? Bridget chuckled again and shook her head. Why did she only start thinking about the future now, when facing the imminent danger of death? *Your timing's lousy as ever, Yang.* She had a job to do. She shut and locked the door and focused on the present.

✻ ✻ ✻

Jamie could tell from the monitor before the pilot's seat that the 'box he was in was fully in space now, suspended within the metal guide tracks of a whirlibang attached to Gharion Preserve. The clackety-clack sounds were different from the noises made by the whirlibangs he was familiar with, but he heard the usual characteristic whine of the rings being charged. He knew what that meant: the trip was about to start. And he was still trapped inside!

Think, dammit! Jamie, think!

Clinging to the pilot's seat, the trader looked around the cabin. Up, down, everywhere—nothing. They'd even taken his oxygen mask when he was boarding; he presumed they were no longer worried about his infecting them with his cooties.

Now he understood.

Jamie wished he had never taken a finance class, never gone to space, never set foot aboard a 'box. He should have fought, screamed, done anything back on Venus—anything to have avoided that first wretched trip with the thugs and Madaki.

"Shouldn't I have a space suit or something?"

"There's one under my seat if we need it," Madaki said.

Jamie's eyes bulged. He looked down at the seat he was clinging to. The 'box he was in was a standard model, just like the one he had first boarded. Pulling up the briefcase from the seat, he pawed at the cushion. *Please, please.*

Beneath the cushion was a compartment with a helmet and a neatly folded SoftSHEL environment suit. There was even a small oxygen canister. All evidently missed by the Xylanx who had prepared the 'box for transit.

Jamie yanked at the helmet. And for the first time in his life, he thanked God for government regulations.

✳ ✳ ✳

Kolvax stood proudly in the control center. His adherents were here, along with a number of other civilians, watching the video image of the 'box in Ring Eleven. Those not in his confidence finally suspected something important was happening, Kolvax expected; if they could only imagine the magnitude of the historic event they were really witnessing!

Borranz certainly had fellow spies on board the station; their suspicions had gone into overdrive when she failed to return from Kano. Some of her squealers had no doubt slipped back to the Dominium to inform on him. He didn't care. It was too late for anyone to stop him. He smiled as he looked at the video image of the 'box in Ring Eleven beginning its move around the track. His ammo was in the chamber, ready to fire.

"Switch again to the surveillance feed from inside the 'box," Kolvax said. "Let's make sure our envoy is behaving like a good—"

Before he could finish the instruction, a siren went off atop a console. "What is it?" he growled.

"Unexpected arrival!" Tellmer said. "Three containers!"

Kolvax forgot about checking on Jamie. He knew the containers couldn't be arriving in the ring where Jamie was to depart from. Kolvax's understanding of transcendental physics was limited, but he knew an already-charged transit ring would never accept an incoming object. The act of powering it up temporarily made it a one-way interstellar street; collisions simply weren't possible. No, it had to be his enemies from the Dominium—and he was prepared for that. "We have Severed-led Stalkers waiting outside the entry chambers at all rings coming from Xylanx space." He didn't care what any bystanders heard now. "Order them to kill anyone who tries to board."

"But honored Kolvax, they're not coming from our space," Tellmer said, breathlessly. "They're coming from Sigma Draconis! *It's the humans!*"

***

Baannng!

"We're here!" Bridget yelled as the rotational motion slammed her body into her seat.

Yeah, but where's here...

***

"This is crazy! This is crazy! This is crazy!"

Jamie snapped the helmet on, completing the suit's vacuum seal. He had no plan at all beyond getting the hell out of the 'box. But the container was beginning to whip around the circular tracks, and he was definitely feeling it. His body had drifted to the floor as he dressed, thanks to the centrifugal force—and now he was standing naturally, under one gee. He knew that force would shortly double or triple, which took the hatch on the top of the 'box out as an escape route. It was the side door he'd entered through or nothing.

The door Kolvax had said released the Spore!

Still—in his mind, at least—he had no choice. The interior airlock door cycled easily, and Jamie paused facing the second, outer door. It was only now, for the first time, that he considered staying aboard—waiting to escape until the 'box was at its intermediate destination. That would be a Signatory space station; they'd know how to deal with the Spore, wouldn't they? It would be better to escape there than to be stuck here with the Xylanx! But before Jamie could give the option any more thought, he heard an ominous glub-glub from the direction of the Spore orb. Under the effects of acceleration, the Spore had turned an angry shade of green, bubbling madly in its prison.

The hell with this! Jamie grabbed the outer door latch.

Nothing. Belatedly, he remembered that Kolvax had said it was locked from the outside. His arms sagged, and not just from disappointment. The emergency space suit didn't have an internal armature to support his frame, like he'd had on Moog. His next move might be the last he was capable of making!

Frantically, Jamie looked around for an ally…

…and found one on the deck.

The briefcase.

Lumbering across the floor, he reached the metal case and tried to lift it. It seemed as sturdy as his official one—and far heavier. Of course it would be, with iron ingots inside. Kolvax had swapped cases on him, yes—but he'd also left him with a weapon.

"Yeah! Yeah!" Jamie wrapped two gloved hands around the case handle and stumbled toward the pilot's seat. With the spinning of the 'box forcing his body downward and backward, it took monumental effort just to cross the floor. Finally he made it. He lifted the case and swung it at the control panels like a drunken samurai.

Krakk! With enormous exertion, Jamie lifted the case again and struck something else. Again! Again! He wasn't looking at what he was hitting, and he didn't know where the strength was coming from. Fear? Panic? Anger at what he'd gone through? All of the above? Jamie didn't care about the answer. He just had to disable the 'box, the door—anything!

Battered panels sparked and smoked. Jamie saw the overhead lights flicker. "Life support system failure," announced a preprogrammed human voice.

"Yeah?" Exhausted by his efforts, Jamie looked at the smashed and useless monitor. "What else?"

"Travel systems nominal. Jump countdown commencing."

"That wasn't what I meant at all!"

51

"Faster! Faster!"

The tramcar could only go so fast, Kolvax knew, but he didn't care. Transit Rings One through Six were mounted on spars that sprang from the far end of the station like giant metal blooms; he had been in the control center at the far end to be closer to the human trader. That meant several kilometers of gardens had to be crossed before he could respond.

The tramcar rode tracks high through the chamber, occasionally grazing the taller treetops. In the front seat of an open car loaded with Stalkers and Severed loyalists, Kolvax ducked branches as he tried to put on his black armor. It was almost impossible in the cramped conditions, and he swore again. He'd already cursed himself for leaving the rings to Sigma Draconis operational. He'd left the link live only to see if any humans would wander through the portal; he'd hoped that he might get a human knowglobe or emissary on the cheap that way. Now that error might cost him everything, he realized.

"They're humans all right," Tellmer said from the seat behind Kolvax. He had been relaying helmet-radio reports from the guards on duty at the far end to his master since the ride began. Now, he was also helping to dress his master—all while babysitting a briefcase in his lap. It was the original platinum-bearing one that Kolvax had switched away from Jamie. The materials had been wheedled at great difficulty from Borranz and the Dominium, and Kolvax had sternly ordered Tellmer not to lose contact with it. It was making his effort to armor Kolvax from the backseat a comical and awkward affair.

"Weapons have been fired, Great Kolvax. Should I order the control station to shut down the transit ring so no one else arrives?"

"Hell, no." Straining to outfit himself in the narrow space, Kolvax could just see some idiot accidentally deactivating all the rings, including the one Jamie was going out on. Or worse, some crony of Borranz's might attempt to abort the launch. "Tell them to form a perimeter. Don't let anyone past.

"Now shut up and find my other boot!"

***

Bridget had handled many first contacts as part of the Visitor Contact Group. None had been as important to humanity as this one. And none had gone quite like this.

Neanderthals were shooting at her.

Neanderthals were shooting at her!

Bridget had allowed herself exactly one second to marvel. The activity had been nonstop since the passenger 'box trundled to a stop on the tracks inside the alien space station. The Xylanx warriors on duty in the receiving area had looked familiar: big, armored, and firing nasty things at them. Bringing the propulsion packs had been the right call. Bridget and her teammates had soared into the zero-gee loading zone, rocketing away at different angles. They'd caught the guards in a cross fire then and were now facing a group of unmasked Xylanx, firing at her from positions of cover.

OVERDRAFT: THE ORION OFFENSIVE

They were evidently workers of some sort, she assumed—and very definitely human—or human-*ish*. They were big on everything but hair—and hospitality. Another projectile glanced noisily off her shoulder plate. Beside her, Gideon fired back at her attackers, scattering them.

"I've picked up the signal from Jamie's badge," Cathe Wu said, pointing to a large open passageway. "He's four clicks that way!"

"Or his badge is." She turned to O'Herlihy. "Take six and hold here. You're our escape route—"

"Got it. Go!"

Bridget triggered her jet pack and soared through the open air, her companions just behind her. The tunnel led downward—a concept that suddenly had meaning as gravity began to increase. They were in a colossal rotating bulb of some kind—and now passing through what almost felt like avenues in a factory town. Multiple-story structures with balconies connected by catwalks bridged the passageway. There were more of the worker bees here—*many* more—all dashing about. A shrill alarm was echoing through the massive hall; Bridget could see that the occupants here were stunned both to hear it and to see their visitors. *Must not get many tourists.*

"Straight on," Bridget said. The residents had *them* in a cross fire now, evidently uncaring whether they struck neighbors across the way. But help in dodging these wild shots came from the surge team's propulsion packs, which were struggling to remain effective in the increasing gravity.

Leading her team, Bridget was finally forced to hit the deck, followed quickly in turn by her teammates. Under a half of a gee, she bounded toward a rectangle of light up ahead...

...before skidding to a stop when she reached a railing.

"I don't believe it!" Dinner said, the first to arrive at her side.

"Welcome to the jungle," Bridget said, gawking with the rest of the team at the vast forest spreading out ahead of them before shouting, "Let's go!"

***

The tramcar screeched to a halt. The helmet slipped from Kolvax's hands, tumbling out of the car and into the greenery far below.

"Dammit! What's going on?"

The driver looked away from his monitor and pointed down into the vegetation. "Eight contacts—we think—fanning out just below us."

Kolvax frowned. It was half a kilometer in either direction to a tram station tower providing elevator access to the surface.

"We've got Stalkers closing in," Tellmer said.

"You're damn right," Kolvax said. "*Us.*" He began to clamber out of the vehicle. The gravity generated by the station's rotation was much less at this elevation; here, the towering trees were within reach even for an armored warrior. "Follow me."

Tellmer froze. "You don't expect *me* to—"

Kolvax stopped Tellmer with a withering glance. "No, you little coward, not you. Take the car to the elevator and bring me my things—and see if you can find me another helmet."

"Yes, Great Kolvax." Sheepishly, Tellmer slipped into the seat vacated by the driver. All around Xylanx warriors reluctantly rose from their seats.

Perched on the edge, Kolvax picked out a sturdy-looking tree within jumping distance. Looking back at his underlings, he said, "In case any of us don't make it, I want you to know I hate you all."

***

The case in Jamie's hands felt as if it weighed a ton. He felt even heavier. He'd pounded and pounded at the controls, and yet his efforts had done nothing to stop the 'box's motion. It was continuing to speed up. By this point during any other trip he'd be strapped into his acceleration chair. Not an option now. He looked around for something, anything that might help…

…when the lights flickered out for good. Only a pulsing emerald glow from the Spore remained.

That was enough for Jamie. While he could still remember where the airlock was, he staggered toward it, forcing one foot after the other. He found the outer door when he fell against it, feeling the handle jab into his gut.

Unable to hold the case anymore, he snapped it open and grabbed two of the iron ingots, one in each hand. Using the bricks as hammers, he began pounding away in the dark.

Something snapped. Explosive bolts fired, sending a door that normally opened inward rocketing from the 'box. The air in the container rushed for the exit, slamming Jamie like a hurricane.

The ingots fell from Jamie's hands, and he felt the enormous force trying to eject him from the vessel. But another force was at work, too—the still-accelerating 'box, rocketing inside circular rails half a kilometer wide. The conflicting motions pushed him outside the airlock—but only halfway. The door frame caught him just under his armpits, even as it knocked the breath out of him. His legs dangled outside, trailing in open space.

"*Heelllp!*" he yelled. But with the wind pounding at his helmet, he couldn't even hear himself.

52

Bridget felt a little like a member of the infantry, making her way through the woods. But only a little. This was no sweep through the Ardennes forest, no Vietnam patrol, no Madagascar recon. They were trillions of kilometers from those places, in a greenhouse being shot at with high-tech weapons. And nothing about her tactics was by the book. Hindered by the full gravity of the terrarium floor, she and her troops were moving as quickly as they could, struck hard occasionally by shots from attackers they couldn't see. Their armor absorbing the fire, they kept on moving.

The saving grace was that in here the Xylanx weren't using incendiary weapons—evidently, they cared whether the whole place went up in flames. But they were still being struck by missile rounds and pulse blasts, and at Surge Sigma's pace, there was no way to avoid being struck entirely. The only thing to do was to keep moving toward Jamie's signal and hope that by staying in motion the trees would offer some cover.

That signal had been moving toward them at a fast rate for several minutes; now, it seemed to have stopped up ahead. And "up" was the operative word. Every so often, through the branches, she caught sight of tracks traversing the "sky" beneath the artificial sunshine; was Jamie up there?

Her eyes widened. "*Look out!*"

Branches above snapped, and in a second a black shape was in their midst. Another figure plummeted from above and landed squarely on Dinner's back, knocking the warrior to the ground. Bridget rolled to avoid a third. Ardennes was wrong, she realized: this was a scene from a war before history. Neanderthals were jumping out of the trees at them!

Bridget fired her rifle at Dinner's attacker. Two more were down now, tangling with Gideon. "I've got this," Victor yelled to her. "Go!"

He didn't seem to have it, but Bridget turned ahead anyway and dashed through the trees. She was meters away when she noticed torn foliage littering the ground. Alerted too late, she looked to one side—and straight into an incoming pulse blast.

The sonic shriek threw her backward. Bouncing off a tree, Bridget hit the ground awkwardly and turned to run. But another full-power blast struck her from behind, sending her hurtling face-first into a boulder. Bridget heard something crack.

She was relieved that it was only her faceplate: whether the rest of the giant garden was artificial or not, the rock was definitely genuine. The isopanel layer of her helmet gave out immediately, and all her data displays winked out. Struggling to her knees, she looked back through the cracked helmet at her attacker.

She had never seen this Xylander bareheaded before—and yet she knew him instantly. His build and armor markings were immediately identifiable, if not his strange face. He touched a control just inside his collar, and she heard his voice in English.

"Ah, the leader. Yang, is it?" Kolvax said. "I suspect you're looking for this." He produced something from a pouch on his hip and threw it to the ground in front of her face.

Bridget reached for it. It was Jamie's trader badge.

"Sturm won't be needing it anymore. And you won't be needing anything either!"

✳ ✳ ✳

The outward pressure from the still-accelerating 'box lessened. Ignoring the pain in his midsection, Jamie heaved against the wall, trying to worm his way back inside. The act raised his head enough that he caught a glimpse of the room he had left behind.

The big fishbowl inside had gone dark; instead, the green glow had shifted to the rhodium supports at the orb's base.

The Spore was loose!

Without thinking, Jamie began wiggling backward out of the airlock. He abruptly stopped when he realized that outside wasn't much safer. There was nothing to keep him from tumbling away from this wild Ferris wheel. Whether he lost his grip or leapt free, the result would be a suicidal slingshot either into space or into one of the support beams rocketing past.

Then he remembered the recessed handholds on the outside of the 'box, the little rungs that gave access to the rooftop. With one arm inside the door frame, he fumbled around looking for a handhold outside. He found one immediately and grasped it tightly as his body drifted away from the doorway.

The first moment of his first spacewalk scared the hell out of Jamie. The transit ring flying by beneath him appeared as a blur of strobing lights: blue, white, orange. The outer airlock door was long gone. Above were the support spokes connecting the whirl-ibang to the Xylanx station's central torus. He saw them whizzing past at an impossible rate. How could he ever get up there when the 'box was still accelerating? Taking his first step onto the rungs was almost enough to stop him from even trying. His feet slipped, and he clutched desperately onto the handholds while his legs bicycled wildly beneath him.

Finding the footholds again, he gasped for breath. This was insane: whirlibangs weren't designed for hitchhikers! What if the 'box achieved its critical velocity? He knew the tunnel through interstellar space, the interdimensional connection, was strictly prescribed; only matter within specific physical confines would make the transit. Would he go with the 'box, subjected to whatever forces were out there? Or would he be scraped off like a bug struck by a windshield wiper? Or, worst of all, would half of him go and the other half of him remain behind?

Jamie decided making the trip might not be so bad. Maybe the Spore would eat slowly, slow enough for him to survive until the next stop. Shifting his weight, he peeked back in through the airlock.

The floor beyond the entryway seemed to be bubbling like a hot pudding, greens now joined by oranges. Jamie blanched. *Dragon vomit?* It looked like it—and it might as well be. It was eating through the deck plating!

Realizing at last that it was no place to be indecisive, Jamie decided the only thing to do was to launch his body free from the vehicle, praying that someone would find him and pick him up. But before he did, the entire 'box quaked. Jamie fought to hold on to the rungs as the container shook violently. Was it slowing down?

The rocking lessened in intensity for a few moments, and Jamie took the opportunity to start climbing. As he scaled the outer wall of the buffeting 'box, Jamie saw a much different sight. The massive metal spokes weren't pinwheeling above him anymore; in fact, the whole production seemed somewhat askew.

The 'box shuddered to a halt. It was abrupt, almost as if the tracks had been gummed up somehow. Recognizing his chance, he started climbing faster.

Upon reaching the rooftop, Jamie found new handholds and looked around to see what had happened. Through the gridwork he saw what looked like a rainbow above, suspended in space. It took a moment for what had happened to register. The Spore, directed into the floor by the rhodium supports and forced downward by the gee forces, had eaten its way through the base of the 'box at a much-accelerated rate. Its appetite in no way abated, it kept going—smearing the outer tracks that bound the container with Spore. By breaking the perfect circle of the transit rings, Formation Seven-Alpha had put a stop first to the interstellar jump and, finally, to the motion of the 'box itself. The circuit looked misshapen to Jamie—almost wilting.

That observation snapped him back to reality. There was only one way to go, with the Spore in all directions. Up, up, up! Back up to the central hub of the station. Jamie saw that his almost-coffin had jammed against one of the spiraling side tracks the Xylanx used to bring 'boxes into the central station; the connection had buckled, explaining why the 'box had stopped exactly here. A four-meter leap through space brought Jamie to the track, now basically just a long, helical ladder back to safety.

As he worked his way from crossbar to crossbar, Jamie chanced to look down. The bangbox that had been his prison was almost gone, a melted meal for a giant jelly. Around it, the tracks were breaking up—but the Spore hadn't stopped. Jamie could see patches on the sides of the support spokes—and even the approach track that he was on. He climbed faster.

Above, he saw armored Xylanx warriors with jet packs emerging from a gateway in the hub. They were toting big guns of a kind he'd never seen them with before: like Gideon's shotgun, only larger. *Oh, great! All I need!*

But the Xylanders passed him by completely, zipping out in all directions on their little rockets. The fire brigade—or was it the Spore brigade?—had gone into action, racing to eliminate the threat.

Good luck with that, Jamie thought. He didn't know if they'd be able to stop the Spore, but at the moment he didn't care. He only saw the open airlock the Xylanders had left from. Climbing relentlessly for it, he prayed for some luck of his own.

53

Kolvax fired another pulse blast at Bridget at point-blank range. Bridget fell to the ground again. She'd been thrown around repeatedly like a Zazzy doll, and Kolvax seemed to be enjoying it. Her faceplate was warped, its internal liquid display leaking; she could no longer see anything. Even the audio telemetry messages from her HardSHEL armor had stopped. Her internal armature was still responding to her movements, but the rest of the armor was dying.

As before, he let her stand again. It was painful to do so—and more painful still to know that she'd let him get the drop on her. She could hear firing from far away; her comrades were still out there somewhere. But would they be able to locate her, with her systems down?

Staggering, she unlatched and removed her helmet. It was more hindrance than help now. She just needed a few seconds' respite to get her bearings and find her fallen rifle...

Kolvax didn't give them to her.

He fired his pulse weapon again, sending Bridget slamming backward into a tree. She heard a loud pop—the propulsion pack giving out. She tried to stand, only to fall back down as Kolvax approached. A dry clicking sound came from her armor's left knee joint. The internal servos were starting to fail from the punishment they'd taken.

Sprawled with her back against the tree, she looked up at him. There was something human in those eyes, she saw—but also something feral and angry. "You know who we are, right?" she asked. "I don't know how—but we're from the same place. Related. We don't have to fight."

"Of course we do." He adjusted his weapon. She heard the whine of a charge building up. "Families always fight. And this fight started long ago."

"We don't have to be bound by that," she said, glaring as he loomed over her. She clutched at the grass, reaching vainly for a rock or something to strike him with.

"Oh, we're not bound by anything. Not anymore. I'm doing this to break our bonds," he said. Seeing her pawing around, he pinned her gloved hand to the ground with his foot. "Your trader is going home with a little present from your old neighbors."

"What—what do you mean?"

"I mean the Earth wasn't big enough for both of our peoples forty thousand years ago. And soon it won't be big enough to land a shuttle on." Pointing the pulse weapon a short distance from her face, he paused. "You have turned out interesting—I'll give you that. We might even rethink the hair thing. I'll see what I can do when I'm in charge."

Bridget tensed, her mind flashing strangely on that moment with Baines back aboard the train in Overland. This was different only in that she was facing her killer. There had to be something she could...

Ah-ooo-gaaahhh!

The clarion echoed throughout the cylindrical greenhouse, louder and more urgent-sounding than the siren she'd heard on her way in. She saw Kolvax's eyes narrow.

"Something you didn't plan on?" Bridget asked.

Before he could answer, she grabbed at his wrist with her free hand and pushed it away. The weapon discharged loudly, its force directed into a nearby tree. Kolvax saw it shatter into a thousand splinters—and then felt both her hands on his metal collar. She butted her head violently against his. That hurt her more than it did him—the neo-Neanderthal's bonier forehead easily absorbing the blow. But it put him in position for the right uppercut she delivered beneath his rounded jaw as she sprang upward.

She was the feral one now. She grabbed his head again, slamming it against her armored breastplate. That was made of tougher stuff, and it stunned him. A high kick followed, her armature responding as it was supposed to. The pulse weapon went flying. Another kick and Kolvax stumbled backward and fell on his armored rump.

He gaped up at her, astonished.

"Something else you didn't plan on," she said.

* * *

The receiving area Jamie had left from had been sedate, with Kolvax's workers professionally preparing the 'box for travel. Now, it was a war zone. Passing through the airlock, he heard a noisy claxon sounding and a battle already underway. Armored warriors with more of the funny guns were blasting at a ceiling that had started to go green.

How in the hell did the Spore get in here so fast? He'd last seen it outside, feasting on the remains of the whirlibang and making its way along the struts toward the station.

He soon found out. To the right, another airlock opened— and a panicked Xylanx warrior floated in, screaming. Jamie realized in an instant what was wrong. The woman's black armor plate was speckled with green goo. It was eating her armor—and would soon eat her alive.

Before Jamie could think of what to do, several of the warriors who had been firing at the ceiling spun and turned their guns on the woman. Their six-barreled blunderbusses fired, spraying her with bluish shot. She wailed again, curling into a fetal position as the gunners peppered her with fire. For a moment Jamie thought they were acting as firemen, hosing down a person aflame. But the barrage was such that the woman stopped moving entirely after a moment.

"Damn fool!" one of the Xylanders who'd fired said. "These people know they shouldn't come back in yet! If you get the Spore on you, stay outside to die!"

Jamie realized there was another motionless warrior floating not far from the ceiling, his armor little more than a greenish sarcophagus. He'd been the one to bring the goo inside.

The gunner pointed in Jamie's direction. "There's another one!"

"Wait!" Jamie said. "I'm not—"

As a group the warriors fired their strange shotguns in Jamie's direction. Still weightless, Jamie pushed off from the door frame of the airlock and somersaulted toward a cargo tender, hoping its bulk would shield him from their fire.

He didn't make it. "*Yargh!*" Tumbling end over end, Jamie felt searing pain in his backside as a spray of blue needles struck his space suit. His motion spared him from the brunt of the barrage, and he reached cover quickly. Regardless, an alarm went off inside his space helmet. The shots had pierced his outfit's sleeve and pants—and more of the projectiles were striking the other side of the cargo tender.

"Forget him," someone yelled. "Look!"

Jamie saw what they were looking at. Above, the ceiling first sagged—and then seemed to bubble outward. The trader had been through this before and knew what was coming. Ignoring the pain he was feeling, he kicked off from the cargo tender and dove toward the doorway leading back into the station.

He was just in time. An emergency protective door slammed shut behind him, even as the loading area beyond explosively decompressed.

Wheezing and smarting, Jamie looked through the window at the carnage. The docking area was open to space now, but the Spore was still visible, at work on the other parts of the room. He couldn't see the warriors who had fired at him. Reminded, he glanced at his arm. It looked like someone had tried space suit acupuncture. Tiny glass-like slivers were impaled in the fabric; the bluish shards hadn't gone through, and they swept neatly away when he ran his other hand across his wrist. But as he turned to move, he realized at least one of the shards had gone through the seat of his pants, lodging in one of his buttocks.

That's fitting, Jamie thought. *This whole trip has been a pain in the ass.* He was pawing at himself to shake any other fragments loose when he heard more troopers charging toward him. He quickly ducked into a side hallway.

Propelling himself through the zero gee, Jamie continued working his way into the station. It was a mob scene. The armored Xylanders were all heading in the direction he'd come from, toward the danger; the unmasked workers were heading the opposite way. Jamie followed the latter group. No one was paying him the least mind now; in his space helmet, he was one more refugee. Jamie remembered from his tour that the whirlibang through which he'd arrived from Kano was at the far end of the station, beyond the big arboretum; that was where everyone was heading. Good enough for him—especially as there were quakes and explosions coming from behind.

Going down a level, Jamie reached the arboretum. Workers were hurriedly cramming themselves into tramcars, rushing to cross over the long cylindrical forest. Joining the stampede, Jamie wedged himself unnoticed into the back of one vehicle.

It stopped at an intermediate station for others to board. Impatiently, Jamie looked out onto the winding staircase leading down from the platform…

…and saw someone familiar. Or rather, *something.*

On impulse Jamie clambered out of the car and onto the loading deck. Another rider called after him. "Hey, you! Are you crazy?"

"Maybe," Jamie called back to the departing car. The station was under Spore attack, and he was pretty sure he was bleeding to death. But he'd just seen the one thing on the station he wanted more than survival. He found the stairs and began to descend.

54

Bridget dashed through the trees. She hadn't found her rifle—and the pulse weapon had fallen too far away, on the other side of Kolvax. And he had produced another weapon from his pack: the strangest thing she'd yet seen.

The hand-weapon fired white-hot cables tipped at either end with glowing weights. Kolvax's first errant shot from the fire-bolo had wrapped around a tree to her right, instantly igniting it. Imagining what one of the cables would do wrapped around her neck, Bridget ran for her life, leaping and crashing through the vegetation.

More sirens went off, as sprinklers buried underground automatically rose to save the primeval forest. Kolvax didn't seem to care, firing again and again, setting more of the woods aflame.

Bridget couldn't recall what direction her troops had been in—if they were even still there. They were occupied themselves, she knew. But they had to see the rising flames. She dashed over a low rise in the landscape. If she could just keep her legs moving for a few minutes more…

Dammit! A metallic snap resounded from one of her knees, and Bridget felt her battered armor's internal servos going out once and for all. The leg locked in position, and Bridget tumbled downward, landing in a puddle.

Bridget struggled to turn and rise again—but it was too late. Kolvax was approaching through the trees, fire-bolo in hand and a murderous look in his almost-human eyes.

✳ ✳ ✳

Jamie trailed along behind as Tellmer picked his way through the bushes. Running in the full gravity, Jamie had still managed to approach unnoticed; the alarms were still going off all around, and the scrawny Xylander seemed entirely focused on finding something—or someone. Kolvax, Jamie figured, which meant he didn't have much time. The trader paused, looking around for a weapon.

Then he remembered how Tellmer had treated him earlier— and realized he had a weapon already. Wincing at the pain in his hindquarters, Jamie dashed ahead, screened from Tellmer by a thick stand of trees.

As Tellmer sprinted past, Jamie leapt from behind a tree while making a scary face. "*Bleaaaggh!*"

"*Gah!*" Tellmer recoiled and dropped what he was carrying.

Jamie quickly removed his helmet, exposing his sweaty and hairy head. He put out his tongue and charged toward the aide. "Germs! Germs! *Germs!*"

"Stay back!" Tellmer cried, tripping over his own boots. The unarmed Xylander stumbled. "G-g-get away!"

Jamie bounded over the grass separating them and screamed in his most frightful, unclean human voice. He tried his best to drool.

"*Brains!*"

"*No!*" Wailing, the timid neo-Neanderthal stood, turned, and bolted into the woods.

"That's right," Jamie said, strutting up. "You'd better run. My cavemen kicked your cavemen's butts!"

He smirked with satisfaction. On the ground to one side he saw part of the aide's abandoned cargo: a spare helmet for someone. To the other side he found exactly what he was looking for…

…and saw something he wasn't expecting at all a long way away through a parting of the trees.

Flames. Smoke. And something else…

"What the…?" Jamie's jaw dropped as the image registered. "I don't believe it!"

✳ ✳ ✳

Here we go again with this scene, the immobilized Bridget thought as Kolvax stomped up. *Aren't I always the one who's telling people not to lose their rifles?*

"You're wrecking your garden," she said.

"I don't care. This is one station. We have many."

She had to keep him talking. "That earlier siren isn't for the fire?"

"No. It's for the Spore, if you must know."

"*The Spore?*"

"Something's gone wrong. And I have to go see what. Goodbye." He knelt several meters away from her this time, drawing a careful bead on her exposed head and neck. Something rustled in the trees behind him.

A helmet went tumbling across the ground to his left. "Eh?" Kolvax's head turned…

…and snapped backward. A heavy object slammed him hard in the face. The Xylander stumbled—and fell like a stone as he was struck again.

Bridget gawked as Kolvax fell to the ground before her. She looked up to see Jamie, space-suited and helmetless, grasping his weapon: a metal briefcase.

"I—uh—couldn't leave this behind," Jamie said, mawkish. He looked up at the blazing forest. "Can we go now?"

***

While Bridget pointed the fire-bolo on Kolvax, Jamie helped strip off the last of her armor plating. Tellmer had returned—fearful of the humans but even more fearful of abandoning his master to the fire—and was cradling his groggy superior.

Jamie had explained a little. They'd have to move, and fast. The Spore had devastated the far end of the station; they'd have to go back the way they came as quickly as possible.

Face red with blood, Kolvax squinted at Jamie and snarled. "The…joke's…on you."

"What?"

Woozy and weaponless, Kolvax pointed feebly at the case beside the kneeling trader. "Those ingots…are only *plated* with platinum-190. Still valuable—I sure wasn't going to let you have it! But it's not enough to do whatever it is you want to do."

"The assayer should've caught that," Jamie said. He glared at Kolvax. "You screwed with the assayer. I knew you screwed with it!"

"Too bad."

Bridget lost hold of Jamie's arm. "Wait! What are you doing?"

Jamie reached for the case. "I'm going to hit him again!"

Another explosion rocked the station, bigger than any before. The ground quaked beneath their feet. That seemed to change Jamie's mind—and the sound of several Surge Sigma members calling out through the burning forest up ahead made up Bridget's mind.

"Congratulations, Kolvax," she said, standing free from the armor pieces. "You keep your head."

"Maybe not," Jamie said, glowering as he held the briefcase close to him. "Not after his people get done with him."

"You don't know anything," Kolvax said. He struggled to stand, supported by Tellmer; he was in no shape to follow them, but he wasn't going to let them leave without a warning. "You Earth people—none of you know anything! This isn't finished!"

"Evolution never is," Bridget said, looking up at the burning branches. "And if you need a replacement tree, you know where to find us. You'll be glad to hear yours is doing a little better now." She winked at him. "You should have tried watering it less." She turned and headed back into the forest, Jamie in tow.

5 5

Bridget had never been a great believer in luck—or in some universal force's predilection for ironic outcomes. There were causes and effects; things just happened.

But all that had happened at Gharion Preserve made her wonder. If it hadn't been for Trovatelli's betrayal, her team never would have thought to use the Echo Ring to chase after Jamie. Surge Sigma's arrival, she suspected, had distracted the Xylanx from their surveillance of Jamie long enough for him to don his space suit and start his escape—thereby triggering the premature release of the Spore.

And craziest of all, their escape had been ensured by, of all things, Trovatelli's bomb. O'Herlihy's small contingent protecting their escape route had been outnumbered almost immediately. But he'd thought quickly—which is exactly what she expected from him—and saved the day. Just as his position was about to be overrun, he'd shown the Xylanx the contents of the munitions 'box they'd had to bring along—a 'box that had already been prepared for easy detonation. He'd spent more than an hour sitting atop the 'box, just as Trovatelli had, prepared to blow up that entire end of the station.

Since that area connected to the only functioning whirl-ibangs that could be used to escape the Spore, the Xylanx decided to meet the crazy human's demands. Bridget and her team-mates had received free passage to their passenger 'box, even as Xylanders streamed to their own pods in an attempt to escape the station. Bridget was glad she hadn't left blast-happy Gideon in charge of the giant bomb; they'd all be stardust by now. Instead, everyone had made it back to the Dragon's Depot—though some were worse for wear.

Passing the infirmary, she saw Jamie charging from the room, with the medic trailing after him. "You've got a nasty flesh wound," Ramiro Garcia-Lopez said. "You need to let me do some-thing about it."

Bridget saw that Jamie had no intention of slowing down—but he was moving forward with extreme discomfort. He had Kolvax's briefcase in his hand. She followed—only to bump physically into Santos, who was heading in from another hallway.

He chuckled as he helped her off his feet. "I heard you were back. You're all right?"

"Bewildered but operational."

Santos looked up the hallway. "Was that Jamie?"

She nodded. "Still want to arrest him?"

He was already moving. "I have a job," he said. He looked back at her with an expression that seemed genuinely remorse-ful. "I'm sorry."

Her brow furrowed. *I have a job, too,* she thought. *Or I did.*

So Bridget followed him. Up at the end of the hall, Jamie and the medic had entered Falcone's office.

The administrator was at his desk, looking more har-ried than usual. The corporate auditor, René Bouchard, stood nearby, looking at the potted tree. Slipping into the room behind Santos, Bridget saw Jamie slam the briefcase on the desk. He opened it.

"That bastard Kolvax was right about the plating," Jamie said. She knew he'd gone immediately to visit the base expert. "Only about a quarter of this material is Platinum-190."

Falcone looked with tired eyes on the shining contents of the case. "Then that means..."

"You're shy by thirty billion dollars," Bouchard said. "I'm afraid this crazy gambit of yours is washed up."

Bridget stepped forward. "You're kidding, right? You know everything we've gone through—everything we've discovered! You're really going to hold us to accounts after all that?"

Bouchard looked over at her. "Quaestor's a business, not a government. I don't care if you discovered the dawn of man—"

"He did," Bridget said. She pulled Jamie's immerse goggles from his vest pocket. "He even brought back video!"

"And we'll purchase it—once its authenticity has been established. But you're still going to be short. There's nothing I can do. We now know it was your efforts that put this expedition in the hole, Mr. Sturm—and Leo here in effect took responsibility for them by making you his trader. I need thirty billion dollars in product—and you can tell time. The quarter ends in forty-five minutes. I'm going to have to shut the expedition down."

"No," Jamie said, slamming the case closed. He looked back at Garcia-Lopez, standing to the left of the doorway. "Wait! You! You wanted a shot at me?"

The medic shrugged as if he couldn't care one way or the other. "You're going to get gangrene and die," he said simply.

"Great! Let's do this!" He looked back angrily at Falcone and Bouchard. "Wait right here."

He charged to the door. Agent Santos started to intercept him. "Mr. Sturm, I'm with—"

"You get the next appointment," Jamie said, limping quickly past the much larger man.

Startled, he looked at Bridget. "This isn't how our arrests usually go."

Bridget shrugged and smiled. "Give him a minute. I've seen that look before. I think he's got another rabbit in his hat. Or something."

***

Jamie hobbled back to Falcone's office forty minutes later, past Santos and his agents, who had agreed to wait outside. He had a bowl in his hand and a pained expression. "There," he said, tossing the bowl onto the desk.

Bouchard looked in the bowl and flinched. "What the hell? That's disgusting!"

Falcone tipped the bowl at an angle so the others could see inside. A long, slivered angle of blue crystal sat in a puddle of blood.

"That's been in my backside since the escape," Jamie said.

"It looks like glass," Falcone said, unruffled by the appearance of something that had been in another man's buttocks just moments before.

"It's from the Xylanx space station. It's the stuff they were using to restrain the Spore."

Brigdet's eyes widened. "This stuff stops the Spore?"

"It does. And I'm prepared to sell this to you for the balance we owe."

Bouchard chortled. "Thirty billion dollars? For a chunk of glass?"

"Yeah," Falcone said. The middle-aged man was calculating as he shook the bowl, moving the shard around. "Think what you're getting. You analyze it and reproduce it, and you've got a product that every species in the Signatory Systems will want!"

Bouchard looked at the bloody fragment skeptically. "We'd have to test it. We'd have to know that it works."

"It *must* work," Bridget said. "How else could they manage the Spore on the station?"

Wincing, Jamie rubbed his backside. "It was containing the Spore aboard the 'box—and it was also in the guns of the response crew. It's got to retard its growth somehow just by contact."

"Still," Bouchard said, "it'll take some time to—"

"No," Jamie said, snatching the bowl back. "You get five minutes to make a decision!"

"Four minutes," Bridget said, eyeing the clock on her palm nervously.

"Four minutes before I go out into that hallway and hand it to the Feds. They'll take possession of it in the name of national security."

"They may do that anyway!"

"Not without a legal fight, once you've filed a claim on it."

Bouchard sputtered. "But you were only out here because you were acting as an agent for Quaestor! That glass belongs to us!"

"But the ass belongs to me. And I wasn't wearing the badge on Gharion Preserve. I was...er, visiting the Neanderthals on my own time."

"Three minutes," Bridget said. "You'd better do this!"

Falcone whipped out an isopanel from his desk and started entering data. He passed it to Bouchard.

"I can't believe we're filing a claim on a chunk of glass!"

"Just do it," Falcone said.

Jamie looked again inside the bowl. "Wait a minute," he said. "I'm thinking maybe I should hold out."

Bridget whacked him on the shoulder. "Jamie!"

"All right, all right!" He looked at her wearily. "Just make sure I get some more painkillers. Soon?"

56

For the second time in three months, Kolvax walked out of the Dominium audience chamber with his freedom.

The fact dazzled him. The humans had escaped, and the entire Gharion Preserve had been destroyed. But the Severed members had remained silent about the Spore scheme, his recorded message of revolution had never gone out, and the truth about Borranz's murder had never been revealed.

Instead, he had cleverly woven a tale that fit the facts—and absolutely suited the Dominium's political needs. He had, on their say-so, stolen the humans' knowglobe. The humans had, in revenge, counterattacked, seeking to steal the secret of the Spore from the Gharion Preserve's labs. Through intent or incompetence, the humans had set it free. Kolvax had heroically driven the humans off and then managed the evacuation of the whole station.

The Gharion Preserve was gone now, and thus the link with Sigma Draconis; no two human and Xylanx systems were connected directly now. That suited the Dominium. He explained it all to Tellmer, who stood beneath the great tree outside the chamber.

"Did they place us on a war footing against the humans?"

"We've never *not* been on a war footing," Kolvax said. "With this they've turned the humans from the imagined villains of the past into a threat that's real. This all feeds into their crazy emergency-powers declaration from years ago—allows the Dominium to tighten their controls on the people."

Tellmer looked away. "Then all is indeed lost."

Kolvax smirked. "Not really," he said. "I've become something more to the Dominium because of all of this. *Useful.* A hero in the war against the humans—the warrior that made the first stand against them. The Severed continues—as a vanguard sponsored by the state."

Tellmer looked down as they began walking from the plaza. "That sounds horrible."

"It's actually pretty good. They're concerned with what the Signatory Systems might do if they find out we created the Spore, so they want more scouting trips. They're going to allow me to lead some recons into the unexplored areas so as to make sure the humans aren't advancing too far. If they do, then they'll be forced to consider something more—invasion, perhaps. And they're giving me offices here—to keep an eye on me, I imagine. It's fine by me. I'll be better positioned to move against the Dominium if they try to send us all underground again."

Kolvax paused before the door to a lavish residence. "This is my new base of operations. We've got a lot to do."

"Yes, Great Kolvax."

"And we're going to start making some changes to this damn fool religion of mine, all right? Enough with the masks—we're all equal now. As I see it, we'll be the trendsetters, in fact." He rubbed at the skin above his eyes. "And maybe we can start growing some hair. That human woman's looked nice."

His aide shuddered. "But these are core principles, Great Kolvax. You can't change—"

Kolvax glowered at him.

Tellmer clasped his hands together, worried. "Well…you *are* the prophet. If—if there was a new testimony, a new holy text from you…"

"Fine," Kolvax said, stepping inside. "I'll write it in the bathroom."

✳ ✳ ✳

The senior staffer in the reception area presented his hand. "I'm Don Ragsdale. Are you Jeanette Bachmann?"

"That's right," the woman replied. She looked every bit the young Washington professional: light brown pantsuit and auburn hair cut short. She shook the greeter's hand firmly.

"Come on in. I read you went to the University of Kentucky," the man said, nodding to the ribbon around her neck.

"As an undergrad, yes." She smiled at him. Her briefers in the safe house in Montevideo had known the recruiter was an alumnus; she'd suggested the ribbon would make a nice understated personal touch. She'd also been the one to suggest making her eyes the same color.

Jeanette Bachmann, née Lissa Trovatelli, followed Don Ragsdale through the crowded and narrow hallways of the Dirksen Senate Office Building. The last few days had been a whirlwind of activity, and she could hardly believe she was here.

She had been concerned about repercussions with the Walled Garden after the failure of her mission. She needn't have worried. Her handler had wasted no time in getting her ready for a new assignment. Talented personnel were few enough, she had been told, that the movement profited little from being vindictive.

And Trovatelli had done something of critical importance by delivering the news of the Neanderthals' existence. The Gardeners were stunned by the revelation, of course, but they wasted little time in formulating a response. It didn't seem likely that Xylanx's connection to Earth could remain a secret for long. Someone would find out. So whereas Trovatelli had attempted to physically close off human space from the Xylanx, the Gardeners chose to work instead on closing humans' minds.

Walled Garden sympathizers in the information industry were already at work, subtly gaming knowglobe search engine results. Once people began their mad dash to learn more information about Neanderthals—and they would—they'd find mostly the scholarly research and fictional treatments that portrayed them as obscenely barbaric, brutal, and not at all connected to the human experience. It wouldn't matter if articles trumpeting the similarities between Homo neanderthalensis and Homo sapiens outnumbered the rest by ten to one. They wouldn't be found easily. Scientific thinking about Neanderthals hadn't changed—but people would presume it had and would react accordingly.

Ragsdale led her to a couple of chairs outside an office door. They sat, and he looked at his portable isopanel. "Your résumé is stellar, Jeanette. But you've been off-planet the last few years?"

"I thought I could be more useful if I broadened my knowledge." She saw in the interviewer's eyes that it was the right thing to say. This meeting was a formality, she knew; the job was already hers. Jeanette Bachmann was a fiction custom-designed for the position. Another agent had been slated to fill the job; Trovatelli had been redirected toward it because of her personal knowledge.

"There's some big news about to come down," Ragsdale said, looking nervously at the door. "We never find out everything, but there have been closed-door briefings on the Hill all morning." He knelt over and whispered to her. "You're going to have your job cut out for you—a possible PR mess first thing. Whatever's going on, it sounds like the senator's son is involved."

The woman tried to appear surprised. "I didn't know she *had* a son."

"We try to keep it that way. He's a wild card, a random element."

Lissa nodded. Jamie certainly was that.

Ragsdale kept his voice down as he eyed the door. "We're still not sure how he got out on the frontier—he doesn't seem the sort. We think he was on the run from Treasury agents."

"Jeanette" gasped. "Can the senator—"

"Make it go away? It'd make our jobs easier, for sure. But she'd rather make him go away, I think…" He looked up. "Oh, Senator!"

Elaine Keeler stepped from the office. "I hope Don hasn't been boring you with my family soap opera, Miss—Bachmann, is it?"

"Yes." Lissa and Ragsdale stood immediately. Lissa thought Senator Keeler looked like an older version of Jamie—if Jamie owned any serious expressions. Hers was stern, as if she'd just learned something dire. Ragsdale looked sheepish as his boss passed.

The senator kept walking, and they followed. "Don't get too caught up in gossip. My new assistant has to be on top of things. But if you care as much as I do about keeping humanity safe, there isn't a better staff to be on—or a better time to be on it." She looked back. "It's about to be a very busy news week, Jeanette. Are you ready to protect the Earth?"

"Always," Lissa said, smiling.

57

Save the world, go to jail.

Surprisingly, Jamie hadn't minded his week in custody at all. Santos—what a straight-laced goofus!—had diligently kept his agents from questioning Jamie, as the nearest lawyer was light-years away, and the Visitor Contact Group people had dibs. Jamie had completed endless interviews with them about the Xylanx from his locked room before they'd left him alone. For the last two days he'd eaten, watched his immerso shows, and slept. Slept plenty. As long as prison was going to be like this, he'd be fine with it.

The news about Lissa Trovatelli had startled him. He hadn't had the best luck with women in his life; most found his excess of competitiveness off-putting. Lissa's interest had developed swiftly, to be sure—but she had really seemed to want him to go with her. It was a rotten thing to be attracted to an outlaw, he thought. But then he remembered his own predicament. Maybe he'd run into her in a parole office one day and they'd do lunch.

A knock came at the door. "Mr. Sturm?"

"Where else would I be?"

Santos entered with one of his federal marshals in tow. "I'm told your attorney has arrived—court appointed, I guess—and the national security people have cleared us to leave for home. Are you packed?"

Jamie looked at the immerso goggles looped around his neck. "Yeah, I have everything." He'd decided to forget about the Xylanx-made suit; the analysts had probably ruined it anyway, trying to see how Neanderthals sewed. "Can you sedate me for the trip? I'd like that a lot."

Santos crossed his arms. "I really don't understand you. I deal with your types all the time—you pull off all these schemes for either money, ego, or both. But you—when you had something worth a mint, you gave it to the expedition!"

"Yeah, well, maybe I don't like it when the black sheep gets pushed around," Jamie said, shrugging. "You know, I could've held out for enough to pay my debts and afford a real lawyer. My fault for taking the first offer." Jamie exhaled and shook his head. He wasn't *really* that upset about it, and the fact surprised him. It was a hell of a time to become a team player. Maybe he could wear the official expedition cap to lockup.

Bridget appeared in the doorway behind Santos. The agent looked back at her. Something was going on between them, Jamie thought—but she was looking at *him* now. "Jamie, you're not going to believe this. Follow me."

Jamie started to walk, confused. Curious, Santos followed.

Bouchard and Falcone were waiting in the counting room— now jokingly called Kolvax's Chapel—along with a half-dozen smartly dressed people Jamie hadn't seen before. Falcone introduced three of them to Jamie as Quaestor's corporate legal team.

His legal team.

Jamie blinked. He looked around, suspicious.

Santos was, too. "Wait. Jamie's attempt to manipulate the rhodium market was completely separate from his inventory-smuggling activities. Quaestor doesn't have a dog in this fight."

"That's where you're wrong," Falcone said. "Those side trades you're accusing him of making weren't unauthorized. They were made on our behalf under the rules set out for corporate trading in the Expeditionary Capital Protection Act. He's a hedger for the company. Well, that's what he was doing. He was hedging *for* the company."

Jamie's eyes bulged.

"What are you talking about?" Santos said, his calm reserve cracking. "He made all those rhodium trades through personal accounts!"

"On behalf of the corporation," Bouchard said.

Santos sputtered. "But that's not what you told me before!" He turned to the administrator. "Falcone, you said you knew nothing about the trades—or about Jamie storing all that merchandise in your Altair warehouse!"

Falcone smirked. "And I told you the truth. This was a special project, above my pay grade."

"Yes," Bouchard said, gesturing to the other suits in the room. "Quaestor was concerned the trading floor had been infiltrated by spies from the competition. We asked Jamie to assist us in a pilot program to help protect some of our inventory decisions, and to make some of our corporate transactions under names that wouldn't attract attention. You know how eager firms are to buy and sell based on what they think the other expeditions are doing! But his trades were made with corporate money in regulated markets—in a perfectly legal manner." Bouchard eyed Jamie keenly. "Here's a draft payment for five hundred and sixty million dollars. Sorry it's late."

Jamie took the isopanel and stammered as he saw the zeroes. "Th-thanks." He knew that everything Bouchard and Falcone had just said was a total lie. They were covering up for him, making it all go away. But why? *What's going on here?*

Bouchard turned back to Santos. "That sum will settle all his margin accounts and should close the matter entirely."

Santos glared. "So you're now going to act as if the company *intended* to ship home all that rhodium that the Spore ate? And you're going to pretend Jamie was just doing his job? Really?"

"That's what our lawyers will say—for as long as you care to contest it. Given the importance of what our expedition has helped your government discover, I hope it won't come to that." Bouchard offered his hand to the investigator. "I'm sorry to have put you to any trouble. I hope we won't detain you any longer."

Santos stared at Bouchard—and then at the hand. "I don't like this," he said. Reluctantly, though, he accepted the handshake. Then he turned to Jamie. "I don't believe this story for a second."

Jamie returned a crumpled smile. *I don't believe it myself,* he thought. The company had just dropped half a billion to bail him out. But why?

"You've got to return home sometime," Santos said. "You'd better watch your step."

Santos turned to the exit—and saw Bridget standing quietly by. Still frowning, he studied her. "This…was *your* idea, wasn't it?"

Bridget's head sunk between her shoulders. "Sorry. It's—"

"Your job. Protect the trader. I get it." Santos shook his head—and a smile returned. He grasped her gently by the arm as he passed. "I was right. You're really something."

"It was good to meet you, too, Saint."

He put his hands together prayerfully and bowed his head. Then he turned and walked down the hall, with Bridget's eyes on his back the whole way.

Jamie looked back at Bouchard and goggled. "What did you just do?" He held up the isopanel. "What is this? Is this real?"

"It's what you owed on your side bets, isn't it?"

Jamie nodded. He didn't have five hundred and sixty million dollars to bet with, of course; he'd traded on margin, using a fraction of that sum. Most of it had come from loans or other people who would now be less than pleased. But Bouchard and Quaestor, it seemed, were intent on settling the entire debt for him. He smiled. "So is this my reward?"

"Reward?" Bouchard laughed. He looked at Falcone. "He thinks he gets a reward!"

Falcone smiled. "The corporation sees this as a loan. A loan you can work off under contract to my expedition, as a trader."

Jamie gasped. "Say *what*?"

"Under contract. I should think five years should do it."

"Five years!" Jamie was apoplectic. "Five years more? As an indentured servant! A slave! In Crazyland!"

"Look at it like this," Bouchard said. "You've got a corporate credit line—with a minor half-billion dollar expense to work off."

"But five years! Three months nearly killed me!"

"And in three months you brought in a hundred billion dollars. We'd like to see if you can get us to a trillion."

The other suits in the room buzzed with excitement over that. *A trillion dollars!* That was bigger than the quarterly revenues of Praetor and Osman combined. Falcone invited them to visit the new map room. "We've got big plans," he said, looking light and happy for a change. "There's a wonderful patch in Cygnus nobody's ever cracked…"

✳ ✳ ✳

One by one the eager executives shook hands with Jamie and stepped out, congratulating each other, Falcone, and Bouchard as they went. Jamie, looking like his bones had turned to jelly, found a pew and collapsed on it.

Only Bridget stayed behind. She'd spent the days after Jamie rescued the expedition studying up on what he was charged with and had convinced Falcone to take the plan upstairs at Quaestor. She hated to undermine Santos—whom she very much wanted to see again. But it was the right thing to do. Somehow she didn't think he would hold it against her.

"You okay, Wall Street?"

"No," Jamie said. "Seriously. Forget it. Bankrupt me. Send me to jail." He looked up at her, weary. "Bridget, you know me."

"I do." She chuckled.

"You know that the things that I know, I know for absolutely certain. I've got plenty of them that have been proven again and again. Things like never listen to stock tips at a bar. And other people don't want to hear your erotic dreams about them. And, most importantly, I do not—*do not*—belong in space!"

She sat down next to him and laughed as he put his head between his knees.

He moaned. "I can't believe this. I'm going to be in debt to these people forever—and that's the way they want it. How could they do this? Why would they even want me after this?"

"Don't underestimate yourself," Bridget said. "You didn't just introduce humanity to a missing link to its past—you brought back video of the Stone Age. And you found something that will allow the Signatory Systems to defend against the greatest threat to interstellar commerce ever seen—all while generating the single biggest sales quarter in expedition history."

Jamie looked up as she stood. "But I'm not a trader! I wasn't trained—"

"Training's overrated." She patted him on the back. "You've got the touch."

His eyes followed her as she moved to leave. "The touch? *The touch?* You can't be serious!"

"Oh, yes." She stopped in the doorway and smiled. "Jamie, I've seen traders come and go. But it takes someone really special to pull thirty billion dollars out of his ass." She slapped the door frame and twirled on her boot heel. "We're heading out in an hour. Don't forget your badge."

She could hear his howl all the way down the hall.

THE END

Follow Surge Sigma again in
OVERDRAFT: THE CYGNUS CAMPAIGN

ABOUT THE AUTHOR

Memphis native John Jackson Miller has been fascinated with storytelling since childhood, producing comics and fanzines with the encouragement of his school librarian mother. He grew up to work in the publishing industry, editing comics industry standards, such as *Comics Retailer*, before moving to the creative side with writing for *Iron Man, Simpsons,* and *Mass Effect.* He also began a long association with Lucasfilm, writing many *Star Wars* graphic novels and prose works. His first novel, *Star Wars: Knight Errant,* reached the Top 25 on the *New York Times* mass-market paperback list, and his first hardcover novel, *Star Wars: Kenobi,* is slated for release in 2013. He also does historical research into the comics industry on his Comichron website. John currently lives in Wisconsin with his wife and two children. His website is www.johnjacksonmiller.com.

NOVELS BY JOHN JACKSON MILLER
Overdraft: The Orion Offensive
Star Wars: Kenobi
Star Wars: Knight Errant
Star Wars: Lost Tribe of the Sith – The Collected Stories

GRAPHIC NOVELS BY JOHN JACKSON MILLER
Indiana Jones and the Kingdom of the Crystal Skull
*(from a story by George Lucas and Jeff Nathanson and a
screenplay by David Koepp)*

Star Wars: Knight Errant series:
Vol. 1: Aflame
Vol. 2: Deluge
Vol. 3: Escape

Star Wars: Knights of the Old Republic series:
Vol. 1: Commencement
Vol. 2: Flashpoint
Vol. 3: Days of Fear, Nights of Anger
Vol. 4: Daze of Hate, Knights of Suffering
Vol. 5: Vector
Vol. 6: Commencement
Vol. 7: Prophet Motive
Vol. 8: Destroyer
Vol. 9: Demon
Vol. 10: War

Star Wars: Lost Tribe of the Sith: Spiral

GRAPHIC NOVELS BY JOHN JACKSON MILLER
WITH MAC WALTERS
Mass Effect: Redemption
Mass Effect: Evolution
Mass Effect: Invasion

GRAPHIC NOVELS BY JOHN JACKSON MILLER
WITH MARK RICKETTS
Avengers Disassembled: Iron Man

Kindle Serials

This book was originally released in episodes as a Kindle Serial. Kindle Serials launched in 2012 as a new way to experience serialized books. Kindle Serials allow readers to enjoy the story as the author creates it, purchasing once and receiving all existing episodes immediately, followed by future episodes as they are published. To find out more about Kindle Serials and to see the current selection of Serials titles, visit www.amazon.com/kindleserials.

Made in the USA
San Bernardino, CA
27 July 2013